W9-BNT-530

A Paragon of Virtue

Christian von Ditfurth

A PARAGON OF VIRTUE

TRANSLATED BY

Helen Atkins

The Toby Press

The Toby Press LLC

First English language Edition 2008
POB 8531, New Milford, CT 06776–8531, USA
& POB 2455, London WIA 5WY, England

www.tobypress.com

First published in German as *Mann ohne Makel*
© Verlag Kiepenheuer & Witsch, Köln, 2002
Translation © Helen Atkins, 2008

The publication of this work was supported
by a grant from the Goethe-Institut.

ISBN 978 1 59264 220 5, *hardcover*

A CIP catalogue record for this title is
available from the British Library

Typeset in Adobe Garamond Pro
by Koren Publishing Services

Printed and bound in the United States by
Thomson-Shore Inc., Michigan

For Gisela

Chapter one

The pain shot into his left knee. He stopped dead, suppressing a cry; then, as the pain eased, he slowly continued on his way. By the time he was crossing the Puppenbrücke he had forgotten about it.

The post office beside the main station was being demolished, though it was not very old. What was left of it, a mass of stones and rubble, lay waiting to be carted away by heavy trucks. Dust hung in the air. At the edge of the excavated site, a section of wall with a window in it was still standing.

The station was older than the post office, but moves to build a new one were continually being put off to some future date. Perhaps when all the long-neglected stations of Berlin's local S-Bahn system had been turned into miniature palaces, the people of Lübeck might hope to get a new main railway station to replace the dingy edifice at the heart of their own city.

Pushing open a swing-door at the entrance, Stachelmann crossed the gloomy station concourse and headed for platform nine, where the Hamburg train was waiting. He got into a first class open carriage and sat down on one of the blue-upholstered seats. At the other end of the carriage an elderly woman was sitting by the window, and he could see a green hat adorned with little silver chains poking up over the back of the seat facing hers. The overhead electronic sign was out of order. Stachelmann had chosen a seat with a table. He opened his briefcase to take out Simone Wagner's essay, which he had been too tired to finish reading the night before. It was about the theories surrounding the Reichstag fire in February 1933. Who had started it? The Nazis? The communists? Or the loner van der Lubbe? Stachelmann liked Simone Wagner: she had lively eyes and a genuine interest in history. She wrote fluently and knew how to handle sources—in relation to other topics, at any rate. But with the Reichstag fire she had walked straight into the obvious trap. Because the fire suited the Nazis' purposes and came at a very opportune moment for them, she was convinced they must have started it. But history is often capricious. Sometimes it produces a combination of events that would normally point to a human conspirator, and then people prefer to see conspiracy at work rather than just chance. You might say that chance is the greatest conspirator of all, Stachelmann thought, as he turned his attention to Simone's essay again. He would challenge her conclusions but still give her a good grade, a 2, in recognition of the effort she had put in. And using her essay as an example, he would explain to the class that while historians might study political beliefs, they must try not to let their own beliefs influence their historical judgments. Though this was easier said than done.

The carriage door slammed shut and a man walked heavily along the aisle and sat down facing Stachelmann across the table. Stachelmann drew the essay closer to him. Wheezing as if his throat was constricted, the newcomer mopped his brow with a handkerchief. After depositing a plastic bag with a supermarket logo on the table, he stood up again and opened the window. There was a whistle, and the train gave a jolt and moved off. The man sat down again, letting out a deep breath. He looked around, eyed Stachelmann for some seconds and then took the *Bild-Zeitung* from his plastic bag. Coughing, he opened the paper.

He was holding the front page up in front of Stachelmann's face. 'Family tragedy', it said in thick red letters, and below that, in smaller, black type, 'Despair of Hamburg property dealer (46)—third murder leaves daughter (6) dead.' A black and white photograph showed a man with his hand covering his eyes. Beside it was a colour picture of a little girl with blonde plaits, above the caption: 'Valentina Holler (6), poisoned like her brother—victims of a serial killer?'

Why does it say '*third* murder', Stachelmann wondered. He tried to read the main text of the story, but the man opposite turned the page, staring intently at Stachelmann for a moment as he did so. Instead of the family tragedy, Stachelmann now had a close-up view of a topless blonde who was giving him a seductive sideways look. 'Sandra knows what she wants,' the caption informed him. Stachelmann did not care what Sandra wanted. He wanted to know what had happened to the property dealer's family. But Sandra was followed by reports on last weekend's national football league matches, which had been waiting behind her back for the page to be turned. While the wheezing man studied Sandra, Stachelmann read about the crisis at Hamburg SV, or at least the part of the story on the top half of the page, for the man was now keeping the rest hidden under the table. Over the top of the paper he gave Stachelmann a hard look. Then he folded it and pushed it across the table. 'All yours,' he said hoarsely, and stood up with a smile in which Stachelmann thought he detected mockery. As though this stranger had heard Stachelmann's oft-repeated assertion that if he ever touched that rag he would only hold it between his finger and thumb, and even then he would wash his hands afterwards. The man moved towards the exit, and the train pulled into Bad Oldesloe.

When it moved off again, Stachelmann turned back to the front page and read the story. The property dealer and his family lived, like other wealthy residents of Hamburg, near the Elbchaussee. Two years ago the dead body of the wife had been found in the Duvenstedter Brook nature reserve by a man out walking there. One year ago his ten-year-old son had been poisoned at a public swimming pool. Now Valentina, too, was dead; that left only the property dealer himself and another son, aged four. A murder a year.

Stachelmann wondered how he would feel after a blow like that. He lived alone in a small apartment in Stietens Gang, a turning off Lichte Querstrasse, which linked Dankwartsgrube with Hartengrube.

In that idyllic part of the old town between the Mühlenteich and the Stadttrave, he sometimes felt lonely. But then he read stories about children who had been abducted and murdered. Or about a Hamburg property dealer whose wealth and status could not save him from losing his wife and two of his children. What you don't have, you can't lose. And you don't have to live with the fear of losing it, either.

Needless to say, the train arrived at Hamburg's main station a few minutes late. Stachelmann took a suburban train as far as Dammtor and then walked the rest of the way to the University. He was sweating; the morning was already hot. It was Monday, 9 July 2001. Soon the summer semester would be over, and then the Von-Melle-Park, with the old main building and the far newer concrete blocks that together house Hamburg's university, would once more be deserted.

Renate Breuer waved a piece of paper at him as soon as he opened the green-lacquered steel door of her office. 'A call for you, just five minutes ago!' she said, as if this were something unusual and special. Renate Breuer found almost everything exciting, even after so many years spent working in the humanities building, the Philosophers' Tower, as secretary of the history department. The paper bore a telephone number and a name, 'Oskar Winter'. In his own small office, Stachelmann sat down at his desk and looked at the paper. It did not take much working out. Oskar Winter—yes, that must be Ossi. Who else? They had been at Heidelberg University together, studying and trying to stir up world revolution. Stachelmann picked up the phone.

* * *

The old man had trouble breathing. Every so often he had to pause for a few moments before walking on. He was wearing a light beige suit of good quality cloth, probably bought at a high-class men's outfitters in Pöseldorf. A tie in an indeterminate mixture of colours complemented both the suit and the sturdy, reddish-brown shoes. He stood out from the other people in the street, who were in summer clothes. At last he reached Kellinghusenstrasse underground station and sank down, exhausted, on a bench that was smothered in blue and black graffiti—both drawings and words. 'Fuck you!' he read on the backrest of the bench opposite.

On the underground train the temperature was bearable, as the open windows let in a flow of air which, though warm, still had a cooling effect. By the time he reached the Landungsbrücken stop he felt much restored. He changed to Line 1 of the suburban railway, heading for Blankenese. It was a longer journey that way, but it saved him changing trains again.

At Blankenese he got out and walked down Dockenhudener Strasse, taking his time: he needed to conserve his strength. Just one more task remained. Actually there were to have been two more, but he had decided that his whole campaign would lose its point if no one was left to mourn. On reaching Gätgenstrasse he headed towards the Hirschpark by the Elbe. There he sat down on a bench close to the natural heritage monument—an ancient tree. It was surprising how many young people were free to stroll about early on a Wednesday afternoon. Pigeons and sparrows were being chased off by seagulls as they vied for the breadcrumbs that children were throwing to them. He resumed his walk, and, reaching the path along the bank of the Elbe, watched the cargo and passenger ships that were either coming into harbour or leaving for England, America, or Asia. Seagulls circled in the blue sky, and the wind sent cotton-wool clouds scudding across it. He went up Jacobs Treppe to the Elbchaussee and walked some way along it in the direction of the city centre. Then he turned left into Holztwiete, and now he could see his goal, a villa in the Art Nouveau style, finished in white stucco with arcs of light blue above the doors and windows. A police car was positioned close to the gateway. The back of the house faced towards a large building site enclosed by a wire fence. A truck was parked beside a site hut, and there was a digger at work, its diesel engine belching out black smoke. Standing under a beech tree close to the boundary, the old man peered into the grounds of the villa. He had found this gap in the hedge on one of his first visits here.

He felt impatient. In recent weeks he had sometimes doubted whether his project made any sense at all. He had started planning the third, most recent attack even before he had carried out the second. Was the deliberation with which he was now preparing the final one a reflection of real doubts about it? He shook his head. No, if he didn't carry out this attack then all the previous ones would have been pointless, and all the effort and risk would have been in vain. This time he didn't have a year to set it up. He could feel the hand of Death on his shoulder. As soon as the commotion over his last strike had died down he would act.

Then he saw him. A little boy with fair hair, sitting astride a toddler's ride-on car, laughing a bright, childish laugh. A woman hurrying after him put a peaked cap on his head to protect him from the sun. The child tugged it off, bit the peak, and tossed the cap away. The woman picked it up and spoke cajolingly to him, though the old man could not make out her words. Still laughing, the little boy propelled himself along on his car, leaving her behind. She followed, holding the cap in her hand. It looked as though she was crying. Once again she tried to insist, but the child just shook his head vigorously. He pointed to something that the old man could not see from where he was, and rode his car in that direction until he, too, vanished from view. Then he re-appeared, heading straight for the hole in the hedge. His face beamed with happiness: he had not grasped the fact that his sister was dead.

A young woman came round the corner, turning her head to look at the old man as she passed. He thought he saw a question in her glance: it was time he went. As he slowly walked towards Klein Flottbek suburban railway station, his brain was busy with his plan. Just once more, he murmured. Then he'd be free.

Seeing the station ahead of him, he quickened his pace. When he reached the platform he sat down on a bench; only then did he realize how exhausted he was.

* * *

Stachelmann had thought at once that the number seemed unusual, and his thought was confirmed when he found he had been connected to police headquarters. He was caught off guard for a moment, but then asked for Oskar Winter. 'I'll put you through to Kommissar Winter,' said the brusque voice at the other end.

'Winter.' The voice came through loudly.

'Stachelmann…'

'Jossi?' Winter asked.

'Yes,' said Stachelmann. He hated that nickname. He could have said, 'My name's Josef Maria', but he knew from past experience that it would be no use. Even in the old days, Oskar Winter, commonly known as 'Ossi', had just laughed at such protestations.

'Well, what a surprise for you!' He sounded absolutely certain.

Stachelmann was indeed surprised, to his annoyance. 'Yes,' he said.

'And now you're wondering how I've tracked you down!'

'Yes.'

'Through the newspaper!' Ossi's voice bellowed. 'Through the newspaper, of course!'

Stachelmann's mind went blank for a moment, then he remembered the short piece about him in the *Hamburger Abendblatt*. The previous week he had given a lecture at the adult education centre in Schanzenstrasse on the subject of the Hossbach Memorandum, and the local paper had had the space to give it a brief write-up. He doubted whether anyone was much the wiser after reading the account, cobbled together by some trainee journalist, of what was in fact one of the most important historical sources on the causes of the Second World War. The article had only confirmed Stachelmann's belief that newspaper offices were full of ignoramuses who had not the slightest interest in anything further back in time than their first girlfriends.

'You gave a lecture!' boomed Ossi, when he received no answer. 'There can't be all that many Josef Maria Stachelmanns.' Ossi laughed.

'Yes, alright,' said Stachelmann.

'Are you doing anything this evening?' asked Ossi.

'No,' Stachelmann replied unthinkingly, not wanting to keep Ossi waiting for an answer a second time. He immediately regretted it.

'Well, let's meet up for a drink, then!' said Ossi. 'A beer to mark our reunion. Or maybe more than one.'

They arranged to meet at eight o'clock in the Tokaya, a student pub close to the university. Stachelmann felt annoyed as he hung up. He had been looking forward to a quiet evening at home with C.S. Forester's naval hero of the Napoleonic Wars, Horatio Hornblower. Overcome by a wave of nostalgia for his youth, he had bought the complete set of novels in a cheap edition. Hornblower's adventures had enthralled him at fifteen, and to his amazement he found that they still did. So now this evening he would not find out how Horny managed to escape from French captivity, but instead how Ossi the revolutionary had ended up as a policeman. This put him in mind of another fellow student, the most ardent revolutionary of them all at the time, a man with unkempt black hair and a huge beard. One day, following a visit to his wealthy father, he had announced his intention of becoming an accountant. This, he claimed, was the most effective way to break the power of capitalism. Stachelmann grinned as he recalled the scene.

His grin faded as his gaze fell on the mountain of papers looming on a small table. In a rhetorical moment he had christened it his "mountain of shame". It was made up of five tall piles of documents, and it graphically demonstrated the hopeless state of his long-overdue *Habilitation* thesis, which would qualify him for a permanent post at the university. These documents had been awaiting his attention for years now; at this point he felt he could barely even remember what his chosen topic was. And because he could not get a grip on it, he'd be sitting in this poky little room, marking essays and test papers, for years to come—always assuming he hadn't been thrown out by then. The sight of that stack of documents reminded him yet again of his lack of self-discipline, and reinforced his belief that he should never have been appointed to this job. He had neither ambition nor talent. He doubted his ability to compose a single decent sentence; it was ridiculous to suppose that he could write a history of Buchenwald concentration camp and someday be rewarded for it with the title of professor. As for an actual chair, he dared not think of it. Yet that had originally been his goal. He had wanted to become a great historian like the Mommsens, like Steinbach, Jaeckel, or indeed Baring as he used to be, though these days he appeared on chat shows voicing wildly irrational views. When Stachelmann thought of his own former aspirations and compared them with what, at the age of forty-one, he had actually achieved, he was filled with despair. Reading the publications of other historians, even the most obscure, made him feel reduced to the size of an ant. He had clearly found his proper station in life: it was to hold seminars and to do preparatory research for Hasso Bohming, the professor—'the Legend' as some people called him, because he loved to boast of his part in all the battles of the recent 'historians' controversy', which had earned him, so he claimed, the hatred of his opponents and the admiration of his fellow campaigners. Others besides Stachelmann had noticed the disparity between these tales of blood and thunder on the front and their reflection in specialist journals and collections of essays.

Stachelmann laughed softly to himself. Of course the affable Bohming was a braggart. But he, Stachelmann, was not even that. He was nothing. If he tried to boast, no one would need to work out what was lies and what was truth because *none* of it would be true. For years he had been plagued by anxieties about his inadequacy. Where would it lead? Would he end up like that perpetual junior lecturer, Weitenschläger, in Heidelberg, who spent more time at wine festivals than in the history department? He could see the man now, red hair, a drinker's face, glazed eyes, leaning against something to stop himself swaying. Stachelmann had curiosity, he was fascinated by his subject, but he simply could not do what that curiosity required of him. It was surely too late now to learn how to concentrate on a subject for years, how to cope with the inevitable tedium and produce something that would secure him a place in the community of historians.

There was a knock at the door, and he called, 'Come in!' When the door opened, he gave a start. *She* was there—Anne Derling. For two years Anne had been working as Bohming's assistant. Since her arrival he had allowed all his colleagues to call him Hasso, though he never left them in any doubt that he was superior to them all. He was especially friendly towards Anne, but then so was everyone, for she was clever and beautiful. A rare combination, one colleague said, and he never spoke a truer word. When Anne joined the department, the whole atmosphere changed. There was a new enthusiasm among the teaching staff which not even a clairvoyant could have foreseen. As time passed the initial excitement died down, but a friendly atmosphere persisted, and discussions were livelier when Anne was in the room. Was she conscious of the effect she had?

Even the handsome political scientist Rolf Kugler had sniffed around her for a while. Youthfully dynamic and newly elevated to the status of professor, he had a reputation for testing out his charisma on every new female colleague. Before Anne's arrival, however, he had not been seen among the historians. And he soon vanished again: evidently he had not found favour with Bohming's new assistant.

With the door open just a crack, she smiled at Stachelmann and asked, 'Shall I get a coffee for you too?'

'Yes,' he said, or rather stammered. She had never made the offer before.

'I'll bring you one,' she said gaily. Her face disappeared; the door stayed open.

Stachelmann felt his palms grow damp. She reappeared and nudged the door wider open with her shoulder, since her hands each held a mug of coffee which she had brought from the small kitchen along the corridor. Her glasses had slipped out of place. She put the two mugs down on the desk, then took her glasses off and polished them on a corner of her blouse, worn loose outside her trousers. Her clothes, bright and summery, looked good with her curly blue-black hair.

'What are you doing just now? I hope I'm not disturbing you too much.'

'No, no,' said Stachelmann, inwardly cursing his awkwardness.

'I've just been talking to a student, I think her name's Alicia or something. She was raving about your seminar.'

'I expect she's confused me with someone else, or perhaps she was drunk the last time she came,' Stachelmann said with a grin. He did hear from time to time that students thought well of his seminars. His courses had been oversubscribed for years. This popularity was gratifying, but it also meant more work. And somehow he managed to persuade himself that it was only the subject matter that, for some obscure reason, appealed to the students. The evening before last, Alicia Weitbrecht had rung him at home, ostensibly to ask him something about the next exam. He had already forgotten the question, but not the call.

'Oh, sure,' Anne said.

Stachelmann shrugged before picking up the mug of coffee from the edge of the desk and taking a sip. Why had Anne come? Just for a natter?

'I need to speak to you,' Anne said. 'Can we have a proper talk sometime?'

Stachelmann eyed her curiously. He hoped he would not break out in a sweat.

'Of course,' he said. 'Any time.'

'Oh, good,' said Anne. She seemed relieved. 'This evening, then?'

Damn, thought Stachelmann. He'd already arranged to see Ossi this evening. 'No, I'm afraid I can't. How about tomorrow?'

Anne looked at him. He thought he saw a shadow flit across her face. 'Okay, tomorrow it is,' she said. 'At my place? I only live just round the corner.'

'Fine,' said Stachelmann. He knew where she lived. He had walked past the building a number of times.

After they had chatted a little longer about the department and the Legend, and bemoaned the apathy of the students they had to teach, Anne got to her feet and gathered up the empty mugs. With a bright smile she said, 'Oh well, back to the grind.' A trace of her perfume lingered in the room. It was nice.

When Anne had gone he felt the pain starting up, right at the base of his spine. He stood up and tried to straighten his back, cursing these continual bouts of pain. He looked at the clock. In half an hour it would be time for his seminar on 'National Socialism, 1933–39'. He had chosen the topic partly in the hope that it would help him with his *Habilitation*, but up to now it had not done so. This seminar group was even larger than previous ones. Some students were having to sit on the floor, which they accepted without protest. Stachelmann and Ossi, in their day, had demonstrated primarily in favour of revolution, but also in protest against poor conditions for students. To them these issues had been related. He was glad that present-day students thought differently on some points, yet it also made him feel a certain contempt for them. The fact was that he had not quite succeeded in abandoning the dream that they had pursued in those days. He took trouble with his students, and they rewarded him with their attendance, if not with much enthusiasm for their studies. Now and again a female student would show an interest in him that was not purely academic: Alicia evidently fell into this category. But that kind of attention left him cold. He had no wish to be idolized by some girl who would then inevitably become disillusioned. Real women were not interested in him, while unsuitable ones chased after him. No doubt this was what a failed historian had to expect. When feelings of inadequacy overwhelmed him, Stachelmann hated himself.

It was time to go to his seminar. He picked up his briefcase, which was bulging with essays. The corridor was busy with people. On its brick walls there were posters advertising diets and techno-discos. The seminar room was crowded, as always. The buzz of conversation died down as Stachelmann entered. Some of the students looked at him expectantly as he sat down at his desk, which was really just a table like hundreds of others in the various seminar rooms. He took out the essays and put them on the table, then pushed the pile towards a student, who looked at it in a bored sort of way before searching for his own essay and passing the pile on. The pile shrank until only three essays remained, written by students who were absent. Stachelmann returned these to his briefcase and told the group that on the whole he had been satisfied with their essays. They were certainly good enough to earn the students their seminar certificates: the only hurdle left now was the exam at the end of the semester. The class received his judgment in silence.

Stachelmann praised Simone Wagner's essay. It was well researched, he said, and excellently constructed, but unfortunately her conclusions were questionable. He cast a quick glance towards the corner where Simone was sitting. Her eyes held a look of incomprehension. She raised a hand to speak, and he nodded.

'The Reichstag fire benefited no one but the Nazis,' she said. She sounded indignant. 'And there was a secret passage between Goering's residence as president of the Reichstag and the boiler and plant-room in the Reichstag itself—that was how the arsonists got into the building unnoticed and made their escape after starting the fire. The police deliberately failed to follow up any evidence that pointed towards Goering—and it was to Goering himself that the police were answerable. And then when you consider how quickly Hitler, Goering and other leading Nazis were on the scene, and how quickly they issued the Reichstag Fire Emergency Decree...' She had worked herself up into a rage and was glaring at Stachelmann. 'Think about it. The Reichstag burns down on the twenty-seventh, and on the twenty-eighth the Decree is ready and in force. That's either magic or else proof that the Decree had already been written before the fire actually happened.'

Stachelmann rejoiced inwardly. He liked it when students defended their opinions so fiercely. It happened far too rarely. He listened patiently as Simone let loose her torrent of words. When she had finished, he said: 'The reason I gave you a two was not because you say that the Nazis set fire to the Reichstag. The reason you didn't get a *one* is because you can't *prove* that assertion. It was based on your instinctive feeling, not on logic. There's no witness and no other source to prove your hypothesis. It's as simple as that.' He stopped short: he should not have added that last sentence. He made an effort to redeem his error. 'You have written an excellent essay,' he said gently. 'If you'd said, "All the indications are that the Nazis set fire to the Reichstag themselves", then I would have given you a one plus if there were such a mark. Though I would have considered even that conclusion to be lacking in balance. But one mustn't present something as a proven fact if it can't be proved. That's the difference between scholarship and politics.' Again he reproached himself: he should not have moved on to general principles. He looked at Simone. Her anger had not abated and she was not prepared to take part in any further discussion. Stachelmann was sorry about that: not many in the group contributed as much as she did.

He saw Alicia Weitbrecht with her hand up, snapping her fingers to attract his attention. A broad, silver-coloured bangle glittered on her arm and she wore striking makeup. She doesn't need that, Stachelmann thought. She repeated his own arguments, keeping her eyes on him all the time. He soon realized that she was trying to score some points with him. He briefly thanked her for her contribution and looked around to see if anyone else was going to speak. He didn't suppose they were. A student in the front row whose name he had forgotten was gazing down at the table in front of him, while others looked away to avoid meeting his eye.

'Okay,' Stachelmann said. It wasn't okay, but what could he do? He spent the remaining time talking about some weaknesses and some good points in other students' essays, and preparing them for the topics to be covered in the next few sessions. He knew that this would all fall on stony ground, but it was only fair to give students the chance. Sometimes he could not help thinking that it made no difference whether he turned up at all. Only one out of all these students got anything out of what he said. But perhaps he should be satisfied with that: in other seminars things were, if anything, worse. Pity, now Simone was angry with him. He hoped she'd get over it.

Back in his office, behind the green steel door, he sat down next to the mountain of shame and looked out of the window. The summer weather seemed to him unreal. It bore no relation to his mood. Yet surely he should be happy? Only yesterday it was an impossible dream, but today Anne had actually invited him to her home. But he would make a mess of things, he knew.

There was a knock at the door. He called, 'Come in', and Alicia Weitbrecht appeared. 'Excuse me, Herr Stachelmann,' she said nervously.

'Well?' he asked. His tone was curt, though he had meant to sound friendly.

She flinched slightly. 'There's something I want to ask you about my essay.'

'Why don't you come at my normal consultation time?'

'I can't, I'll be away.'

'I'm afraid I'm not free just now,' Stachelmann said in a friend-lier tone. 'Can you manage tomorrow afternoon, at about four? Here in my room?'

She smiled. She was a pretty child. That's just it, Stachelmann thought: she's only a child.

Chapter two

The air in the Tokaja was hot and smoky. Stachelmann, who had turned up early, searched for Ossi but could not see him in the dim light. He found an empty table in a corner, from which he could watch the door. A gaming machine nearby was emitting computer-like bleeping tones. Gradually his eyes adjusted to the darkness and he picked up the menu, which offered all the usual things—vegetables *au gratin*, noodles, pizza, cheap wine.

A woman dressed in black was standing beside him; he had not noticed her arrival. She looked at him expectantly and asked, 'What can I get you?' There was smoke in her voice.

'I don't know yet,' he answered. When she raised her eyebrows slightly, he added hastily, 'I'm waiting for someone.' He stammered, and cursed himself for it.

The woman in black shook her head and departed. She had a ponytail that hung down to her waist.

The gaming machine went on bleeping.

The door opened and a couple came in. Stachelmann was just about to look away again when behind the couple he saw a familiar head. Ossi's face had grown broader, but Stachelmann recognized him at once. He half rose in his seat and waved, forgetting that Ossi, coming in from the light, would not be able to see him. Watching Ossi peering at each table as he drew nearer, Stachelmann stood up, and finally Ossi saw him and spread his arms wide.

'Oh, there you are, old man!' he said. 'You haven't changed a bit.'

Stachelmann hated that sort of remark. Of course he had changed. And not for the better. He avoided Ossi's bear hug by keeping his distance and holding out his hand. Ossi's handshake was vigorous but a bit flabby: he had put on a lot of weight. His red sideburns made him look older than he was.

He sat down opposite Stachelmann and looked into his face. 'Just the same,' he muttered. Gazing over Stachelmann's shoulder at the wall behind him, he added: 'Those were the days, eh?'

Stachelmann nodded.

The woman in black reappeared and asked for their orders. Her voice sounded shrill. They each ordered a Pils.

'Well, so now you're at the university here,' Ossi said. 'A historian. That's what you always wanted to be.'

'Yes,' said Stachelmann.

'And you give lectures,' said Ossi.

'Yes, sometimes.'

'And I've ended up in the police. Murder squad.'

'But you wanted to be a lawyer, didn't you?' asked Stachelmann.

'Yes, I did, really. But then it all went pear-shaped just before my professional exams. Women, you know.' Ossi made a dismissive gesture.

Stachelmann didn't know, but nodded anyway. So Ossi had dropped out just before the last round of exams. He suspected it had had less to do with women than with Ossi's lack of staying power. Ossi had always been good at sidestepping difficult hurdles, but you couldn't sidestep exams. He had passed the first set: when it was a matter of small obstacles, Ossi would leap over them with a triumphant whoop. But then, don't policemen need staying power? Stachelmann remembered that at one stage Ossi had wanted to become a lawyer for the protest movement. That was why he'd moved from Heidelberg to Marburg: the law faculty at Heidelberg was too conservative for his liking. But he must have failed to make the grade in Marburg. Perhaps because by that time their movement had fizzled out.

'Murder squad?' Stachelmann asked, as if he was not sure he had heard correctly.

'Yes. I've been with the police for eleven years altogether, and just about five years with the Hamburg murder squad. So now I'm a Kommissar in the detective force, instead of a lawyer. I haven't done too badly.'

Stachelmann thought of dead bodies, but said, 'Not badly at all.'

'And what brought you to Hamburg?' Ossi asked.

'My doctorate. There was a professor at the university here who was interested in my thesis. At least he pretended to be.' Stachelmann was not being totally honest. Bohming had been supportive about his research on Buchenwald, and had even urged him to develop it further for his *Habilitation*. But for Stachelmann, completing his doctoral thesis had been a torment, and despite all the praise it had received he did not think it was as good as people had claimed. On the whole, the reviews it had received in the historical journals had been restrained, as they generally were, yet one of them had said that perhaps a new star had risen in the firmament of historiography. Stachelmann had not forgotten that—not least because of the extravagant formulation. They had wanted to keep him at Heidelberg but had been unable to offer him a proper job. That was why he had moved to Hamburg. And here they would throw him out at some point if he didn't get on with his *Habilitation*. He was on a fixed-term contract which would run out in just over two years. Would the Legend keep a failure in his department? Hardly. Members of his department had to be successful, because their success rubbed off on him.

'So you've achieved everything you wanted, Jossi.' Ossi was beaming.

Stachelmann did not want to be dragged back into the past. How he hated that nickname! It was stupid, and it reminded him of events he had long since put out of his mind. Ossi and Jossi—

they had made a name for themselves at university. They had often shared a platform at political meetings and demonstrations and had almost always held the same views. Politically they had been like twins. Stachelmann had taken it for a real friendship. But when their dreams evaporated, nothing had held the 'twins' together any more. Now Stachelmann looked at Ossi and did not like what he saw. Ossi would soon be fat, and he was probably a heavy drinker, to judge by the redness of his nose and the enlarged pores on it. 'No, I certainly haven't achieved everything I wanted, far from it. They can still throw me out. I've got to make it to professor one of these days, or the game's up.'

Ossi laughed: 'But that'll be child's play for you!'

'I wish,' Stachelmann replied. 'If only it were. There's a mountain of documents waiting to be cleared away first.'

Ossi looked at him, and saw he was not smiling. Stachelmann knew that Ossi didn't understand. How could he? In the world of dead bodies there was no mountain of shame to keep you awake at night. Stachelmann saw no point in telling Ossi about his anxieties. It wouldn't do either of them any good. But equally he didn't want to pretend to be more successful than he was. It was time to change the subject . 'Anyway. So what particular dead body are you busy with at the moment?' he asked, with an attempt at humour.

'It's the murder of a child,' Ossi said. His voice sounded sad and exhausted. 'I don't know if we'll ever solve it.'

'Why not?'

'We can't find a motive, and we've no clues either. It's clearly not a sexual killing. It seems almost as though death came upon the girl like a ghost and then simply vanished again.'

A change had come over Ossi; Stachelmann was surprised at his stilted way of talking. Perhaps that's how he copes with the horror of it, Stachelmann thought. Then he remembered the picture he had seen on the train that morning. A little girl with plaits. 'Is it that business with the property dealer?' he asked.

Ossi nodded. 'Yes, how did you know?' His hand gave a momentary twitch. 'Oh, of course, the newspapers.'

The woman in black appeared: 'Would you like to order?'

'Odd name, isn't it—Valentina Holler,' said Ossi.

The woman in black hissed something under her breath and shook her head in annoyance. She walked off, her ponytail swinging.

'And an odd case,' Ossi added. He was running his thumb and forefinger up and down his beer glass. His eyes were blank. 'She was playing,' he said. 'Just playing. She was playing with a doll, pushing it around the garden in a doll's pram.' He looked up from the table and, seeing the woman in black, signalled to her. She came over, giving him an unfriendly look. Ossi ordered another beer, and, after an enquiring glance at Stachelmann, made it two. Then, saying, 'Back in a minute—call of nature', he stood up and went in search of the toilet.

Stachelmann was amazed at the complete change in Ossi's mood. Of course the murder of a child was upsetting. In many murder cases there were tangible motives, some of them even good enough to count as mitigating circumstances in court. But the murder of a child was always incomprehensible. There was no question of jealousy, envy, competition, revenge, or any of the other reasons people might put forward for killing another human being.

Ossi returned. Stachelmann noticed a stain on his trouser leg.

The woman in black came and set two beers down on the table.

The gaming machine bleeped.

Ossi took a mouthful of beer. 'Valentina was pushing her doll's pram, and then she collapsed. She died instantly. Poisoned. Cyanide.'

Stachelmann was startled. The paper had said nothing about that. 'Cyanide?'

'Yes, someone poisoned a six-year-old child with prussic acid.'

'How was it done?'

'There was a sweet lying somewhere in the garden, a caramel filled with cyanide. At least, that's what the pathologist said. We shan't get the autopsy report until tomorrow. We found the sweet wrapping. It was there next to the body. Valentina found the sweet, wrapped in blue paper, she unwrapped it and evidently put it straight into her mouth. A couple of sucks and she was dead. Just as the killer intended.'

'That's extraordinary,' said Stachelmann. 'You wouldn't use a sweet to kill an adult.'

'Who would do that—fill a sweet with cyanide and throw it into a garden so that a child will find it and die? I just don't get it.'

They sat in silence for a while. Stachelmann gazed around the pub, which had filled up in the meantime. The woman in black was busy now, doing her job calmly and efficiently. By the time she knocked off tonight she would have shifted a couple of hundred-weight on her tray.

'And this is the third murder in the Holler household. I wouldn't be surprised if there were two more in due course.'

'Is the man being blackmailed?' Stachelmann was surprised to find himself so interested in the case. He felt that it was not only because of Ossi's involvement with it. Something about it must have struck a particular chord with him. Holler—who was Holler?

Ossi took some seconds to reply. 'No—at least it doesn't *seem* to be blackmail. We're not even sure it's a case of serial murder.'

'Aren't three deaths in one family enough?'

Ossi lit a cigarette, drew deeply on it and explained quietly and despondently: 'With serial killings there's a single killer or group of killers, which usually means the same methods. Holler's wife was bludgeoned to death, the son was poisoned and so was the daughter. Someone put cyanide in the son's Coke. Two poisonings, but the first death doesn't fit in. Beating somebody to death is quite different.'

'But all the same—three deaths in one family in a couple of years?'

'You're right. The only thing is, no one knows of a motive. Holler is a highly respectable businessman. We've gone through everything on him with a fine-tooth comb. He almost seems like a saint. He's involved with all sorts of charities, but doesn't make his generosity public. For instance, he donated half a million for the victims of Chernobyl, but when we found out about it he was livid and told us in no uncertain terms to keep it out of the papers. His business associates and his clients praise him to the skies. He's honest, dependable—a kind of Jesus of the Elbchaussee.'

Continuing, Ossi told Stachelmann that he had visited Holler at his home in Holztwiete that morning. The man had obviously been crying and had not slept. Holler was a tall man with short fair hair, who looked younger than his years, but his eyes held a look of despair. No, he had no idea why his daughter had been poisoned. Holler had assured Ossi that he could look at anything he liked, he would tell his bank and his doctor to waive their duty of confidentiality. The police could turn the house and the business inside out if they wished. 'Do anything you think might help track down the murderer,' Holler had said, his voice breaking.

Ossi was baffled, which was why he was speaking so freely about the case—that much was obvious. Once again Stachelmann was conscious of a nagging question in his own mind about Holler—who he was and why these terrible things were happening to him. Deep inside, he thought he could hear a voice trying to remind him of something. But of what, damn it? And what connection could he possibly have with Holler? He didn't know the man, had never been anywhere near his house. What had he to do with property dealers, or charities, or a madman who injected cyanide into a sweet and threw it into a garden in the hope that a child would eat it? Had the murderer watched the little girl suck the sweet? Had he been glad when his plan worked? Surely there had been a strong possibility that someone else would find the sweet and throw it away, or eat it themselves, so was the child the real target of the crime at all, or was it a matter of chance? Was someone wandering around the city with a bag of caramels laced with cyanide in his pocket, scattering them haphazardly in the hope that somebody would die? Would there be further poisonings? How did you get hold of cyanide, anyway? Who produced it? What kind of a death did you suffer when you swallowed cyanide? Question after question surged through his mind. No, it was just one sweet, and one dead child. And the murderer had meant it for that particular child. But how could he know that the child would eat the sweet? Whichever way you looked at it, the mystery remained.

Ossi had ordered a third beer from the woman in black, and a schnapps to go with it. 'I'm not on duty,' he said. 'Are you disappointed?'

Stachelmann looked at him, puzzled.

'I mean because this isn't how an old pals' reunion ought to be.'

Stachelmann laughed. 'Why, how should it be?'

'Oh, you know, clapping each other on the back, laughing so loud that it annoys people at other tables, laying into the booze, telling each other what good shape we're in, or else patting each other's beer guts, all that stuff. Anyway, I'm divorced and I've got two children.'

'I know that name,' said Stachelmann. 'It's there somewhere in the back of my mind, I just can't put my finger on it.' He gazed blankly into the smoke-laden air.

'What name?' asked Ossi.

'Holler.'

'I was hoping to forget that name for an hour or two,' said Ossi.

The gaming machine bleeped.

Ossi wiped his mouth with the back of his hand. He looked tired. 'Why are you so interested, anyway? Do you know how many murders there are every year in Hamburg?'

Stachelmann shook his head.

'In 2001 I think there were thirty-seven.'

'But a child?' Stachelmann rejoined.

'A child, a child.' Ossi sounded angry. 'I'm sick of hearing that. Everybody keeps going on about it being a child—how awful that is, killing a child. I'll give you my opinion, for what it's worth: murder is murder whether it's a child or an old granny. Or do you think one life's worth more than another, a thousand marks rather than two hundred? Perhaps it *is* worth more to industry, because they can expect to unload more stuff onto a child in the course of its life than they can onto an old granny whose time is nearly up and whose days of frenzied consumerism are over. It's a load of bollocks.'

'Still the old class warrior!' said Stachelmann. It did not sound funny.

'Idiot!' said Ossi. 'They're at their wits' end at headquarters. The press is really going to town on the story, especially *Bild* and the *Morgenpost*. And Holler's a kind of Messiah figure who knows the mayor, the Senator for the Interior, the head of the Chamber of Industry and Commerce, the boss of the Trade Union Federation and all the rest.'

'A foot in every camp, then?'

'No, not in any camp, but he knows everybody. And it rather seems as if he and the Chief of Police are bosom pals. At least that's the way it sounded when the Chief was bawling us out about this case.'

Stachelmann desperately racked his brains. Damn and blast, where had he heard or read that name? He'd read it somewhere, he could see the letters before his eyes. They had been typed. Or was his memory playing tricks on him? It wasn't as good as a historian's ought to be. It was sometimes embarrassing when people asked him, a specialist in the subject, for dates or names. All too often they just wouldn't come to mind.

'Well, you seem to be full of gloom and despondency,' said Ossi.

'No, I'm just thinking.'

'By the look of you, that's the same thing.'

Stachelmann felt irritated. He had often been told that. 'I can't get that name out of my head...'

'Holler?'

'I've read it somewhere.'

Ossi looked at him, suddenly alert. 'Where?'

'I wish I knew.'

'Well, think!'

'What d'you think I've been doing for the last half hour?'

No, it wouldn't come. Not today, perhaps not ever. It was probably just some resemblance, perhaps a similar name he'd come across in a book or journal. Or maybe it was a case of *déjà vu*? Anyway, even if Holler wasn't a common name like Schmidt or Müller, there was nothing wildly unusual about it. Another thing struck him. In the old days Ossi had never been so persistent, or so serious. He had always had a quip for every occasion. Back then Stachelmann used to wonder what crack Ossi would come up with if the world were about to end. Probably his best ever. Everyone else would be standing at the edge of the abyss, screaming, but Ossi would have a joke at the ready. Hey, guys, have you heard this one? But faced with the Holler case Ossi had run out of jokes. Maybe even before that. Did he still know his friend, he wondered—or had he perhaps got him wrong back then? He had envied him because he seemed able to shrug off the kind of problems that kept Stachelmann awake at night. But perhaps Ossi had had sleepless nights too?

It was late by the time Ossi and Stachelmann paid the woman in black for their drinks. Stachelmann gave her a good tip, but she did not smile, and barely looked at him. He almost felt like apologizing.

Only when he was on the train heading back to Lübeck did Stachelmann realize how tired he was. There was a *Bild* lying on the table in his first-class carriage. He took another look at the pictures. Valentina Holler, six years old, poisoned with prussic acid. Cyanide kills quickly, but before you die you suffer excruciating pain. The photograph of the father, the property dealer, was black and white, blurry. He did not know the man. Why had Holler's name been buzzing around in his head ever since the morning?

Chapter three

The old man had to admit he'd been lucky so far. No one had seen him carry out his killings, and so no innocent stranger had had to die. And he had managed to dispatch each victim at the first attempt. It had been easier than he'd expected. The old man lay on his bed gazing up at the ceiling. He could see pictures. Breakfast—his mother giving him a bowl of semolina. His father getting up from the table, about to leave for work. 'Selling houses', he called it. He himself going to school; they had their own special one. He had loved his teacher, who was called Esther and taught every subject. In the evenings—Papi was often still at work—Mami put him to bed. She always read something to him: fairy tales were what he liked best. He closed his eyes. The one where the Angel of Death had his sword taken from him—he still remembered that one vividly.

One day God said to the Angel of Death: 'Go forth and lead the soul of Joshua to Paradise.' The rabbi Joshua was a just man, but his time had come. Because he had never sinned, the Angel of Death was to grant him one last wish. 'Show me my place in Paradise,' said Joshua. 'But give me your sword to hold: it frightens me.' The Angel of Death gave him the sword and lifted him up onto the sheltering wall that enclosed Paradise, so that he could get a view of it. When Joshua saw Paradise in all its glory he did not want to return to earth, but jumped down into Paradise, still holding the sword. The Angel of Death asked for it back, since he could not do his work without it, but Joshua would not give it to him. Because Joshua was a pious man, God allowed him to keep the sword for seven years. During all that time nobody died. After the seven years were done, God yielded to the Angel's pleas, and death returned. The first to die was Joshua, but he felt no pain. The Angel of Death drew his soul out of his body just as you might pull a thread out of some milk. Gently borne aloft, the rabbi floated to his allotted habitation in Paradise.

That had been the old man's favourite story when he was a child. Death could be beautiful. For him it would bring release. Life was so much unwanted ballast, dragging at his soul like a ton weight.

Would his luck hold? He thought of the woman. Her scream when he had emerged from behind the bush. She stood there rooted to the spot, making no attempt to defend herself. He had hit her on the head with a club, harder and harder, working himself into a frenzy. When at last he stopped, exhausted, her head was a shapeless lump, covered in blood and brains.

*   *   *

Stachelmann hardly slept that night, and when he did nod off he dreamed of corpses. He was in a bad way when he woke up. His back ached and he was stiff: the tablets were not effective for long. He struggled out of bed, his eyes burning. He spread two pieces of bread with jam, and as he drank his mug of instant coffee he glanced at his local paper, the *Lübecker Nachrichten*. On the page devoted to the weather and non-local news he found a small item on the Valentina Holler murder. Hamburg was less than an hour away by train, yet even that short distance meant that the crime was given less prominence.

Stachelmann stood at the window in his dressing gown, looking out into the rear courtyard. It was raining and the sky was overcast. Then he remembered what this evening held in store: the meeting with Anne that he had dreamed of for so long. His stomach contracted, as it always did when he was nervous or excited. Then sometimes he would get diarrhoea. Not on the train, he hoped. He found train toilets disgusting.

He survived the train journey better than he had feared. When he saw the mountain of shame his spirits sank momentarily; then pleasurable anticipation gained the upper hand again until it was superseded by the fear that he would mess everything up as usual. He picked up a pile of historical journals that he should have read long ago. He did not like them, seeing in them nothing but a parade of vanity. The scholarly debates in them reflected the desire for self-advertisement rather than the sincere search for truth. Present-day scholarship was a primeval jungle in which each scholar stood up on his hind legs, beating his chest with his fists to let the whole forest know who was an alpha male or aspired to be one. That drumming reverberated through the journals. To become a silverback you had to bow and scrape and write a lot, quoting copiously from the crowned heads of historical research. Stachelmann gave a mirthless laugh. Things had not changed so very much since mankind first started walking upright.

He discovered an article on the Mittelbau-Dora concentration camp, where the v-2 rockets were produced. This article was different. In plain language it described the sufferings of the prisoners at this camp near Nordhausen, and assessed the camp's significance for the development of arms technology. So, not everyone was striving for alpha-male status. The Dora camp had originally been a satellite camp of Buchenwald. A ray of sunlight shone in through the window; the rain had stopped. He marked the page with a slip of paper: later he would photocopy the article and add it to the mountain of shame.

He did not go to the university canteen, for fear that if Anne saw him there she might come up to him and cancel their meeting. Instead he walked to Harvestehuder Weg, on the bank of the Aussenalster, where the ducks had lost almost all fear of humans.

Why had Anne invited him? He wished he had asked her. As it was, he would have to suffer this uncertainty for many hours yet. What could she want from a failure like him? He was suddenly gripped by panic. Every time he saw Bohming in the history department he was afraid that he would call him into his office and ask him when he expected to finish his *Habilitation*. Of course Bohming would put it in a friendly way. He would speak of the great hopes he placed in him, perhaps repeating what he had said when Stachelmann first came to Hamburg: 'You have every chance here, Stachelmann, I'm not as young as I used to be.' He had hinted at how one could get round the taboo on internal appointments. 'Look, I have friends in Cologne. What do you say, two or three semesters there, you can manage to put up with those garrulous Rhinelanders, and then you come back to Hamburg. You see, I've got it all worked out. Now all you have to do is finish your *Habil*. But that's nothing to you, after that doctoral thesis—"new star in the historians' firmament" and all that—and if you run into a sticky patch I'll always be there to help.'

Could anyone have wished for a more auspicious start? Stachelmann felt guilty when he remembered the friendliness of his reception in Hamburg. Bohming and the others were still friendly, but Stachelmann thought he detected a sense of disappointment. That would only grow. Why did he lack the strength to jump that last hurdle? It was not just Bohming who was disappointed in him—he was far more disappointed in himself.

He sat down on a bench near the water and watched the ducks. A few swam up and waited for the crumbs which they supposed Stachelmann had in his pockets. Others had had enough to eat and were dozing in pairs on the grass. He watched sailing boats drifting past on a slack breeze.

His parents would also be disappointed if his contract was not extended. He must become a professor if he was ever to attain peace of mind. But he lacked the peace of mind needed to *become* a professor. He felt that his doctoral thesis had said everything there was to say about his topic. He should have held back some of his material, thinned out what he put in his doctoral thesis—he would still have got a good mark. But if he'd done that then the periodicals would not even have mentioned his thesis, and he would not have got his present appointment in Hamburg. But he could have done a *Habil* at some lesser university. He lived in fear of the day he would have to acknowledge that he would never do it. That fear often robbed him of his sleep.

The ducks had given up on him. They swam or waddled towards the next bench, where a grandmother and grandson were throwing crumbs into the water and onto the grass. At every throw the little boy gave a piercing shriek. It was time to go.

At four o'clock there was a knock at his door. Alicia—he had forgotten all about her; he hoped it didn't show. Then he told himself that maybe it would be a good thing if it did. She had made herself look pretty and was wearing a short skirt. She's a lovely child, Stachelmann thought, not for the first time. But he was not attracted to her. He tried to make this obvious, adopting a cold, harsh manner. But this had no effect, or at least none that she chose to show. Softly saying, 'Hello,' she gazed into his eyes for a little too long before sitting down on the chair facing his desk and leaning forward a little. The top two buttons of her blouse were undone.

A lovely child. Why did the same phrase spring to mind whenever he saw her?

There was a knock at the door, and Anne poked her head in. She opened her mouth, then shut it again when she saw Stachelmann's visitor. Stachelmann thought her smile faded for a moment. 'Oh, sorry,' Anne said and closed the door.

Stachelmann listened as Alicia talked, but he couldn't really work out what Alicia wanted. Was she trying to find out why she had got a 3 and Simone Wagner a 2 even though she couldn't prove her theory? She didn't seem particularly upset. She was merely complaining a little, explaining that her essay agreed with the opinion of almost all reputable historians. Stachelmann wondered if he should tell her the truth: that he had given her a 3 because her work hadn't shown even the smallest spark of originality. But there had been another reason, too. Alicia's attentions were making him nervous, and he didn't want to encourage her by giving her a mark that she might see as flattering.

When Stachelmann had been a student there had been almost nothing but 1s and 2s. The professors and lecturers had been happy if a student even submitted work for grading at all. Stachelmann had benefited from that, but did not feel able to award marks on the same basis. He was strict in the marks he gave, and tried to be fair. He wondered if he would ever be able to give Alicia a 1. If he did, she would probably ring him at home twice a week and pursue him in the department on the other days. He would never be able to take his seat in the new canteen in the Philosophers' Tower without fearing that she would come over and join him.

He tried to be objective and friendly but detached. She smiled radiantly at him. He told her that in future she should take less notice of the majority view of historians and instead pay closer attention to the sources. She nodded eagerly. When he thought he had covered all the necessary points, he said, 'I'm glad you're willing to take my criticism on board,' and stood up, hand outstretched, as a signal for her to go.

She stood up too and held out her hand. Then she drew it back and said, 'Herr Stachelmann, just one more question.'

'Yes?'

'Can I invite you out for a coffee? I know a nice café not far from here, on the way to the Klosterstern.'

'Why?' asked Stachelmann. He felt embarrassed. Why had he asked the question instead of simply saying no?

'Does everything have to have a reason? I just think it would be nice. And if you also thought it would be nice, that would be a good enough reason to have a cup of coffee.' Her smile both attracted and repelled him.

Stachelmann held out his hand again and said, 'I'm afraid not. Sorry.'

'Oh, I see, you're busy. Never mind, we can do it another time.' She said this with a smile that some men would have found unsettling; then she turned and left the room, still with a spring in her step.

He continued to sit at his desk for a while, feeling annoyed with himself. Why had he not spoken more plainly? Why did he prevaricate whenever he felt pressured? Why, in such situations, could he not simply say no?

The phone rang; it was Bohming. 'Listen, Herr Stachelmann, would you mind coming over to see me in my room?'

'Of course,' Stachelmann said. 'When?'

'Shall we say in a quarter of an hour?' As always, Bohming was speaking a little louder than necessary.

'Right, I'll be there,' Stachelmann said. He looked at the clock: he hoped it wouldn't take too long. Bohming liked to spin things out. In discussions he would talk endlessly about himself and his achievements. And yet, as Stachelmann had gathered from gossip at a historians' conference, Bohming had not always been such a hero. He had been a timid bag-carrier when he was assistant to some professor at the Free University in Berlin—a professor so insignificant that no one could even recall his name. Bohming had apparently never uttered a word, or if he had, he had spoken very softly to make sure no one would hear. But this knowledge of his boss's far from glorious past was no help to Stachelmann in the present situation. What did Bohming want him for? Was it about his *Habil*? Stachelmann could feel his stomach contracting. He could see his hands trembling. When would this fear come to an end?

He hoped Bohming would have finished with him by the time he was due to go to Anne's.

* * *

Sitting in the conference room on the third floor of police headquarters, Ossi was recalling his conversation with Stachelmann about the Holler case when the Chief of Police came in, followed by the head of the murder squad, Kriminalrat Schmidt, and an assistant of nondescript appearance. The Chief of Police sat down at the head of the table, around which the members of the No. 3 Response Unit of the murder squad were assembled. The assistant passed the Chief an attaché case of brown leather with silver fittings. Opening it, the Chief took out a notebook and a heavy black fountain pen; the nib glinted under the neon lighting. He wrote something in the notebook before raising his head and looking severely around the table.

'Gentlemen,' he said. 'Lady and gentlemen,' he corrected himself, with a nod to Kommissarin Ulrike Kreimeier. In a chilly tone he explained why he had convened this afternoon's meeting. He was sure, he said, that they were all doing their best to solve the Holler case. All the same, no progress was being made. 'This state of affairs is not acceptable.' He reminded them of the anxiety felt by the city's population. Three members of a highly respected Hamburg family had fallen victim to one or more murderers, and yet so far the police had not come up with anything at all. The press was growing more and more vehement. Criticism was being levelled at the police and at the Senator for the Interior. He himself had been personally attacked that morning in the *Hamburger Abendblatt*. He was being accused of doing nothing, but what more could he do than take his best people off every other case and put them on this one? But his best people were obviously not good enough. He paused for a moment, staring angrily down at the table.

Ossi cast a quick glance at his neighbour, Hauptkommissar Werner Taut, who gave him a wink with his left eye. Of course, the elections for the Hamburg city parliament were taking place in six months' time, Ossi thought. That was why the top brass were getting edgy. The Chief of Police owed his promotion to the Senator for the Interior, who in turn owed his appointment to the Mayor. Not that the Senator for the Interior was responsible for pursuing criminals— not even the most mysterious serial killer in the whole of Hamburg's criminal history. But just as the opposition in any country would condemn a minister of justice as incompetent if, somewhere in his jurisdiction, a prison warder let a prisoner escape, so the Hamburg public would blame its Senator for the Interior if a man who had taken it into his head to destroy the Holler family, root and branch, was still at liberty after two whole years. This was the constant refrain of the media, even though it was still unknown whether the same person had committed all three crimes. There might equally well have been three separate killers. The murder of Frau Holler was totally unlike that of Valentina. The murders of the two children, on the other hand, were very similar. But that was still not proof that the same killer was responsible for both.

When the Chief of Police reached the end of his diatribe, he asked, 'Do any of you have anything to say?' He looked at Werner Taut, the team leader of the response unit. When no one offered to speak, he demanded, 'What about you, Herr Taut, have you no thoughts on this? What have you done to track down this madman?'

'We're doing everything we can,' Taut replied. He had a calm, deep voice that matched his big, corpulent physique. He gave an impression of sluggishness, but Ossi and his colleagues knew that their boss had a quick mind which he liked to conceal behind his deliberate manner. Many people had underestimated him, some to their cost.

'And you placidly sit around here, while out there somebody may already be planning or committing his next murder!'

Ossi had to suppress a grin. The Chief was just worried that there would be yet another mysterious murder before the elections, giving the media even more grounds to question the competence of the police.

'We're sitting around here because we were summoned to this meeting,' Taut said, in what seemed to be a relaxed and amiable tone.

The Chief snorted. 'You've been working on the Holler murders for years, and you've nothing to show for it. Nothing at all!'

There was a lengthy pause. 'That's true,' admitted Taut eventually.

The Chief looked at him, his eyes wide. 'So you really do know nothing.'

'You could say that.'

'And you look forward to getting your salary every month?' The Chief's voice sliced through the air in the room.

'I'd be sorry to do without it. I'm sure I'm not the only one in that position.'

The Chief closed his eyes for a moment. Then he stood and went over to one of the windows, which gave a view of the City Nord. He gazed out for a while. Then he turned to the others and said, almost sadly, 'What *have* you found out so far?'

In a bored voice Taut summarized: 'On the morning of the thirteenth of April nineteen ninety-one, a man who was out walking found Ruth Holler dead in the nature reserve, the Duvenstedter Brook. A tall individual, probably a man, had beaten her head to a pulp. He must have been in a terrible rage.'

The Chief grimaced.

Taut continued serenely: 'She was murdered on April twelfth, in the late afternoon. The murderer left her lying on the path. So it looks as if he wanted her to be found quickly. We have found no clue at all to the identity of the perpetrator, not even the weapon. The forensic pathologists say that it was some sort of big club, possibly a baseball bat...'

'No footprints?' asked the Chief.

'No. There were a lot of footprints left by joggers or people out walking, most of them impossible to identify. Since the murderer and the victim were presumably the only people to use that path in the time between the murder and the finding of the body, one would expect the murderer to have left clear prints. We were able to identify Ruth Holler's. But apart from those, the scene-of-crime officers could only find slight, indeterminate indentations. The ground there is mostly soft and springy, which doesn't make it any easier. We think that the murderer put plastic bags or something similar over his shoes. Or cycling gaiters. But really we don't know whether those indentations are linked to the murder at all. It makes no difference, since we can't learn anything from them anyway.'

The Chief snorted.

'We searched the databases of both the regional and the federal Criminal Investigation Agencies, but didn't find any parallels to this case. Obviously we checked the victim's family: the husband has an alibi, he was having dinner with the mayor, and there's no question of suspecting the children.'

The Chief frowned. Perhaps he was annoyed to hear Holler being named as a possible suspect; perhaps it was a warning to Taut not to treat him like a fool. His career had been in administration, and he had never actually seen a body at the scene of a crime. He sensed the contempt that the detectives felt for him.

'We turned Holler's house inside out looking for any possible lead. Nothing.'

The Chief shook his head.

Ossi noticed with alarm that he was drumming his fingers on the tabletop. He put his hands under the table. This chewing-over of the meagre results of their investigations was getting on his nerves. The Chief was right, they were at fault, but nothing was to be gained by going on about it. There was work waiting for him down below, on his desk on the first floor, while they were sitting up here jawing. Taut must be feeling the same way. By now he was speaking almost in a monotone. He always did that when he was angry.

'Sebastian Holler died on the third of September 2000, at more or less exactly four-thirty P.M., in the Aschberg swimming pool in Rückersweg. He was sitting on the edge of the pool, probably watching the children coming down the big slide. He took a sip of Coke and fell into the water. The pool attendant was there in an instant but was unable to do anything. He thought the boy had drowned. He called an ambulance straight away and tried to revive the boy, but of course he didn't succeed. When the emergency doctor arrived, the boy had been dead for some time. Cyanide does a thorough job.'

The Chief looked enquiringly at Taut.

'The ambulance crew notified the police, and officers were on the scene within minutes. Scene-of-crime and forensic medical teams got there very soon afterwards. Witnesses were identified and questioned immediately. We have a long list of names on file. No one saw anything unusual, and most of the witnesses didn't even notice that a child had died in the pool.'

The Chief shook his head disapprovingly.

Of course, Ossi thought, *he* would never fail to notice if something happened. He'd come speeding to the rescue like Superman.

'The latest victim, Valentina Holler, was found dead in her garden by the nanny on the seventh of July. The autopsy showed that she had eaten a caramel that someone had filled with cyanide. The sweet wrapping was lying next to the dead girl, close to the hedge that screens the garden from the street. We assume that the girl found the sweet lying on the lawn, picked it up, unwrapped it and ate it, all in the space of about two minutes. Death occurred at approximately

5:13 P.M. The time can be pinpointed very accurately because the nanny went inside the house to visit the toilet...'

Ossi grinned inwardly at the prim and proper phrasing. Just among fellow officers, Taut would have said that the nanny had gone inside for a pee.

He himself had interviewed the nanny. She was just a girl of nineteen. She blamed herself. 'If I'd taken Tina into the house with me it would never have happened,' she had sobbed. No one, not even Holler, was blaming her. The nanny had been touchingly devoted to the child. And Valentina had been alone in the garden so many times before. Nothing could happen to her there—after all, she wasn't a baby. No, the guilt rested on nobody but the person who had injected the sweet with cyanide and tossed it into the garden. The nanny would probably suffer for the rest of her life because she had had to go to the toilet at the wrong moment.

After the Chief had exhorted them to make 'a greater effort'—'the honour of the Hamburg police is at stake!'—he and his retinue withdrew. Schmidt gave Taut and his colleagues a penetrating look before closing the door behind him. The members of response unit 3 remained sitting in the conference room.

'At least we know now that we're meant to catch the guy,' said Roland Kamm.

Ossi sniggered.

Taut was staring at the wall.

Ulrike Kreimeier was examining one of her fingernails.

Wolfgang Kurz was picking his nose with his little finger.

'Well,' Taut said. 'It's understandable. He wants to keep his job.'

'I thought a Chief of Police was supposed to *support* the police in their work,' complained Ulrike.

'Are you suggesting he hasn't boosted our motivation?' Ossi asked with mock indignation.

'Okay, calm down,' Taut said. 'He's right about one thing: this doesn't make us look good. Here's some maniac wiping out a whole family and we're just standing by and watching. We've found no evidence and no motive and we haven't got a single suspect. For more than two years now this person's been making fools of us.'

'Person?' asked Ossi.

'My hunch is that it *is* one person,' said Taut. When Taut had a hunch it was no good contradicting him.

They went downstairs to the first floor, and gathered in Taut's office.

'What if the murderer was only interested in one victim, and killed the others as a smoke screen?' asked Kamm.

'What if there are two or three killers?' asked Ossi. It irritated him that the others insisted on assuming that there was only one murderer.

Taut shook his head.

'You must know more than we do, Ossi,' said Ulrike.

'No, I know just as little as you do. That's why I refuse to draw any far-reaching conclusions.'

'Okay, okay,' said Taut. 'But I do think our working hypothesis is the right one. We must concentrate on one killer. When we've got him, we'll see if he's the only one. Alright?'

After a few moments they all nodded. They were surprised at how simple it could be to provide a guideline for their work, and equally surprised that Taut had actually told them his reasons, giving them what, for him, was quite a full explanation.

'The idea of the serial killer who really only wants one person dead works very well in detective novels, but I've never come across it or heard of it happening in real life. Just imagine—murderers are human, too—what stress these people suffer, how frightened they must be, and how, perhaps, they are tormented by conscience. After all, they're generally not the monsters or killing machines that the press likes to portray them as, but people like you and me who for some reason have gone completely off the rails. What we have to find out is how and why that happened.'

If you took down those remarks, spiced them up a bit and sold them to the tabloids, there'd be a fine scandal just in time for the elections, Ossi thought. He could picture the headlines: '"Murderers need sympathy and understanding", says top detective', or 'The Hamburg killer: give him a hug', or 'Hamburg murder squad cop says: "I love you all"'. But Taut was right. They would never catch any murderers if they thought of them simply as monsters. What had sent their mystery killer off the rails? What drove a person to commit three murders in two years?

'By the way, there's one thing you've obviously all forgotten: Where's the report from the profiler submitted after the second murder? Did anyone read it?'

Ossi remembered the psychologist from the Federal Criminal Investigation Agency, a beanpole of a man with a brick-red face. 'I did take a look at it.'

'Well?' asked Taut.

'Don't tell me you found it convincing?'

'Well, he knew a lot more about the possible killer than we do.'

'Oh, come on,' said Ulrike. 'He had a screw loose.'

'Ever heard of modern police methods?' Taut demanded. He took a folder out of a drawer, opened it and leafed through the contents. 'Ah, listen to this, I marked a bit here:

> "The crimes are clearly not directed against the victims themselves: the killer wants to hurt the head of the family, Maximilian Holler. The systematic way in which he has killed two members of the family indicates a borderline personality rather than a psychopath. The murderer is probably someone who had some contact with Holler, either long ago or possibly in the more recent past, and who may even have been more or less a friend. He probably idealized and envied Holler on account of his success and above all because of his integrity as a person. Deficits in the structure of an individual's identity may lead to a wish to merge with another person. Holler, who represents an ideal and a model even for many well-balanced people, became, for this individual whose own sense of self has not undergone a normal development, the object of a projective identity. Then something that Holler said or did made him feel so hurt and rejected that it unleashed an atavistic rage. This swing from idealization to an impulse to destroy is typical of borderline personalities, who otherwise appear well-adjusted

and unremarkable. Therefore, any persons with whom Holler had fairly close contact, either privately or professionally, but who at some point suddenly distanced themselves from him should be considered. A female perpetrator is also a possibility, for example a former lover who had perhaps entertained the fantasy of becoming his wife. The nature of the killings— poison, and blows to the head—could just as easily point to a woman as to a man. Thus the criteria for identifying the killer are as follows: a close personal link with Holler which led to a pathological idealization of him, followed by a sudden breach after a hurtful action or rejection. The time frame is indeterminate—it could be someone Holler knew in his youth, or else a much more recent associate."'

Ulrike groaned. 'We went into all that. Holler didn't have a girlfriend, and he couldn't think of any friends who had suddenly distanced themselves from him.'

'How do you know he didn't have a girlfriend?' Taut challenged her.

'You can't prove a negative. I asked him—you were there, Ossi.'

Ossi nodded.

'I promised him that we would treat any information in the strictest confidence, although in practice that might have been difficult.' She sounded bored.

'Just suppose he was lying?' asked Ossi. 'Do you think he'd let his girlfriend go around committing murder to her heart's content rather than let the truth come out? Jesus, you read about adultery in the papers every day. Nobody gives a toss anymore. No, that's taking us down the wrong track. For God's sake don't inflict that wretched shrink on us again.'

Taut grinned.

'We ought to have another look at Holler's business rivals. We know there are some who would be richer but for him,' said Ossi. He couldn't summon up any enthusiasm: he was pretty sure nothing would come of this line of investigation.

Taut nodded.

Ulrike said: 'I've had a suspicion in my mind the whole time.'

The others turned to her in surprise. Then why haven't you said anything before, their looks seemed to say.

'You don't have to blurt everything out as soon as you think of it,' she said, sounding slightly offended.

'Never mind that,' Taut said. 'What's your idea?'

'I think it might be Holler himself. He seems just too good to be true.'

'You're kidding!' said Kamm. He was not expressing disbelief.

'Such things do happen,' she said. 'It might sound mad, but all murder is mad.'

'You mean he killed his own wife and two of his children?' asked Ossi.

'He could have,' she said.

Taut looked round the table: 'Let's hear what Ulrike has to say. This may be the first sensible idea we've had for some time.'

'Well, Holler's a man with no flaws at all, a kind of Jesus figure,' said Ulrike. 'Now, I've never met a person without any flaws. He knows just about all the top people in Hamburg. He gives enormous sums to charity and tries to prevent it from becoming public knowledge. Of course it does come out, and so he emerges as a saint complete with halo, because most people who do good works do it mainly for their own benefit. Holler acts like someone who's not of this world. Now that really would be a first. Perhaps he's been working to a plan for decades. Perhaps his wife was standing in his way. Perhaps he wants to get rid of his wife's offspring—'

'But he's their father!' said Kamm.

Taut waved that aside.

'Oh yes? But has a father never killed his children because he thought they *weren't* his? And besides, a father often regards even his own children as being in effect part of his wife. Especially if he's a businessman who's hardly ever at home.'

Kamm gave a slight nod.

'Just suppose the man's planning some big coup, bigger than

anything we mere mortals can imagine. Something absolutely huge. And to achieve it he needs good contacts with important people and a big shiny halo. And his wife is standing in his way. Perhaps he's got another woman. Perhaps she'll only take him without children. But the details don't matter at the moment. Whatever his scheme is, it won't work unless he commits these crimes.'

'Alibi,' said Ossi.

'Have we checked it?' queried Taut. He looked round at them each in turn. No one answered. 'Do I have to do everything myself?' he demanded.

'I'll do it,' said Ossi. He knew that Taut hated all physical exertion, unless it consisted of going to the pub. He sat as if he were welded to his seat; soon he'd fall asleep on it.

'It would be better for the guv'nor to go and see the mayor,' said Kamm.

'No,' said Taut. 'The mayor is only a witness like any other. All the same, Ossi, it would be best to tread carefully. I'd rather the Jesus of the Elbchaussee didn't immediately realize what line of enquiry we're following.'

Ossi saw that Ulrike's eyes were shining.

Taut turned to her: 'It's a nice theory. To be frank, there's a touch of Hollywood about it. But taking everything into consideration we really have got only one suspect at the moment, and that's Maximilian Holler. And he's the leading property dealer in Hamburg, if not the whole of North Germany, besides being the epitome of human virtue. So be warned, my friends, if we make a mess of this, the Chief will eat us alive. And he's not the only one: everybody who's anybody in this city loves Maximilian Holler.' He gazed earnestly at each of them, before asking Ulrike: 'What do you propose we do?'

'Have him shadowed around the clock. Question his business rivals. Search his house, with his agreement of course, but we already have that; he's practically begged us to do it. Look into his bank accounts. Check what trips he's made recently. The works.'

'And we're supposed to do all that with the handful of people we've got?' asked Kurz. He was sitting stiffly upright on the office chair. Even sitting down he was almost a head taller than his colleagues.

Taut shook his curly head from side to side. 'We might be able to get some reinforcements, at least for the surveillance.'

'Then make sure the Chief doesn't find out,' said Ossi.

'Tomorrow, or the day after at the latest, I'll tell you some more about my theory. Or perhaps a completely different version. But there are things I need to check out first,' said Ulrike.

'Why all the secrecy?' asked Kamm. 'That's stupid.'

'Let her do it her way,' said Taut.

Ossi was glad when they were finished. It was late by the time they reached the end of their discussion. In their unit it always took a bit longer than you'd expect. Taut hated to pull rank; he did not issue instructions but encouraged debate. And this method produced results, even if it seemed cumbersome. Ossi thought it made the team gel; there was a good working atmosphere and each of them made an effort to contribute something to solving their cases. Ulrike, in particular, had blossomed. When she had first been transferred from vice to the murder squad she had seemed like a little grey mouse. For a long time she had had nothing to say. But just over a year ago she had come up with an idea about the Sevchenko case that had given them their breakthrough. One morning some schoolchildren had found a dead Russian with a lot of money in a small side street near Altona railway station. The case had seemed insoluble until Ulrike's idea had set them on a new tack. This led them not to the Russian mafia or the St Pauli underworld, but to a smart young woman in Eppendorf who had shot her Russian lover dead because he was about to leave her. After that there had been remarks from time to time about feminine intuition, until Ulrike had lost her temper and said that men didn't have a monopoly on thinking, and that if they had no ideas it wasn't because of a biologically determined lack of feminine intuition but because some people totally lacked imagination and would be better employed franking letters than hunting down murderers. That had shut them up, and Ulrike had won full acceptance in the murder squad. She could look forward to a brilliant career.

Ulrike and Ossi left the building together. It was late. The summer evening seemed likely to stay warm, which was unusual for Hamburg, where it tended to turn cool as soon as the sun had gone down. 'Shall we go somewhere for a beer?' asked Ossi.

'Good idea,' Ulrike smiled. She was in high spirits. 'Where shall we go?'

'Along there, and then round the corner and a few yards further on there's an Italian place where you can sit outside...'

'And where I don't have to drink beer,' Ulrike said. She took his arm, and he relished the physical contact. Then she stood still, saying, 'Hang on a minute, I need to go back to my car and get a jacket. Unless you want to hear my teeth chattering later on.'

When she reached the zebra crossing on Hindenburgstrasse the light was green for pedestrians. As she stepped into the road, a black Mercedes shot out of a side street and drove towards the crossing at breakneck speed. Ossi saw it, took a moment to register what was happening, and then yelled, 'Ulrike, watch out! Mind that car!' She didn't hear him, she was absorbed in her own thoughts and engulfed in the noise of traffic. When the car hit her, she flew through the air like a doll.

Chapter four

Don't misunderstand me, Josef Maria,' said Bohming. 'I'm very patient with everyone, especially my colleagues.'

He liked to refer to his subordinates as colleagues.

'I have consistently spoken up for you, but not even I can convince everyone in the department that you're going to produce the best *Habil* in living memory, and that that naturally takes a bit more time. I'm picking up signals here and there which I'm afraid will only get louder. We have to economise; the Senate is putting us under enormous pressure. And what do you think will happen if the other side takes control after the elections?'

Stachelmann would have been amused at the Legend's prevarications if this were not all about his own imminent downfall. Or at any rate about his *Habilitation*, and specifically the mountain of shame. No doubt about it, Bohming was holding a pistol to his head. Of course as a full professor with a chair, Bohming had the power, if he so wished, to prolong Stachelmann's dismal existence almost indefinitely. But, typically, here he was, the great superhero, playing down his own influence and claiming he had to defer to higher authority, simply because he hadn't the guts to say, *Listen, I'll give you two more years. And if in those two years you can show that you've a good prospect of finishing, then I'm willing to give you two more. But after that you've had it.*

Stachelmann couldn't say much. He had foreseen this, but how could he defend himself? Bohming might be no hero, but he was right. I'm not up to it, Stachelmann thought. How did I ever manage to finish my doctorate, and *summa cum laude*, too? The Stachelmann he had been in Heidelberg seemed like a different person from the present Hamburg Stachelmann. In Heidelberg he had radiated confidence, whereas in Hamburg he was paralysis and depression personified.

He assured Bohming that his preparation was well advanced; soon he would be going to the Federal Archive in Berlin and from there to the former Buchenwald concentration camp. That would complete his research, and then he would start on the writing.

Bohming patted him on the shoulder. 'I don't have any doubts about you, Josef Maria. I'll stand up for you, believe me. I'm sure you'll manage it.'

Back in his own room, Stachelmann sat down at his desk. He stared at the mountain of shame. He felt like a mountaineer who plans to climb the north face of the Eiger but is buried by an avalanche at the very foot of the Matterhorn. He had known that fate would catch up with him some day. He could already see himself trudging off to the job centre. But who would employ a failed historian? What would he say at interviews? *Well, you know, that ossified academic world was getting on my nerves. You've no idea how stressful it is trying to get something across to students who just aren't interested. And then to spend your whole working life trawling through documents, writing specialist articles that nobody reads except to savage them and pull them to pieces. I need to try something new.* No human resources manager would buy that rubbish. That's what they all say, people whose university careers have ended in failure. And a person who's failed there will fail anywhere else, too. No stamina, no resilience, no commitment. He could feel himself starting to perspire. Was this the hour that presaged his doom?

His eye fell on a pile of unread historical journals. Those scribblers who filled them with their mostly insignificant articles, spray-ing their perfume on history's every fart, those pushy, self-important show-offs, indistinguishable from one another—were they any bet-ter than he was? They simply lacked the scruples that paralysed him. Or was he imagining it? Was he just putting a favourable gloss on his lack of ability by calling it scruple? A scrupulous distaste for the self-advertisement that, in this profession, was undeniably a factor in determining your success or failure?

Stachelmann knew he only had one last chance to make some-thing of his life. He looked at the clock. It was almost time to go to Anne's. An inner voice told him that it would be wiser not to go.

* * *

It was a small one-bedroom attic apartment in Winterhude, not far from police headquarters. Living room, bedroom, galley kitchen, a meagre bathroom. On the living room wall hung a poster from a 'Modern Painting' exhibition at the Kunsthaus and a reproduction of a Kandinsky. A television, a stereo, a few pop CDs. A bookshelf with a few good novels of recent years, a concise encyclopedia, no detec-tive stories. An old brown sofa and an armchair that didn't match it. A small bureau-style desk. On the floor a greying flokati rug. In the bedroom a double bed, bedside table, wardrobe. In the hall a coat rack consisting of a wooden board with hooks, screwed to the wall, and a mirror.

Ossi had never been inside Ulrike's home before. Now she was dead and here he was. He could still see the scene: he would never forget it. The black Mercedes that killed her. The car skidded momentarily, hit the curb of the central reservation and went rac-ing on. Ossi had not managed to get a good view of the driver; he thought it was a man. Ulrike was lying motionless on the pavement, eyes staring blankly at Ossi. Her face was smeared with blood, and her hands and legs were red too. Her left leg was bent outwards. Ossi felt her neck, then her pulse, and put his ear to her chest. Nothing: she was dead, had probably been dead before her body hit the pavement. Ossi used his mobile to call an ambulance and to order a search for the Mercedes. Then he sat down beside the body and cried.

A few minutes later the place was teeming with police, doctors and journalists. Taut pulled Ossi to his feet, put an arm round him for a moment and said, 'We've got to find him.'

The media published descriptions of the Mercedes, and police officers did the rounds of repair garages and car parks. No one had seen the car. And now Ossi was standing in Ulrike's apartment. He thought he could detect her scent. He had no idea what he was looking for. He opened the flap of the bureau—the key was in the keyhole. Felt pens, a notebook, a pile of papers. He took the notebook and papers over to the sofa and sat down, putting the papers down on the seat beside him. He started on the notebook. On the first page there was a shopping list, on the next some measurements—perhaps she'd been planning to make a dress or something. He looked around, but could not see a sewing machine. On the third page she had sketched a face: rough, quick strokes, but the proportions were good. It might be a doodle she'd done while talking on the phone. On the fourth page there was a coloured nude drawing of a man, prominently showing the sexual organs. The other pages were blank. Ossi put the notebook into his briefcase.

The papers were a motley collection, possibly gathered together when she had been tidying up. Or maybe this was the pile for things she meant to look at properly when she got round to it. There were letters from her mother; Ossi struggled to decipher the shaky handwriting but soon gave up. There would be time to read the letters later. They weren't likely to contain a clue to the identity of the murderer. Ossi found recipes, mostly for Italian dishes, torn from newspapers and magazines. A brochure about fitted kitchens from a mail-order furniture company. Was she planning to replace her dilapidated kitchen? Perhaps just dreaming of it, Ossi thought when he saw the prices. You can die in the service of the state, but don't expect to get rich first. Beneath that brochure he found a letter from the publishers of an encyclopedia, promising a discount if you ordered the set of over twenty volumes within fourteen days. Why had Ulrike kept that? Even with the discount, the encyclopedia still cost a lot of money. Next came a leaflet from a supermarket. Ulrike—presumably—had put a cross in blue Biro by a lawnmower. What would she want with a lawnmower, when she had no garden? Underneath that he found a blue cardboard folder. In it was a page torn from *Der Spiegel*, about the 'Death's Head' units of the ss, the *Totenkopfverbände*. How odd. Ossi couldn't ever remember Ulrike showing an interest in history. Under the article there was a piece of paper with a diagram on it. Starting at the top, it began with a vertical line which, roughly halfway down the sheet, met a horizontal line. Four vertical lines descended from the horizontal one. At the foot of the one furthest to the right was the name 'Maximilian Holler'.

Ossi sat there without moving. It was a moment before he could think clearly. He stared at the piece of paper: the diagram looked like a family tree, but there were no names on it except that of the property dealer. He rotated it, looking at it from each side in turn. What had been in Ulrike's mind when she took a pencil and ruler to draw this diagram? Perhaps it was meant to show a relationship between the victims and the suspects. But why, in that case, was Holler's name at the bottom right-hand corner? What names ought to be attached to the other lines? Or was there no real meaning behind it? Ossi often drew nonsensical things on a piece of paper or card when he was concentrating. A lot of people did that, including, apparently, Ulrike. Ossi leaned back and remembered the times when they had all sat together to pool their ideas about crimes, suspects and clues. Ulrike had had more imagination than any of them.

When you are on your own, a fertile imagination can lead you astray, but with a team working together it can often show you the way out of an impasse. At first Ossi had occasionally been surprised at the ideas Ulrike would suddenly come out with, but he soon saw that she was clever and that her ideas helped the rest of them to move forward, either by working to refute her ideas or, if Ulrike stuck to her guns, by following them up. Ossi had often envied Ulrike: she had a special place in the team. When she said something, everyone paid attention. In the hectic atmosphere of day-to-day police work, that was unusual.

Now Ossi remembered what Ulrike did when she was concentrating. She didn't doodle, nor did she roll paper up into little balls like Taut, or stare vacantly up at the ceiling like Kurz. She would have a marble in her hand and fiddle with it. Occasionally it would clatter to the floor, making her jump, and then she would hunt around until she found it again.

What was it, then? Had Ulrike found out something and drawn a diagram to clarify it in her own mind before telling her colleagues about it? He went quickly through the rest of the papers but found nothing else of interest, and put them back on the open flap of the bureau. He felt like an intruder. It was her home. But she was dead. She had left behind a folder with a diagram and a name. Holler was the only person Ulrike suspected. Ossi couldn't think of any other suspect either.

He drove back to police headquarters, trying hard not to cause an accident. Returning to the murder squad's offices, he almost collided with Taut in the doorway. 'Result!' Taut bellowed, 'We've got—'

'Who?' demanded Ossi.

'The car. We've got the Mercedes.'

*   *   *

His knees were hurting as he climbed the stairs. Stachelmann stopped at one of the landings, but the pain persisted. He went on. On an enamel plate the name was inscribed in a curving script: Derling. People you visited always lived on the top floor. Stachelmann was panting, and he waited for a few minutes until his breathing had steadied. He ran his hand through his longish curly hair, wondering if he should have gone to the barber's. He could see his hand trembling as he lifted it to the bell; he heard it ring in the apartment, a two-tone chime. Then there were footsteps, light and unhurried. The door opened, light shone out through the gap, and there was Anne giving him a radiant smile. She looked as if she were just going out, her hair done and her make-up freshly applied.

'I didn't recognize you at first,' she said. 'Why are you standing there in the dark?'

Stachelmann hadn't noticed that the light in the stairwell had gone out. 'Oh, I don't know,' he said.

She invited him in. The apartment was decorated in warm tones. There was an aroma of garlic and herbs.

'Dinner's almost ready,' said Anne. The bell of a timer rang in the kitchen. 'I'll just check that nothing's burning. I'll be right back.' She vanished through a door on the right at the far end of the passage. He heard clattering sounds. She came back, said, 'I haven't given you a proper welcome,' laughed and embraced him, lightly and fleetingly. Her perfume smelled nice, a subtle rose fragrance.

She had laid the table in the main room, which had a dining area in one corner. There were two candlesticks on the table. She passed him a bottle of red wine. 'If you're happy with this one, could you open it for me, please?' There was a corkscrew lying on the table. The wine was a Bordeaux, but one that Stachelmann didn't know. He pulled out the cork. Anne appeared holding a roasting pan between oven gloves. 'Lamb and vegetable bake,' she said. 'I hope you'll like it.'

'I'm sure I will,' he said. 'It smells great.' She was acting as if it were perfectly normal for her to invite him over for a meal for no particular reason. What had they ever had to do with one another, except as colleagues? In the canteen one of them might happen to see the other and go over and join them, but that was all. Stachelmann was not the only one who was convinced that Bohming had taken a fancy to Anne. He was married, but what of it? But instead of Bohming it was Stachelmann, who merely hoped to become a professor some day, whom she had invited to dinner at her apartment; she had taken trouble with her appearance and must have spent hours in the kitchen to produce a meal like this. What did she want of him? He was surprised, and was waiting for an explanation. He didn't dare ask.

They ate, and the food was good. Stachelmann drank only a little wine; he felt unsure of himself. They chatted about the history department, and then about Anne's family. Her father had shot himself four years ago, without leaving a suicide note. No one knew why, or where he had got the pistol from; it was of a type used in the last war. Anne was quite calm as she told him all this. She put a CD in the player. Stachelmann knew the music, it was Mozart's piano concerto no. 23, gentle, harmonious, almost kitschy. It was a perfect evening. But he had no idea why they were spending it together.

'And what do you do when you're not seducing female students?' she asked. She had a frank, open kind of laugh: surely there couldn't be anything concealed behind it.

'Normally I eat female students for breakfast,' he said. 'A bit of garlic and cayenne pepper, and they taste perfect. But only blondes.'

'So I'm in no danger—that's a relief,' said Anne, tossing back her hair with its blue-black sheen. 'And anyway, ugh, garlic for breakfast, that's abnormal.'

'That's how I am,' said Stachelmann. 'You can't change the way you are, even if it would make you more popular.'

'And when are you going to eat that Alicia girl?'

'How come you know her?'

'She's in my seminar group. If only she were half as keen as she is pretty.'

'She's pursuing me,' said Stachelmann.

'How flattering,' said Anne, rather cheekily. 'But I'm afraid her quarry isn't entirely innocent.'

Stachelmann looked at her, startled. It sounded almost as if Anne were jealous. Or was she only making fun of him? 'Rubbish,' he said. Then, 'Sorry.'

She smiled. 'It's all right. It would be very understandable.'

Silence.

'Oh, by the way,' said Anne. 'Before I forget.'

Pause.

Stachelmann stretched a little. He hoped she would not notice his agitation.

'I had a talk with the Legend,' said Anne. 'He thinks that if I ask you nicely you might be able to help me now and then.'

'With what?' It just slipped out.

'Well, with my thesis for my doctorate.' She looked at him expectantly.

At first Stachelmann didn't understand. He had just come from Bohming, who had told him off and threatened to show him the door because he wasn't getting his *Habilitation* finished. And this same Bohming was advising Anne to ask him for help. What kind of help? Anne had to write her doctoral thesis by herself, anything else would be cheating. Bohming obviously wanted her to get it finished. But, as her supervisor, he mustn't help her more than he helped his other doctoral students, otherwise the rumours would gain real currency. Why should Anne get her doctorate quickly? Was Bohming hoping to put her in Stachelmann's place after he had thrown him out? He felt everything tensing up inside him.

Anne was eyeing him with an air of surprise.

'Yes, of course I'll help you,' he said. He was afraid he'd start stammering.

'You know what my topic is,' she said.

He said nothing.

'The origins of the Nazi concentration camp system.'

He nodded. He had heard nothing about that; he had thought Anne was grappling with some subject relating to the Wilhelmine era. But it seemed her topic overlapped with his. Bohming knew that Stachelmann had assembled a mass of source material. He wanted Anne to have the benefit of it before he threw Stachelmann out, so that Anne could have his job and Bohming would have earned her gratitude. What a devious plan! The more he thought about it, the less he really believed that Bohming could be so underhanded. But maybe it wasn't a plan but just an inspired idea, a vague possibility that might become more concrete and provide a solution if Stachelmann didn't manage to conquer the mountain of shame. Bohming often spoke of receiving inspiration as if it was a gift granted only to a chosen few. But they weren't characters in some Greek drama! Stachelmann's destiny was in his own hands. He simply had to carry out what he had set himself to do. How humiliating, if Anne were to get his job just because he had failed to get a single line down on paper! Did Anne know about this?

'Yes, of course,' he said. 'I'll give you a hand. But how, exactly?'

'I've got a confession to make. I'm scared of archives. That's odd for a historian, isn't it?'

Stachelmann couldn't help laughing: it was funny. 'So why did you become a historian?'

'Yes,' she said. 'That's a very fair question.'

Silence.

She went into the kitchen, he heard clattering sounds, and she returned with two glass dishes. 'Ice cream, homemade,' she said. 'Well, at least, the milk was produced by cows, the eggs were laid by hens, the sugar comes from somewhere or other, sugar beet or sugar cane, and Sarotti made the chocolate. But I mixed it together with my own fair hands and put it in the freezer.'

Stachelmann forced a smile. Why would somebody become a historian if she was scared of archives? He had once heard of a historian who was allergic to paper dust but who still went to the archives, putting on white cotton gloves and taking a tablet every so often. He had admired that man. What greater proof could there be of a genuine enthusiasm for history? She hadn't answered his question and was trying to steer the conversation in a different direction. Departmental gossip, the next staff meeting. She also still hadn't told him what kind of help she wanted.

'So how can I help you?'

She looked at him nervously. Her bright smile had gone. 'Bohming said you've collected enormous quantities of source material. He says it would be enough for three theses. Since our topics overlap, I'd be really grateful if I could have a look at some of it.'

Stachelmann remembered his research trips to Berlin, Koblenz, Weimar, Nordhausen and various other places. He had stayed at cheap hotels on noisy streets, and had hardly slept because his joints hurt despite his medication. It had been sheer torture, although not so bad that he wouldn't go again, at least to Berlin and to Buchenwald. He thought it was important to have far more material than he would actually use, because that was the only way to see the material in context and assess its value. Apparently not even the Legend appreciated that sources are not sacred, that they often contradict each other, and you have to compare them. Only when you know *all* the sources can you decide which ones to use. It takes time, far more than is apparent from a casual reading of the piece of scholarship that results from all the research—

and who gives it more than a casual reading? That said, Bohming was wrong: Stachelmann did not have too much material, but if anything, too little. He would undertake another research trip, and the mountain of shame would grow even taller. Perhaps when it was tall enough he would manage to dismantle it. If he was not thrown out first.

So now Bohming was eager to award a doctorate to an assistant who had a fear of archives or sources, or both. Stachelmann should have been angry: Bohming really had a nerve expecting him to do this. Yet instead of feeling angry he was touched. There was Anne, petite and beautiful, and he thought he could see her hands trembling. He was sure she knew what she was asking. She must be under a lot of pressure, to make her confide in him as she had done. He ate a mouthful of ice cream and then asked, 'What is there about archives that anyone could possibly be afraid of?'

'I'm afraid of libraries, too. Archives and libraries are monsters to me. I don't understand the system.' She swallowed, and spoke quickly. 'I'm afraid of the staff. I'm afraid of asking stupid questions. I feel that with my historical knowledge I ought to be able to understand how archives are organized, but I'm completely at sea. I can cope better with libraries now that you can search and order online. It's anonymous, and on the Internet you can't look stupid.'

'But when you were studying you must have used libraries?'

'Only in the run-up to the exams,' she said. 'Then I had to, and it wasn't too bad. There was one librarian who was very friendly and even asked me out for a coffee. So that gave me more confidence.'

Stachelmann could imagine the reason for the librarian's friendliness. He felt jealous, but that seemed absurd. He would often be with Anne now, and they would go through the mountain of shame together. Only hours ago that would have been the stuff of dreams, but now he suddenly felt afraid that he and Anne together would be sawing off the branch he was sitting on—a branch that was already dangerously thin. Then he was seized by an idea. He had to ask her.

'I'm about to go on a research trip, to Berlin and Buchenwald. Why don't you come with me? There's no need to carry your phobias around with you for the rest of your life. Our topics are related, so why don't we go on a paper-chase together?'

She looked at him in astonishment: 'You'd be prepared to do that?'

He nodded. Her surprise showed the distance between them. 'Yes,' she said. 'I'll come.'

As he was leaving, she put her arms round him and kissed him on the cheek. She held him for a few seconds.

It was raining. The pavement reflected the light of the street lamps. Ignoring the few passersby, he walked quickly to Dammtor station: time was short if he was not to miss the last mainline train back to Lübeck. When he reached the main station, the Lübeck train was already waiting, and he got into the end carriage. As he walked through to first class, he scanned the seats and luggage racks for a newspaper. Eventually he found a *Morgenpost*, stained and crumpled. The Holler murder had been relegated to page three. 'Police still in the dark. How much longer?' it said. A policewoman had been run over. 'Was it deliberate?' She had been one of the team investigating the Holler case. Was there a connection? To judge by the newspaper's speculations, its editors knew nothing. And neither did the police. Stachelmann thought of Ossi. Then his own pain hit him, leaving him almost dazed as he rode homewards through the night. Raindrops clung to the windows.

* * *

The old man tried to push the toy locomotive across the table but the wheels were jammed. Something had broken the connection between the wheels and the flywheel-driven motor inside the engine. Getting to his feet, he went over to a cupboard and took a box of precision tools out of a drawer, and with the help of a screwdriver he separated the tin coachwork from the chassis. He studied the motor and the axles. When the locomotive was pushed along to make its wheels rotate, cog-wheels were supposed to transmit the energy of the movement to the motor, and then the energy stored in the motor's lead flywheel was returned to the wheels to make the engine go along of its own accord. The power was transmitted via the rear axle. He gently tried to turn the rear wheels. The cogwheel fixed to the rear axle was intended to drive another, which in turn drove the gearwheel on the axle of the flywheel. The middle cogwheel was jammed; it was out of alignment because its axle bearing was bent. The little boy who had brought the locomotive to him had probably pushed it along too hard, or stopped it too abruptly. Or it could just be normal wear and tear, and the bearing of the middle axle was the natural weak spot. Every toy had a weak spot, a spot where it would inevitably break. The old man would often comment angrily on this when children brought along toys that hadn't lasted even a few hours, but after his anger abated he would patiently repair their cars, dolls, or trains.

With a small pair of pliers he straightened the support of the axle bearings. He carefully turned the flywheel. Now the gearwheels were failing to engage. He bent the support a little more and rotated the flywheel again. This time the force he applied was transferred through the gears to the rear axle. He rotated the rear axle and saw the flywheel turn. He was pleased with himself: he had found the cause of the problem. But the repair wasn't complete yet, the axle bearings were still weak and would bend again the first time they were put under strain.

Going over to the cupboard again, he got out a small welding torch with a tiny gas canister, and a box. He rummaged in the box until he found two small metal plates. He bent them into an L-shape and adjusted them to the shape of the axle bearings on the toy locomotive. He had to bend them carefully, checking all the time to make sure that they fitted into place. Then he put on welding goggles, took a length of welding wire and fixed the metal plates to the axle bearings and to the chassis. He applied the heat a little at a time; tin softens very quickly. When he turned off the gas the flame went out, and he laid his goggles on the table. His face was reddened. He blew on the two welds and waited. After a few minutes he gently pushed the engine along. The flywheel turned, and when he released the engine it continued to run forward by itself. He had done it. A smile spread across his face. He was popular in this apartment building in Hansastrasse. Eight families lived here, and they found the old man helpful and kind.

The children in particular loved him. Even children from neighbouring buildings came to him when their toys were broken.

The old man could mend almost anything. When the parents turned up with their wallets and purses he waved the money away, saying that he enjoyed working with his hands. He used to own a toyshop, he told them, and so in a way he was continuing in his old line of work. That was why he did it. Mending things was better than sitting around doing nothing. What else was there for an old man to do? The parents ended up believing that their children were doing him a favour by taking him their broken toys to repair. Now he was looking forward to the moment when the doorbell would ring and the little boy with the tousled ginger hair would be standing there, asking for his engine back.

He leaned back. He was content: soon he would have completed his mission, and then at last he could die. He smiled as he remembered the doctor and how he had tried to prevaricate until at last it came out: metastasized prostate cancer. But perhaps chemotherapy and radiotherapy might do some good, at least slow down the spread of the disease. The old man had laughed. No, he would not subject himself to that ordeal. He welcomed the signs of release. Soon it would all be over. He looked back over his life: nothing but injustice, pain, death. Why prolong it?

His thoughts went back to his years in London. At first he had been in a camp with more than forty other children. The rooms were damp. When more and more bombs fell nearby, the children were evacuated to the country. He was sent to stay with a couple who ran a farm. They were dirty and bad-tempered, they slapped his face and called him Jack because it was too much bother to pronounce his real name. If they thought he hadn't worked hard enough they gave him no supper. He slept in a tiny room just big enough for a bed and a chair. Mice scrabbled about in the attic above, and at first their noises frightened him, but after a while he was only frightened of his foster parents. The husband drank, and then he would hit out at anybody, including his wife. Sometimes they sent him out gleaning in a field, and then he would be alone for hours. That was wonderful. Jack saw airplanes in the sky, slow-moving twin-engined Heinkel bombers and ultra-fast Spitfire fighter planes taking on the Messerschmitts. He would lean against a tree and look up at the sky. He was delighted if a German plane was shot down, and would dance around in the field. The stricken plane would trail a plume of smoke behind it as it fell to the ground. Sometimes you could see white dots in the air, parachutes, airmen seeking safety in captivity.

Once the thing he had both hoped for and feared actually came to pass: a pilot parachuted down onto his field. At first Jack did not know what to do. Then he ran towards him, tripping over a clod of earth, standing up and finally reaching him. The man was lying on the ground, bleeding from a head wound. The eyes stared at him, the goggles had slipped down to his chin. The glass on one side had shattered. On his chest he wore a medal, a cross. Jack stood there motionless, staring at the pilot, who was not moving. Then people approached, carrying pitchforks and hunting rifles. When they saw the airman they lowered their weapons. Someone said, 'The bastard's a goner, thank God.' Soon afterwards a policeman arrived, and the body was taken away.

Perhaps the dead pilot came from Hamburg. Jack imagined him at the central station, saying good-bye to his wife before travelling to France, to the Channel coast. There he and his squadron took off—knights of the air in the service of the devil. And then, over England, a Spitfire or a Hurricane brought him down. He imagined the dogfight, a British ace chasing the Nazi aircraft. He could easily picture it—there were aerial battles here almost every day. When a British plane was shot down his fears grew, especially at night. When it was a German one he was happy. He sensed the determination of the people around him, but also their fear. What if the Nazis *did* make it across the Channel?

At school the teachers tried to stop the other children attacking him. Once four of them lay in wait for him and beat him up. He came home with a bloody nose, and was punished for that with more blows. Some of them called him Kraut; it took him a while to work out what it meant. Once some people from a Jewish aid organization came and asked if he would like to go to a boarding school. But they looked stern, so he stayed in the small village called Steyning, with his foster parents. Better the devil you know. There was an old cherry tree in the school playground, a favourite spot for playing.

One day Jack saw some boys there playing with a toy car. It was an expensive one, with steering and doors that opened. Jack would have liked to join in, but the others elbowed him aside. One boy, who was in his class, dropped the car, and when he tried to push it along the ground it would only go in a circle—the steering had jammed. The boy was trying to turn the steering wheel, but couldn't. Overcoming his nervousness, Jack picked up the car and said he would repair it. The boys were surprised at first, and then laughed at him. Only one didn't. That was Tony; it was his car, he had taken it to school and there would be trouble at home if it was broken. Next morning the car was on Tony's desk, mended.

Before Jack had become Jack, while he was still Leopold, he had often spent time in a workshop belonging to one of his uncles. This uncle was a clockmaker, who understood the very soul of clockwork movements. Leopold had watched, bright-eyed, as his uncle, a lens clasped to his eye, peered at little wheels and with diminutive tools got them going again, all the while talking to the clocks and the cogwheels as if to spur himself on. That was when Leopold started to study mechanical things with a child's intense concentration. One wheel had to engage with another; anything that was not perfectly aligned would prevent them from moving freely. This knowledge helped him to survive in Steyning. Repairing a toy car, he found a friend, Tony. The others stopped making fun of him, although Jack still felt the looks they gave him when the German army won victories or, later on, suffered defeats. What did they think? That one always remained a German, even after being driven into exile by one's compatriots? Jack did not yet know the things the old man knew now. He was a German, but he hated the Nazis more than any English person possibly could. They had robbed him of everything, his parents, his brothers and sisters, his grandparents. When he went back to Germany, they took his inheritance from him, too. Soon after that Tony died in a road accident. He could not attend the funeral: Germans were not allowed to travel to England.

The old man stood up and went into the kitchen. It was time for his afternoon tea. He put the kettle on the stove, spooned some tea into a china teapot and waited for the water to boil. He poured the boiling water into the teapot, glanced at the clock and sat down. He would give the tea plenty of time to draw. While he was waiting, the idea came to him. He would buy a toy car and fill it with explosive. He considered whether to set it off by remote control or using a sensor that would react to movement nearby—he had read about sensors in a model-making magazine. The first option exposed him to the risk of being seen; with the second, there was the danger of killing the wrong person. He would think about it and come to a decision. At any rate, he knew now that he would stage his attack either in the house or in the garden. And this blow would finish Holler off.

The old man took a second china teapot and poured in the rest of the hot water from the kettle. He waited for a moment before emptying it down the sink. He poured the tea through a strainer into the second teapot, then filled a cup and added some sugar crystals from a sugar bowl. Having given his tea a stir, he took a sip and leaned back in his chair. He was content: he had solved the question of how to do it. Not down to the last detail, but in principle he knew it would work.

Chapter five

The Mercedes 260E was in an underground car park in Rahlstedt, a district in the northeastern part of Hamburg. When Ossi got there the scene-of-crime team was already at work. Later they would take the car to police headquarters, where the forensic technicians would take it apart. Taut had established that the owner, a businessman from Poppenbüttel, was away, and his wife had assumed that the car was in the car park at his office in the city centre. The ignition had been hotwired. The left-hand headlight was smashed, the radiator grille was bent, and on the roof there was a large indentation left by the impact of Ulrike's body. The car had thrown her up into the air and she had crashed down on to the roof, then slid backwards and to the left when the Mercedes skidded. As it skidded, the car had hit a pillar with its right-hand rear wing. There was a deep dent and some paint had flaked off.

There was not much for Taut and Ossi to do. The scene-of-crime officers were doing their job and would soon make their report. Ossi feared that it would not help them much. Something told him that Ulrike had been murdered by a professional hit man because she was on the trail of the Holler killer.

Back at headquarters, Ossi told his boss what he had found in Ulrike's apartment. He showed him the diagram and the *Spiegel* article. Taut shook his head and said nothing for a long time, carefully studying the paper with the diagram.

'If it weren't for the name Holler, it would never occur to anybody to connect this with our case.' He turned it round. 'Perhaps it makes no difference which way up the name is written. If the name's upside down the diagram is still just as meaningless. It looks like a family tree, but the other names are missing. If this *were* the Holler family tree, it would be easy enough to put the other names in. Above Maximilian one would put in his father, Herrmann—who was just as highly regarded as his son is now; he was even in the city parliament for a while. Maximilian inherited the business from him, but it was only under him that it really expanded. I've been going into that. Maximilian Holler bought up a whole string of rival firms. We'll have to look into all of them. My guess is that he took unfair advantage of someone, or that there's somebody who thinks he was cheated. That's still the likeliest motive for the murders. If we leave aside our mysterious friend, jealousy.'

This was typical of Taut, thought Ossi. His poetic cynicism would break through at times when they were completely at sea with an investigation, and right now they were not so much at sea as going down with all hands. Instead of clues they were finding puzzles, just more and more puzzles.

Taut put the paper down on the desk. 'Let's regard this as Ulrike telling us to take another look at the family.'

Ossi could tell from Taut's tone of voice how little hope he had that this would lead anywhere. He admired Taut's intuition. Taut was seldom wrong—almost never, in fact.

'I think there *is* a connection between this drawing and Ulrike's death,' said Ossi. 'At least to the extent that Ulrike knew *something*, and the murderer knew that she knew. I saw the Merc shooting out of Wesselyring. It was aiming straight for her. The driver meant to kill her.'

Taut nodded. 'Yes, that's possible. We must follow up that line of enquiry. But things often look different from the way they really are. A lot of things seem so plausible that we can't help believing them. And that's dangerous.' Standing up, he went over to the window and looked out. 'Which of us has been to see Holler most recently?'

Ossi thought for a moment. 'Ulrike,' he said.

'And what came out of that meeting?' asked Taut.

'No idea.'

'You mean the two of you sat here together and Ulrike didn't say a word about her visit to Holler?'

'Not quite,' replied Ossi. 'She said she'd been there again. And she also said that you hadn't told her to go. She wanted to have a good look at the man herself, and hear what he had to say. That was all.'

'Strange. Since when did she have secrets? And shortly after your conversation she was run over.'

'That's right,' said Ossi. 'Shortly after that she was run down and killed.'

'And what has this article to do with it?'

'Haven't a clue, but I know someone I can talk to about it. He spends all his waking hours dealing with this stuff.'

'With the ss?'

'With the ss,' said Ossi.

*   *   *

Disguised as Napoleonic customs officers, Captain Hornblower and his companions had crept down the Loire in a boat they had built themselves. At Nantes they seized back the *Witch of Endor*, which the French had captured not long before, and shook off their pursuers; Hornblower excelled as a gunner. Out at sea they happened to encounter a British ship of the line, so they were safe, and Hornblower could look forward to promotion and fame and new adventures.

These were the first images in Stachelmann's mind when he woke up. His next thoughts were of his visit to Anne. On his way home he had thought of nothing else. He still could not make sense of it. What was Bohming up to? Was it some sort of plot? Were he and Anne in it together? Were they having an affair? Only one thing had become clear. Anne was not nearly as self-confident as he had always assumed. Like any beautiful woman, she had seemed to him to be unapproachable. Stachelmann was intimidated by beauty.

While he was having his tea and muesli he read the *Lübecker Nachrichten*. Now the Holler murder had ceased to be headline news and merited only a column on one of the back pages. Probably *Bild* would fire off a few more shots at the Senate, complaining that there were not enough police, that Hamburg was one of the most dangerous cities in Germany. The elections for the city parliament were looming.

The phone rang. Stachelmann hated being called first thing in the morning. He went into the living room and answered brusquely, just giving his name.

'I'm sorry to bother you, Herr Stachelmann.' It was Alicia.

'I thought we discussed everything there was to discuss,' said Stachelmann. It did not come out as gruffly as he wanted it to.

'Yes, we did,' said Alicia.

Stachelmann said nothing.

'I just forgot one thing. I meant to ask you when the essay has to be handed in.'

'Before the beginning of next semester,' said Stachelmann. 'But you know that perfectly well.'

Alicia took a deep breath. 'I'm in Lübeck right now.'

Stachelmann felt the stirrings of arousal. For a moment he hesitated. It was a long time since he had slept with a woman.

'It's a beautiful city,' he said, and hung up.

It took him some time to calm down. He went into his small study. There were bookcases around the walls and piles of books on the floor. The desk was a wooden board resting on two trestles. It was covered with books and papers. When he was in a good mood Stachelmann would refer to the chaos in his study as a palaeontological challenge: in order to find anything, he had to delve down through the strata of papers. Sometimes the urge to tidy up took him and he was amazed at the things he found. But the urge was never more than transitory.

Stachelmann switched on his PC, which occupied one corner of the desk. He had no fondness for it, but had got used to it. He had stopped writing anything by hand, because whatever he put on the computer was searchable. Similarly, while he could not understand some people's total infatuation with the Internet, it did make his life easier. To him it represented an enormous data resource, and he had learned how to find his way around it.

Today his e-mails consisted almost entirely of spam, but there was one from Ossi asking if they could meet again for a beer. Well, why not? Besides, Ossi must know more about the Holler case than had appeared in the papers. Why am I so interested in that crime, Stachelmann wondered. After all, there are murders happening every day. Is it because the destruction of this family is being carried out in such a horribly systematic way?

The telephone rang and he left his study to go and answer it. Not Alicia again?

He lifted the receiver. 'Yes?' His voice sounded angry.

There was a silence at the other end. Then a voice said softly, 'Shall I ring again later? I'm sorry to have disturbed you, it's Anne.'

'No, *I'm* sorry, that was rude of me,' he apologized.

She hesitated. Then she asked, 'Was I too pushy yesterday?'

'No,' said Stachelmann.

'When will you next be coming into the department?'

'On Monday, as usual,' he answered.

'Shall we go out for some lunch, instead of eating in the canteen? My treat.'

'Yes, fine,' said Stachelmann. He was pleased. But he also had some doubts. What was she after?

He would have time to think about it over the weekend. He knew he wouldn't come up with an answer. Perhaps Anne herself didn't know.

Going back into his study, he returned to an article that he had been trying to read for some time. It was appallingly badly written, in an affected style and bristling with foreign words—you had to write like that if you wanted to get on. Stachelmann did not write much. His own articles seemed to him too simple and straightforward, and they completely lacked the tone of superiority that impressed people. He had to read this article because it was controversial and students would ask him what he thought of it. It was about the conflict of opinion among the Nazis in connection with the first concentration camps. Some wanted most of the prisoners to be released quickly, on the grounds that the deterrent effect that was the main purpose of this so-called 'preventive detention' had already been achieved. Others—notably Himmler, who was head of the (still quite small) ss and was in charge of the concentration camps in Bavaria, especially Dachau—wanted to keep the prisoners where they were. Himmler had a vindictive hatred of all those who for him embodied the Weimar system. He wanted them—especially the Jews—to pay for the years of Germany's humiliation. Himmler's view prevailed, and soon all the concentration camps were under his control. The writer of the article kept going on about the attempts that were made to preserve basic elements of the rule of law in the Third Reich. He made it sound as if Hitler's Germany would have gone on being a state founded on the rule of law if only Himmler had not had his way.

Stachelmann again did not read the article to the end, but put it aside on one corner of the desk.

He stood up and paced to and fro through his small apartment. The living room had a two-seater sofa, an armchair, a built-in stereo, and that was all. Visitors noticed that he had no TV. It addles the brain, he would say when asked. Even so, he thought he might buy a set one day; he sometimes found it frustrating when people talked about a good film they had seen on television. Not that that happened very often.

He was too restless to stay indoors, so he went out, and walked around the old centre of Lübeck, with all its reminders of the wealth the city had once enjoyed as a member of the Hanseatic League. Little now survived of either the wealth or the League. The city was in debt, with the mayor and the city council constantly embroiled in quarrels whose original cause and subject no one could remember. Nothing you heard or saw recalled the city's former greatness. He went along Königstrasse to the big bookshop that he visited now and then, always coming away depressed after seeing how many other historians had managed to complete their books. There the volumes stood, in their serried ranks, in the section marked 'History'.

Tomorrow he would go and see his parents in Reinbek. It would be a brief escape from the morass in which he lived, but it was not something that he looked forward to.

Immediately after breakfast Stachelmann got into his old vw Golf: the trip would take much longer by train. He joined the freeway at the Lübeck-Mitte junction and headed towards Hamburg. There was congestion in the opposite direction: a great many people were off to spend the weekend on the Baltic coast. As he cruised along at a leisurely speed, he wondered how long it was since he had gone away anywhere on holiday. The last time had been when Karin had persuaded him to fly to Majorca with her. It had been ghastly, packed with tourists, almost all of them German or British. When he went on holiday he wanted to see some different faces, and in Majorca that was impossible. He found the mixture of plebs and petty bourgeois repellent. They were loud-mouthed and drank too much. He and Karin had quarrelled, and that holiday had marked the end of their relationship. That had been just about three years ago. He had hardly thought of Karin since.

He left the freeway at the Reinbek exit. A few minutes later he was parking in front of a white, two-storey detached house with a steep red roof. It was in a development of white detached houses with steep red roofs. Each house had a front garden, some with a garden gnome, some without. Some with a hedge, some with a fence, some not enclosed by either. His parents had opted for a rabbit-wire fence.

On this Saturday afternoon they did what they always did when he came. They had tea and cake and talked about his life at the university. He did not tell them his troubles. They would only have worried, and there was nothing they could do to help. His father sat at the table, thin and straight-backed, and talked about Gaxotte's biography of Frederick the Great, published in 1938 but still unsurpassed. It was to his father that Stachelmann owed his early interest in history, or rather, in tales of Prussian heroes. Occasionally he observed in himself, with some amusement, a tendency to dislike southern Germans, especially Bavarians. He remembered with nostalgia how his father used to give him books from his library, full of the glory of Prussia and the low cunning of her enemies, especially the French. With every thrust a Frenchman bites the dust! His father had realized long ago that his son did not share his prejudices. They agreed to differ. Generally his father recounted stories of his time in the Hamburg postal administration and complained about the meagre pension awarded to him after so many years of service—this despite the fact that the pension was sufficient to cover two holidays a year, as well as the upkeep of a house that many other old people would have considered too big.

His mother always pressed more cake on him than was good for his incipient paunch, but since he stepped on the scales even more rarely than he visited his parents, he readily accepted another piece of apple pie with cream. His mother raised her coffee cup to her lips, took a sip and carefully replaced the cup on the saucer. Then she said, 'I suppose you've heard about that child that was murdered in Hamburg.'

His mouth full, Stachelmann nodded.

His father said, 'A nasty business.' He helped himself to another piece of cake. 'Incidentally, I knew old Holler—splendid chap.'

'How did you know him?' asked Stachelmann.

'It was when I was in the police. He stayed on there afterwards.'

Stachelmann was startled. His father had never mentioned serving in the police. 'When were you in the police?'

'Only for a short time, during the war, as a sort of auxiliary policeman.'

Stachelmann thought for a moment. How had a post office official found himself in the police? 'You've never told me about that before,' he said.

'Nothing much to tell,' said his father. 'It was only for a short time. But after the war I came across Holler again at the police sports club. Just a couple of times. Later he set up in business by himself, became a property dealer, got elected to the city parliament and all that. He was a splendid fellow. Gave himself no airs at all, was ready to listen to anybody.'

'Was?'

'Yes, he died sometime in the seventies. In Majorca—fell off a cliff.'

'And why were you in the police?'

For a moment the old man closed his eyes, tilting his head backwards. Stachelmann's mother had her eyes fixed on the tablecloth. Then he said, 'I wasn't fit for active service. And then when that idiot Goebbels declared total war they combed every department for people to mobilize. The front needed fresh meat, especially in the east. They had me by the scruff of the neck, but then they found out that I had arthritis. Thank goodness that's not the only thing you've inherited from me. But I was fit enough for the police. We had to do guard duty, that sort of thing.'

'And why have you never mentioned it?' asked Stachelmann.

'It wasn't worth mentioning. You ran around with a shotgun in your hand but didn't actually do anything.'

Stachelmann didn't believe his father. He wasn't lying, exactly, but he was certainly keeping something back. If it had been as innocent as all that he would have talked about it, the way he talked about so many other things. But was there any point in pressing him on the subject?? Maybe his father had guarded prisoners of war, forced labourers or concentration camp inmates. Or possibly gangs of men put to work defusing unexploded bombs. Stachelmann's mother was staring at the wall; she looked as if she was miles away.

Stachelmann did not stay to supper. Every time he visited his parents his mother urged him to stay on for supper, and every time he said no. 'You shouldn't work so hard,' his mother said, every time.

He drove back by the same route. The congestion had eased and he was soon home. He sat down on the sofa, put on the CD of Mozart's piano concerto no. 23, with Horowitz as the soloist, and started on the next volume of Hornblower's adventures. He didn't get far; something was bothering him. He turned his computer on, and there was another e-mail from Ossi, saying he needed to speak to him. An article had cropped up in connection with their investigation of the Holler case, an article about the SS *Totenkopfverbände*.

Stachelmann paused the CD player and rang Ossi. He got the answerphone, and left a short message. He set the piano concerto going again. This was the CD that Anne had put on when he had visited her. And now she wanted to go on the trip with him.

He picked up the volume of Hornblower and started reading again, but could not concentrate. It wasn't the fault of the book, he knew. He was always like this when there was something nagging away at the back of his mind.

The phone rang; it was Ossi. They agreed to meet at the Tokaja the following evening. 'This time it's work-related,' Ossi said. 'We've found something about the SS *Totenkopfverbände*, or whatever they're called.'

*   *   *

In the morning they got the results of the forensic examination of the Mercedes. The only find, apart from traces of the car's owner, was a single white hair. Well, thought Ossi, that doesn't get us much further at present. He did not think that the Federal Criminal Investigation Agency would learn anything from the hair. For DNA testing you need something to match your sample against. All the same, they would report a discovery: the suspect was a man whose hair had gone white with age. Ossi was prepared to put money on it.

He set off to go and see Maximilian Holler. Holler's offices were in Palmaille, next to the city's Building Control Office. The furnishings and décor were modern; everything was very understated and looked fiendishly expensive. He did not have to wait: Holler came towards him at once, his hand outstretched. Perfect composure—Ossi could think of no better term. It summed up everything about him; his walk, his expression, his reactions. Above all, the way he looked at you: there was something warm and inviting in it, but also something that kept you at a distance and discouraged you from accepting the invitation. Ossi knew that this man was superior to him.

'We have to work on the assumption that your wife, your son and your daughter may have been murdered by the same person,' said Ossi. He felt acutely uncomfortable, but how could one talk about murder without sounding brutal? Still, Ossi doubted that that had been the right way to open the conversation.

If Holler was shocked he gave no sign of it. When he spoke,

his voice was quiet and pleasant, though he sounded sad. 'Yes, that's what everyone says.' He spoke calmly, but what he clearly meant was, 'Now tell me something I *don't* know.'

'It is possible, however, that the crimes are not linked,' said Ossi. He had started stupidly, like a small boy babbling at random, trying to cover up his agitation.

Holler nodded.

'We haven't really got a clear lead,' said Ossi.

'And what about the policewoman who was run over? I met her, she came to my house on one occasion.'

Ossi would have liked to know what questions Ulrike had asked. 'Yes, that is a possible lead. Perhaps she found out something that we don't know about.'

'Oh?' Holler prolonged the 'o' sound.

'We have to consider every possibility.' Ossi hesitated, choosing his next words carefully. 'Are you sure that you have no business associate who hates you...'

'Hates me enough to kill my family?'

Ossi nodded.

Holler did not take even a second to think. 'No, none. But I've already been asked that a number of times.' It was said in a pleasant tone.

'When was your firm founded?'

'My father founded it in nineteen forty-six.'

'And it was always based here?'

'No, my father founded it in Schenefeld, but the business changed premises a few times before his death. In the end he established the office in Wandsbek. He preferred not to be located in the inner city. He liked a quieter setting. After his death the firm moved from Wandsbek to here.'

'Have you still got your father's business papers?'

'What do you mean?'

'Correspondence, contracts, accounts and so on.'

'Yes, those things are all here.'

'And all those for the time since you've been in charge?'

'Of course, we keep them here, down in the cellar.'

'May we look at those papers, today?'

He did not hesitate for a second. 'Of course. Take them with you. But I don't know what you expect to find. If you like I can ask my chief bookkeeper to help you. Documents of that kind are very complicated.'

'Thank you, but we have our own people for that sort of thing,' Ossi said, although he suspected that it might not be easy to prise any forensic accountants free for this case. Those people were up to their eyes in work. 'May I make a phone call?'

Holler stood up, indicated the telephone on his desk—'Dial zero for an outside line'—and left the room.

Taut answered after the second ring. He sounded irritable. Ossi told him that Holler was releasing the firm's documents for them to examine. But that would be useless if they couldn't find anyone to interpret them.

'Don't worry about that,' said Taut. 'I'll send you some people with packing-cases. In about an hour and a half.'

Ossi hung up, and a moment later Holler reappeared. He looked enquiringly at Ossi. 'Well?'

'Some of our men will come with packing-cases in about an hour and a half from now.'

'Fine,' said Holler. 'What shall we do in the meantime?' He looked at the clock, went over to the telephone, pressed a button and said without lifting the receiver, 'Frau Mendel, will you please cancel the meeting at twelve-fifteen and reschedule it? Thank you.'

'You don't have to cancel the meeting on my account,' said Ossi.

Holler waved away this intervention. 'It suits me quite well. Come on, if it's not in breach of your official oath I'll buy you lunch.'

Ossi tried not to show his surprise. Well, why not? I'll get to know him better, he thought.

They took Holler's Jaguar, which was like a living room in wood and leather. Holler's driving style was relaxed and safe; he had the car perfectly under control. They stopped at a small restaurant called Le Chapeau. Holler went ahead and opened the door. A black-suited waiter held out his hand to Holler. Taking it, Holler asked, 'Can you fit us in, Jakob?'

'Of course, Herr Holler,' said Jakob. He led them to a corner where a wall screened them from the rest of the diners. They had an unimpeded view of the Elbe. 'May I bring you something to drink, sir?' Jakob asked Ossi. Ossi ordered a mineral water. Jakob disappeared.

Ossi said, 'I see you come here often.'

'Yes,' Holler said. 'It's quiet and the food's good.'

On the Elbe a large freighter was heading for the port. Ossi tried unsuccessfully to make out its name. On the stern was a flag he did not recognize.

'That's the *Esmeralda*,' said Holler. 'She's from Argentina, with a cargo of meat for the steakhouses.' Ossi thought he detected a touch of contempt in his voice.

Jakob reappeared, carrying a tray with a bottle of mineral water and a glass. He had a white napkin over his left arm. He turned to Ossi: 'Shall I bring the menu, sir?' He somehow managed to convey the impression that it would be a *faux pas* for Ossi to ask for the menu.

'What do you recommend, Jakob?' Holler intervened.

Jakob named a few dishes. Ossi hardly understood a word. As soon as he heard him say 'chicken' his mind was made up.

For his starter he chose tomato soup. Holler ordered some wine, with a name that sounded French. Ossi stuck to mineral water.

'How long have you been in the police?' Holler asked.

'Sixteen or seventeen years,' answered Ossi.

'I thought that as a policeman you would know exactly.'

Ossi knew fellow officers who would. 'I'm not really bothered. It's only promotions that count in the end.'

'And how are you doing in that respect?'

'Could be better, but there's still time.'

They fell silent. Ossi looked out onto the Elbe. A suspicion was taking shape in his mind. At first he was barely aware of it, but as they sat chatting, it grew stronger and stronger. Why was Holler buttering him up like this? What did he want of him? He wouldn't be so friendly unless he had some ulterior motive, Ossi was sure of that. And there was another thing. It had not struck him at first, but now it seemed monstrous. Only days before, this man had lost his daughter; she had been murdered. And now here he was, showing not the slightest sign of grief. Back in his office he had acted as though the matter scarcely concerned him, but at that stage Ossi hadn't noticed, he had just been glad that for once he wasn't having to deal with weeping, desperate parents or spouses. The weeping and the despair were normal; Holler's sangfroid wasn't.

'I'm sure you're asking yourself, why does this man show no feeling? He's just lost his daughter and he goes out to eat in a smart restaurant.'

Ossi was startled. 'No,' he said. 'Not at all.'

'Really?' Holler said. 'Now that does surprise me. It's what *I* would think.' He scratched his nose with his little finger. 'But of course policemen are different.' He did not indicate in what way he thought policemen were different.

A few minutes earlier Ossi had thought that Holler was trying to influence him in some way; now he was afraid he was playing with him, trying to trip him up, showing off his own superiority. This was about the murder of his daughter, and Holler was playing games.

'And you're quite certain that you've made no enemies, either in business or in your private life?' asked Ossi. He had to get back to the matter in hand. He thought he had seen a hint of a smile on Holler's face.

'No, not as far as I know. But perhaps someone bears me a grudge for no reason.'

'Perhaps,' said Ossi. 'Or perhaps you've done something to a competitor that has really enraged him. Your firm has expanded greatly in the last few years, so I hear.'

'In the past twenty-five years we have increased our turnover by several thousand percent.'

'I thought there was some kind of crisis in the property market a while back,' said Ossi.

'Yes, but it didn't affect me. Anyway, that was long ago. It was when I had just taken over my father's business, and since then the business has done well. You see, when the market shrinks you have to buy up your competitors, so that despite the inauspicious conditions you are able to increase your share of the market. And I took advantage of the crisis to buy property at favourable prices. No crisis lasts forever. When it was over I made some good deals.'

'And there was really no one who felt you had taken advantage of him?'

Holler smiled. 'I paid good prices for the other firms. It may be that some of the owners wish they hadn't sold, now that business is good again. But they can't be as angry as all that—they got large sums of money from me. I didn't exploit their situation. And when I talk about buying cheaply, I didn't force anyone to sell to me. There was hardly anyone buying in those days. Dealers were ringing me, asking if I wouldn't care to have this or that house or plot of land. And if I liked something I bought it, at the market price.'

'But that must have cost you a lot of money?'

'Yes, it did. The banks helped a bit. It was easier to get credit then than it is now. And my father had left me a really sound business. The assets were very healthy indeed. And the additional property I bought did my position in the market no harm at all.'

He talked about his business as casually as if he were talking about some film he had just seen. Ossi longed to ask him how he really felt. His daughter's body had not yet been released for burial. It would be released tomorrow, the pathologists had said. Then Holler would have to bury his daughter. Would he deal with that just as casually?

Jakob arrived with the first course. Ossi's tomato soup was a splash of red in a huge plate, the edge of which was decorated with cream or something of the kind. It smelled of basil.

Holler was having lobster soup: his plate had a splash of something closer to beige.

Ossi enjoyed his soup, the best tomato soup he had ever had. He would have liked to order another.

They ate in silence.

During the second course they still did not talk much. After that they had an espresso and then drove back to Holler's office. Kamm and Kurz were waiting outside the entrance, together with two uniformed policemen they had brought along. Holler led them down into the cellar. It was clean and light, not really a cellar, Ossi thought. Holler opened a door and showed them into a room. Against one wall there were shelves holding dozens of folders, and against another a huge metal cabinet. The folders were sorted by year. The writing was neat and legible. It was some time before Ossi noticed that the room was dry and the air fresh. He looked around and saw a box under the window. He could hear it humming. Air-conditioning. Ossi had never been in an air-conditioned cellar before.

'Why do you have air-conditioning here?' he asked Holler.

Holler pointed to the metal cabinet. 'There are some things in there that need good air, above all the right level of humidity.'

'Pictures?'

Holler nodded.

'Could you please open it?'

Holler hesitated but then drew a key from his jacket pocket. In the cabinet were three flat rectangular objects wrapped in linen sheets. Holler took one out and unwrapped it. It was a painting of a Madonna. 'This means nothing to you, does it? It's valuable, very valuable indeed. Do you want to see the other two as well?'

Ossi shook his head.

The uniformed officers had brought some packing-cases, and they filled them with the folders. Everyone apart from Holler carried a case out to the van. After all the cases had been loaded in, Ossi took his leave of Holler. As they drove back to headquarters Ossi had a strong sense that they had been wasting their time. And they would waste a lot more time. They wouldn't find anything in the thousands of pages. Holler's documents were as clean as his cellar. If not cleaner. It was sickening.

Chapter six

Monday.

Stachelmann sat at his desk, reading a student's seminar paper. He was bored. The paper simply regurgitated the facts established by eminent historians. There was a knock at the door: it was Anne. She was smiling at him, and she had brought him a mug of coffee. 'To help you wake up,' she said. He did not feel like coffee, but accepted it and thanked her. Anne placed a slim folder on his desk. 'This is the outline of my thesis.'

'I thought you were still looking for sources.'

'This is based on the secondary literature and some collections of source materials. Of course it's only provisional. Will you have a look at it?'

He nodded. He hadn't even produced an outline for his own thesis.

She came round to his side of the desk. Her hand brushed against his shoulder. It gave him goose pimples. 'What's this you're reading?' she asked, but then Stachelmann saw her give a start. 'Oh, I'm sorry,' she said, retreating to the other side of the desk. 'I'm sorry, sometimes I don't think and then I poke my nose in where I shouldn't.'

'No, no,' Stachelmann said. 'It's all right. It's just a paper by a student.'

'When do we go on our trip? We still haven't talked about it.'

'I've told the Federal Archive that I'm coming on the twenty-ninth, and I'll stay for about ten days. Then I'll be going on to Weimar. I can get in there at very short notice, I know the chief archivist.'

'Oh really?' she said, highly amused. 'It sounds just like the Mafia. You scratch my back and I'll scratch yours. What do you do in return?'

'Nothing,' said Stachelmann. 'He probably has some idea that with me his documents are in good hands. He says he once read something by me. Ever since then he's occasionally pointed me towards something useful, and I haven't had to announce my visits in advance.'

'Well, I'll be able to see it all for myself and then pass judgment.'

'I'm against the death penalty, especially in my own case.'

'So am I, except when it's a matter of illicitly receiving documents,' said Anne. She was silent for a moment. 'So that puts paid to my holiday. I was planning to go to Greece at the end of this month, right at the height of the season. Oh well, never mind, it would be too hot anyway. I've got cancellation insurance and a friend who's a doctor.'

'Now there I have to make an exception,' said Stachelmann. 'When it comes to insurance fraud I'm in favour of summary justice, execution by firing squad.'

'How cruel!' said Anne. 'What are you doing this evening? You might help me enjoy my last hours before sentence is carried out.'

'This evening I'm meeting a friend in the Tokaja, just round the corner from here.'

She thought for a moment. Then she asked, 'Someone from the university? Sorry, my nosiness again.'

Stachelmann felt awkward. 'No, he's in the police.'

'So the illicit receiver of documents is best friends with a policeman. I suppose you've got him involved in your shady schemes.'

'Not yet, but give me time. No, this evening there's only murder on the agenda.'

Anne's eyebrows shot up. 'Murder?'

'The Holler murder. You must have heard about it.'

'Yes, of course.' She hesitated and then asked, 'But what have *you* to do with it?'

'Nothing at all. But something seems to have cropped up in the course of the investigation, some link with the Nazi period.'

'And how did the cops hit on you?'

'I told you, I've got a friend who's one of them.' He sounded impatient, and instantly regretted it.

Anne thought about it, the tip of her little finger in her mouth, and then asked, 'Can I come?'

'Where to?'

'This evening, to the meeting with your friend.'

'I might have known,' said Stachelmann. 'You're a bloodthirsty wench, aren't you?'

'They call me the Vampire of the Von-Melle-Park.' Anne bared her teeth.

'Well, only a very young one,' said Stachelmann. 'But then your kind live a bit longer than we ordinary mortals do. Try using something to make your teeth grow.'

'I have done. Only it takes so long.' She looked at him sadly. 'So is it boys only this evening?'

Stachelmann laughed. 'No, I'd be delighted, please do come along. We'll leave just before eight.'

When she had gone he realized how confused he was. The unapproachable Anne could be very playful, as well as quite pushy. He looked at the clock: it was time for his seminar. He grabbed his briefcase, and on the way to the seminar room he thought of a question he might ask right at the beginning. He was conscious of how much his mind was still on the evening.

The seminar room was quite noisy, and some students went on talking after he had come in. Others seemed to be dozing, or were reading the paper or a book. He dropped his briefcase down on to the table. The thump made some of them look up. 'Good morning,' he said, although it was afternoon. 'May I interrupt your conversations and your reading?' he asked amiably. The students eyed him curiously: they had never seen him so brisk and self-assured. There were a few giggles. They took their seats and gazed at him expectantly. Alicia Weitbrecht was not there—a good sign. Simone Wagner seemed relaxed and was looking at him in a friendly way. Her anger had obviously subsided.

'Today we're jumping ahead a bit, but the question I want to ask you is important for this whole course. The question is: what were the ss *Totenkopfverbände*? What functions did they carry out?'

At the front, on the left, a hand went up. Stachelmann was pleased that someone was responding so promptly. The student, whose name Stachelmann did not know, said, 'What about my seminar paper? I'm supposed to be giving it today.'

'We'll get to it, if not today then next week,' replied Stachelmann.

'But then *my* paper will get squeezed out, because it's the holidays in two weeks' time, in case anyone needs reminding.' This was said in a whining tone by another student who had also never uttered a word before.

'I read every paper and give it a grade. We knew from the start that not everyone would get a turn to deliver their paper.' He was amazed; he couldn't understand students who never opened their mouths for months on end but then insisted on their right to read out their paper to the seminar group. They would be able to discuss at most three-quarters of the papers, because the summer semester was short and the group was too big. At the end there was an exam; Stachelmann would have to mark the exam papers after he got back from his research trip. He thought of Anne.

'Let me return to my question,' he said.

Slowly and hesitantly a discussion got under way. It emerged that the students knew virtually nothing. They did not even know who had guarded the concentration camps.

After the seminar was over, he was just opening the door to his office when he heard a voice behind him. 'Herr Stachelmann! Herr

Stachelmann!' It was Renate Breuer. She came tripping towards him on her high heels, waving a piece of paper. She was breathing heavily when she reached him. 'A call from the Eppendorf Clinic. Alicia Weitbrecht. There's a phone number.'

Stachelmann asked her to come into his office and listened to her excited account, from which he eventually grasped that someone from the Eppendorf Clinic had called to say that Alicia Weitbrecht had been admitted, and would he please ring back. On the piece of paper was a name, Dr Möller.

Stachelmann sat down at his desk and said nothing. Was it a trick? The secretary was observing him. What was she thinking? Did she suppose he was having an affair with Alicia? He indicated that she should leave, and got an angry look. Then he picked up the receiver and dialled the number. A woman answered and said she would put him through to Dr Möller. It was some minutes before Dr Möller came on the line.

'You are Dr Josef Maria Stachelmann?' asked Möller. Stachelmann had already given his name, but he repeated it.

'I have to ask you that because my patient has authorized me to inform you of her condition.'

'What condition is that?' asked Stachelmann.

'Physically she is alright, but not psychologically. She tried to commit suicide.'

'I beg your pardon?'

'Suicide,' said Möller. 'If you can spare a few minutes, could you come over here, to the psychiatric department? I'd like to have a word with you. I think it's important.'

'Right now?'

'If possible.'

Stachelmann called a taxi and was at the hospital in under ten minutes. Amid the maze of concrete buildings he located the psychiatric department and asked at the reception desk for Dr Möller. The receptionist gave him directions, and Stachelmann found the room at once. A plate on the door of room 35 said 'Consultant'. Stachelmann knocked gently. A forceful voice called out, 'Come in!'

The doctor's body did not match his voice. Möller was a small, wiry man; his black pupils were magnified by the thick lenses of his round glasses. He was balding a little, though Stachelmann would have put his age at no more than thirty-five. Another one who had achieved more in life than he had himself.

Dr Möller offered him a seat. Scratching his chin, he said: 'Perhaps you can help me.'

'I'm afraid that's unlikely,' said Stachelmann. 'What happened?'

'She tried to kill herself by asphyxiation. One end of a hose attached to the exhaust, the other coming into the car, windows shut, motor running. You sometimes see it done in films. It's not difficult and it doesn't hurt.' Möller spoke in an even tone and with apparent indifference.

'But it didn't work.'

'It couldn't. She has a relatively new car. The catalytic converter filters a lot of the poison out of the exhaust emissions, the carbon monoxide for instance. The cars they produce these days still make it nice and warm on Mother Earth, but people looking for a reasonably painless death need to go for older models. It still works with those.'

Stachelmann did not answer at first, but felt he was expected to say something. 'So what happened?' A silly question, he thought.

'She sat in her car and puked her guts out, if you'll forgive the expression. Breathing in car exhaust fumes isn't exactly a health cure. She was in a lay-by on the B75, near Reinfeld. Two workmen found her. They'd been called out to deal with a blocked pipe and were on their way back. One of them needed to relieve himself and he noticed the car with the motor running and the hose.'

'When was this?'

'Yesterday evening.'

So she'd spent the whole day in Lübeck, or at least in the vicinity. 'And where do I come in?'

'That's something known only to you and Miss Weitbrecht,' said Möller. He looked Stachelmann in the eye as if to say, *You know perfectly well what you did to her.* 'She talks about you all the time.

She says you cheated on her, or dumped her. Were you friendly with her?' Möller looked at him distrustfully.

'No, she's in my seminar group, that's all.'

'Ah,' said Möller.

Stachelmann was furious. This man thought he'd been engaging in what lawyers call abuse of a position of trust, or something like that. And now he was being held responsible for the crazy actions of a hysterical girl who had been pursuing him. He was the victim, not Alicia. What fault was it of his if she was unstable? He had done nothing to encourage her. At the first sign of her infatuation he had rebuffed her. The last time she phoned he had hung up on her. You could hardly make it any clearer to a person that you didn't want to have anything to do with her. At least, not the kind of thing she obviously had in mind. If it began to be rumoured in the department that he'd been having a relationship with Alicia, that would spell the end of his career. Her suicide attempt would be used against him. He could feel Möller studying him closely.

'You know, this sort of thing happens quite often. Women work themselves up into a state of mind where they convince themselves that there's something between them and a particular man, and when they're faced with the truth there's enormous disappointment. Some of them get depressed, others kill themselves, others develop an intense hatred and try to harm the man who has rejected them.' To Stachelmann, he seemed to be saying, *So I wouldn't like to be in your shoes.* 'Do you want to see her?'

'No,' said Stachelmann.

'It would be better if you did,' said Möller. 'Certainly better for *her.*'

Stachelmann's throat tightened. He was afraid. He wanted nothing to do with this. He was innocent, and yet Alicia was dragging him into something that sickened him. And she was succeeding. Now he was being made responsible for her, even though his one wish was never to set eyes on her again.

Dr Möller showed him the way to her room. After a momentary hesitation Stachelmann knocked and pressed down the door handle.

There was only one bed in the room. She lay there looking like an angel. White face, long blonde hair that looked freshly combed. Her eyes were closed. Stachelmann looked at her and could tell that she was not asleep. Her face was not relaxed enough. She opened her eyes and said, 'Come and sit here, Josef.' She sounded wide awake. She patted the edge of the mattress. There was a chair standing next to a table that had a bunch of flowers and a bowl of fruit on it. He brought it over and placed it by the bed.

'Why did you do this?' he asked.

'No, let's talk about something else.'

Silence.

'How did the seminar go today? Did you notice I wasn't there? I've never missed it before.'

'Yes.'

'Come a bit closer.'

Stachelmann moved the chair fractionally nearer to the bed.

She stretched out her hand towards him.

He hesitated, then took it, squeezed it gently and let go. He put his hand on his knee, then moved it to his thigh.

'I'm glad you're here.' She was talking as though they were close friends, but he had no intention of reciprocating.

'How long will you be staying in the hospital?'

'I don't know, certainly for the rest of this week. And you must come and see me every day.'

He made no answer.

'Promise you will?' Her voice was gentle, but there was an undertone of determination.

'Yes,' he said. 'But I have to go now.'

'Already?'

'Yes. Work, you know.'

'Well then, give me a kiss and off you go.'

Stachelmann bent over her, catching the scent of her perfume—light, slightly arousing—and gave her a quick peck on the cheek. She smiled. He left her without a backward glance.

He walked back to the Von-Melle-Park. The drizzle did not

bother him, it matched his mood. How would he ever get rid of her without her killing herself?

Anne came to his office at half past seven. She sat down opposite him and looked at him. 'Good heavens, what's the matter? You look terrible!'

He shrugged his shoulders; he felt thoroughly miserable. Since his return from Alicia's bedside he had been sitting at his desk doing nothing. He told Anne what had happened.

After that they sat in silence for a long time.

'It's not your fault,' said Anne. 'You didn't encourage her.' Was that a statement or a question? 'Absolutely not,' said Stachelmann. 'Quite the reverse, if that's possible.'

'Perhaps your rejection of her made her think you were somehow suppressing your true feelings. Perhaps there was some situation in her childhood where a really strong "no" was only the cover for a "yes." Where one had to dig down to deeper levels to extract the "yes."'

'That sounds like a cross between mining and amateur psychology,' said Stachelmann. His knees were hurting. He had already been tired when he arrived at the department that morning. During the night he had paced around in his apartment, lain down, got up again. He was hurting all over. In the end he had taken more painkillers than he was prescribed so that he could at least lie down for two or three hours.

'Excuse me!' Anne sounded huffy. 'It doesn't take a psychologist. I had a school friend who—well, in her family all sorts of things went on. And I've never had anything to do with mining. You swallow too much coal dust!'

Stachelmann was grateful to her. Instead of taking offence at his moodiness, she was trying to cheer him up. 'I'll never be able to get rid of Alicia,' he murmured.

'I know lots of men who'd love to suffer your plight. She's really gorgeous, and not stupid.'

'Perhaps you could point one of them in her direction. You seem to know about these things.'

Anne laughed. She looked at her watch. 'Time to go,' she said.

*   *   *

They had left the documents stacked up in an office that belonged to a colleague who was off sick; it was not certain when, or even whether, he would return. Taut had acquired the services of two forensic accountants. This had not been easy; Kriminalrat Schmidt had had to use his influence with the Chief of Police, though how Taut had managed to persuade Schmidt to do this no one would ever know. Schmidt was fully aware that the Chief knew Holler well. So he had probably sounded out the Chief, and no doubt the Chief had not wanted it to be said that he wasn't doing all he could to further the investigation, after the dressing-down he had given them. Taut had evidently caught Schmidt at the right moment. Besides, how would the Department for Internal Affairs look in the election campaign if it was whispered that the Chief of Police had shielded a suspect? Pity there weren't elections every year, Ossi thought. Then you'd see some progress.

While the forensic accountants were taking a preliminary look at Holler's books, the members of the response unit assembled in Taut's office. They summed up what they had found out so far; not much, and no clear picture was emerging. They had had photographs of Ulrike and the Mercedes published in the papers and shown on the regional TV channel. This had produced a great many phone calls, mostly from crazies. Some of them claimed to have seen Ulrike long after she was dead.

Ossi had photocopied Ulrike's diagram and the article about the *Totenkopfverbände* and distributed them to the team. Kamm said nothing. Kurz looked at the diagram from every angle and growled, 'Fat lot of help that is. Okay, it looks like a family tree. But what good is that? It's perfectly easy to fill in the names in the right places. What then?'

Taut said, 'Do it.'

'What?'

'Fill in the names.'

Ossi said, 'It'll turn out that all this has nothing to do with our case and that we're barking up the wrong tree. The whole thing's probably quite different from what we imagine.'

'Have you got a better idea?' asked Taut.

Ossi shook his head.

'And what does your historian say?'

'I'm meeting him this evening.'

This time Ossi was already sitting at a table when Stachelmann and Anne entered the Tokaja. Stachelmann introduced Anne to Ossi. Instead of giving a reason for her presence he just said, 'A colleague of mine.' He was not pleased to see the hint of a grin on Ossi's face.

The woman in black appeared and sullenly took their orders. Anne and Stachelmann ordered sautéed vegetables au gratin and red wine, Ossi a beer and a schnapps. 'I've lost my appetite,' said Ossi.

'So have I,' said Stachelmann. 'But starving yourself doesn't make anyone feel any better.'

Ossi brought him up to date on events since their last meeting.

'I read about your colleague in the paper,' Stachelmann said. 'You're sure that her death is connected with the Holler case?'

'No,' Ossi replied. 'To be honest, we're completely in the dark. Of course I never said that and I don't want to see it quoted in the papers.'

'I understand,' Anne said. She did not sound offended. 'I vow to be as silent as the grave. Honest Injun.'

Ossi did not smile. He looked tired. He reached into the inside pocket of his jacket and took out a piece of paper. 'I found this article in her apartment. She cut it out of the *Spiegel*. It may have some bearing on the case, but probably not. But when you know nothing, even speculation seems like a lead.' He pushed the article across to Stachelmann, who skimmed through it and passed it to Anne.

'Why would someone cut out an article like that?' asked Anne. 'Was she interested in history?'

'Not to my knowledge. She would surely have mentioned it sometime. She liked reading, but she read novels, contemporary things. She followed the recommendations on the *Literary Quartet* programme.'

'A policewoman with an interest in literature,' Anne said in wonderment.

'You shouldn't watch so many crime series on TV,' Ossi said. He turned to Stachelmann: 'And who are the *Totenkopfverbände*?'

'They were the units that guarded the concentration camps. Some of them also fought at the front as units of the Waffen-SS. They were headed by Theodor Eicke, and he was one of Himmler's most ruthless murderers He was killed in battle in nineteen forty-three, so the Allies weren't able to hang him. If he'd still been alive, he would have been tried as one of the principal war criminals.' Anne rattled off the facts before Stachelmann was able to get a word in. He could only nod.

Then he asked, 'And you found that in Ulrike Kreimeier's apartment together with this diagram?'

Ossi nodded. 'They were together in a folder.'

'Have you looked into the Holler family tree?'

'We're just doing that.'

'What's known about the family?'

'Worthy and admirable in every respect.' He told them about his lunch with Holler. 'And while I'm giving away professional secrets, I may as well tell you that we're going through his books.'

'So you *have* got some grounds for suspicion?'

'We're poking around pretty much at random, trying to find a loose thread we can pull at and hope that what's on the other end isn't just a red herring. Holler says he has no enemies. But then why is someone wiping out his family? Surely it's possible that he caused the ruin of a business rival or associate, perhaps unintentionally. Otherwise where would so much hatred be coming from?'

'But it could just be a madman,' said Anne. 'Someone who envies him.'

Ossi nodded. 'Could be,' he said. 'That's the theory favoured by our psychological profiler. But you try catching a madman who has no links with his victim and who makes no mistakes.'

Anne got up and went in search of the bathroom.

Ossi grinned at Stachelmann. 'You've picked a good one there.'

Stachelmann shrugged.

'So she's still available?' said Ossi.

Stachelmann felt a twinge of jealousy.

Anne came back.

Ossi turned towards her, half turning his back on Stachelmann. Stachelmann saw how Ossi was trying to get a conversation going between the two of them. He listened with only half an ear. Ossi was telling her about their wild days in Heidelberg, showing off a bit.

Ossi's voice grew louder: 'Once I had to rescue him. He was daydreaming as usual, and all of a sudden he was in the middle of a bunch of ultra-right-wingers. The day before, he'd been denouncing them at a plenary meeting at the university, and they'd got wind of it. I rushed into the mob, grabbed Jossi by the arm and dragged him into the student refectory building, so fast that it was all over before they'd cottoned on. It's always like that. If most of the far right weren't brain-dead they'd be in power by now.'

The woman in black brought their drinks. Ossi gulped his schnapps down in one go. 'Another one,' he said.

Anne turned to Stachelmann: 'So you were quite a hero, Jossi.'

'Don't get into the habit of using that name, or I'll make you call me Dr Stachelmann.'

'Yes, Dr Stachelmann, sir.'

The gaming machine bleeped.

The woman in black brought their food. Ossi ordered a beer and another schnapps. Then he leaned back and said, 'What might the *Totenkopfverbände* have to do with our case? See if you can think of anything. Let's have the benefit of all your studying!'

'Was Holler senior imprisoned in a concentration camp?' asked Stachelmann.

'No idea,' said Ossi.

'Well, check it out. Perhaps there's still an old score to be settled, something to do with the concentration camps.'

'I don't get it,' said Anne. 'If there *is* an old score from that time to be settled, why should someone be killing off the family of the son? That's rubbish!'

'Rubbish is just about right,' Ossi responded. 'My whole job—everything I ever think or do—involves picking over rubbish. But just occasionally we strike gold. That's how it is in difficult cases, anyway. Usually it's all very simple and straightforward—husband bludgeons wife, wife stabs husband—because of boozing, jealousy, money problems or whatever. You see the body and within a few minutes you know who did it. Then there are the masterminds who commit the perfect murder but make a mistake, or several. We soon collar those geniuses, especially now that we've got DNA analysis. The most difficult cases are the opportunist killings, where the murderer has never even seen the victim before. Now suppose he's from a different town and has left no usable traces behind except perhaps a hair. Are we to extract hairs from heaven knows how many million Germans? It can't be done.'

He was addressing himself almost entirely to Anne. Stachelmann was certain he wouldn't be delivering this lecture if she hadn't been sitting there.

'But there's probably never been a case like this one before. Not in this country, anyway. So all suggestions are welcome, including rubbishy ones.'

The woman in black brought Ossi his drinks.

'You need to investigate the family down to the last generation.'

'Ah, Dr Stachelmann is becoming quite biblical,' said Anne.

'Yes, I suppose we'll have to,' said Ossi. He tilted his head from side to side, his eyes fixed on Anne. 'We've got nothing, absolutely nothing.'

'And what have you found out about the death of your colleague, leaving aside this article?' asked Stachelmann.

'Nothing there either. We haven't found the driver. The owner of the car was in America at the time, and can prove it. The car was broken into and the ignition hot-wired. The criminal, or criminals, even deactivated the alarm system. They were professionals when it came to electronics.'

The gaming machine bleeped.

Stachelmann looked idly around while Ossi talked intently to Anne. From the scraps he overheard he gathered that Ossi was boasting about his job. Stachelmann wondered what either the Hollers or the dead policewoman had to do with him. Nothing, nothing whatsoever. It was ridiculous for him to concern himself with the case. He had enough on his plate without that. After all, the police weren't helping him with his *Habilitation*, were they?

The woman in black appeared. She loaded the empty plates and glasses on to a tray and looked at each of them in turn: 'Anything else?' Her tone was not friendly.

None of them ordered anything. 'Can we have the bill, please?' said Stachelmann. She turned on her heel and stalked off.

They parted outside the door. Anne turned to Stachelmann. 'Will you just see me home? I'm afraid of robbers.'

'I'd be better, I'm a policeman,' said Ossi. His speech was slightly slurred.

'Yes, I'm sure you would, but not this evening,' said Anne. 'Besides, what I need is moral support, after having been immersed in the world of crime. It gives me the creeps.' She pretended to tremble with fear.

Ossi went off with a despondent look.

Anne took Stachelmann's arm. Tiny drops fell onto his face: it was still drizzling. After a while Anne said, 'He's quite nice really, but he has an awful job.'

'I don't know,' Stachelmann said, 'sometimes I like him and sometimes I find him too inclined to barge in and take over.'

Anne turned her face towards him and smiled. 'Yes,' she said. 'That's one way of putting it.'

She was so light. He could have gone on walking with her like this forever. He was sorry when they reached the entrance to her building. She went up to the door, then turned round and asked, 'Can I offer you something?'

He felt a fluttering in the pit of his stomach. 'My last train leaves soon.'

'Ah,' she said.

He stood there for a few moments, then went towards her and held out his hand. She took it, pulled him to her, embraced him quickly and kissed him on the mouth, lightly, little more than a touch. 'Then you'd better hurry,' she said. She was smiling.

'Otherwise I shall have to sleep on a park bench,' he said. He had rarely felt so unsure of himself. He felt a fool. Such a fool.

'In this weather you'd be sure to catch cold.'

'See you tomorrow.'

'Yes, see you tomorrow, don't miss your train.'

He sat on the train, feeling dejected, and looked out of the window. He saw his face reflected in it. It looked ugly, devoid of expression. He did not understand what had just taken place. He could not understand himself. Anne had given him a clear invitation, only an idiot could have failed to realize that. He was afraid of disappointing her.

You're ill, he told himself. Sometimes you have to lie down because you're incapable of walking and you feel as if you've been given a dose of valium.

So what, you should still have gone up to her apartment with her.

But if she finds out that you're ill, first she'll feel sorry for you and then she'll send you packing.

Maybe, but it would have been better to risk it, rather than just assume you'd fail.

But you've become somebody who can only live alone. You've been on your own for so long that you've got used to it. You're happy that way.

No, you're a neurotic and a coward. You're on the edge of the abyss. You'll never be a professor. You're afraid of everything and everybody, you've no self-confidence. You're ripe for the loony bin.

During the night his various pains dragged him from his sleep. His ribcage felt like a steel corset, and breathing was painful. He could feel every single joint, big or small. He got up, went into the bathroom and swallowed five tablets. In the living room he put on Mozart's piano concerto no. 23 and sat down on the sofa. As the music started, he felt the tears coming.

* * *

The boy had been thrilled when he had got his toy engine back. It ran beautifully, it was as good as new. The old man went into his bedroom and lay down. He was tired. Lying on his back, he stared at the ceiling, knowing he would be unable to get to sleep. He remembered his second attack. It had been simple. He had followed the boy around for months until the idea came to him—such a simple idea, and so effective. The poison was there in Goldblum's cellar, almost as if it were waiting for him. Goldblum had told him how he had bought the cyanide capsules from a Nazi on the black market. He might as well have said: take the cyanide and do what you have to do on behalf of all of us.

He had sat down at the edge of the pool next to the boy. Choosing his moment, he had emptied the contents of the capsule into the bottle. Then he had stood up and left.

Chapter seven

When he woke up his eyes were burning, as they always did when he hadn't had enough sleep. It was a wonder he had slept at all. He ate some breakfast and took a shower. He remembered last night and felt terrible. He dreaded the very thought of going to the university. He got dressed and went anyway.

On his desk in the Philosophers' Tower there was a note asking him to ring Dr Möller. Renate Breuer had also written down the telephone number. Stachelmann groaned to himself. He dialled the psychiatrist's number but did not get him. He was not available, a woman's voice said: he should try again in half an hour. Stachelmann was tempted to ask just who was trying to get in touch with whom here.

There was a knock at the door, and it opened. Anne put her head in. 'Well, did you catch your train?'

'Yes,' he said.

'You look awful. Are you ill?'

'No, no,' Stachelmann said. 'I slept very badly, that's all.'

'Me too,' said Anne. 'Oh, I meant to ask you: have you phoned the Federal Archive to say that there are two of you now?'

Stachelmann clapped his hand to his forehead. 'Damn, I forgot. I'll do it today. I'll smuggle you in as my assistant, then they can hardly say no.'

'Aha, assistant, is it?' said Anne. 'How nice that I can fulfil that wish for you.'

Stachelmann said, 'No, no, I didn't mean it like that. It would just be the easiest....'

She grinned and left.

What a wonderful day.

He leafed through a copy of *Deutschlandarchiv*, which he had found in his pigeonhole. For several issues a debate had been going on about Soviet policy towards Germany in the early 1950s. With each successive issue the attention he paid to these articles dwindled, as their authors concentrated less on substance and more on point-scoring. It was always like that when there was a dispute among historians. At the start Stachelmann would eagerly follow the debate, but then he would rapidly lose interest. At first there was content, but by the end only posturing. Stachelmann liked to compare these controversies to contests between rutting stags. A few of the prima donnas among the historians were quick to take offence, and when they did they wouldn't even acknowledge that two and two make four if a rival claimed it was so. Some got themselves into untenable positions because they would never admit to being wrong and would cling to an opinion even if it was liable to be misunderstood. Bohming, the Legend, a satellite circling now one planet, now another in the historical cosmos, would wait to see how a dispute developed before deciding which side to back. Stachelmann couldn't help smiling. Bohming was a charlatan; he had reached the highest level of all debates, the level where disputes were carried on merely for their own sake.

Stachelmann put the journal aside and picked up the phone. This time Dr Möller deigned to accept his call. 'Could you come here again?' he asked. Naturally it had to be right away, because the doctor was free just now. And, he observed, one never knew what tomorrow might bring—in times like the present one must expect to be summoned to tend to victims of an accident at any moment.

Stachelmann felt he was surrounded by crazy people. Möller was a hysteric, Anne was odd, and Alicia, of course, really was crazy.

This time Stachelmann was free, so he walked over to the hospital. Dr Möller greeted him pleasantly, offered him a chair and sat in silence for a while, before saying, 'I'm quite sure that you didn't always reject Miss Weitbrecht. I realize that this is difficult for you. And you might have some trouble with the university.'

Stachelmann stared at him. He shook his head. He could not understand this. 'No, she's in my seminar group. That's all.' Then he raised his index finger. 'No, that's not all. Shortly after the seminar course began this semester she started pursuing me.' He thought he saw pity in Möller's eyes.

'And then you couldn't resist,' said Möller gently.

'No, damn it!' Stachelmann was startled by his own voice, which was loud and penetrating. 'She's a hysterical young woman! She rings every couple of days wanting to come and see me. God knows why she's taken it into her head to chase after me.'

Möller smiled. His smile said, as eloquently as words could have done: *Go on, have your say—I don't believe a word of it.* Only after this did he speak. 'Well, be that as it may, I think you have a responsibility towards Miss Weitbrecht. If you prefer, you can regard it simply as part of the general duty we owe to every human being because we ourselves are human.'

Stachelmann almost groaned aloud. Möller was at least as mad as Alicia. She must have given him an Oscar-winning performance, Stachelmann thought.

'It would be nice if you could visit her straight away. And when we discharge her you shouldn't break off contact with her. At least not immediately.'

Who had appointed this idiot? Stachelmann struggled to control his anger. 'I am not Miss Weitbrecht's personal therapist. She may have managed to convince you that I'm a heartless monster—'

'Oh no,' Dr Möller said. 'She thinks you're a wonderful person.' His eyes shone.

'I will not visit her. And I would be glad if she'd keep right away from my seminars and from me. I gave her no reason even to dream that there was the slightest possibility that I wanted to have more to do with her than with any other member of my seminar group. I can't even say that she was one of the brightest.'

Dr Möller gave a friendly smile: 'It seems to me that your agitation speaks for itself—'

Stachelmann stood up. 'Do you know what? Tell her to use a knife next time. But to cut the arteries lengthways, otherwise it won't work. I read that somewhere. And now I wish you a pleasant day with your patient. Perhaps *you* have a use for her.'

He walked out, banging the door behind him. After taking a few steps he felt he had been a bit harsh; after a few more he thought he had been cruel. He had a momentary impulse to go back, but he could picture Dr Möller's triumphant expression if he did. He walked faster. A cold breeze was blowing through the wind tunnels formed by the buildings along the streets, even though it was the height of summer.

*   *   *

The man was short and fat, and wore horn-rimmed spectacles. He spoke slowly, as if talking was painful for him, and Ossi grew increasingly impatient. The man was one of the two forensic accountants whom Taut had roped in to work on the case. They had taken a preliminary look through Holler's papers, and Taut had persuaded them to present an interim report.

The fat one was called Steinbeisser. 'You know, gentlemen, that my colleague Tannhuber and I find it, well, let's say, not really professional to tell you anything at this stage about documents which we have not yet been able to study thoroughly. We have not had time to do that, it will take us at least two more weeks. But you said you couldn't wait—your deceased colleague, urgent case, we can understand that. But we hope *you* will understand that we absolutely cannot give you an interim report in writing. It is quite conceivable that the information that we give you now may prove, in the light of the final outcome of our investigation, to be partly or even wholly incorrect. Admittedly that is not likely, but it is not impossible. This being so, what I am about to tell you has no value as evidence. That is why I still cannot see how it can be of any use to you.' He shrugged his shoulders and ran a hand through his greasy hair.

'Well?' said Taut.

Steinbeisser muttered something, too quietly for anyone to hear. Then he squared his shoulders. 'Herr Holler is a wealthy man, unless he has handed over his firm's considerable profits to the casino. He owns the largest property dealing firm in Hamburg—'

'I gathered that much from the newspapers,' Ossi blurted out. Steinbeisser's way of talking was intensely irritating to his listeners.

The forensic accountant gave Ossi a sharp look. 'The firm's books are audited every year by an accountant from one of the best firms in Hamburg. Niemeyer and Sons, you may have heard of them. I had a period of training with them, almost twenty years ago.' He looked around proudly. 'But only since nineteen seventy-five.'

'*What* only since nineteen seventy-five?'

'Holler's books have only been audited by Niemeyer and Sons since nineteen seventy-five. Prior to that, we find in the documents the name of a firm we do not know and that no longer exists: Hansen, Notaries and Accountants. That's what their stamp says, and it's the letterhead on their invoices. The firm only lasted for five years, from nineteen seventy-one to nineteen seventy-five.'

Ossi became aware that his fingers were drumming on the table. Taut was looking at him in annoyance, eyebrows drawn together in a frown. Ossi put his hands in his pockets.

'Since we consider the firm of Niemeyer and Sons to be utterly reliable—well, no one is infallible, but it wouldn't be likely that they made any mistakes—we've looked at the books for the year nineteen seventy-four.'

'Aha,' said Taut.

'Herrmann Holler died on the sixteenth of June nineteen seventy-four. His son was evidently his sole heir, at least the books contain no reference to anyone else. Herrmann Holler left the property-dealing business to his son. It was already doing very well. The firm's bank accounts contained more than a million marks in liquid assets, which was a very considerable sum at the time. And then there was a special account that contained more than eleven million marks.'

Taut whistled through his teeth.

'That is not necessarily significant,' Steinbeisser said indifferently. 'Suppose that shortly before his death he had sold an office block or an apartment building and had channelled the money destined for his clients through his own account. That would easily explain such a sum. Be that as it may, the money was not passed on to a client: instead Holler kept the account open. And at the start there was no activity with the account. He did not invest the money and so missed out on a large amount of interest.'

'You mean to say that for years he had eleven million marks stashed away and did nothing with it?' asked Ossi.

'Precisely.'

'But later he did do something with it?'

'After a few years he began to draw on it. It seems to have been all transfers, not money taken in cash.'

'Transfers to whom?' asked Taut.

Steinbeisser looked hesitantly at him. 'I have a list of the recipients here.'

'Do you know what the money was transferred for?' Taut was tense.

'I'm not yet in a position to judge that. My colleague and I will need to sort through the documents a bit more first.'

'You've no idea at all?'

'Oh yes, I think I know,' said Steinbeisser. He gnawed at a fingernail and then whipped his hand quickly behind his back when he noticed the others' eyes on him. 'This really is most unprofessional.'

'We'll treat it as mere supposition, not as evidence. We'll hold back with it until you've got evidence that will stand up in court.'

Steinbeisser seemed somewhat reassured. 'Very well then. He used the money to buy up other firms. Property dealing firms, competitors. But so far I haven't found any contracts or legal documents relating to these acquisitions. I'm more or less guessing.'

'But you think your guess is right?' asked Taut.

Steinbeisser nodded.

'Well, we can soon find out.' He gave the list of names to Kamm. 'Go and look these up.'

Kamm left the room.

Steinbeisser stood in the middle of Taut's office, beads of sweat glistening on his forehead. Taut thanked him and saw him out.

After Steinbeisser had left, no one spoke for a while. Ulrike had always sat in the corner next to Taut's desk. That seat was empty now.

Taut looked at Ossi. 'Did anything come out of your meeting with the historian?'

'He's got a good-looking girlfriend,' said Ossi, shrugging.

'Great,' said Taut. He sounded irritated.

'Those eleven million were a sort of war chest,' said Kurz.

'Better still.' Taut stood up and stretched. 'But where did the money come from? Old Holler's firm was sound, but small. Eleven million put by, just like that?'

'I wonder if they paid any tax on it.'

'I doubt if we'll be able to find that out. Anyway, it's too far back to be punishable now. And if anyone was on the fiddle it's more likely to have been Holler senior. I don't think we'll be able to harass the sainted Maximilian about it.'

'But he might at least have asked himself whether it was all above board,' said Ossi.

'Maybe he did.'

'We'll have to ask him,' said Taut. 'Ossi, you've become his bosom pal. Why don't you do it?'

Ossi nodded. Typical, he thought. In crime series the senior detective officer does that sort of thing himself. In response unit no.3 of the Hamburg murder squad he sends one of his minions, while he sits like a spider on its web, waiting. Taut was patient, a master of logical deduction—he was better at that than any of them. Still, Ossi welcomed the opportunity to visit Holler again. He wanted to ask him whether his father had been in a concentration camp. Even though he now felt fairly sure that that was a false trail, he had made up his mind to put the question to him. Anything for a change, he thought.

'Can I take my friend, the historian?'

Taut thought for a while. 'As long as he stays in the background. I don't want any trouble. This is a police investigation.'

* * *

Jack served an apprenticeship as a mechanic. There was no question of continuing his school education or going to university: his foster parents were not well off, but even if they had been, he wasn't their son. He was amazed to find how good he was with his hands. He learned to use a file, and grasped the principles of mechanics. Soon he was well thought of in the workshop. He came in for fewer blows than the other two apprentices, Joe and Phil, but they made up for it by beating him up themselves, accusing him of deliberately showing them up. They could not bear the fact that he was better than they were. And they hated him even more because he was German. They regarded tormenting him as their contribution to the war effort. They maligned him, pretended that shoddy pieces of work were his, and stole things he had made. They messed up his part of the workbench with iron filings and oil. Their master had a good idea of what was going on, but did nothing to stop it, and sometimes punished Jack for things that Joe and Phil had done in order to get him into trouble. The punishment usually took the form of overtime, which Jack soon realized suited his master: it was profitable for him to have Jack working extra hours for nothing.

Despite all this, Jack was glad to have discovered something that gave him satisfaction. He learned how to use his hands to make works of art. That was how he privately regarded the objects that he filed and assembled during his apprenticeship. He loved gear wheels best of all. You could use them in a variety of ways to transmit energy. He learned how to calculate transmission ratios and to build elaborate drives. Soon he could repair the gearboxes of tractors, which brought his master new customers and more money, and induced him to take Jack on as a hired hand. Jack was grateful—it was not easy for a German to get a job. The country people were full of distrust. It made little difference that Jack was a Jew: to the English, a German was a German. But at least they had let him learn a trade. He was better off than his family: there were rumours suggesting they were long dead. The Jews were being murdered, some said. They had heard it on the wireless. Yet at the same time, they didn't seem to believe it. As they said to Jack, there had been propaganda lies in the Great War, so why not in this war too?

Chapter eight

Anne had offered to buy him lunch in the canteen. She chose spaghetti and a salad, while he had cabbage roulades. The food was better than people claimed: it was simply the in thing to find fault with it. Stachelmann was irritated by the clatter and talk all around him, but it didn't seem to bother Anne.

'So we're off the day after tomorrow. I'm really looking forward to it,' Anne said.

'Don't forget your toothbrush.' The thought of going away with Anne gave him a sense of elation. He had heard nothing more from Alicia. By now he was feeling rather proud of the way he had stood up to Dr Möller. He told Anne about it.

She listened intently, letting her spaghetti get cold. 'And you're not worried that she'll do it again?'

He shrugged. 'I don't know. I think there's method in her madness, and I suspect she knows more about cars than she lets on.'

'But what if you're wrong?'

'I did nothing to bring on this crazy behaviour. Nothing at all. And therefore I'm not responsible.'

'I agree. But all the same it's not a nice feeling, is it?'

'No. But does that mean I have to sit at her bedside, holding her hand? Or worse, heaven forbid?' Stachelmann felt strong, as he always did when he had no doubts. He had managed to extricate himself from a mess. When things got desperate he always found a way out. But he often let things drag on and got into difficulties as a result. He thought of the mountain of shame, and his spirits sank again.

'By the way, Ossi rang this morning. He wants me to go with him to see Holler and hear what he has to say. Ever since they found that article about the ss in the dead policewoman's apartment they won't let it rest.'

'I'm sure it's all nonsense. But quite interesting nonsense. So Dr Stachelmann is turning detective!'

Stachelmann grinned. 'You could be my Dr Watson!'

'Very funny! But tell me what Holler's like.'

'My lips are sealed,' said Stachelmann. 'I refuse to confide in someone who doesn't want to be either Dr Watson or an assistant.'

'Oh, you're wrong there. I *am* an assistant, only not yours but Professor Bohming's. And very happy to be one.'

Ossi came to pick him up.

'No flashing lights?' asked Stachelmann.

Ossi did not reply. He was driving fast along the Reeperbahn towards Blankenese.

'The only lead we have will probably prove to be a complete waste of time. If there was anything in it my boss would shift his ass and follow it up himself. He wouldn't want it said afterwards that he missed a trick. "We even involved a historian in our investigations, and forensic accountants, and the Salvation Army, and Hamburg sv!"' Ossi was fed up.

'You don't like being the errand boy,' said Stachelmann. 'When do you get to be head of department or whatever it's called?'

'I could have been, long ago, only there were some courses I didn't take. And now they don't even ask me anymore.'

'Well, tell them that now you're really keen to be a top cop.'

'If only I knew whether I really am that keen. I am right now—I always am when I'm angry. But at other times I'm not so bothered.'

Stachelmann laughed. 'So you're in the same boat as I am.'

Ossi looked at him in surprise. Then he swerved sharply. 'Damn it,' he said. 'Those cyclists are like bluebottles, always where they're not wanted.' He ran a hand through his red hair. 'In what way am I in the same boat as you?'

'I don't produce the goods either. Not properly. They'll be throwing me out one of these days.'

Ossi pulled up at a traffic light. He looked at Stachelmann. 'I'd never have thought it,' he said.

A car behind them sounded its horn.

Ossi waved an apology to the driver behind and moved off. '*He*'s in a hurry.'

When Holler opened his door to them, Ossi introduced Stachelmann as a colleague. Stachelmann could not judge the quality of the objects he saw as Holler led them from the vast entrance hall into an even more spacious room. He could only see that everything looked very expensive—the polished marble floor, the tapestries, the paintings and chandeliers. A harmonious mixture of antique and modern. The room contained a huge bookcase; some of the books were bound in leather, and some had slips of paper sticking out of them. Holler motioned them towards a corner where some armchairs were grouped around a table. The only other furniture in the room was a small desk with a leather-upholstered chair. There were telephones on both tables. On the desk Stachelmann could see a notepad and a few books lying open. He tried to make out the titles of the books; they were all about yachting.

They exchanged a few remarks about the weather and the season, and then Ossi said, 'We see from your papers that, as well as the firm, your father left you a sum of around eleven million marks, in a separate account. Only one payment was made into the account, and that was the eleven million. Where did that money come from?'

Holler looked at him for a while. 'I don't know. Good heavens, it was a quarter of a century ago. He must have earned it. He was a hardworking man. I owe him a lot.'

Ossi gazed out of the French window, which opened on to the garden. That was where Holler's daughter had been poisoned.

'Well, I can still remember the time thirty years ago when my father put two hundred marks in my hand so I could buy a bike,' said Stachelmann.

Ossi looked at him crossly.

Holler stood up and began to pace up and down. 'People vary, not least with regard to their powers of memory. Please don't take this the wrong way, but in my business one is often dealing with very large sums of money. Last month, for instance, I sold an office complex in the City Nord for about thirty million.'

Ossi scratched his chin. 'If either your father or you, shall we say, forgot to pay some taxes, I'm not interested in that. It's too long ago, and besides, I don't work for the tax authorities.'

Holler gave an almost imperceptible nod. 'Very kind of you to point that out. But I've never yet *forgotten* to pay any taxes.' He stressed the word 'forgotten'.

'So you can't tell us where the eleven million came from?'

'Perhaps my father did some good deals just before his death. I wasn't involved at that time.' Holler was still pacing. 'Besides, what has this to do with the murder of my daughter?'

'Maybe there is some old score to be settled. Maybe your father did something that someone else resented—resented so much that they want to kill off everyone bearing the name of Holler?'

'Then that person should have come to me. We would have found some solution. If there were any grounds even to suspect that my father might have wronged him, and he had demanded money from me, he would have received some.'

Stachelmann admired his choice of words. A bit stilted, but very precise.

The door flew open. A child ran into the room calling, 'Papa! Papa!' and holding out a toy car.

'Is is broken?' asked Holler.

'Car boken,' said the little boy.

A woman appeared in the doorway, young and beautiful. There was a hint of something Asian, something exotic about her. 'I'm sorry, Herr Holler. I went into the kitchen just for a moment and that's when he came in here.'

'It's all right,' said Holler. 'It doesn't matter.' His face darkened. 'You can't keep a child chained to your side twenty-four hours a day. And that's why Sebastian and Valentina died.'

The woman turned pale.

Holler made a placatory gesture. 'Will you take him now?'

The child readily took the woman's hand and they left the room. Holler put the toy car on the table.

'We need to speak to the property dealers whose firms you bought up,' Ossi said.

'If that's what you need to do.'

'None of them have any reason to seek revenge on you?'

'I've been asked that before. Look, I got independent valuers to assess the value of each firm that I wanted to buy. I bought eight firms, and in every case the sellers got a lot of money. It's left them very comfortably off, so why should they hate me? There was no haggling, just the kind of prices that are paid when the market is good, even though in fact there was a recession in property prices at the time.'

'Have you got the names of the sellers?'

'They must be in the papers that you took away.'

'We'd have to hunt for them. I'm sure you have them to hand.' Ossi was hoping to find some discrepancies between the forensic accountants' list and Holler's. Perhaps he would find something that Holler was trying to hide. But he was not hopeful.

Holler picked up the telephone handset. He pressed a button and asked someone to put together a list of the sellers and fax it to police headquarters. 'When you get back, the list will be on your desk,' said Holler.

Ossi glanced towards Stachelmann. 'Thank you. Now for a completely different question. When did your father found the business?'

'Nineteen forty-six. I told you that before.'

'Where did the money come from?'

'I've no idea. But it wasn't hard to start a business like this. It still isn't. When I think of some of the people who have set themselves up as property dealers! No, what you need is clients, and above all their trust, which is built up over the years if you treat them properly. I learned from my father that sometimes you have to forgo immediate profit in order to earn a better reputation in the long run. That is more or less our firm's philosophy. In this business you only get somewhere if you behave fairly not only towards your clients, but also towards your competitors.'

'What did your father do before he dealt in property?'

'The same as you, he was a policeman. He never told me much about it. You can understand that, it was a terrible time. He had a congenital heart defect, so he wasn't called up to serve in the Wehrmacht, but stayed in the police. He didn't tell me any more than that.' Holler sat down. He was calm. 'Now I'm sure you're going to ask me what position he held in the police. I don't know.'

'And he spent the whole of the war in Hamburg?' asked Stachelmann.

'Yes, I think so.' He hesitated. 'No, I vaguely remember him saying, "It was lucky for me that they sent me to Russia for a few months"—which meant that he wasn't working in Hamburg when the terrible bombing raid took place.'

'And what did he do in Russia?'

'Police work, I suppose. He never talked about it.'

'And he never mentioned being in the ss or under the direction of ss departments?'

Holler looked sternly at Stachelmann. 'I didn't catch your name.'

'Dr Stachelmann.'

'You're not a policeman, then.'

'I'm a historian.' Stachelmann cursed the perspiration that he knew was about to break out on his forehead.

Holler turned to Ossi. 'You certainly go to great lengths.' He looked again at Stachelmann.

Stachelmann did not know what to make of that remark. He nodded.

'Do you think that I murdered my daughter, and my wife and my son, too?' This question was addressed to Ossi.

'No,' said Ossi.

'Then why are you investigating me?'

'We're not investigating you. I admit that we're just groping around. We're trying to get hold of anything we can.'

'And as likely as not, it will lead nowhere. You'll stir things up, do a lot of damage and still not find the murderer. If you carry on like this I shall lose my good name, and as I have already told you, that's what my livelihood depends on. You are supposed to be catching my daughter's murderer, not ruining me. You do understand that?'

Ossi nodded. 'We'll be as discreet as we can.'

'But you're not going to find the murderer in my firm's books, nor in my father's life history. My daughter hadn't even been born when he died.'

Stachelmann noticed with surprise that the self-possessed Holler was getting angry, but within seconds Holler had reverted to a more friendly tone. 'Well, you're only doing your duty. Please forgive my agitation. After all, this is'—he wiped his eyes with the back of his hand, and his voice failed for a moment—'this is about my family.' He turned to Stachelmann. 'Tell me something about yourself. Why are you concerned with this case?'

'Herr Winter asked me.'

'But he must have had a reason.'

'My research area is the Nazi period, particularly the concentration camps.'

'The ss, the Reich Security Department, the Gestapo and all that?'

'Yes.'

'What are you working on at the moment?'

'Buchenwald.'

'Buchenwald concentration camp, near Weimar. I went there once. Horrible. The things that human beings can do to other human beings.' Holler stood up and went over to a bookcase. 'I'm sure I had a book about Buchenwald.' He scanned the shelves for a few moments. 'Oh well, I can't find it right now, besides which, I expect you've read everything there is to read on the subject.'

'Hardly. In particular I haven't read all the documents. During the coming vacation I intend to fill in some of the gaps.'

'You're going to look in the archives?'

'Yes, in Berlin and Weimar.'

'There's something fishy there,' said Stachelmann when they were back in the car. 'He was more upset by our questions about his father than by those about the money. And then he suddenly switched back to oozing friendliness.'

'Yes,' said Ossi. He wrinkled his nose. 'Our friend Holler is definitely not as saintly as he tries to appear. He's got something nasty in the woodpile and doesn't want us to find it. But it may have nothing at all to do with the murders. Personally, as an old crime hand, I think it's all about money.'

'Maybe,' said Stachelmann. 'But I'm not an old crime hand.'

Ossi braked: they had joined a long tailback. He swore. The car phone rang, and Ossi answered it: 'Kastor three.' He listened and then said, 'OK. I'm stuck in a traffic jam. I'll be as quick as I can.' He opened the window, put the blue light up on the roof, and switched on the siren. Slowly the other cars made way for him. Ossi squeezed past them. The drivers glared.

'What is it?' Stachelmann asked.

'We're to go to the Chief of Police. Right away.'

The Chief of Police admitted them at once. He did not offer them a seat. The instant Ossi shut the door, the Chief started on them. 'Who are you, may I ask?' he demanded of Stachelmann.

'Dr Stachelmann.'

'And just what have you to do with an investigation by one of my departments?'

'I was asked to take part.'

The Chief looked angrily at Ossi. 'Was this your idea?'

'In a way,' said Ossi. It was clear to Stachelmann that although it had been Taut's idea, Ossi had no intention of getting his boss into trouble.

'In a way?!' bellowed the Chief. 'In a way! Perhaps you'll deign to give me a proper answer?'

'Yes,' said Ossi.

'Yes, what? Yes, it was your idea? Or yes, you'll favour me with a straighforward answer?'

'Both.'

'Are you taking the...' The Chief broke off. He sat down on a big chair behind a massive desk and paused.

Stachelmann was amused by the large, pretentious oil paintings on the wall, evoking the glorious past of the Hansa League. Cog in heavy seas; market place and harbour. He saw Ossi's fingers quivering behind his back.

Impatiently, the Chief motioned them to sit down. Ossi fetched a chair that was standing against the wall, Stachelmann sat down on the one facing the desk.

'Whatever put it into your head to involve an unauthorized person in an investigation?' he asked Ossi. He was visibly struggling to keep his temper.

'There may be a historical angle to the case,' Ossi replied. 'It's possible that the key to it lies in the past. Besides, if I may say so, we regularly draw on the help of experts who have not been formally authorized by the police.'

The Chief nodded. 'But we don't invite them to be present when questioning people.'

'We do sometimes, with psychologists. Besides, we weren't questioning Herr Holler, we were simply trying to get some information that might set us on the track of the criminal. And I felt it was important to have someone there with a knowledge of history.'

'And what emerged from your enquiries?'

'That Holler's father may have had a skeleton in his cupboard. But that doesn't get us much further.'

'Holler's father?'

'You could say he was a colleague of ours.'

'I know,' said the Chief. 'And I'm afraid many policemen from those days have skeletons in their cupboards. The police were under Himmler's command. Of course not every ordinary uniformed policeman, nor every detective, committed crimes. But the police as a whole certainly couldn't boast a clean record after nineteen forty-five. Take the persecution of the Jews. The Nazis couldn't have done it without the police. Serving the deportation orders, taking the people from their homes, guarding them in the Moorweide, taking them to the trains. The ss didn't do that all by themselves. And do you think that every detective resisted acting as a sort of auxiliary to the Gestapo? Nazi sympathies keep on manifesting even today.' He turned to Stachelmann. 'I'm sure that's how you see it, too.'

'Yes.'

'You know, my father was a Social Democrat party official and member of the Hamburg parliament. In nineteen thirty-five the Nazis forced our family into exile. You could say I'm a Frenchman by birth. Well, that's just by the way. But Maximilian Holler has nothing to do with all this, even if his father was a Nazi.'

The door opened. The Chief's secretary appeared, with a note in her hand; he read it and looked at his watch. 'Cancel the lunch meeting.' Almost imperceptibly raising her eyebrows, the secretary turned on her heel and vanished.

The Chief blew his nose. 'No doubt you'll have guessed straight away that Herr Holler telephoned me as soon as you had left him. He complained that your investigations seem to be directed against him rather than towards finding his daughter's murderer. You're digging up old matters that might interest a historian'—he nodded in Stachelmann's direction—'but not the police. Have you no other leads?'

Ossi shook his head. 'We've gone over everything in minute detail. We've had no success in tracing the driver who killed Ulrike Kreimeier. We don't even know if the two cases are linked. In the Holler case we haven't the ghost of a suspicion or a motive. The one thing we know is that there's something dubious in the Holler family.'

'And what's that?'

'There's a bank account containing eleven million marks and it's not clear where the money came from—'

There was a knock at the door. 'Come in!' the Chief called. Taut entered. 'Where on earth have you been? The amount of money we spend on radios and mobile phones, and it's still impossible to get hold of anybody!'

Taut did not answer. He fetched a chair and sat down beside Ossi.

'We're just talking about the Holler and Kreimeier cases. You're making no progress, Herr Taut. Why is that?'

Taut and Ossi exchanged glances.

'We haven't really got anything to go on,' said Taut.

'"Really"—what do you mean by "really"?'

'We haven't got anything concrete. But there are a few inconsistencies in relation to Herr Holler...'

'...whose family have been the victims of a serial killer.'

'We don't even know that.'

The Chief leaned back in his chair. 'We can't say to people: there's someone out there who has killed the wife and children of a respected resident of this city, and the police know nothing and do nothing. The press have been badgering me for days. They keep urging me to hold a press conference, so that they can tear us to pieces even more effectively. I can't put that off forever. Herr Taut, I'm not expecting you to hand me the murderer on a plate by tomorrow morning, but I would like to be able to say that we're following up significant leads.'

'The lead relating to Holler is good.'

When Stachelmann saw the others' faces he knew he should have kept quiet.

'Dr Stachelmann, you think I should appear before the press and say: we haven't got a murderer, but as for the victim—and Holler *is* a victim—we think there are some discreditable things to be discovered about him.' The Chief shook his head.

Stachelmann was unperturbed by the Chief's outbursts. He could get up and leave whenever he chose. He felt as if he were watching a play. 'I don't think that Holler's father was doing police work, at least not while he was in Russia. He may well have belonged to one of the police battalions that murdered Jews and Bolsheviks there.'

Taut and Ossi stared at him in astonishment.

The Chief snorted. 'This gets better by the minute. So the father of the victim is a mass murderer.'

'It's possible,' said Stachelmann.

'And that's what I'm supposed to tell the press?'

'No,' said Stachelmann, 'but I would follow it up if I were you.'

'Even supposing you were right, what has that to do with the murders of Holler's wife and children? And even if Holler senior *was* in one of those police units, why should that cause someone to kill his daughter-in-law and grandchildren? And who would it be? Obviously not the Russian victims, and as for their descendants, how are they to know who killed their relatives? To them they were foreign soldiers—they were simply Germans. These are just wild speculations, Dr Stachelmann.'

Stachelmann stood up, saying, 'I just wanted to give you my opinion, but if you have no use for it, I'll go and carry on speculating wildly at the university. Good day to you!'

The Chief made no reply. Taut and Ossi also remained silent.

As Stachelmann was about to leave, standing with his hand on the door handle, the Chief said: 'I hope you'll keep what we've discussed to yourself?'

What you mean is, you're shitting bricks because we're so close to the elections, thought Stachelmann. It gave him satisfaction to think in such crude terms. He made no reply and closed the door behind him.

There was a note on his desk in the Philosophers' Tower. It said, 'Please contact me. Anne'. Stachelmann went to her office, which was smaller than his, but more homey—an effect created simply with the addition of a plant and two pictures on the walls showing views of the city of Hamburg. Like the ones in the Chief's room, in a way, only not oil paintings.

'Sorry, I'm just curious. How did you get on with Holler?'

Stachelmann gave her a brief account of the interview with Holler, and a fuller one of the meeting with the Chief of Police.

Anne laughed. 'So you really got into hot water! If you carry on like this you'll find yourself joining the old lags in Fuhlsbüttel prison. And don't expect me to smuggle a file in to you in a cake!'

'No, but perhaps you'd like to come to the beach?'

She looked at him and asked, 'You mean go for a swim?'

'If you like. I was thinking of the beach out towards Scharbeutz and Haffkrug.'

* * *

Ossi swore. He was trying to ring Stachelmann but getting no answer. Eventually he got hold of Renate Breuer. She didn't know where Stachelmann was. She didn't know his mobile number. Ossi banged the receiver down. 'I'll try again later.'

He picked up the fax that was lying on his desk. It was the list of property dealers who had sold their firms to Holler. 'Shall I contact them all?' Ossi asked. 'Kamm's found the addresses.'

'Yes, why not,' said Taut. 'It's so long since we've been in trouble with the Chief.'

Ossi gave him an inquiring look.

'What do you think will happen when you talk to these associates of Holler's and then one of them complains to Holler and he complains to the Chief?'

'I didn't hear anyone telling us not to talk to them.'

'Well, the Chief's not a fool. If one of them does turn out to be the murderer, the Chief will be the first to have suspected it.' Taut sounded bitter.

'It's not as bad as all that.'

'By the way, the new woman's turning up later.'

'How long have you known that?'

'I forgot about it.'

This was not the first time Taut had kept things from his colleagues. Ossi let it go—that was just the way Taut was. He brooded on things and sometimes forgot about other people. He had more good points than bad.

'She's just finished her training to be a Kommissar,' said Taut. 'Her grades were first-rate.'

She can't replace Ulrike, Ossi thought. He closed the door behind him. Now Taut would sit at his desk for a long time, leafing through papers or staring at the wall. As if walls could solve problems.

Chapter nine

I need to get my bathing things,' said Anne. 'I hope Bohming won't find out. I feel as if I were back at school, playing truant!'

'The Legend isn't here,' said Stachelmann. 'Or at least his car isn't in the car park. He's probably the biggest truant of all.'

'I'll be back in half an hour, and then we'll be off.'

Stachelmann took a seminar paper from the pile. It was one of the many which wouldn't be presented in an actual seminar. Too many students, or too little time, depending on how you looked at it. This paper was about the Röhm putsch, and simply reproduced what had already been written dozens of times before. Stachelmann called himself to order. He couldn't expect his students to write history afresh. He himself had still not managed to write the first sentence of his *Habilitation* thesis.

The Röhm putsch, then, in which Hitler eliminated the leaders of the SA, his brownshirted stormtroopers, because, after having brutally cleared his opponents off the streets for him, it was now in his way. The Wehrmacht wanted to be the only armed force in the Reich, and Hitler was granting the generals' wish by removing the competition. Now nothing stood in the way of war. After Germany's defeat, some of these same generals would claim that Hitler had forced them to go to war, but even during the Weimar period they had been plotting revenge for the diktat of Versailles. The seminar paper did not mention this point. Stachelmann considered whether to draw attention to the omission. But it would have been expecting too much of the student, and he decided to give the paper a 2.

He looked out of the window. A bank of cloud was blocking out the sun. It would rain before long.

There was a knock, and at the same instant Anne opened the door. 'I can't see us going swimming,' she said. 'Not in the sea, anyway.'

'Well, let's at least go for a walk,' said Stachelmann.

The telephone rang. Stachelmann hesitated but then lifted the receiver. It was Ossi.

'The Chief's annoyed with you, really furious.'

'So?'

'So you're off the case.'

'I wasn't the right person for the job anyway.'

Anne, listening in, looked at him sternly.

'No, that's not true,' Ossi replied. 'But the only worthwhile lead is the one pointing to the dealers that Holler forced out of the market.'

'But then you'll be in trouble again,' said Stachelmann. 'The Chief will go mad.'

'Maybe, but if it puts us on to the murderer, or murderers, he'll love us.'

'That's how it is with love. Either you find it or you don't. You've probably chosen the best road to happiness,' said Stachelmann.

Anne grinned.

'How's your pretty colleague?'

'Quite well, I think.'

'We could go out for a drink again soon.'

'You'll have to buy drinks all round, anyway, when you catch your man.'

'I'd better get a move on, then,' laughed Ossi.

It took them an hour to reach Scharbeutz. There was relatively little traffic on the roads, even though the Baltic seaside resorts had already received their first influx of summer visitors. Many of them were from towns in North Rhine-Westphalia, as their car registrations showed. It was drizzling, and a cold breeze was blowing along the beach. The tall, hooded wicker chairs were unoccupied. An old woman wearing a rain hood was walking her dog, defying the notices banning dogs from the beach. Seagulls and crows were picking out anything edible from the sand. On the horizon a ferry was passing, perhaps on its way from Travemünde to Sweden.

Anne had linked arms with him.

An idea took hold of him. He did not know why, or why it came to him just then.

'What do you know about the police during the Nazi period?' he asked.

'Not a lot. It's not my field. They acted as a sort of auxiliary force to the Gestapo. Well, not quite, perhaps, but something of the kind.'

'They rounded up the Jews. In the East, reserve police battalions carried out the same extermination work as the task groups.'

'I've read that book too,' said Anne. 'Sound scholarship and well written. Unlike Goldhagen.'

'A lot of Goldhagen's book is second-hand,' said Stachelmann. 'It gives the German chattering classes a bit of excitement and plays on the guilt complex which is strongest in those who aren't guilty.' He threw a stone into the waves. It bounced twice before sinking. 'My father was in the police. I had no idea. He mentioned it, just in passing, a couple of days ago. While I was talking to him about Holler.'

'That case is really preying on your mind,' said Anne.

'Not as much as the question of what my father got up to. He was conscripted into the police, he says.'

'Well, ask him about it!'

'I hardly dare to, but I will. Soon. God, he's an old man.' He looked out to sea. The ferry had shrunk to a dot. 'Or perhaps I won't. Supposing that there *was* anything, it can't be remedied now. And, damn it, who knows what I would have done in his shoes.'

'Even so, one has to ask.'

'Does one, really? He's almost ninety.'

'I'm sure I would have looked very pretty in my League of German Girls uniform,' said Anne.

'Pretty, yes. But the wrong colour hair.'

'You can't have everything.'

They walked on in silence as far as the jetty at Haffkrug, and then walked back along the promenade to the car; surprisingly, Stachelmann had been able to park on the road, close to the Scharbeutz roadsign.

'I know a nice pub in Lübeck with students and musicians and so on. But no Hamburg students.'

'Speaking of them, how's your girlfriend doing?'

'Who?'

'Alicia.'

Stachelmann tapped his forehead. 'I hope somebody else is lumbered with her by now. Don't change the subject, I'm asking you out for a meal. The pub's called Ali Baba, they have Turkish stuff.'

'Fine. If you're paying, I'll even eat a doner kebab.'

He laughed. 'I think they do other things as well.'

Stachelmann felt the electricity between them as they sat side by side in the car. Neither spoke. But he could guess what she was thinking. And he knew she could guess what he was thinking. Then he began to feel afraid; afraid of his lack of courage, afraid of revealing his quirks—he knew he must have them, but could not see them because they were as much a part of him as his nose or eyes. Other people's reactions sometimes made him conscious of them. And today his back was tormenting him more than usual.

She glanced at her watch. 'Looks as if we're going to be out late tonight.'

* * *

'We've got him!' shouted Wolfgang Kurz, flinging open the door to Taut's room.

'Who?' asked Taut.

'The driver!'

'Who is it?'

'Oliver Stroh. Lives in Steilshoop. A lot of previous: GBH, drunk driving and so on.'

Two uniformed officers dragged a man into Taut's room. He was cursing, almost unintelligibly. Taut waved him away, wrinkling his nose. 'Take him to an interview room.'

The officers dragged the man back out on to the corridor.

'And how did you find him?'

'He was sitting in a bar, knocking back the drinks. Apparently he was quiet enough at first, but then he started to get noisy. The landlord heard him boasting that there was no car he couldn't break into. And then he started coming out with all sorts of rubbish. Said he'd shoot anybody who got in his way; nobody should expect any mercy from him. Then one of the people in the bar told him to stop his ranting, they wanted some peace and quiet for their game of cards. That really set him off. They could all shut their traps, he wasn't afraid of anybody, he'd just run over a policewoman. The landlord pricked up his ears at that. He'd read about Ulrike's murder. He phoned us and we went and picked the guy up.'

Taut changed his mind about the interrogation. 'He's drunk, let him sleep it off. We'll give him a good grilling tomorrow.'

Ossi, in Taut's office on other business, had not said anything. So it seemed Ulrike had not been murdered, but had been mown down by a drunken car thief. They would soon find out. He had come to Taut's office to tell him about his visit to Otto Grothe, the first dealer on Holler's list.

* * *

Otto Grothe occupied the first floor of an old house, not a large villa, but big enough to suggest that it was not cheap to live in. Grothe gave Ossi a friendly welcome. He was an old gentleman with a refined air, who walked with the aid of a stick topped by a silver knob in the shape of a dog's head. He showed Ossi into his living room and offered him a seat. Ossi sank into a deep sofa. Old furniture, perhaps Biedermeier or Art Nouveau, Ossi thought. But he knew nothing about such things; to him everything in the room was simply antiquated and kitschy. There was a musty smell. The sunlight showed up a layer of dust on the table, and the windows had not been cleaned in months. On the walls were shelves full of old books. A big old-fashioned radio stood on a cupboard. The man was living in a different age.

'May I offer you some coffee?' asked Grothe. 'Though I can't promise that it will be up to my wife's standard.' Without waiting for an answer, he went out of the room. Ossi followed him into the kitchen. Grothe put a kettle on the gas stove and switched on an electric coffee grinder. It made a noise like a circular saw. When the coffee had been ground, Ossi asked, 'Where is your wife?'

Grothe pointed heavenwards. He looked sad.

'I'm sorry to disturb you.'

'You're not disturbing me. You know, an old man on his own is glad of any distraction.'

'You used to be a property dealer?'

Grothe's eyes lit up. 'Yes, until nineteen seventy-eight. Since then I've lived on the proceeds of the sale of my business, Grothe & Co.'

'And who was Co.?'

The kettle whistled and Grothe poured the water into a china filter. 'By the time I sold the business, he was there in name only. I founded the company in nineteen fifty-two with a colleague, Gerhard Klump. Unfortunately he died in nineteen sixty-three. He was unmarried and had lost all his family in the war. He left his share of the business to me.'

'So he was a friend, too,' said Ossi.

'More than that,' said Grothe. 'He was everything to me.' The old man looked taken aback when he saw Ossi's expression, but he quickly recovered his composure. 'He was immensely capable and the epitome of honesty.'

'And you sold the business in nineteen seventy-eight.'

'Yes, I received an offer from Herr Holler junior—the father was dead by then, of course. At the time the property market seemed to be heading for a crisis. The post-war reconstruction phase was over.

Although as it turned out, it was only a slight downturn. Anyway, I was glad to get such a good offer from Herr Holler.'

The coffee was ready, and they both returned to the living room. Ossi sat down on the sofa. 'That was a good move by Herr Holler.'

'Yes, otherwise I might not have sold the firm. But he offered me a good price.'

'You've never regretted selling up?'

'Oh yes, I have. I would have saved myself years of boredom. I only realized afterwards that you can actually miss dealing with problems and worrying about your livelihood!'

Ossi chuckled. 'Thanks for telling me that.'

Grothe laughed, too. 'There you are, your visit has done more than just relieve an old man's boredom for half an hour.'

'How well do you know Herr Holler?'

Grothe thought for a moment. 'I don't really know him at all.'

'But you sold your business to him.'

'That's true. I spoke to him several times. He was pleasant, very accommodating. Altogether he has a tremendous presence, there's something exciting about him. But perhaps that's only how he appears to *me*.'

'And yet you say you don't know him.'

'Well, perhaps the best way to describe it is that he seemed to me like someone wearing a mask.'

'A mask?'

'You could have told him Hamburg was going up in flames, and he would have gone on smiling and holding the door open for the ladies. How could anyone say they knew him? I saw him, talked to him, negotiated with him and sold my company to him. But I don't know him.'

'And that makes you sad.'

Grothe stood up, went over to a shelf and took a leather-bound volume from it. He sat down next to Ossi with the book and opened it at one of the later pages. There were seven photographs. 'This is my wife,' he said. 'She died just over two years ago. Cancer. It's only to be expected at our age.' His eyes were moist. The photos dated from different periods. In one she was standing, holding a handbag, in front of the house. It probably dated from at least twenty years earlier, and the roughcast plaster on the house was white. Now it had turned brown and was flaking off in places. In another picture she was leaning against the bonnet of a Borgward coupé, white and elegant. She was beautiful. Two other pictures showed her in a park. In the most recent photo she was with her husband. They were sitting at a table, obviously in a restaurant. 'That was taken on her last birthday,' said Grothe. 'I have to be grateful to Herr Holler for letting me sell my company to him. It allowed me and my wife to spend many happy years together with no financial worries. Earlier in my life there were times when I was convinced I was about to die.'

'In the war?'

Grothe nodded. He refilled Ossi's cup. Ossi did not refuse the coffee, although his stomach was becoming unsettled. Grothe made a strong cup of coffee. 'I learned the art of enjoying every day to the full. But now that Martha's gone....' He turned his face away. 'I got to know Holler's father during the war. I've been wondering ever since how such a devil could beget a decent human being.'

'A devil? I don't understand,' said Ossi.

'Old Holler was in the Gestapo in Hamburg. I never had any dealings with him personally, but I know people who know other people whom he treated very badly. He was a murderer and a thug.' Grothe had become agitated.

Ossi could not understand why Grothe was getting so worked up. 'A lot of people were murderers and thugs in those days.'

For a long moment Grothe looked him in the eyes. His face had reddened. He nodded. 'We were all guilty,' he said. 'All of us. There was almost no one who didn't play a part in it. On the front, in the police, in the party, in the civil service. Including me.'

He rose, went over to a small table and picked up a silver cigarette box which Ossi had not noticed before. Grothe passed it to him. 'Look at the inscription inside.' Ossi opened it. The initials 'B.R.' were engraved on the inside of the lid. 'B.R. stands for Bernhard Rosenzweig. He was my neighbour. One day, it was shortly before the invasion of

Poland, there was a sort of bazaar outside his house. They were selling household objects, jewellery, crockery, cutlery, clocks, a radio similar to this one here.' He pointed to his radio. 'And that's where I bought this box, for six Reichsmark, a giveaway price, solid silver.'

'And what happened to Rosenzweig?'

'I don't know, suddenly he was gone. I never saw him again. Perhaps he escaped, perhaps they gassed him. But I bought his cigarette box for six marks. It was worth a hundred times that.'

'If you hadn't bought it somebody else would have,' said Ossi.

'Yes, and that person would have been happier with it than I've been. It always reminds me of Bernhard Rosenzweig. He was an ordinary shopkeeper, he had a clothes shop in Fuhlentwiete. He had a lot of regular customers, including my wife and me. The business was doing well, he was riding out all the anti-Jewish propaganda. Until November nineteen thirty-eight, until Kristallnacht. They burned his shop down. And what he did manage to salvage from the fire he had to surrender to the state. His property was made over to the state. And the state sold it off at knock-down prices.'

Ossi's hands were sweating. He turned the box round to face Grothe and set it down on the table.

'Listen, why don't you take the box? Martha always said I should throw it away. And once I almost did. But then I asked myself what Rosenzweig would say if I threw his box into the rubbish. And as for selling it to a stranger…'

'I couldn't possibly accept it,' said Ossi. 'In any case, it's against regulations.'

'Why should I want to bribe you?'

'Of course you wouldn't, but rules are rules.' Ossi took his list out of his pocket and laid it on the table in front of Grothe. 'Do you know any of these people?'

Grothe put on a pair of spectacles; his hands shook a little. 'I know them all. They were all in the same business as me. Some of them also sold their firms to Holler.'

'They all did,' said Ossi. 'According to Herr Holler, anyway. This is a list that he gave me.'

Grothe read through the list again, screwing up his eyes behind his glasses. 'I should have gone to the optician long ago,' he said. 'But it's not worth it now. It's the same with my memory. You know other people in the same business, and even when you've retired from it you still pick up some of what's going on. Of course news got around of who had sold their firms to Holler. I still remember that. The one that surprised me the most was Enheim. His business was booming, he was doing far better than I could ever have hoped to do. He had specialized in administrative buildings and he practically monopolized that market. And then suddenly Holler bought him up. He must have paid a fortune.'

Grothe looked at the list again. He shook his head. 'The name's not there. My memory isn't as bad as all that.'

'What name?'

'Enheim.'

* * *

They were sitting in a sheltered corner of the restaurant garden. It was a warm evening, and the food had been good.

Anne looked at her watch. 'The witching hour.' She thought for a moment, then said, 'Damn, the last train's gone.'

Stachelmann was surprised at how little dismay she showed. He would not have been so calm. 'I'll drive you back to Hamburg,' he said.

'You're crazy. An hour there and an hour back—that's two hours! And you've got a seminar tomorrow.'

'Not till the afternoon. It's all right.'

'No,' said Anne. 'We'll have one more Turkish Chianti, and then you can clear your sofa for me. You do have a sofa?'

'Only a two-seater.'

'Well, I'm not all that tall.' She smiled into his eyes. 'You haven't had a lady visitor for quite some time,' she said. It wasn't a question. Her speech was a little slurred, after only two glasses of wine. But Stachelmann had no doubt that what she said, she meant.

'The place is a mess.'

'My place always is, except of course when I'm expecting

a distinguished visitor, such as the aspiring professor Josef Maria Stachelmann.'

'Stop it.'

'You don't know how good you are,' she said. 'Everyone in the department really respects you. They rave about your doctoral thesis, and can't wait for your *Habil.* The Legend was saying only last week'— she mimicked his speech and gestures—'"He's having problems with the starter. But when the engine fires, Stachelmann will wipe the floor with everyone, or I'm a Dutchman. And one of these days he'll be putting me out to grass. This, my dear colleagues, is the history-writing of tomorrow: politics, economics, the military, technology, culture. It won't be just maps and chaps and moving your divisions around, it won't be just the intrigues of the Papens and the Meissners, the making and breaking of treaties, the big dramatic events. When Stachelmann analyses a thing, he looks at it from every angle—Marx, Daimler, Weber, Keynes and Rilke, and who knows, perhaps Gottfried Benn, too. And modern sociology and psychology. And he gives things their due weight, at least most of the time—"'

'That'll do,' he said. 'It's nice of you to try to build me up.'

'Me, build *you* up? You've got it the wrong way round. The only one who needs building up here is me. Why do you think Bohming sent me to you? So that you can teach me how to do history. I haven't told him about my fear of documents, but I'm afraid he suspects I have a problem.'

Stachelmann felt like someone waiting at the wrong bus stop. One bus goes by after another, always the wrong one, and time passes until the last one goes. He couldn't understand what Anne was getting at. She was obviously tipsy. What would happen if she had another glass?

The waiter arrived with the wine. He had also brought a glass for Stachelmann, though he had not asked for one. 'They're both on the house,' the waiter said.

On the way to his apartment she took his arm. Whenever she spoke, she leaned her head against his shoulder. They walked for a quarter of an hour, passing only a few other people and two or three taxis.

By the Trave river, two prostitutes were looking out for punters. He took his key from his inside pocket and opened the door to the apartment. 'I even have a spare toothbrush for you,' he said.

She went into the bathroom, while he sat down in the living room. He put on some music, Mozart's piano concerto no 23.

She came out of the bathroom and sat down beside him. Their knees touched. 'Mozart is lovely,' she said.

He sat there, enjoying it. After they had listened for a while without talking, he stood up. 'I'll make up the bed for you. You sleep in the bedroom, I'll sleep here.'

She shook her head and gazed at him.

'Yes,' he said. He went into the bedroom and put a cover on the duvet, and then took a sheet from the cupboard and laid it over the mattress. The door opened, and Anne came up to him and put her arms round him. He was holding the pillow. 'I haven't finished,' he said.

She slipped out of her shoes and lay down on the mattress. 'This is fine.' She closed her eyes, giggling softly. 'It's about time,' she whispered. 'It's about time, Josef Maria.'

He looked at her and switched the light off. A beam of light from the hallway shone on to her head. She's much too beautiful for you, Stachelmann thought, and much too intelligent to waste her time on a man who's a failure. Then he saw that she had fallen asleep. He covered her with the duvet and quietly left the room. At the door he turned round to look at her.

* * *

The old man sat on the bank of the Alster feeding the ducks. He had read that this was bad both for the ducks and for the water, but he did not care. He was thinking back to the time just after he had returned from England. When he turned eighteen he had decided to go to Germany. He did not know why. He could remember nothing. His parents' faces were like blurred outlines in a mist; he had forgotten what they were like, and this forgetting hurt him more than their actual loss. At first his foster parents refused to let him go—he had completed his apprenticeship and was going to be earning money—

and he argued with them for six months. He gave his master notice and did not look for another job. He *had* to go back, even though his foster parents told him that Germany was in ruins. The newspapers said the same thing. Once Jack met a soldier who had been in Hamburg and who told him about the bombing raids. Hamburg was nothing but rubble and dust, he said, and he could not imagine that it would ever be rebuilt.

He left the lake, went to Klosterstern underground station, and took a train to Kellinghusenstrasse. There he changed to the U3 for Barmbek. Sometimes he felt he knew every single underground train carriage in Hamburg. He travelled this route once or twice a week. At Barmbek he got off the train, came out of the station on to Drosselstrasse and turned into Bramfelder Strasse. He had to wait a long time for the light at the pedestrian crossing to turn green. Across four lanes of traffic, heavy trucks jostled with private cars on their way into and out of the city. After crossing the road he went along Wachtelstrasse as far as the junction with Adlerstrasse, then turned left into Adlerstrasse until he was outside number 17. He had lived here as a child. When he first came back to Hamburg, he would never have found the house had the address not been in an old city directory. He had gone to every address where families called Kohn had once lived. There were no Kohns at any of them now. But when he found himself in front of his childhood home he recognized it at once. Some of the buildings in the street were new, but the one where he had lived on the second floor with his parents and sister had escaped both the bombs and the post-war building craze. He retained only a few scraps of memory from that time. A round table in the living room. A bookcase. A red toy car. A thick carpet, red and black, on the floor.

I'm mad, thought Leopold Kohn. I keep coming back to a house that I lived in for such a short time, decades ago. I'm drawn to the place, but everything that draws me here has been gone for more than half a century.

Soon after his return to Germany the Red Cross had informed him that his parents and sister had been deported. 'Probably to Treblinka,' the man had said. Treblinka was death. He hadn't understood everything the man said—he had forgotten almost all his German. But he did not need a translation to know what Treblinka meant. Jewish community representatives had explained it to him soon after his arrival. Until then, Kohn had not known much about the death camps or what it meant to be sent 'east'. The people at the Jewish community centre had also told him who his father had been: a property dealer, honest and not especially successful, dealing mostly with Jewish clients. They advised him to fight for compensation, and helped him write to the appropriate authorities. It was not their fault that he had no chance of succeeding. It took Leopold Kohn a long time to grasp the full picture. But once he had understood what he needed to understand, he began to consider what had happened, and how he could set it right.

Chapter ten

Vacation began next week. He would pick Anne up and they'd hit the road together. First stop would be the Federal Archive in Berlin, and then Weimar and Buchenwald. He had booked two rooms in Haus Morgenland, a small hotel close to the Archive in Berlin-Lichterfelde. He was excited. He could still see Anne lying on his bed, her features harmonious, serene.

He had made breakfast. It had not been hard to get up; he had barely slept anyway. The sofa was too short for him. The pain in his back was excruciating. Anne gave him a bright smile as she emerged from his bedroom. 'I don't know when I've slept so well,' she said. Then she went into the bathroom. Stachelmann could hear the splashing of the shower as he poured the tea into a thermos jug. When the splashing stopped, he called, 'Tea or coffee?'

'I don't mind. Well, perhaps coffee.'

He put some water on and looked for the coffee jug and filter.

She came out of the bathroom fully dressed, but with wet hair. 'I couldn't find a hair dryer.'

'I don't have such luxuries. I'm only a poor lecturer, after all.'

'If you had more lady visitors you'd have got one by now.' She said 'lady visitors' in a derogatory tone.

'My female visitors all have short hair and aren't as vain as you,' he said, startling himself.

She grinned, but looked a little crestfallen. 'What a pity I'm not more to your taste.'

'Well, it's not as bad as all that. One has to make these compromises in life.'

They sat on opposite sides of the small kitchen table, on which lay the newspaper, the *Lübecker Nachrichten*. Stachelmann could never eat breakfast without reading his paper, but now he didn't dare open it and put it beside his plate.

'May I?' Anne took the paper and leafed through it. 'Fancy, a rag like this in Lübeck, international city of culture,' she commented.

After breakfast they drove to Hamburg together. At the university they went their separate ways. Anne wanted to go home. 'To start packing a few things for our big trip,' she said, smiling.

In his office, Stachelmann sat down at the desk and looked at his mail, but with little interest. A thought had occurred to him; he had tried to put it out of his mind, but now it had returned with greater urgency than before. He must speak to his father, and soon. The prospect filled him with anxiety.

* * *

The man sitting slouched on the chair facing Ossi's desk had the bloated face of a boozer. He was scratching his head. He had black, greasy hair which left his ears visible but hung down in separate strands over his collar. With his little finger he picked something out of his teeth, rolled it between his index finger and thumb and flicked it onto the floor. He wore jeans and a black studded leather jacket, and a heavy gold chain around his neck. He reeked of beer and schnapps. Ossi found him repellent. A uniformed policeman sat in a corner, watching.

'Your name is Oliver Stroh and you steal cars,' said Ossi.

The man raised his head. In broad Hamburg dialect he replied,

'My name's Oliver Stroh and sometimes I have a drop too much to drink.'

'On the tenth of July, between seven and ten P.M., in the private car park in Steinstrasse, you broke into a black Type 260E Mercedes and drove it away,' said Ossi.

'On the tenth of July, from the late afternoon onwards, I was on a tour.'

'What sort of tour?'

Stroh laughed. 'Around the pubs. I was on a pub crawl in St Pauli. I started in La Paloma, and if my memory serves me I finished up in the Kaiserkeller. If my memory serves me.'

'Do you do that every day?'

'D'you think I'm a millionaire?'

'What do you live on?'

'Unemployment benefit, and financial subsidies.' He pronounced the last phrase carefully, in standard German, as though it was one he had picked up somewhere.

'What sort of financial subsidies?'

'What nice people give me.'

'You mean you beg.'

'Call it that if you like, pal.'

'I'm not your pal.'

'Suit yourself.'

'So how come you were boasting of having killed a police-woman?'

'It was in the paper.'

'Oh, you're a newspaper reader! What paper would that be, I wonder?'

'Depends what people have left lying around. It might be the *Bild*, the *Morgenpost*, the *Frankfurter Allgemeine*.'

'Well, which one?'

'Which one what?'

'Which paper was it where you read about the murder of the policewoman?'

'Can't remember.'

'And why did you boast about it?'

'Lay off me, pal, it's none of your business.'

'Stop calling me "pal"!'

'Okay, okay.'

'But it wasn't in the papers.'

'What wasn't?'

'The fact that a policewoman had been run over by a stolen car.'

The man fixed his bloodshot eyes on him, and shook his head. For a moment Ossi thought he wasn't going to fall for the lie. Then the penny dropped. Ossi beckoned the uniformed man over and whispered in his ear, and the officer nodded and left the room, returning after a short while with a copy of the *Morgenpost*. Ossi took the paper and laid it on the desk in front of Stroh.

'Here's the *Morgenpost* for you. Perhaps you'd be good enough to read me the headline.'

Stroh stared at the paper. He shook his head. 'What's this in aid of? Can't you read it yourself? Is there a law saying that every policeman can get somebody to read to him?'

'Just read it,' said Ossi.

'No,' said Stroh.

'You can't read! That's it, isn't it, *pal*?'

'Don't call me "pal"!'

Ossi rephrased his question. 'Am I right in thinking you can't read?'

'None of your business.'

Ossi stood up and left the room. He got a coffee from the machine in the corridor, then went over to a window and looked out, sipping. He was convinced Stroh was lying, but was he Ulrike's murderer? He must take his time with the questioning. Stroh might be stupid, but he was cunning. Ossi finished his coffee and went back into his office. He wished he had used an interview room: it would take quite some time to get rid of the smell.

'I want a smoke,' said Stroh, as Ossi came back in.

'Later, perhaps,' said Ossi. 'When we've finished.'

'We *have* finished.'

'That's for me to decide.' He leaned back in his chair. 'You lied to me. You said you read in the paper about the, let's say, accident, but you can't read. Why don't you just admit that you ran over the policewoman? That'll save you and us a lot of hassle.'

'I want a lawyer.'

Ossi stood up and brought him the Hamburg telephone book. He sat down again and looked at Stroh, who was sitting motionless, his eyes fixed on the cover of the phone book. He sniffed and wiped his nose with the back of his hand. He coughed. 'All right. I saw it.'

'What did you see?'

'I saw the Merc run over the woman.'

'You told me one lie, and now you're telling me another.'

'No, it's true, I did see it.'

'You were driving the car that ran over the woman.'

Stroh shook his head.

'Where were you when it happened?'

'In Sydneystrasse, somewhere round there. I'd just had a beer with a friend, and this car came racing round the corner with the tires squealing. And then there was a hell of a bang. It skidded and then just zoomed off.'

'You're lying. We've found traces in the car that definitely point to you. We haven't had the hairs analyzed yet, but there's a fingerprint of yours on the steering wheel.'

Stroh stared at Ossi in disbelief. 'I want a lawyer.'

Ossi pointed to the phone book. 'It's your right to have a lawyer, but not to have me read the phone book to you. You give me a confession and then I'll pick out a good lawyer for you.'

'You're lying,' said Stroh. 'You're trying to pin this on me! I had nothing to do with it!' He was almost screaming.

'Then why are you lying?' Ossi shouted back at him. 'If it wasn't you, tell us the truth!'

'I am!' Stroh sounded desperate.

Ossi gestured to the uniformed officer in the corner. 'Take him away.'

The policeman handcuffed Stroh and led him out of the room. Stroh turned in the doorway and yelled, 'There can't be any fingerprints of mine in the car!'

Ossi turned away. After the door had closed he sat silently at his desk for a long time. Stroh was a down-and-out and had committed a few offences in his time, but he had nothing to do with Ulrike Kreimeier's death. If he had, he would have reacted differently to Ossi's attempt to catch him out with the tale of the nonexistent fingerprints. And if somebody like Stroh had driven the Mercedes, fingerprints wouldn't be the only traces he'd have left behind. Still, at least they now had a witness. Stroh had seen what happened. But it was doubtful whether his evidence was worth much.

* * *

Stachelmann had rung his parents. His mother answered, and was surprised when he said that he must talk to his father about his time in the police. But when she spoke again she seemed to accept that this conversation was inevitable. 'This evening would be fine,' she said, but there was sadness in her voice. 'You can come any day, old people are generally just sitting around at home.' This was true of Stachelmann's parents, but not of all retired people. Many of them were seized by wanderlust in their old age.

On his way to Reinbek, Stachelmann thought about the older generation, partly to take his mind off the impending conversation. What have today's pensioners done to deserve their affluence, he wondered. Pensioners would never again be as rich as they were now. When he saw old people in cafés or on park benches, such frail, sometimes pathetic figures, he tried to imagine what they might have done when they were younger. What did they do during the war? What have they done to atone for the crimes of their generation? He was sure that most old people had never asked themselves these questions.

They were sitting in the living room, facing one another. He thought his father looked like a very old man. He was bent forward, his hands resting on the table. Stachelmann wondered if it had been wise to forewarn him of the purpose of his visit, but the shock would have been all the greater if he had suddenly come out with his questions without any prior warning. They sat in silence for a while, and then his father said, 'You're right, we need to talk about it. Even after such a long time. Most of us are fortunate enough to die without being asked, but it seems I'm not. That's the price of living to an advanced age.' He shook his head. 'You know, a lot of people keep quiet not only because they're ashamed but because they're afraid they won't be understood.'

'How do you mean?' Stachelmann was glad to be able to say something.

'Because today things are judged differently. Because now no one can imagine what it was like then. There are history books and memoirs of those times, but the printed word can't convey the fear we felt, fear of our own people, of the enemy and of the victims. Fear of the end, of defeat. We didn't experience it as a liberation but as what it was, at least for a time—the end of all hope. Ruin. We didn't find ourselves starving until after the defeat. Earlier on we were afraid but at least we had food to eat. After May nineteen forty-five we were afraid and had nothing to eat. Looking back now, we know that after the ruin there was a quick recovery, at least in the west, but if anyone had predicted that at the time, we wouldn't have believed them. Nineteen forty-four and nineteen forty-five were the worst years of my life. The prospect of certain defeat, and fearing for your life every day. And at the same time knowing that you were taking part in something that would later be seen as criminal.'

'You were a post office official and then became a policeman? I didn't know that that could happen.'

'I was in the SA, and back in nineteen thirty-three I was an auxiliary policeman, at the time of the Reichstag fire. Later they remembered me and conscripted me into the regular police.'

'So you were a Nazi,' said Stachelmann.

'Yes.'

'A party member?'

His father nodded.

'And then they moved you, as an SA man, from the post office to the police. What rank did you hold in the SA?'

'Senior squad leader—Oberscharführer.'

'And what did you do as a policeman?'

'Nothing very important. Guarding bomb-clearing squads and things like that.' He spoke almost tonelessly.

'They were concentration camp inmates.'

'Some of them were from the concentration camp at Neuengamme, but others came from prisons, mainly from Fuhls-büttel.'

'And you stood there with your gun and made sure that none of them tried to escape.'

'I carried a pistol, I was in command of the guard detachment.'

'Did any of them try to escape?'

'Yes, but we recaptured them. They usually tried to hide in ruined buildings or in cellars. The thing is, we didn't go with them right up to the bombs that they had to deactivate.'

'Because you were afraid of being blown sky-high.'

'Yes. There were bombs with timing devices, and some that had failed to explode for some reason but could easily go off. It was a dangerous business.'

'But not too dangerous for concentration camp inmates or convicts.'

'Somebody had to do it.'

His father's face wore a bleak expression. He seemed almost immobile, though his left hand was trembling slightly. He looked as if his thoughts were elsewhere. His words had the ring of necessity: whatever he had done, he had had to do. He reminded Stachelmann of the sort of official who parrots the regulations with a shrug, knowing full well that they make no sense but still have to be obeyed.

'So you recaptured concentration camp inmates and convicts.'

'Yes, those were my orders. The bombs had to be defused, otherwise there would have been even more deaths.'

Stachelmann leaned back in his chair. He fixed his eyes on the angle where the wall met the ceiling. He said nothing. Had his father's involvement been unavoidable? Had the involvement of so many people, the precondition for all the murder, been unavoidable? His father was not a murderer: he was quite a gentle sort of man. But in that case what had he been doing in the sa?

'How long had you been in the SA?'

'Since thirty-two.'

'And did you take part in Kristallnacht?'

'I was ordered to. I had to guard German shops.'

'Weren't the Jews Germans?'

His father looked at him angrily; it was the first time during the conversation that his face had shown any emotion. He raised his voice slightly, in what sounded like indignation: 'That's just what *I* said.' His voice reverted to a monotone. 'They didn't count as Germans at that time. Their citizenship was withdrawn…'

'But only later, not in nineteen thirty-eight,' objected Stachelmann. He could feel the pain creeping into his back. He shifted his body so that he was right up against the chair-back. He knew that the pain would get worse. His mother came in, her eyes wet with tears.

'Would you both like some tea?' she asked. Receiving no answer, she looked from one to the other of them and went away again. She was probably standing outside the door, listening. *Why doesn't she come in*, Stachelmann wondered. *Has all this nothing to do with her?* He extracted a tablet—his emergency supply—from the small pocket in his jeans, and swallowed it. He didn't need any water. His father watched him raising the tablet to his mouth.

'But they were treated like foreigners.'

'Like enemies,' Stachelmann said. 'And then their property was confiscated as enemy property.'

'I had nothing to do with that.'

'It's bad enough that you caught concentration camp inmates. How many?'

'From my gang, perhaps a dozen tried to escape. We picked up eight of them.'

'And what happened to them?'

'We had to hand them over to the police.'

'The Gestapo.'

'No, we gave them to the ordinary police, and they probably turned them over to the Gestapo.'

'And why didn't you let them go?'

'I'd have been in hot water. Anyway, the bombs had to be cleared. It was important.'

'You'd have been in hot water if you'd said you hadn't managed to catch the escapees? I can't believe that.'

'If you keep on failing to catch any, they'll stop believing you. You don't understand. You can't understand. I don't blame you for that. Those were completely different times.'

'It never occurred to you to think that what you were doing was wrong?'

'No. I had my orders. It was wartime.'

'A war that Germany started.'

'That Hitler started.'

'Führer, command us and we will obey?'

'Otherwise you faced a charge of undermining military discipline. Then your head was on the block.'

'You're saying that if you live in a criminal state you have to obey criminal orders.'

'We had no choice about what state we lived in. The law determined what we had to do. What could the ordinary individual do about it? Until thirty-nine everything was on the up and up. Think of the unemployed. Think of Versailles: Hitler restored Germany to what it had been before, a great nation. That's how we saw it then. And we weren't the only ones. At the Olympic Games it wasn't only Germans who were filled with enthusiasm. Weimar was ruin, chaos, humiliation; Hitler put us back on our feet again. That's how *every-body* saw it then.'

'Except for those who had fled into exile or who were locked up in concentration camps.'

'No one could understand them. And what if the communists had come to power? Then even more people would have found themselves in camps and been killed. Besides, in thirty-three even communists went over to the Nazis. In my own SA unit there were two ex-communist-party members.'

'And later you were catching concentration camp inmates. What colour were their badges?'

'Red, I think. So they were politicals. Communists or socialists—I don't know which for certain. One of them looked terrible, like a skeleton, I sometimes slipped him a piece of my bread. It was against the rules, but he looked practically starved to death.'

Stachelmann's mother came in. She was carrying a tray with a pot of tea, three cups and a plate of chocolate biscuits. 'Why don't you leave it now,' she said. 'You can't change the past.'

'Doesn't it strike you as remarkable that this is the first time Father has told me what he got up to in the Nazi period?' His words sounded harsher than Stachelmann had intended.

'You never asked,' said his mother. 'If you'd asked before, he would have told you.' Putting the tray down on the table, she distributed the cups, placed the biscuits in the middle, and poured the tea. Then she sat down on the sofa. 'Has Father told you that he warned our neighbours?'

Stachelmann's father made a self-deprecating gesture.

'Warned them of what?' asked Stachelmann.

'It was shortly before Kristallnacht. Father had heard that his SA comrades were going to pay a call on a neighbour of ours—he was a Jew. Father suggested to him that it might be a good idea if he went away for a few days. He did, and he was very grateful. When he was sent east he gave us that.' She motioned to a gold picture frame which held a photo from a holiday his parents had spent in Italy many years ago.

Stachelmann was longing for the painkiller to take effect. He took a sip of tea. 'While we're on the subject, how did you come to know Holler?'

'Holler was a big shot in the Hamburg Gestapo. I think he was also involved in the deportations.'

'And after forty-five, did nothing happen to him?'

'I never heard of anything. He'd probably taken precautions. Collected enough testimonials and denazification certificates. Perhaps some denazification court or other *did* find evidence against him, but that soon ceased to matter any more. He was a leading figure in the police sports club, at any rate, and always very jolly.'

'What was he doing in the police sports club when he wasn't a policeman any more?'

'Old comrades,' said his father. 'Just like me. I went back to the post office, but I still belonged to the police sports club for many years.'

'And what about Holler junior?'

'Don't know him. But why should he have anything to do with all that, any more than you do?'

Driving home, Stachelmann kept trying to ease himself into a less painful sitting position. The tablet was having almost no effect. Soon after the Reinfeld exit he found himself in a tailback: holiday traffic and a long stretch of road works. He had noticed the congestion on his outward journey, and had planned to leave the autobahn at Reinfeld on his way back, but had forgotten. Now he pressed the radio buttons until he found some classical music, a Baroque organ concert. He switched off the engine and put his hands behind his head. He stretched, but it did no good. He could still hear the monotone of his father's voice, conveying not indifference but a voluntary surrender of the will. His father was one of the countless people of his generation who were complicit in that great murder which in Germany, too, ever since the screening of a poor-quality American television series, had come to be known as the Holocaust. Strange how we use abstract terms to refer to the victims, thought Stachelmann. It helps us to suppress the thought of the reality. The Germans build a Holocaust memorial to show the Americans that they have learned their lesson. After all, we want the Yanks to go on buying Mercedes and vws. Why don't we call it the murder of the Jews? And *was* it a burnt offering, which is what 'holocaust' means? A sacrifice? Did the Jews sacrifice themselves? For years Stachelmann had been frustrated by the use of the term, which was supposed to express solidarity with the victims but in fact represented a lack of thought and a suppression of the real facts. He never used the term himself.

His father had played a part in the great murder. He had been the proverbial small cog without which the big murder machine could not function. He had stood guard over camp inmates and recaptured those who tried to escape. He was like the train drivers, part of a production process whose end product was ashes.

What would *he* have done? Would he have had the courage to disobey orders? Would he have found a way to stay out of it?

The driver of the car behind him sounded his horn. The column of cars had crept forward a few yards and a gap had opened up between Stachelmann's Golf and the old Ford Taunus in front. He started the car and edged forward, and then switched the engine off again.

He and his father had never been close.

*   *   *

Ossi was fiddling with his key ring. Among the keys of various sizes was an Aquarius charm. The keys jingled. Ossi had the phone to his ear and was waiting. From the switchboard came a gruesome rendering of some Bach. Then Holler was on the line. He sounded annoyed. 'Yes?'

'Just a quick question. Is it possible that you left someone off your list?'

'What list? Oh, you mean the list of property dealers. I didn't put it together myself and I haven't seen it. I'll ask my secretary. Is that it?'

'Did you buy a firm belonging to a Herr Enheim? Norbert Enheim?'

Silence.

'Yes, I did. Is he not on the list?'

'No,' said Ossi. 'He isn't.'

'That's an oversight,' said Holler.

'The only one?' asked Ossi.

'I'll check it. If any other name is missing I will let you know.'

'How soon?'

'If you hear nothing from me within two hours the list is complete. Except for Enheim, of course.'

'Of course,' said Ossi. He was pleased that the infallible Holler had been caught out in a mistake. He hung up, still fiddling with the Aquarius charm. Then he looked at the desk chair opposite, and his spirits sank. That was where Ulrike had sat, for over two years. Now she was dead, and the murderer was eluding them. Ossi thought the term 'murderer' because he refused to believe it had been an accident.

He considered whether to open the bottom left-hand drawer of his desk, which contained a bottle of schnapps and some peppermints.

Instead, he reached for the telephone book and looked up the name Enheim. There were three entries.

He couldn't resist the compulsion to open the drawer, but on seeing the bottle he closed it again. He leaned back. Then he reached for the drawer handle again, pulled out the bottle, unscrewed the cap and took a swig. Replacing the cap, he put the bottle back. When he popped a peppermint into his mouth, it tasted disgusting in combination with the schnapps. As long as Ulrike had been sitting opposite him he had not been able to drink. He guessed that she knew. But she had never said anything.

He started dialing the numbers to find Enheim, and the very first person he reached confirmed that he had been a property dealer.

'You sold your firm to Maximilian Holler?'

'Yes, in nineteen seventy-six. The swine came and took the firm off me. That's the way he does things. If he could, he'd like to be the biggest dealer in the whole of North Germany.'

'How do you mean, took the firm off you? I thought you sold it to him.'

'Well, you could put it that way. But why don't you come over, this afternoon if you can. I'll tell you a nice story. Then you'll see the wonderful Maximilian in a very different light.'

Ossi checked that Enheim's address in Ohlsdorf was correct, and sat still for a while after he had hung up. The conversation with Enheim had left him confused. The man had sounded quite calm, not like a habitual grumbler. This might turn out to be their first useful lead. Ossi got up from his desk and went along to Taut's office.

'Shall we go out for a bite?' he asked his boss.

Taut growled something undecipherable in reply, and then stood up. They went to Erna's Snack Bar in Wesselyring. While Ossi ate sausage with curry sauce and Taut had meatballs, Ossi told Taut about his calls to Holler and Enheim.

'Well, go and check out Enheim,' said Taut, his cheeks bulging. 'That sounds interesting. It *is* odd that he wasn't on the list. You can take your new colleague with you.'

'My new colleague?'

'She's called Carmen Hebel. That's all I know.'

'Makes no difference anyway,' said Ossi.

'Rubbish. It does make a difference, because you've got to get on with her for the next few years. She's supposed to be good, one of the best at police training college, and nothing but praise ever since. She does martial arts. She's from Stade.'

'An ambitious type of girl, then,' Ossi commented. 'Fell off an apple tree and rolled along here.'

'It's not all apple orchards around Stade. They produce cherries, too. A good policeman shouldn't go for the most obvious assumption.'

'Alright, know-all.'

'Introductions after lunch, and then you two go off to Ohlsdorf to see Enheim.'

'Yes, *sir*,' said Ossi, touching his right hand to his forehead in salute. But he knew that Taut, too, had stopped finding this banter amusing. They were only keeping up the pretence that they could go on just as before.

The new woman had short black hair. She was small, with a confident manner and a firm handshake. The introductions were over quickly. They all said the usual things, and expressed the usual hopes for a good working partnership and successful outcomes.

Ossi took her into the office they would be sharing.

'So this is where your colleague used to sit, the one who was killed,' she said.

'The one who was murdered,' answered Ossi.

She shot him a quick glance but did not reply.

He told her briefly about the Holler case, but soon found that she had already read up on it. When he spoke about Enheim she listened intently, watching him closely. She had alert black eyes.

Then she said, 'Call me Carmen.'

'Oskar.' He held out his hand.

'Ossi, then,' she said, shaking it.

They used Ossi's police car, a Passat, to drive to Ohlsdorf. Ossi put a cigarette in his mouth. Carmen said, 'Please don't.'

He looked at her, taken aback, then raised the cigarette packet to his mouth and put the cigarette back. 'I can see I'm going to have a hard time with you,' he said.

'But a healthy time,' she answered.

Enheim lived in Jupiterweg, a small street of two-storey houses of red clinker bricks. Ossi parked outside number twenty-seven. There were four doorbells; at the top right a row of faded handwritten capitals spelled ENHEIM. Ossi pressed the bell. They waited. Ossi rang again, for longer this time. Nothing happened. 'But we had an appointment,' he muttered. 'Has he chickened out?'

Carmen pressed each of the other three bells in turn. In response the entry buzzer sounded twice. As Ossi opened the door, an old woman with broad hips came waddling towards them, eyeing them suspiciously. Carmen held out her police ID card.

'Police!' said the woman, startled.

'We'd like to see Herr Enheim,' Ossi said.

'Has he done something?' the woman whispered.

'No,' Ossi replied. 'Nothing at all.'

'And why did you ring *my* bell?'

'Herr Enheim didn't answer.'

A man was on the stairs, looking down. Ossi saw that he had a walking stick over his left arm. He was bald and had a fleshy face with pendulous cheeks. Carmen went up the stairs.

'You rang my bell,' said the man.

'Yes, we want to see Herr Enheim.'

'So why did you ring *my* bell?'

'Because we got no answer from Herr Enheim.'

The man shook his head and went back into his apartment. Enheim's door was opposite. Carmen knocked loudly. Ossi came up the stairs. They looked at each other, and Ossi shrugged his shoulders. Carmen delved into her jacket pocket. When her hand emerged it was holding three skeleton keys. 'One of these may fit.' She inserted the smallest one into the old lock, jiggled it about, there was a click and she opened the door. It all happened so quickly that Ossi forgot to protest. 'We'll be in trouble for this,' he said.

'Only if someone notices and grasses us up.' She grinned at him.

'God, some partner they've landed me with this time!'

'You should be glad,' she said.

Ossi wondered what he was supposed to be glad about.

Carmen called into the apartment, 'Herr Enheim, are you there?'

No answer. Ossi and Carmen exchanged a glance and tacitly decided to go inside and take a look round

In the hall there was a worn imitation Persian runner, and against the wall an old cupboard with a telephone on it. Above it hung a copperplate engraving of the port of Hamburg. There was a musty odour. Three doors opened off the hallway. Carmen opened the one on the right. It was the kitchen. There was a smell of burnt fat, and dirty crockery was piled up in the sink and beside it. The tap was dripping. A sudden humming noise made her jump; the refrigerator had switched itself on. Carmen came out of the kitchen, shaking her head. 'Nothing,' she whispered. Ossi opened the door on the left-hand side of the hall. The bathroom. A stained washbasin, the mirror tarnished in places. Black and brown marks on the shower curtain. In two corners Ossi could see patches of bluish-black discoloration: mould. The tiles on the walls and on the floor seemed small to Ossi. A frayed towel hung on a rail. The uncovered toilet bowl looked grey. Ossi came away from the bathroom, shaking his head. Carmen pointed to the door at the end of the hall and then at herself. Ossi stayed in the hall while she approached the door. Cautiously she pressed down the handle, opened the door just a crack and put her head round it. Her head jerked back again and Ossi found himself looking into wide, staring eyes. 'Oh my God,' said Carmen. Then she vomited.

*   *   *

Stachelmann opened his eyes with caution. A gap between the curtains was letting in a ray of light. Dust particles danced in the air. The light dazzled him. He closed his eyes, conscious of a general numbness. He felt as if he were someone other than himself. Opening his eyes again, he noticed that his vision was poor. He raised his arm; it felt heavy and was slow to obey him. This dulling of sensation happened every few months. When it came he could not think clearly, and the fine movements of his fingers, arms and legs were impaired. His joints felt like rubber. The pain was muted, like his perception. It would be a few days before he was back to normal. He felt like a tortoise on its back. This damned helplessness. Later he would summon up all his strength and phone the department to tell them he was ill. Flu, he would say, as he had said the last time.

He got up and went into the living room, using the wall for support. The answering machine was blinking. He pressed 'playback'. 'Hi, Josef, Anne here. I can't come with you on Monday. Bohming is planning to put on a big show at the Historians' Conference and has asked me to help him. I'm sorry. I wanted to tell you straight away. Shall we go out for a meal before you go to Berlin?' She sounded exhausted.

Stachelmann sat down in his armchair and tried to make some sense of it all.

Then he went into the kitchen and carefully made himself some tea. He had a piece of white bread with marmalade and a glass of orange juice. When the tea was ready he took a mug with him into the bedroom and put it on the bedside table. On it was a book with a cover showing a ship-of-the-line in full sail—*Hornblower in the West Indies*. Stachelmann lay down and reached for the book. He tried to read, but gave up after one paragraph. The text was swimming before his eyes, and he was not taking in the sense of what he read. He closed his eyes and soon fell asleep.

When he woke up it took him a few seconds to work out where he was. He looked at the clock: three in the afternoon. He must ring the department without delay. He got up and went into the living room. His knees felt rubbery. He picked up the cordless phone and dialed the secretary's office. Renate Breuer answered at the first ring. Stachelmann tried to inject some firmness into his voice. 'I've got a bug, some sort of flu. I don't think I'll be coming in for the rest of the week.'

'Oh dear, I'm sorry to hear that. But it doesn't mean cancelling anything. And then it'll be the vacation. I'll tell Professor Bohming. I hope you'll soon be feeling better.'

Stachelmann thanked her and hung up. He rang Haus Morgenland to cancel the room for Anne. Then he took the phone with him to the bedroom and lay down. He gazed up at the ceiling, thinking of nothing in particular. He felt neither happy nor sad. He hardly cared that Anne would not be going with him. Everything seemed far away. So it was Bohming, he thought. He fell asleep.

* * *

Leopold Kohn opened the door to the toyshop, which set some bells ringing loudly. There was no one serving in the shop, but then a short, fat man appeared, his long ginger hair tied in a ponytail.

'Afternoon. I expect you're after something for your grandson.'

Kohn smiled. 'Yes, a remote controlled car or something like that.'

'Come this way,' the man said. He led Kohn into a side room. 'We specialize in model-making.' In the room there were piles of boxes of kits for cars, ships and airplanes. Every possible size, material and price. 'Perhaps the boy would be interested in an airplane?'

'No, it has to be a car.'

The salesman shrugged his shoulders. 'If you say so.' He sounded disappointed.

'I'll have a look round,' said Kohn.

'Call me when you find something, or if there's anything you want to know. I'll be next door.'

Kohn looked at the boxes of cars. He compared the functions and effective range of the remote controls. Then he returned to the main part of the shop, where the salesman was sitting over an open notebook, writing something. When he heard Kohn he looked up.

'Haven't you got any more powerful remote controls?'

'No, you'd have to have those custom made.'

'What about the remote controls for airplanes?'

'They're specifically meant for planes. And in any case their range on the ground is very much reduced by any obstacles. If you ran a plane along the ground its remote control wouldn't have a much better range than a car's.'

'But it would be possible to build a remote control with a longer range?'

'Yes, you can build anything. You could get a powerful transmitter from a place that supplies electronic components, or by mail order, or on the Internet, I'm sure. But why does your grandson need that sort of thing? He must be quite an unusual little chap. How old is he?'

'Twelve. He's a bright lad.'

'Yes, before you know it they're way ahead of you.'

'Thanks anyway,' Kohn said, and left the shop. He was annoyed: he should not have had that conversation. The salesman might remember it later and tell the police. Up to now Kohn had made no mistakes: this was the first. That made him all the more angry with himself.

'Perhaps two more years,' the doctor had said, 'if you refuse to have therapy. Nowadays there are some very effective treatments available for prostate cancer.' And that had been almost a year ago. *How long can I keep going,* Kohn wondered. He imagined the secondaries spreading from his prostate to the rest of his body. He wanted to die soon. It was better than going on living.

Chapter eleven

Carmen had thrown up in the corner near the door. Her face was white. She looks like a corpse, Ossi thought. He moved past her to the door and opened it wide. The desk immediately caught his eye. It was covered in blood and brains. What was left of the head lay face down, a large hole gaping in the back of it. Greyish-red matter was spattered on the floor. One arm rested on the desk, holding a pistol. Ossi noticed the long barrel. A silencer. Since when did people use silencers when they shot themselves?

He returned to the hallway. Carmen had vanished. Ossi dialed police headquarters on his mobile and asked for a scene-of-crime team and the pathologist to be sent. No need for the emergency doctor, he thought.

He came back out of the apartment. Carmen was sitting hunched up on the stairs, her hand covering her face. When she heard him coming she lowered her hand. 'Sorry,' she said. 'I'm really sorry.'

'I feel sick, too,' Ossi replied. 'I've never seen anything like that before.'

He sat down beside her and took her hand. 'Bloody awful job we're in,' he said. But only for the sake of saying something to comfort her. Her hand felt cold. Beads of perspiration were gathering on her forehead. Ossi took his mobile out of his jacket pocket and dialed headquarters again. 'Winter here. Send me an emergency doctor. Fast!'

'No,' she said quietly.

'Oh yes. You don't have to play the heroine. You might not believe it, but even police officers puke sometimes, just like anybody else.'

They sat on the stairs, not speaking. He held her hand.

The forensics team, the pathologist and the doctor arrived almost at the same moment. The doctor took Carmen's pulse and blood pressure, then gave her an injection. 'To stabilize your circulation. Shall I take you home?'

She shook her head.

'I think I should.'

'No,' she said.

She went into Enheim's apartment. The door to the room with the desk was ajar. A light had been set up for the camera. Three of the forensics officers were searching the room, taking care not to tread in the pools of blood and brains. Ossi was in the hall. Carmen stepped past him and stood watching the men at work in the room.

'Suicide?' she asked from the doorway.

The pathologist was tall and bony, with longish fair hair thinning at the temples. He raised his arms. 'Maybe, maybe not.'

'When?'

'How should I know? I haven't got that far yet.'

'Is he already cold?' asked Carmen.

The pathologist threw her a look of surprise. 'I'd say this morning between eleven and twelve. I'll be more precise later.'

'Thanks,' said Carmen, giving him a smile.

'The first considerate suicide,' said Ossi. 'Didn't want to startle his neighbours.'

'Possibly. We'll have to talk to them. Somebody may have heard something despite the silencer.'

People had gathered at the entrance to the building and were whispering among themselves.

'Will anyone who doesn't live here please leave now,' said Ossi.

Three women turned to leave, one of them glaring at Ossi as she did so. The man with the walking stick and the woman with the broad hips stayed where they were, looking at him expectantly. He nodded to Carmen: 'Can you go down to this lady's apartment with her?'

She nodded and went downstairs.

Ossi asked the man to take him to his apartment. 'Please lead the way.'

A copper-coloured nameplate on the door read 'MORTIMER'. The man led Ossi into his living room. It was dirty—like the rest of the place, no doubt. Ossi sat down on a sofa, the covers of which had probably been beige at one time but were now brown and threadbare. Soon the stuffing would be bursting through. No pictures on the walls; the sun's rays were refracted by the dirty panes of the two windows.

'You are Herr Mortimer?'

The man was sitting in an armchair. He nodded. 'Heinrich Mortimer.' Brown stumps of teeth were revealed when he spoke. Threads of spittle hung between his upper and lower lip.

'Unusual name.'

The man nodded.

'You're a pensioner?'

'I was a travelling salesman. Now I draw a pension.'

'What line of business were you in?'

'Insurance.'

'Did you know Herr Enheim?'

'Is he dead?'

'Yes.'

'What did he die of?'

'You knew him?'

'After a fashion. He was my neighbour. Lived in the apartment opposite.'

'Did you have any contact with him?'

'Not a lot. Now and then we'd talk about the weather or Hamburg SV. That was all.'

'Did Herr Enheim have many visitors?'

'Very few. Women from time to time—you know what I mean.'

'Prostitutes?'

Mortimer nodded. 'Sometimes I'd see one on the stairs. They looked like tarts, anyway.'

'Do you know any of the ladies?'

'No.' Mortimer grinned. He looked as if he was thinking, *no such luck.*

'Any other visitors?'

Mortimer thought for a moment. 'Yes, now and then an elderly man came to see him.'

'Can you describe him?'

Mortimer shook his head. 'Medium height, maybe five foot seven, face very brown, bushy eyebrows, they were white.'

'Very brown?'

'Yes, as if he'd just come back from holiday. Or had a daily session at a tanning studio.'

'How many times did you see him?'

'Just once.'

'But you said "now and then".'

'Well, I used to take a look through the spyhole in my door whenever his bell rang.' He evidently regarded his curiosity as quite normal. 'And then I would see this man from behind.'

'From behind. It could have been someone else, surely?'

'No. He always wore a grey jacket. Oh, and he had white hair, a bit long. It curled at the back of his neck.'

Ossi wondered how often Mortimer changed his clothes. 'Do you know how this man used to get here?'

'By taxi.'

'Always?'

'Always, including today.'

'He visited Enheim today?'

'Yes. This morning. I saw the taxi from my window. And he rang Enheim's bell, too.'

'And he was wearing that jacket again?'

Mortimer nodded.

'But it's summer. Who would wear a jacket in this heat?'

Mortimer shrugged. 'I mean quite a lightweight jacket.'

'Did you hear anything after the doorbell rang?'

'No. Or rather, yes. The door slammed when he left.'

'You didn't hear that the other times?'

'I don't hear Enheim's door unless I happen to be in my hallway.'

'Were you in the hallway today?'

'No, I was in the living room. I was watering my rubber plant when I heard the door. And footsteps, too.'

'So somebody was in a hurry, slammed the door and ran off.'

Mortimer nodded. 'Maybe.'

The woman with the broad hips was a Frau Schmidt. She had seen little and heard nothing. She remembered various ladies who came into the building and went up to the first floor. On one occasion she had seen an elderly gentleman. He had been wearing a grey jacket. She couldn't give much of a description: medium height, a lean face, white hair. Carmen was disappointed with the results of her questioning.

'That's not bad at all,' said Ossi. 'We can't expect to get the killer served up on a plate.'

'And what if the forensics team don't find any traces apart from Enheim's?'

'There's still the silencer.'

'That doesn't prove it was murder,' Carmen objected. 'He might really have had some reason for not wanting to be found straight away.'

'And the man with the jacket? He positively fled from the apartment. I wonder if he had told the taxi to wait for him.'

'Let's ask around among the neighbours. Though there are any number of reasons for leaving an apartment in a hurry. Not everybody who does that is a murderer.'

'But not every apartment that someone leaves in a hurry turns out to have a dead body in it.'

They left Enheim's building and started ringing at the neighbours' doors.

They did not turn up anything new, except for something that one young woman had seen. She told Carmen that an elderly man wearing a jacket, grey or dark green, had hurried down the street in the direction of the cemetery. He had a deeply suntanned face: this had struck her particularly because of the contrast with his white hair.

'He may have hailed a taxi. Or gone on foot as far as the Kornweg S-Bahn station. Whatever,' said Carmen. 'We should still get the taxi firms to ask their drivers. One of them might remember something.'

'Sure. But we'll do something else first. We'll ask Herr Holler where he was today between eleven and twelve.'

Carmen looked at him in surprise. She seemed on the point of asking him if he thought Holler was stupid. Or a master of disguise.

'Well,' said Ossi. 'You never know.'

'Unless what you've put in the case-notes is rubbish, Holler is tall and youthful-looking, the sort of man that women fall for. But we're talking about an old codger of only medium height. And probably a case of suicide.'

'I thought you'd like to meet the object of your desire at last.' She grinned. 'Okay, let's go, and I'll take a look at wonder-boy.'

* * *

By Saturday he was considerably better. He still felt weak, but his joints were no longer like jelly. He could type again without missing the keys. On his computer he found an e-mail from Anne. 'Hope it's nothing serious. Get in touch.'

He gave some thought to what he needed to take with him when he went to Berlin on Monday morning. He rummaged in the chest of drawers in the living room for his mobile phone and found it in a drawer under some newspaper articles that he had saved, reports of historical finds in Lübeck and on the Baltic coast. That gave him the idea of going for a seaside walk that afternoon.

He followed the same route that he had taken with Anne. There were hordes of people in swimming costumes. Children were shrieking, and teenagers were playing ball games. He took off his sandals and walked along the beach, paddling his feet in the water. Seaweed caught between his toes. A crowd of children racing noisily by splashed him with water. The effort of walking began to tell on him, but the light breeze cooled his forehead. He felt as though he was seeing and hearing all the hurly-burly through some sort of screen. Bohming came into his mind. One minute he was urging Anne to go to Stachelmann for help, the next he was commandeering her for one of his self-glorifying performances. Stachelmann was angry. In the message she had left on his answering machine, Anne had not sounded especially disappointed. Several times he had been tempted to dial her number, but there was no point. She had evidently not put up enough resistance. And now she was doing research for the Legend and possibly accompanying him to the conference to add a touch of glamour to his appearance there. It was disgusting. Why had she not told Bohming that everything was already booked, including the hotel, just a stone's throw from the Archive? Because she hadn't wanted to go. She didn't want to be alone with him. Her friendliness towards him was just a ploy so that he would help her bring about his own dismissal. For that was Bohming's plan. Stachelmann the failure, the one-time up-and-coming historian, had to be got rid of to make room for Bohming's protégée. But not until she had squeezed him dry. For the moment he still had his uses.

Stachelmann almost walked into somebody. Startled, he gazed at the man's fat belly and the mat of black hair on his stomach and chest. Some emblem or other hung from a thin gold chain round his neck. The front of his scalp was completely bald, but further back a growth of long hair reached down to his shoulders. He was just how Stachelmann imagined a pimp from St Pauli. Stachelmann swerved to avoid him, while the man ignored him, eyes fixed on two bikini-clad girls playing with a ball in the water.

Stachelmann left the beach just before the Seebrücke causeway. He sat down on a bench on the promenade next to an old lady and closed his eyes. He was exhausted.

He was roused from his thoughts by a deafening noise. A lowered Volkswagen Golf, its rear passenger windows tinted black, was roaring along the beach road. The young man at the wheel had his arm hanging nonchalantly out of the window. Stachelmann stood up and headed towards Scharbeutz. On the windscreen of his car he found a parking ticket, which he pulled out from under the wiper and dropped on the ground. He had forgotten to get a ticket from the machine. He did not care. He drove to the intersection, where he turned off onto the B432 towards Itzehoe. At Ahrensbök he left the main road and headed towards Stockelsdorf and Lübeck. Why did so many places near the Baltic coast have to be so ugly?

He parked his car in the street known as An der Obertrave. In his living room the answering machine was flashing. It was his mother, sounding upset and asking him to call her back. He picked up the cordless phone and lay down on his bed. Then he dialled his parents' number. His mother answered after the first ring.

'Your father's not well,' she said.

'Nor am I.'

'Perhaps there are still some things you need to discuss.'

'What more is there to discuss?'

'I think your father would be glad to tell you more about that man Holler. You seemed so interested in him.'

Stachelmann made no reply. Of course he was interested in Holler.

'Why don't you say something?' his mother asked.

'What does he know about him?'

'He wants to tell you himself.'

'Then can you get him to come to the phone, please?' Stachelmann was sure his father was sitting beside her, listening through the earpiece.

His mother hesitated, and then said, 'He's gone out for a walk. Anyway, I think it's better if he doesn't tell you over the phone.'

'I've got to pack, and then I'm driving to Berlin and Weimar. I'll be in touch when I get back,' said Stachelmann. He would have liked to hear what his father had to say about Holler. He could have driven over to see him straight away, but he didn't want to. His mother sounded even more upset when he said good-bye. The breach with his father was an unspoken one; there had been no quarrel, or at any

rate they hadn't shouted at each other or whatever else people normally did. Stachelmann had said good-bye and driven home. But he
was in no doubt that his father had been as conscious of the breach
as he had been himself.

And what more had *he* to do with Holler after the short shrift
he had received from the police chief? Ossi hadn't contacted him
again either. He considered phoning Ossi, but decided not to. He
turned instead to Hornblower's Caribbean adventures.

The A24 freeway was packed with holiday traffic—heavily laden cars
with bicycles on the roof and sometimes a trailer behind, caravans
and camper vans. Most were travelling in the other direction, away
from Berlin. Still, the service areas were overcrowded and noisy. On
the Berlin Ring Stachelmann drove southwards for a stretch and
then turned off at the Zehlendorf junction. From there it was only
a few miles to Lichterfelde, where the Berlin section of the Federal
Archive had been set up a few years earlier. Stachelmann was familiar
with some of the files held there because following German unifica-
tion he had made a small foray into the history of the GDR. On that
occasion he had had to go to the former SED Central Party Archive
in Wilhelm-Pieck-Strasse, now renamed Torstrasse, in the Prenzlauer
Berg district of Berlin. The SED Central Committee building had
once housed the Institute for Marxism-Leninism, near the Pieck
and Grotewohl entrance, and the Institute had been the repository
for the SED and KPD party files. On the top floor, right up near the
roof, hardworking staff had been hauling out tons of hitherto secret
documents for people eager to read them. It had been quite an experience for Stachelmann, and for many others, too. But for years now
the Torstrasse building had been idle, as the files were now at Lichterfelde, in the former barracks of Hitler's SS bodyguard regiment,
the Leibstandarte 'Adolf Hitler'. It was here, on the parade ground,
that during the Röhm putsch of June 1934 dozens of actual and supposed opponents of the Führer had been murdered. Stachelmann's
visits here always brought that episode to mind.

He parked his ageing Golf on the street outside Haus Morgenland, which proved to be an old pile with creaking floorboards. At

the reception desk he completed the registration form and received the keys to his room and to the hotel's car park, where he left the car after first depositing his suitcase at the main door. Coming back in, he lugged the case up two flights of stairs and took possession of a small room facing away from the street, as he had requested. He flexed his aching back and lay down on the bed. This was where he had planned to spend some time with Anne; he had booked the adjoining room for her. He felt sad.

For breakfast he just had a cup of coffee. He felt excited, as he always did when he visited an archive. How many enigmas might be concealed in the files, in all those millions of pages! It was like the expeditions of modern treasure hunters: a hundred searches and just one find, if that. Even so, it offered better odds than playing the lottery.

In the reading room Stachelmann signed in. The chairs and desks were arranged in rows, and most of the desks were occupied, chiefly by young people with laptops hunting for pearls from the archives for their dissertations or theses. He saw a few older men too, some of them no doubt grappling with their own history. Once Stachelmann had even seen Egon Krenz poring over some files here, when he was preparing for his trial. It would be some consolation if even a few of those once prominent in party and state in the GDR were prompted by their consciences to search in the archive for what nearly all of them had suppressed from their memories.

Stachelmann was pleased when one of the reading room librarians recognized him. He was a tall, elderly man with a long nose, who had been working at the Institute for Marxism-Leninism when Stachelmann had first got to know him. He had forgotten the man's name—an embarrassment he often suffered—and was relieved to be able to decipher the name 'Bender' on his nametag.

'It was a good thing you let us know in advance which of our files you wanted. Demand is very heavy at the moment. It was NS 3, wasn't it?'

Stachelmann nodded. 'NS 3—for the SS's economic enterprises administration, the WVHA—and NS 4.'

'Come this way, please,' whispered Bender. He led Stachelmann over to the massive shelves where the catalogues, mostly blue-bound, were located. He pointed to several volumes, on the spines of which Stachelmann recognized the shelf marks NS 3 and NS 4. 'Have a look in these. Though you won't be able to get absolutely everything this week. A government department is having to investigate something or other, all very urgent and so forth. As a citizen I have to be glad if a government department acts quickly on anything, but in this instance you'll be inconvenienced by it.'

'What department is it?' whispered Stachelmann.

'Come out to the corridor,' said Bender. Once they were outside the reading room he whispered, 'Some branch of the Hamburg revenue department. A tax investigation would be my bet. Mind you, any tax evaders in the documents we have here are in the clear by now, it's long past the expiry of the limitation period. Not much good trying to bring an action now against the SS, or against Oswald Pohl, the head of the WVHA, to make them pay back tax!' Bender tittered. 'I asked the two revenue gentlemen what they were after, but I got no answer. The only thing I did learn is that politeness isn't their strong suit. It was always like that in the old days, too.'

It was only because Bender was obviously angry that Stachelmann voiced his own complaint: 'So now, after putting in my application months ago, I still don't get access to the documents I want.'

'It's not quite that bad,' Bender answered. 'You'll get most of them, just not all.'

'And when will I get the ones that these wretched taxmen have made off with?'

Bender grimaced and raised his eyebrows. 'I don't know. Nor do the two gentlemen from Hamburg, I rather fear.'

'And which documents are they?'

'Right now it's a whole lot from the SS economic enterprises administration, and also NS 4 Ne—that's Neuengamme concentration camp. They've taken all the Hamburg files and all the central files that might possibly relate to Hamburg. Quite a lot.'

'Great,' said Stachelmann. 'Maybe I can come to some arrangement with them?'

'You can try. If you want to ruin your day.'

'Please show me where they are.'

Bender made a face as though he had eaten something sour. 'Fine, I won't stand in the way of your unhappiness.' They approached the door and he pointed out two men whose backs were turned towards them. 'Those two. But don't disturb the other readers.'

Stachelmann went over and stood behind the two men for a moment. Each had documents open in front of him, and the headings showed that they were letters and notes from the WVHA. The man sitting next to the aisle turned round, possibly aware that he was being observed.

'Excuse me,' whispered Stachelmann. 'Have you got a moment?'

The fellow was short, with a small, thin face and a bald patch. He wore horn-rimmed spectacles that seemed unduly heavy and sat almost on the very end of his nose. 'Not really,' he said. 'But I'll come out to the corridor with you.'

He led the way on slightly bowed legs. In the corridor he swung round abruptly. 'Well?' he demanded. His voice had a tinny quality.

Stachelmann was surprised, and irritated at his own reaction. He spoke in a sharper tone than he intended. 'I applied in good time to reserve, among other things, the documents that *you* have now taken. My trip here is costing me time and money.'

'I'm sorry to hear it,' said the little man. 'But it can't be helped.'

'And when can I have them?'

'Don't know.'

'Will you be able to let me know when you have finished with them?'

'That's not something I can do.'

'What department are you from?'

The man turned on his heel and went back into the reading room.

Stachelmann went out into the open air. He walked across the former parade ground towards the chapel, which now served as a library. The chapel bore witness to the barracks' earlier use in the days of Kaiser Wilhelm as the principal cadet school. First Prussia's elite, then the elite of the ss. He took his mobile out of his shirt pocket and dialed Ossi's number at police headquarters.

'Winter.'

'Stachelmann.'

'You're still around, then?'

"Fraid so. Tell me, have your lot sent some people to the Federal Archive in Berlin?'

There was a silence. Then Ossi asked, 'Have we done what?'

'Sent people to the Federal Archive to look through files.'

'Sorry, have you been drinking?'

'I drink very rarely and very little, unlike you.'

Silence. 'Anything else?' asked Ossi.

'No. Is something the matter?'

'Why should it be?' There was a click.

Stachelmann continued his walk. It took him a few minutes to realize that he had offended Ossi. He was one of those drinkers who are ashamed of their addiction. Stachelmann hadn't known that, or guessed that it was such a sore subject.

* * *

Ossi put the receiver down and stared at the wall.

'What's the matter?' asked Carmen. She was sitting facing him, typing a report on her computer. Her fingers danced over the keyboard.

'Nothing,' he said. 'Nothing at all.'

'That's alright, then.' She typed on for a while. 'By the way, what's happening about that financial report?'

'What financial report?'

'You know, the examination of Holler's accounts.'

'Well, well, you seem to know the case files by heart.'

'I'm a good police officer.'

Ossi laughed. 'And modest with it.'

'I'll have to work on that.'

'And meanwhile I'll organize us a round of coffee.'

When Ossi returned with coffee in two plastic cups, Carmen said cheerfully: 'Steinbeisser's on his way. He was keeping his arse parked on his nice comfortable office chair until one of *us* got in touch with *him*. Very much one of the old school.'

They drank their coffee. Ossi remembered his phone conversation with Stachelmann, and his mood darkened.

'Who's rattled your cage?' Carmen asked.

Ossi was amazed at how quickly she had made herself at home. She could be very loud-mouthed and coarse at times. 'How many brothers and sisters do you have?'

'Six, why?'

'Nothing really. I just wondered why you're so mouthy.'

'Well, now you know.'

There was a knock at the door.

'Come in,' bellowed Ossi. He sounded angry, aggressive.

Steinbeisser appeared in the doorway, looking intimidated. He surveyed the room as if to identify all possible sources of danger, then stood there in his worn-out grey suit and grey tie in front of Ossi, saying nothing. He had a file of documents under his arm.

'Sit down, Herr Steinbeisser.' Ossi drew forward the chair on the other side of his desk. Steinbeisser sat down and still said nothing.

'What has your investigation turned up?'

'Nothing irregular, if you take into account the fact that even the irregularities follow a regular pattern.'

Ossi wondered if he was mocking them. He glanced over towards Carmen, who had turned away with a hand over her mouth. He hoped she wouldn't burst out laughing.

'Aha,' said Ossi. 'And you've considered these regular irregularities?'

Steinbeisser nodded.

'And what emerged from your considerations?'

Steinbeisser opened his file. He leafed through the pages, then sat up straight and said, 'I have a complete list here.' He opened the metal rings of the file. 'If you like, you can take a copy of this summary.'

Ossi took the sheet and gave it a quick look. It was a spreadsheet. The first column was headed 'Name', and then came 'Purchase date', 'Purchase price', 'Repayment', and 'Date of repayment'. Under 'Name', eight people were listed, of whom the second was Enheim and the fourth Grothe. Ossi read out: 'Helmut Fleischer, Norbert Enheim, Karl Markwart, Otto Grothe, Otto Prugate, Johann-Peter Meier, Ferdinand Meiser, Gottlob Ammann.'

Carmen had regained her composure and now looked at him, interested. 'And what about them?'

'They are the property dealers who sold to Holler, listed in order of the date of selling.' He glanced at Steinbeisser, who nodded. 'If we add the purchase prices together, we get thirteen million. That's two million more than were in that eleven-million account. Holler could have gained those by careful day-to-day management of the business.'

Steinbeisser looked on impassively.

'And then there's this item that conveys nothing to me: "Repayment". What does that signify here?'

Steinbeisser leafed through his file. 'It means that each of the sellers paid money over to Herr Holler after the sale. I worked out that in each case it was about eight to twelve percent of the selling price. Herr Enheim, for instance, sold his firm for one point seven million, and then paid Holler a hundred and eighty thousand marks.'

'When?' Carmen asked.

'Seven months after the sale.'

'Seven months? That's a long time. Why?' Ossi gave Steinbeisser a searching look.

Steinbeisser shook his head. 'The item is referred to as a repayment. I don't know any more than it says in the documents. But it's rather unusual, in my view.'

'In your view,' said Ossi in a tone of resignation. 'No ideas? No suspicions?'

'No, I can't put a name to something that is not in the documents.'

'Then you can be glad that the Good Lord made you a policeman.'

Steinbeisser shrugged and stood up. 'Can I go now? I've got work to do.'

'Thank you for your help,' said Ossi as Steinbeisser departed.

'Come on, we're going to call on Holler,' said Ossi.

'Just a minute, I want a quick look at the list.' She took it and left the room, returning two minutes later with two copies. 'The original can go into the case file. We can immortalize ourselves artistically on the copies.' She handed Ossi one sheet and sat down at her desk with the other. She picked up a ballpoint pen and ticked off the various columns. 'Actually it's all quite clear when you see it presented like this. Steinbeisser may be a comic turn, but he knows his onions when it comes to accounting. He's compiled this straightforward list on the basis of Holler's books. I couldn't do that.' She looked at Ossi: 'What about Enheim? What does the pathologist say?' She picked up the phone and pressed a speed dial button. 'Herr Ablass, please.' She waited, then said, 'Well, doc, what have we got? Murder, suicide, any clues?' She listened. 'Okay, we'll be right over.'

In the forensic pathology department of the Eppendorf University hospital they found Dr Ablass waiting for them. His predecessor, Dr Werner Hauschildt, the city's most experienced forensic pathologist, had retired the previous month. Ablass was short and wiry, with a thin moustache and round, thick-lensed glasses. 'Glad you've come,' he said by way of greeting, giving each of them a swift handshake. 'Ah, the new one,' he commented when Carmen introduced herself. She made no reply.

'It's very clear-cut,' said the doctor. 'Enheim was shot.'

'Not suicide, then?' Ossi asked, then wished he hadn't.

Ablass shook his head. 'No chance. You try shooting yourself without leaving traces of gunsmoke on your hands. Enheim should possibly have washed his hands more often, but we've found nothing to suggest that he could have fired a bullet into his own head. And of course the silencer is another argument against it.'

Now it was Ossi's turn to shake his head.

'Makes no difference,' said Ablass. 'Nine millimetre calibre, my guess would be a Walther P 1 or P 38.'

'That's army issue,' Ossi said.

'Not exclusively. From the late fifties it was in use with the army, the Federal Border Police and the ordinary police. Together with the SIG P 210–4 or P 49, it was the standard pistol of the post-war years. During the war the P 38 replaced the Luger 08, in the police as well as the army. In 1957 production was resumed, and the gun got a new light metal grip and a new name, P 1. Or so I'm told by my forensic technology colleagues. But it's a bit much to think that police in the sixties and seventies were running round with the same shooter as the Gestapo had used. Charming. And of course some of those policemen never did accept the new democracy after forty-five.' He shuddered slightly as if he had just bitten into a lemon.

'Can it be established whether the gun dates from the war years or the fifties?'

'Hang on, not so fast. Don't forget that I'm just thinking aloud. There are a few marks on the bullet that I've seen a few times before on bullets fired from a P 1. But that doesn't prove anything.'

'But surely you wouldn't mention it at all if you weren't reasonably certain?'

Ablass did not answer. Carmen chewed her lower lip.

'When was Enheim shot?' she asked.

'Between eleven and twelve, probably very close to half past eleven.'

'Then the guy in the grey jacket is the chief suspect.'

'The *only* suspect, we don't know of any other,' said Ossi.

'We must go and talk to Mortimer right away and make sure we get a better description and an identikit picture. Come on!' said Carmen.

Any second now she'll be pulling me along by the arm, thought Ossi. God, she's always in such a hurry!

He trotted along behind her, deliberately taking his time. On the way to the car she kept turning round impatiently.

'Police work is brain-work,' he called out to her.

'And sometimes it's leg-work. However quick your brain is, it's no use if you're slow on your feet. What's the good of knowing who's committed a crime if you won't stir yourself to catch him?'

Ossi thought she was walking even faster now. By the time he reached the car she was already in the driving seat with the engine running. He got in on the passenger side, and she accelerated away with a screech of tires. 'All we need now is our flashing blue light.'

'Good idea.' She put it in place on the roof and turned on the siren. She raced towards Ohlsdorf.

She was a good driver, but her hectic pace got on Ossi's nerves. It made no difference whether the identikit picture, always assuming that they managed to construct one, was distributed ten minutes earlier or later. 'You get a kick out of this,' he said.

'A little.' She cursed the driver of an Opel who failed to give way quickly enough.

'Suppose you cause an accident by going so fast? Then it will be a while before there's any identikit picture at all.'

'I'm not going to cause an accident,' she said.

Nor did she. With another screech of tires she stopped outside the building where Enheim had been murdered.

They were in luck. Mortimer was at home. He looked at Ossi in surprise, and then grinned when he saw Carmen, and asked them in. 'Brought reinforcements with you,' he said. 'And very nice, too.' He hobbled on his walking stick to the living room.

'Yes, alright,' said Ossi.

'Well, have you caught your murderer?'

'We're looking for several just now, which one do you mean?' Carmen asked.

'Several,' repeated Mortimer. 'Hamburg gets more dangerous every day.'

'So you'll probably vote some crazy district court judge into the city parliament,' said Carmen.

Mortimer stared at her, then shook his head. Threads of spittle hung between his upper and lower lips. 'I don't think that's what you're meant to be questioning me about.'

'We're not questioning you,' said Ossi. 'We've a request to make. We'd like you to come down to headquarters with us, we need an identikit picture of the man who came here from time to time, the one in the grey jacket.'

'Oh dear,' said Mortimer. 'I don't think that will be much use. I hardly saw him.'

'But you came face to face with him.'

'Yes, but he looked away as soon as he saw me.'

'And didn't that strike you as odd?' Carmen demanded.

He gave her a stern look. 'Of course it did.'

'The best thing will be for you to come with us now. I'll bring you back here afterwards.' Ossi got to his feet.

'Do you have good coffee at police headquarters?'

'You'll get some from the canteen, not from the machine, okay?'

Mortimer nodded, picked up his stick and stood up. He negotiated the stairs quite nimbly, but struggled to lever himself on to the back seat of the Passat. Carmen drove back to police headquarters. Once there, she accompanied Mortimer to the police artist, while Ossi fetched coffee from the canteen. On the way he encountered Taut. 'We must all get together and talk some time,' said Taut. 'Maybe then we'll get a line on this case. Let's say this evening, six o'clock.'

'That's after knocking-off time.'

'Yes, it's the only time we'll get some peace and quiet.'

Precariously, Ossi carried the three mugs of coffee to the room where Mortimer was telling the artist what the man in the grey jacket had looked like. As Ossi came in, having pushed the door open with his elbow, Carmen looked across at him with raised eyebrows. That might mean that they were getting nowhere—or the opposite. Ossi put down the coffee and watched. The artist was finding Mortimer irritating, and was getting impatient. A sure sign that nothing would come of this. They could give up any hope of getting a picture to put out. The artist was no psychologist, certainly, but Mortimer's imagination would have left even a psychoanalyst floundering.

Mortimer took a sip of coffee and pulled a face. 'Is it always this bad?' Instead of waiting for a reply he immediately turned to the artist again. 'You need to make the cheeks narrower.'

'Just now you wanted them broader.'

'Broader?' Mortimer gave him a look. 'Fatter. But now they're too fat. And besides, come to think of it, he had tremendously bushy white eyebrows.'

'I'll leave you to get on with it,' said Ossi.

Carmen stood up. 'Give me a ring when you've finished.'

They went back to their office. 'Oh Lord,' said Carmen. 'That's a complete waste of time.'

'You were the one who was so keen. We've got a meeting with Taut at six.'

'Great, that's all I need.'

'Don't you like your new colleagues?'

'I don't know them yet. But that isn't what I'd planned for this evening.'

Ossi made no reply. He settled down to study the file on Ulrike Kreimeier's death. No progress in the Kreimeier case, none in the Holler case, none in the Enheim case. Mortimer would be no help. If any sort of identikit picture emerged, it could go straight into the wastepaper basket. Who was the man in the jacket? Ossi reached for the phone and called Kurz. 'Have you people questioned the taxi drivers?'

'We haven't got hold of them all yet. We're just ordinary mortals, not miracle-workers.' Kurz was annoyed.

'It surely ought to be possible to find a super-tanned, white-haired man in a grey jacket who has taken a taxi several times to the same address in Ohlsdorf!'

'Oh sure, piece of cake.'

Ossi put down the receiver. 'We're taking another ride to Ohlsdorf,' he said.

Carmen shook her head. 'There's nothing to be gained by that.'

'First you charge around like a madwoman, and now you sit there frittering away our time.' He gave her a furious look. He couldn't make her out. One minute she was alert and ready to go, positively hyperactive, thirsting for action, and the next she seemed like a snail. All that was missing was a trail of slime. When he first met his new colleague he had been pleased. She seemed quick-witted and uncomplicated. And she was pretty, too. But her tendency to take charge got on his nerves. The way she kept grabbing the initiative. At first he had tolerated it, found it amusing. But now, as she lapsed into lethargy, he had had enough. He looked across at her. She was staring absently past him, gazing at the wall. Like a toy mouse that somebody had wound up and let go. First it races around, then when the spring runs down it just lies on the floor, spent.

What next? They needed to do the rounds of Enheim's neighbours again in the hope of finding someone who remembered the white-haired visitor. Perhaps, after all, they might get a description of the criminal that would lead somewhere. Perhaps finding the old man would set them on the right track. Did he have something to do with Holler? The one thing that was clear was that Enheim had done a deal with Holler that raised some questions. Above all, the question of the repayment. Why would someone pay back part of the purchase price? Why hadn't Holler and Enheim just agreed a lower price in the first place? Why hadn't Holler agreed lower prices with *all* the people he had bought out? And why had Enheim been so angry with Holler?

He needed to ask Holler again. But it wouldn't solve the murders, Ossi was certain of that. What was equally certain was that after this evening's meeting with Taut he would buy himself a bottle of schnapps.

*   *   *

Stachelmann finished his walk and returned to the reading room in the Federal Archive. He made do with the files that were available to him. There was not much in them that he did not know already. At the weekend he would drive to Weimar and try his luck there. He was studying the structures in Pohl's WVHA, which controlled the ss-operated economic enterprises and the concentration camps. Pohl was the manager of death—not fanatical, but efficient, a modern mass-murderer. His life ended on the gallows at Landsberg in Bavaria. His grave in the cemetery next to the prison had since become a place of pilgrimage for Nazi sympathizers from all over Germany. His personal files traced the career of a model Nazi, starting with membership in the Freikorps, the right-wing volunteer militias, after the First World War and culminating in the rank of Obergruppenführer in the ss. Stachelmann went back to the catalogue shelves. Perhaps some other file would hold the answer to the question of whether

Pohl himself had wanted to take control of the concentration camps or whether this had happened on Himmler's orders. After the war Pohl had argued at great length that he was not responsible for any of the killing, though he did not deny the fact of the mass murder of Jews. That was an astonishing position to adopt, given that he had been the administrative head of all the concentration camps, at least during the final years of Hitler's regime.

Stachelmann had reason to fear his compulsive research habit, which had often led him to go far beyond what he actually needed. What was the good of new insights that could not be put to use, and specifically not in his *Habilitation* thesis? How could he bridge the gap between the first beginnings of the concentration camps and their later being placed under Pohl's control? As he leafed through the catalogues, his thoughts strayed back to the mountain of shame in his office. What was the point of following up clues about Pohl if he couldn't even manage to work through his stack of documents back in Hamburg? That stack already included a large number of copies made in the Federal Archive in Lichterfelde. He had had many of them done just on the off-chance of their being useful, in the days when he was still regarded as a rising star and his photocopying bills were paid by the department with no questions asked.

He returned the catalogues to the shelf, tucked his laptop under his arm, gave Herr Bender a wave, and went to the cloakroom that was shared by a coffee vending machine and rows of steel lockers. Opening his locker, he stowed the laptop in his briefcase, then left the Archive building. The weather was sultry, with white clouds in the sky. He was perspiring by the time he reached the main gate. He handed in his reader's card and stepped out on to the pavement of Finckensteinallee. He would drop off his things at the hotel and then take the S-Bahn to Friedrichstrasse, for a stroll around the Reichstag district and East Berlin.

Suddenly he had a sense of being followed; of eyes drilling into his back. He stopped dead and swung round. An old lady was pushing a stroller along the pavement. A BMW came past in the opposite direction, driven by a Turk, judging by the kind of music he was playing full blast. Stachelmann walked on. On arrival at Haus Morgenland he left his briefcase in his room. Then he set out again for the Lichterfelde-Ost S-Bahn station. As he walked along Königsberger Strasse he knew there was somebody behind him. He stopped, and two girls with rucksacks overtook him. He scanned his surroundings. Nothing out of the ordinary. Once inside the station he stopped at a kiosk and bought a copy of the *Berliner Zeitung*. When he reached the platform there was a train for Friedrichstrasse waiting to leave. He sat down at the front of the last carriage, with his back to the direction of travel. There were about a dozen other people sitting in the carriage, none of whom seemed to be paying any attention to him. He opened the newspaper and started to study the 'what's on' pages. Perhaps he might find a film or a show to go to one evening. The prospect of spending every evening in a small hotel room in the company of Horatio Hornblower was not all that appealing.

The train reached Potsdamer Platz, and on an impulse he got out. At one time this had been Berlin's biggest building site. He strolled around among the steel and glass structures which bore the emblems of Sony and Mercedes-Benz. He still had the feeling of being watched, so again he turned round abruptly, but again saw no one. So now you're a no-hoper with a persecution mania. Off to the loony bin with you. Perhaps that was a better place for him than the Philosophers' Tower of Hamburg University.

He returned to the station. Taking the S-Bahn for Friedrich-strasse, he once again sat at the front of the carriage, observing the other passengers. An old woman sat constantly moving her lips as though talking to herself or chewing something. Two young men were speaking in a foreign language which sounded like Russian. Engrossed in their conversation, they were oblivious to their surroundings. Two young women sharing a Discman pulled the ear-pieces out of their ears from time to time and chatted, perhaps exchanging views on new songs by their favourite bands. They were a picture of harmony as they talked and laughed and then listened intently, sometimes humming along with the music. At the far end of the carriage, in the middle of the row of seats, sat an elderly gentleman reading a paperback book. He was wearing a grey jacket and his face was deeply tanned, which accentuated the whiteness of his hair.

Stachelmann left the train at Friedrichstrasse. He felt relaxed and had forgotten his fears. He mingled with the tourists at the Reichstag building, and looked for bullet holes from the war, but found none. Before Reunification you could see the bullet-riddled façade as you crossed the sector border by S-Bahn. There the war had still seemed like a recent event.

He spent the evening in the Mitte district. He strolled down Unter den Linden, once the most beautiful place to walk in the whole city but now oppressively dominated by ostentatious buildings of steel and concrete. Here it was cold even at the height of summer. He turned off into Friedrichstrasse and entered the station, where he had a fish dish in one of the fast-food restaurants. Then he went up to the platforms. The station was full of tourists and people going home late from work or from shopping. He sauntered along to one end of the platform. As he came back again he recognized the man in the grey jacket sitting on a bench near the stairs, reading a paperback.

Stachelmann looked at him for a few seconds, but then moved on: it was embarrassing to stare at strangers. But it seemed the man had not noticed, or at any rate had not let himself be distracted from his reading. Stachelmann walked to the opposite end of the platform and back again. His mind was troubled: he could no longer see clearly why he was visiting the Archive. He had not come to Berlin to do research, he told himself, but to escape. To flee from the mountain of documents at home to yet more documents in the Archive here, which in reality he didn't even need. It was true that he might lack this or that, but how could he know what he *hadn't* got when he didn't know what he had? Was it necessary to drive all the way to Berlin simply to realize that he had no business coming here before finding out exactly what there was in the mountain of shame back in Hamburg? If he carried on like this he would just heap up more layers of documents, adding to the misery that was already so bad that he had to run away from it. The higher the mountain in Hamburg grew, the greater would be his fear of never conquering it. That was his mistake, running away from failure, only to sink deeper into the morass. Until there was no way out.

Then he remembered Anne. In his thoughts she was smiling;

she had a smile that drew one to her. Perhaps she wasn't just planning to exploit him. Why didn't he give himself a chance? If he didn't try, he certainly wouldn't win her. That would be the worst thing of all. And the way he was behaving, that outcome was already a fait accompli: he was accepting failure so as not to have to fear failure. This is crazy, he thought. He laughed softly to himself. I know I have a few peculiarities, but I'm not mad—just doing my best to drive myself mad. I really am one of a kind! He laughed, and a man walking past looked at him and shook his head.

The elderly man was still sitting on the seat near the stairs reading his book. He seemed oblivious to what was going on around him. Stachelmann once more resumed his stroll along the platform. He passed the bench where the man was seated. Then he went right to the edge of the platform to see whether the train shown on the indicator board was coming. He felt a sense of urgency, an eagerness to get a grip on things at last. He looked for the headlamps of the approaching train and saw two points of light, and then also the light from inside the carriages. The train was rapidly approaching. Soon he would hear the squeal of the brakes. Something pushed him in the back. Not hard, but with enough force to throw him off balance. He was drawn irresistibly down towards the rails. Arms flailing, he thrust his torso backwards. The train was almost upon him. He froze, and just had time to see a woman, wide-eyed, with her hand clapped to her mouth. Then he heard a scream. It came from far off. Or had *he* screamed? A face looked down at him, an old man with white hair and a grey jacket. Stachelmann saw him as though through a mist. The man was smiling at him. A smiling, suntanned face.

*   *   *

They sat in Taut's office. Kamm and Kurz were smoking; Ossi coughed and lit a cigarette, too. Taut was sitting, sphinx-like, behind his desk, not speaking, the small eyes in his heavy face resting on his colleagues. The door opened and Carmen appeared, breathing quickly. 'Sorry, I had to nip out to the shops. By the time we're through, they'll be closed.'

Taut muttered something, then said, 'Let's make a start. Anyone got anything to say?' Nobody had.

'Same old story,' Taut complained, as though it were not up to him, as the superior officer, to lead the discussion. 'We've got two cases here, Holler and Enheim, and a dead officer who was run down by a car. In the cases of Holler and Ulrike Kreimeier we're groping around in the dark; with Enheim we've got a very shaky witness. There's even an identikit picture.' Taut looked at Ossi.

'That's right, we've got an identikit picture and a description. Kamm and Kurz'—Ossi gestured towards them—'have been working through all the taxi drivers since yesterday. The man we're after supposedly arrived by taxi, and he may also have left by taxi, but we don't know that for certain. He's an old man, white hair, fairly long and curling at the ends. Wearing a grey jacket.'

'The question is whether we should go public with this description and the picture,' said Kamm.

'Why not?' Carmen replied.

It was on the tip of Ossi's tongue to tell Carmen to keep her trap shut for the next half-hour. Instead, he said, 'The description is poor, and it's questionable whether the picture is anything like the man who used to visit Enheim. If we start a search based on an identikit image that may match a hundred other people but not our suspect, then at the very least we'll make ourselves look stupid, and almost certainly we'll be overwhelmed with idiots reporting false sightings.'

'Better than nothing,' said Kamm.

'I agree,' said Kurz. 'Maybe we'll get some assistance from Kommissar Luck.'

'He only ever phones,' said Carmen.

'Thank you for your intelligent contribution,' growled Taut. 'This is what we'll do. We'll use the image and the description in an appeal for a witness to come forward. That might save us from the worst of the time-wasters. Officially the fellow in the grey jacket is a witness and that's all. What he may be if we get hold of him is another matter. We've got nothing else to go on. I'd rather not repeat to you what the Chief whispered in my ear this morning. And after this I've got a meeting with Kriminalrat Schmidt. By instituting a search we achieve one thing, whatever else happens, and that's to ease the pressure on us. The Chief and the Senator for the Interior will be happy, and we'll be able to get on with the job in peace for a while. And we may even have some success with the picture and description, even though I share your reservations, Ossi. I'd like you to tackle Holler again, with Carmen. Even if it turns out to be a red herring, I want to know the significance of those repayments that Steinbeisser listed. Kurz and Kamm, you carry on working your way through the taxi drivers. And I'll get the search under way.'

Ossi did not say a word as he drove to Holler's with Carmen, though she kept trying to start up a conversation. Ossi was annoyed. Her brash manner got on his nerves. She always wanted to take the initiative, always knew best and thought she was really smart. It was a shame, at first he had looked forward to working with her. He could see that she was trying to be less pushy; she had let him drive.

'I'm really curious to see what this Jesus is like,' she said. She was pretending not to notice Ossi's bad mood.

Ossi said nothing.

'So far I only know Holler from the notes in the files, and they paint him in glowing colours. And his photo's not bad, either. He's a good-looking man.'

As Ossi parked in front of Holler's office building, Carmen gave a low whistle. 'This guy's stinking rich. That makes him a bit different from Jesus.'

'You're an expert on Jesus, I suppose,' Ossi could not resist saying.

'Up to a point,' she answered. 'Never let it be said that all those religion education lessons were wasted on me.'

'And you're a saint, too, no doubt.'

'I'm certain of it.' She sounded almost jolly.

Ossi led the way into the foyer. The receptionist was elegantly dressed, so elegantly that Ossi wondered if she was made of porcelain. But she was real enough to dial Holler's number. 'Someone will come for you in a moment,' she said. She spoke with a broad Saxon accent, which sat ill with her appearance. Ossi almost burst out laughing. Carmen looked at him in surprise, but a gesture from him told her it was nothing.

'We weren't expecting you,' said Holler's secretary. 'But you're in luck, doubly so. Herr Holler is here, *and* he can give you ten minutes.' She led the way to the lifts.

Holler rose from his seat and advanced to meet them as they entered his office. 'Hello, Herr Winter, I hope you bring good news. I haven't met your colleague before, have I?'

Ossi introduced Carmen as Ulrike Kreimeier's successor.

'Ah, yes, the police officer who died so tragically,' he said. His expression was sorrowful.

'My fellow officer who was murdered,' said Ossi coldly.

Holler offered Ossi and Carmen seats in the comfortable sitting area of his office. 'What brings you to me?'

'Where were you on the sixteenth of July—that was a Monday—between eleven and twelve o'clock?' asked Carmen.

Ossi was irritated: once again she had rushed in. But she had asked the right question.

'What is the point of that question?'

'Just answer it, if you would,' Ossi said.

Holler went over to his desk and pressed a button on his telephone. 'Frau Mendel, would you join us for a minute, please, and bring the appointments diary.' He returned to his seat.

The door opened. It was Frau Mendel, carrying the diary, a large book bound in black.

'Where was I on July sixteenth, between eleven and twelve o'clock?'

Frau Mendel turned over the pages, then said: 'You were looking at a property in Alte Wöhr street.'

'Alone?' asked Carmen.

'No, with the seller, Herr York.'

'You were with Herr York the whole time?'

'Yes,' replied Holler. 'He came at nine and left to return to Frankfurt at around two o'clock.' He turned to Frau Mendel. 'Please give Herr Winter and his colleague Herr York's address and telephone number.' He looked at Ossi. 'That would have been your next request.'

Ossi nodded.

'May I ask why you want to know where I was at the time in question?'

'Herr Enheim was murdered.'

'Murdered?'

'Yes,' Ossi said. 'Murdered.'

'I read in the newspaper that it was suicide.'

'It was murder.'

Holler leaned back in his armchair. 'That is terrible. I knew Enheim. Not well, but he did entrust his company to me.'

'You bought it for one point seven million, less the repayment,' said Carmen.

'Repayment?' Holler looked puzzled for a moment. Then he gave a chilly smile. 'Ah, yes,' he said calmly. 'There were a few deficiencies that only showed up after the sale was complete. Herr Enheim and I came to an agreement without involving the lawyers.'

'What sort of deficiencies?'

'I am trying to recall the details,' Holler responded. His brow furrowed. 'Enheim owned a plot with a house on it. The house was in an appalling condition, dry rot in the roof, mildew in the cellar. He had not told me that. That was point one. And point two was that his client index was basically worthless.'

'What client index?'

'Well, you see, a property dealer is not primarily an owner of real estate, even if it sometimes happens that a dealer does in fact own properties. Like Herr Enheim, for example.'

'Like Herr Holler, for example,' said Carmen.

'Like Herr Holler, for example,' said Holler. 'We property dealers make our living by letting or selling apartments or houses. Every property dealer sets very great store by maintaining a database of buyers and sellers, and landlords and potential tenants. His function is to bring these groups together and opposing interests. We create harmony where t' extreme conflict. Landlords would like to doub would prefer to see them halved. The seller price, the buyer tries every ploy to lower ' voice mellow.

He'd have made a good doctor, Ossi thought. The kind that patients trust. Or a good con man, whose way with words is his stock in trade.

Holler was silent, apparently reflecting, and then he continued: 'The value of a property company is no more and no less than the value of its database. Our capital takes the form of contacts. True, we occasionally buy something ourselves, when an offer is irresistible. But that is the exception. I have to confess that I am less successful as a property owner than as a dealer. As an owner one has to be hard-hearted, execute actions for eviction, raise rents, all things that are distinctly unpleasant. In the two apartment blocks that I own in Altona, I have never yet raised the rent. I am afraid there are people living there whom other landlords would have evicted long ago. In some cases I allow the rent to be deferred from month to month, until the debts are so big that I cannot see how those poor folk can ever repay them. You can imagine what happens in the end.'

Truly Jesus-like, thought Ossi.

'You recovered a sum of money from all the dealers who sold out to you, generally after a few months,' said Carmen.

Holler was taken aback. 'Possibly. In that case there must have been deficiencies each time, of one kind or another. With Enheim the chief one was not the sorry state of the house, but his failure to maintain a good client list. In effect he was broke when he sold to me. His list contained nothing of value in it. If I remember rightly, we did not gain a single client for our own portfolio. So all we acquired was one decrepit house.'

'But it's still unusual for money to change hands again after the sale.'

'So you may think. But there is a legal period of liability. During that period my people examine anything that I buy. Sometimes they say to me, boss, you've been a bit rash again. I am afraid they are right. They are good employees.'

'So it's usual in property deals for money to change hands after ᴀᴀle?' Ossi returned to Carmen's question.

ᴀWith me, certainly.'

'Would you mind giving us the addresses of your two apartment blocks in Altona? Are they the only buildings you own for letting?'

Holler looked at Ossi and Carmen as if he were about to ask what on earth they were after now. But instead he called Frau Mendel again. When she appeared, he said, 'Please write down the addresses of our two buildings in Altona and also the apartment house in Alster-blick, and give them to these two officers.' He turned to face Carmen. 'Please collect the addresses from Frau Mendel when you leave.'

Frau Mendel disappeared.

Ossi stood up.

Holler remained seated. 'May I ask if you are solving the murders of my wife, my daughter and my son, or whether you plan to go on spending your time studying my bookkeeping?'

'We shall find the murderer or murderers sooner or later.'

'Obviously later,' said Holler sharply.

'Possibly later,' said Ossi. 'We're doing everything we can.'

'Not at the moment, clearly. You are investigating the death of your fellow officer, what was her name again, and the murder of Enheim, and my books.'

'It may all be connected,' said Carmen.

'How long have you been a policewoman?'

Carmen stood up. She nodded to Ossi. 'We'll leave now.' Ossi followed her out. As they opened the door to the front office, they saw Frau Mendel waiting with a piece of paper in her hand. Without a word she gave it to Ossi.

Ossi settled himself into the driving seat. Carmen gazed at him for a while. 'Why aren't you driving off?' she asked.

Ossi dialed the number of the murder squad on his mobile. 'Is that you, Frau Kurbjuweit?' he enquired. It really got up his nose that the secretary never gave her name when she answered a call. The reception on the mobile was poor, so Ossi had not been able to identify her voice. 'On my desk you'll find a file box labeled Holler. The top sheet of paper in the box has a list of names and addresses. Please get the list, look up the telephone numbers of the men listed, and then phone me back on my mobile.' He ended the call.

'What's that about?'

'Do you believe all that stuff about deficiencies and repayments? With his tenants he's all Sermon on the Mount, but when people sell to him he applies the thumbscrews. It just doesn't add up.'

'And if all the dealers on the list confirm that, yes, there *were* reasons for repaying some money, what will you do then? Will you say it's impossible? This is daft, a complete waste of time. We ought to be doing something towards finding the old boy with the Tenerife tan.' She was angry. Ossi could not understand why.

'You can go back to headquarters if that suits you better,' he said. He gestured with the back of his hand. 'Go on, no problem, I'll just give the dealers a going-over on my own. At least then I won't have somebody chipping in the whole time.'

She opened the door of the Passat and walked away without looking at him. He watched her go.

His mobile rang. Frau Kurbjuweit gave him four telephone numbers. She couldn't find the rest because there were too many listings under those names in the phone book. Ossi dialed the number for Otto Prugate. There was a delay before someone answered.

'Yes?'

'Am I speaking to Herr Prugate, Otto Prugate?'

'Who is that?'

'Kommissar Winter, Murder Squad.'

Silence.

'Are you still there?'

'What have I to do with the murder squad?'

'Can I come and see you?'

'Only if you tell me what it's about.'

'You know Herr Holler?'

'That swine.'

'Are you still living in Sprützwiese?'

'That filthy swine. I don't have anything to do with Holler now. Nor he with me.'

Ossi drove to Sprützwiese, which was in the Lurup district of the city. Trees lined the street. Children were playing on the pavement. House number 9 was smothered in ivy, with gaps cut into it to

He'd have made a good doctor, Ossi thought. The kind that patients trust. Or a good con man, whose way with words is his stock in trade.

Holler was silent, apparently reflecting, and then he continued: 'The value of a property company is no more and no less than the value of its database. Our capital takes the form of contacts. True, we occasionally buy something ourselves, when an offer is irresistible. But that is the exception. I have to confess that I am less successful as a property owner than as a dealer. As an owner one has to be hard-hearted, execute actions for eviction, raise rents, all things that are distinctly unpleasant. In the two apartment blocks that I own in Altona, I have never yet raised the rent. I am afraid there are people living there whom other landlords would have evicted long ago. In some cases I allow the rent to be deferred from month to month, until the debts are so big that I cannot see how those poor folk can ever repay them. You can imagine what happens in the end.'

Truly Jesus-like, thought Ossi.

'You recovered a sum of money from all the dealers who sold out to you, generally after a few months,' said Carmen.

Holler was taken aback. 'Possibly. In that case there must have been deficiencies each time, of one kind or another. With Enheim the chief one was not the sorry state of the house, but his failure to maintain a good client list. In effect he was broke when he sold to me. His list contained nothing of value in it. If I remember rightly, we did not gain a single client for our own portfolio. So all we acquired was one decrepit house.'

'But it's still unusual for money to change hands again after the sale.'

'So you may think. But there is a legal period of liability. During that period my people examine anything that I buy. Sometimes they say to me, boss, you've been a bit rash again. I am afraid they are right. They are good employees.'

'So it's usual in property deals for money to change hands after a sale?' Ossi returned to Carmen's question.

'With me, certainly.'

'May I ask why you want to know where I was at the time in question?'

'Herr Enheim was murdered.'

'Murdered?'

'Yes,' Ossi said. 'Murdered.'

'I read in the newspaper that it was suicide.'

'It was murder.'

Holler leaned back in his armchair. 'That is terrible. I knew Enheim. Not well, but he did entrust his company to me.'

'You bought it for one point seven million, less the repayment,' said Carmen.

'Repayment?' Holler looked puzzled for a moment. Then he gave a chilly smile. 'Ah, yes,' he said calmly. 'There were a few deficiencies that only showed up after the sale was complete. Herr Enheim and I came to an agreement without involving the lawyers.'

'What sort of deficiencies?'

'I am trying to recall the details,' Holler responded. His brow furrowed. 'Enheim owned a plot with a house on it. The house was in an appalling condition, dry rot in the roof, mildew in the cellar. He had not told me that. That was point one. And point two was that his client index was basically worthless.'

'What client index?'

'Well, you see, a property dealer is not primarily an owner of real estate, even if it sometimes happens that a dealer does in fact own properties. Like Herr Enheim, for example.'

'Like Herr Holler, for example,' said Carmen.

'Like Herr Holler, for example,' said Holler. 'We property dealers make our living by letting or selling apartments or houses. Every property dealer sets very great store by maintaining a database of buyers and sellers, and landlords and potential tenants. His function is to bring these groups together and to reconcile their opposing interests. We create harmony where those interests are in extreme conflict. Landlords would like to double their rents, tenants would prefer to see them halved. The seller demands an exorbitant price, the buyer tries every ploy to lower it.' He spoke calmly, his voice mellow.

expose the windows. Ossi pressed the bell next to the name Prugate and the entry buzzer sounded. A tall, bald-headed man was waiting for him. There was perspiration on his forehead. He showed Ossi into his kitchen, which looked simple and practical. It reminded Ossi of the IKEA kitchen he and his wife had bought years ago. The chair that Prugate gave him wobbled, so Ossi did his best to sit still. The coffeemaker had a full jug of coffee on it. Ossi cast around for an ashtray, but could not see one and so suppressed his desire to have a cigarette with his coffee. Without asking, Prugate put two gold-rimmed cups and saucers on the table, and then a can of condensed milk and another tin container with individually wrapped sugar cubes. He poured the coffee and motioned to the sugar and milk. Ossi took two cubes.

'Why is Holler a filthy swine?' he enquired.

Prugate had a line above his nose. 'I can be rather—impulsive, shall we say. It just slipped out.'

'Twice,' Ossi said.

'What do you mean, twice?'

'It slipped out twice. Once I'd swallow, but when it's twice I take it seriously. For me to call someone a filthy swine, he has to have done something pretty significant. And even then it's abusive language.'

'Are you trying to pin something on me?'

Ossi shook his head. 'I just want to know why you said it.'

'Because he took me for a ride.'

'How?'

'He bought my company off me, and then he re-opened the deal.'

Ossi was getting restless, but was careful not to put too much strain on the chair. 'What do you mean, re-opened the deal?' he asked.

'He paid the asking price and then held out his hand.'

'Do you think you could possibly manage to tell this story coherently?'

Prugate looked him in surprise and said nothing.

'Held out his hand—what does that mean?'

'It means he demanded money.'

'On what grounds?'

'On the grounds of what he claimed were deficiencies.'

'What sort of deficiencies?' Ossi gave the impression that nothing could disturb his equanimity. He spoke to Prugate as one might speak to a frail, helpless old man. It was the right approach.

'He complained about my index.'

'The client index?'

'Exactly.'

'And what was his complaint?'

'That it was no good.'

'Was the information out of date?'

'No, I always made sure to keep it in good shape.'

'So Herr Holler had no grounds for claiming anything back?'

'None whatsoever. But he still did it.'

'And you paid up. Why?'

'He threatened to take me to court and ruin my business reputation. In plain language, it was extortion.'

'You can't extort money from somebody by threatening to take them to court,' said Ossi. 'If what you say is true, Holler would have lost his case, and you would have kept your money.'

'Can't you understand that an old man like me doesn't want to be dragged through the courts? Possibly with appeals and all the rest of it?'

'I can understand that,' said Ossi, who did not believe a word the old man was saying. 'What sum of money are we talking about?'

'A hundred and sixty thousand marks. And he even said I should be glad that he wasn't demanding the whole selling price back and bringing an action for fraud.'

'Perhaps he wasn't entirely wrong?' suggested Ossi.

Prugate stared at him, wide-eyed. A bead of sweat ran down past the bridge of his nose to the corner of his mouth.

'Was the client index the only bone of contention?' Ossi queried.

'Not entirely, but it was the main cause of complaint. He also objected to the condition of the house that I sold him. It was old and in a bad state, but I'd told him that beforehand. And he'd dismissed it as unimportant. It didn't matter, he said, he intended to put up something new anyway. But six months later he suddenly remembered the state of the house. He said he'd get me for that, in the courts, regardless of how things stood with the client portfolio.'

'So Holler knew before the sale went through that the house was no good, and was going to pull it down.'

'Yes.'

'Did he dispute having said before the sale that it didn't matter?'

'What he said was—and these were his very words—"How will you prove it, Herr Prugate? In law the contract is all that counts. There's nothing in the contract about a ruin." And then he laughed out loud.'

Why was Prugate sweating? Ossi was certain that he was under some pressure. The deal, or the fraud, had taken place more than twenty years ago. Something was not right. But what was it?

She was sitting at her desk and did not look up when he came into the office. They sat in silence for minutes on end.

'I'm sorry,' said Ossi. He was not sorry, but he couldn't stand the silence.

'What did you find out?' asked Carmen.

'I keep wondering about Prugate. He was ripped off a good twenty years ago, or so he believes. And yet he's as angry as if it had been this morning. There's something not right there.'

'Maybe. But some old people are a bit funny. They live in the past. So it could be that something makes him as angry as if it had happened yesterday because in his mind it actually did.'

'That's a roundabout sort of logic,' said Ossi. 'Too complicated for me.'

'That doesn't make it untrue. A thing is not more likely to be false because it's more complex.'

'Now she's going all philosophical on me,' Ossi muttered to himself.

Carmen laughed. 'You curse the fate that put me here at this desk.'

'I curse the fate that killed Ulrike. And any time now I'll be cursing us for going round in circles and just producing crap. It makes me sick.'

Carmen was silent. Then at last she said, 'I'm sorry.'

'What for?'

'The business with Ulrike. You don't show it, but you miss her.'

'Yes.'

'It's not my fault. If it were up to me, Ulrike would still be alive and I'd be on patrol on the Ochsenzoll.'

'Ochsenzoll?'

'Or the Reeperbahn. Would you prefer that?'

* * *

It was as if he were on a pre-set track. Or as if, like a puppet under someone else's control, he were being made to walk the same route over and over again. To Adlerstrasse. Nowhere was the past as close to him as here. The individual is his own past. The past is real, the future just a promise or a threat, depending on circumstances. He was only surprised that so far no one had accosted him. Week after week he stood outside number 17, gazing at it. Strange behaviour, he thought. Somebody ought to notice it. Perhaps they had all known for a long time who he was.

Standing here, he remembered how it had started. It had started right here. Long before that night in November 1938. Two men had appeared, he remembered it clearly. One wore a black uniform, the other a leather coat. The one in the leather coat had been friendly to start with, had sat down at the table in the living room. Kohn recalled quite clearly how his parents had not known at first what to make of the visit, and then had wept. His father had shouted, then wept some more. His mother had sent Leopold to his room. He would never forget the fear in her voice. In his room he stood listening at the door. He understood little of what was said, but it sounded horrible. Suddenly his door was thrown open. The two men burst in and looked around. 'Nice,' said the leather-coated one. 'Very nice indeed.' He went to the window. As he came back towards the door, he trod on the toy car that Leopold's father had given him. A Maybach, red, made of metal. The man seemed not to notice that he had wrecked the car. Leopold was too afraid to say anything. From the living room he could hear his mother sobbing. The two men went into the other room. 'Nice,' said the leather-coated one, 'Really nice.'

'Why are you taking everything away from us?' His mother's voice. Tearful, angry, desperate.

'You'll get good German money for it. Be glad that we aren't just confiscating the house. We've got the right to do that, if we liked. We'll pay you for something that we could just as well have had for free. We're being generous.' Kohn had reconstructed the conversation from remembered scraps. 'We're being generous.' They had said that. 'We're being generous.'

The authorities allocated the Kohns a tiny rented apartment. It was in Schlachterstrasse, near the Grossneumarkt, where other Jews to whom the same thing had happened were also living. Some of the fathers were in the Neuengamme camp.

Kohn could not remember when the idea of sending him to England had first come up. It was after Kristallnacht. His mother heard about the Kindertransport scheme for sending children to England, and lost no time in putting Leopold's name down. 'So that one of us survives, at least,' she said. Leopold didn't understand what she meant. He would see his parents again, why ever shouldn't he?

Chapter twelve

He heard the squeal of the brakes. It hurt when he hit the rails. Somewhere people were screaming; one female voice drowned out all the rest, a soprano of horror. He felt as if he were somewhere else, not lying on the railway tracks. As if through a mist he had seen the train rushing towards him, red, two headlights, above them the windscreen and behind it a ghostly shape, the train driver, Kostas Ionanides. It was to him that Stachelmann owed his survival. He had been paying attention, he was new and still nervous. Stachelmann later learned that Ionanides had listened to other drivers who had run over people, suicides who made you an accomplice and a victim. You can't avoid them, a train takes a long time to stop, hundreds of tons pulling against the brakes. Steel on steel, it's stoppable but there isn't the same braking power as with rubber. The first time Ionanides heard about dead people on the rails he had vowed to keep an even better lookout. He did not want to be woken up by nightmares of body parts, bodies that he had ripped apart. If anyone else had been in the driver's seat, Stachelmann would probably be dead. Later, after he had got over the shock, there were moments when he wished that

Ionanides had been confined to bed with flu that evening. It would have saved him much pain and despair.

The train's leading carriage had stopped only inches from his body—he could have leaned back against it. He looked up at the platform, saw all the eyes fixed upon him and raised one arm. Eventually a man detached himself from the crowd and climbed down on to the track. He was slightly built and had a rucksack on his back. 'Are you alright?' he asked. Stachelmann nodded, and the man helped him to his feet. His right shin hurt, and so did his ribs. He had hit his head, and his hand reddened with blood when he passed it over his forehead. Hands reached down to him. The man on the track pushed, others pulled, and at last Stachelmann was sitting on the platform, with people staring at him. The crowd parted and a woman in a white coat appeared, followed by two men with a stretcher. The woman knelt down. 'How are you feeling?' she asked, as she reached for his hand and took his pulse. She looked at his forehead and waved the two attendants forward. They put the stretcher down beside him. Saying, 'I can manage,' Stachelmann stood up and promptly fainted. When he came to, he was lying in the ambulance with a drip attached to his left arm and the emergency doctor sitting next to him. He looked at her and she smiled. 'So you're back with us,' she said. She reminded him of Anne.

The ambulance was using its siren and blue lights. Then it came to a halt and the door was opened. The two ambulance men pulled the stretcher forward onto a trolley and wheeled him to the hospital entrance, with the emergency doctor walking alongside. He was pushed into a treatment room and lifted on to the examination table. A doctor appeared, shook Stachelmann's hand and murmured something which he did not catch. He examined Stachelmann, speaking quietly, almost to himself. 'Bruising' was all that Stachelmann managed to make out. The other doctor stood by the wall and looked on; now and then her eyes met his. Then she said, 'You've been lucky, nothing serious. All the best.' She opened the door and was gone.

Then a nurse appeared, a large woman of about fifty. She asked: 'Okay?' and took Stachelmann by the arm without waiting for a reply. Saying 'Yes', he walked to a lift, leaning on her arm. Two floors up, she led him into a room. One bed was occupied by a patient who was asleep. Stachelmann lay down on the other.

'Now we need to take your details,' said the nurse.

'I'm privately insured and I'm entitled to a single room.' Stachelmann had raised the level of his insurance when he learned that he had rheumatoid arthritis.

'Your head's obviously getting clearer,' the nurse said, 'if you can think of that sort of thing.'

If I *have* to be in hospital, I'll have the deluxe treatment, Stachelmann thought.

'There is a single room free,' said the nurse. She released the brakes on his bed and wheeled him into a room at the end of the corridor. It had only a wardrobe in it. 'I'll get you a table and chairs, right away,' she said as she went off.

She returned with another nurse, both of them carrying chairs. They left the room and came back again with a table. 'Do you want a television?' asked the other nurse, who had a squeaky voice. Stachelmann shook his head. They both left, shutting the door behind them. Peace reigned.

What had actually happened? He closed his eyes and reflected. He had felt a deliberate push from behind. He had not been accidentally jostled, as sometimes happens. It had been a quick, hard shove with the flat of somebody's hand, intended to propel him onto the tracks, to be run over by the train. Stachelmann imagined what he would have looked like if the train had not stopped in time. 'A miracle!'—he could still hear the exclamation from someone in the crowd. Yes, it was a miracle that he had survived.

Who could have any reason to push him on to the line? A madman? Were there people who killed other people just for fun? Surely not. What would Ockham say, the man with logic's razor? If somebody pushes you, he does it to move you somewhere. Who wants to kill me? Or is it a case of mistaken identity? That must be it: he knew no one who hated him enough to want him dead. Alright, you can't be sure of that, you can't get inside other people's heads. But even allowing for every conceivable exaggeration, he couldn't think of the slightest reason.

As he reached for his mobile phone, he realized that he was wearing hospital pyjamas. He got up and went over to the wardrobe. Inside hung his clothes, all dirtied of course; he had not noticed anyone putting them there. In his jacket pocket he found his mobile, its display screen shattered and difficult to read. He switched on, searched for Ossi's number and called him.

'Murder squad.'

'Can I speak to Kommissar Winter?'

A few seconds elapsed. 'Winter.'

'Ossi, it's me.'

'Hello,' Ossi said. He sounded as if he had been keeping his voice in the freezer.

'Ossi, somebody tried to kill me.'

'What?' He paused. Then he asked, 'Where and how?'

'Friedrichstrasse S-Bahn station, in Berlin. Somebody pushed me on to the rails.'

'You're having me on.'

'No, you idiot. I'm in the Charité Hospital, with bruising and a bump on my face.'

'You're sure it wasn't an accident? Someone not looking where they were going, or kids playing tag, or something?'

'Somebody pushed me with his hand, hard enough to make me fall into the path of a train.'

'Give me your room number.'

Stachelmann stood up, went to the door and opened it, and read the number on the outside. He relayed it to Ossi.

'Aren't my Berlin colleagues on your case yet? They must have been called to the S-Bahn station. Now they probably don't know where the unfortunate victim was taken to. What a shambles! Have they got another state visit going on? I'll put them in the picture and get them to send somebody to take down the details. The things you get up to! When the officer's been, give me another call.' Ossi rang off.

Before long there was a knock at the door, and a uniformed policeman came in. He was fair-haired and very young, with soft features. Far too young for a policeman. 'Good evening, sir. The

Hamburg police have asked me to come and talk to you. They want me to take down some details. I gather someone made an attempt on your life.' His tone was sceptical.

Stachelmann gestured towards a chair, and the policeman sat down, resting a notebook on his knee. He looked at Stachelmann expectantly. If I'd met him in the street I'd have taken him for a schoolboy, Stachelmann thought. Maybe that's the only way we realize we're getting older. His back hurt; he didn't know whether the pain was caused by the fall or his arthritis. He raised himself up slightly in the bed, placing a pillow under his back.

'Yes, somebody pushed me on to the rails at Friedrichstrasse station.'

The policeman made a note. 'Did you see who pushed you?'

'No, how could I have? He did it from behind.'

'You might have turned round as you fell.'

Stachelmann stared at him. 'With or without a pirouette? Or perhaps a triple loop?'

The policeman looked at Stachelmann as though he were from Mars. 'How do you mean?'

'I mean I had other things to think about than trying to see who pushed me. Like not falling on my back. It's instinctive. Only, humans aren't as good at it as cats.'

The policeman chewed his pencil. 'But you're certain you were pushed. Why?'

'Wouldn't you notice if somebody gave you a push in the back? With the flat of the hand, to make sure you fell? Maybe "push" isn't quite the right word, maybe I should say "a firm thrust".'

The policeman chewed his pencil. 'Okay, I'll type up a statement and bring it back for you to sign. So you didn't see who did it.'

'No, I didn't.'

'Is there anybody who did?'

'I don't know.'

The policeman rose to his feet, shook Stachelmann's hand and left. Stachelmann was sure that the young man didn't believe him. He probably thought he was a fantasist. Or that he had just tripped and fallen on to the rails and didn't dare admit it. Stachelmann pulled the pillow out from under his back and put it under his head. The door opened and the doctor appeared with a syringe in his hand. Stachelmann had a horror of injections. The doctor told him to bare his buttocks. The injection was not painful, and in a matter of minutes Stachelmann was asleep.

Next morning he vaguely remembered dreaming. The fat nurse appeared with his breakfast. She was in a cheery mood. 'So how are we today?'

'I don't know how *we* are. *I've* got a headache.'

'Shall I bring you something for it?'

Stachelmann declined the offer. He heard her whistling a tune in the corridor.

The breakfast consisted of rye bread and black bread, a small tub of margarine, miniature pots of jam, and cheese sealed in plastic. There was a steaming mug of tea. He spread himself a slice of bread and strawberry jam and took a sip of tea. He ate three mouthfuls and put the rest of the bread back on the plate.

His head was throbbing, and his ribs were painful when he breathed, a stabbing pain. His back hurt, and felt as though it had set rigid overnight. Cautiously he got out of bed. A white bathrobe was hanging from a hook on the door. As he moved towards it he felt giddy, with pains everywhere. He went back and sat on the edge of the bed. As the giddiness subsided he tried again. This time his circulation seemed to be performing better. He put on the bathrobe and opened the door. In the corridor were other people in bathrobes, some holding infusion bottles. A man in a white coat was hurrying off somewhere. Stachelmann's room was at the end of the corridor. He went to the window and looked down. Rain was falling on a large car park. He moved carefully along the corridor; his legs were obeying him, but the pain was a torment. From one room whose door was not quite shut came the sound of a number of women laughing. The door was marked 'Nursing staff'. He knocked on it and pushed it wider open. Five or six nurses were sitting around a table that was laid with plates and mugs. There was an aroma of coffee. He recognized the fat nurse, who stood up when she saw him. 'Really, Dr Stachelmann,' she said.

Stachelmann asked for a tablet for the pain and a glass of water. After taking the tablet, he continued his peregrinations through the hospital. In a room with a glass door some people were smoking; you could smell it out in the corridor. He saw a man in a dark blue dressing gown with a hip flask in one hand and a cigarette in the other. As Stachelmann turned away he came face to face with a woman who had a catheter, or at any rate she was carrying a bag of pale yellow liquid in her hand. Halfway along the corridor were the stairs and two lifts. One landing down he discovered a green metal door marked 'Emergency Exit'. He descended the stairs and opened the door, which gave on to a concrete stairway. It was dark, but he felt about on the wall until he found a light switch. As he pressed it, dirty stairs showed up in the dim light.

'What do you think you're doing?' The voice behind him was peremptory.

He turned round to find a short, red-haired nurse staring fiercely at him.

'I just wanted a look,' he stammered.

'There's nothing to look at here.'

'Right, fine.' He shut the door and returned to his room. He lay down on the bed. Tomorrow he would discharge himself, regardless of what the doctors said. His door opened and the doctor appeared, accompanied by the fat nurse. Sitting down at the foot of the bed, he said, 'Well now, back on your feet already, Herr Stachelmann?'

Stachelmann nodded. 'What's your diagnosis?'

'You're as fit as a fiddle, as far as I can judge.'

'I have arthritis.'

'That's not our field. Apart from some bruising and the elegant lump on your forehead, you've nothing to worry about.'

Nothing to worry about, thought Stachelmann. That's not true.

'And at all events you're sufficiently recovered to be receiving visitors.'

'He was from the police,' said Stachelmann.

'That's not who the doctor means,' said the nurse.

'That's the only visitor I've had.'

'Because I sent him packing,' said the nurse, making it sound as if she had won a victory.

'Sent who packing?'

'Your father.'

It hit Stachelmann like a punch in the solar plexus. He gasped.

'What's the matter?' she asked.

'Why did you send my father away?'

'I said I'd see whether it was okay just then, but when I looked in you were asleep. I'm sure your father can come back another time. In fact he said he would. He's a very understanding man.'

'How does my father know I'm here?'

'Didn't you tell him? You've got a telephone in the room, and you've got your mobile, too.'

She had evidently gone through his jacket pockets. Had Ossi told his father? There was no reason why he should have. Ossi didn't know his father, nor where he lived, or even whether he was still alive.

'What did my father look like?'

'How can I describe him?' the nurse pondered.

The doctor interrupted her. 'Herr Stachelmann, I'd like to keep you in for another two or three days. Just for observation.' He left.

'What did he look like?' Stachelmann persisted.

'Oh dear, I'm not good at describing people. I probably see too many of them.' She hesitated. 'White hair, with the ends coming down over his ears. And he was wearing a grey jacket, a bit old-fashioned, the way old people's clothes tend to be. Oh yes, and he must just be back from his holidays, he looked very fit and brown.' The nurse went away.

It was the man he had seen yesterday. On the S-Bahn train, he had been in the same carriage as Stachelmann. And he had also noticed him on the platform at the Friedrichstrasse station. Obviously there were other men who wore grey jackets, but his father was not among them. Nor did he have hair reaching down over his ears. And he certainly didn't have a tan.

His mobile rang. It was Ossi, who still sounded distinctly cool. 'I've just had a call from an officer in Berlin. They can't do much, I'm afraid. Are you sure you didn't see anybody who might have pushed you?'

Stachelmann reflected, then decided not to say anything about the man in the jacket. Ossi was already angry with him, and he didn't want to give him a reason to laugh at him as well. If Ossi was dismissing the murder attempt as fantasy, a tale about an omnipresent old man would only confirm him in that opinion. 'No,' said Stachelmann, 'I didn't see anybody.'

'Well, there's nothing to be done, then. Take care. Cheers.' Ossi hung up without waiting for an answer.

Stachelmann spent the rest of the day in bed, with his eyes closed, thinking things over. The nurse brought him his supper. Outside the sun was shining, and its rays were dazzling. Lunch had been a stew; now the tray was laid with slices of bread, sausage and cheese. A steaming pot of tea had a healthy smell but tasted foul. Instead of eating, Stachelmann closed his eyes again and continued to think. For the first time his belief struck him as mad. Perhaps people were right after all to think him crazy. Why should anyone try to push him in front of a train? There was no reason. Looking at it the other way round, though, if somebody *had* pushed him in front of the train, that person must have had a reason, unless he was out of his mind and took delight in killing other people. That was possible, but it would not be reasonable to assume it. Ockham's razor again. The only person who would push him into the path of a train was someone who intended to do it and had a motive. Unless it was a case of mistaken identity. That was a possibility, though it was again one that William of Ockham's blade would cut away. No, somebody was intent on killing him, and that person had his reasons. That was the best assumption to work on. (And if it actually was a case of mistaken identity, so much the better.) He needed to discover the motive. Nothing occurred to him immediately. Then he remembered the two men at the Archive. They had behaved very strangely and had commandeered the very files that he had wanted. Hamburg Finance Department my foot, thought

Stachelmann. The period of limitation had expired for anything like that. Unless the finance authorities were being driven by bad conscience. But since when did authorities have a conscience? Perhaps it was something to do with GDR property? But then they were looking in the wrong files. If those two were involved in the attempt to kill him, what was the role of the old fellow in the grey jacket?

If there *was* a motive for killing him, why should one suppose that that motive no longer existed? On the contrary, it made sense to assume that someone out there still wanted to see him dead— him, the historian without prospects. The man who had claimed to be his father was clearly a liar and was probably a murderer, too. He had come with the intention of killing Stachelmann. Friedrichstrasse station had been an ideal location. But so was the hospital, which was full of people coming and going. All the killer had to do was to choose a moment when bystanders' attention was diverted to something happening in another room.

What conclusion could he draw from all these assumptions that seemed so logical and yet might be false? If he wanted to stay alive, he must not stay in the hospital. He must get out of there, that very night. He had had one lucky escape. And yet perhaps it was all nonsense. Perhaps I really am nuts, he thought. But if you rely on probabilities for your survival, you're dead. He felt no fear because it all seemed so unreal. He saw himself as an actor in a film. He could not help laughing. This is me, the failure, terrified of a pile of documents and destined to end up sleeping underneath a bridge, and I'm the one somebody wants to bump off? He thought of Hornblower, who was plagued by self-doubt but did not let that prevent him from taking brave decisions. To learn from him meant learning how to win. Stachelmann laughed, but then fear *did* creep into his body, invading his guts and rising up to grip first his heart and then his mind. Sitting on the edge of the bed, he could see his hands shaking.

He made his decision. He waited until it was dark outside, then switched off the light in his room and looked out of the window. The car park was only dimly lit, but watching carefully, he picked up on some movement. There was an asphalt path, fringed by bushes, which led from the car park to one of the hospital entrances. A bush had stirred, even though there was no wind. He kept his eyes fixed on the bush, but nothing more happened. A bird or a cat, long gone. He let his gaze sweep to and fro. A car arrived and parked, and a woman got out. Stachelmann went out into the corridor and pretended to be taking a stroll, paying close attention to whatever activity was going on. Gradually everything quietened down. Now and then a nurse would hurry along the corridor and vanish into a room where a small light was showing above the door.

He went back to his room and waited until after midnight. Then he put his clothes on. In his wallet, which was in his back trouser pocket, he found a little over two hundred marks and his credit card. Cautiously he opened the door and looked out into the corridor, which was empty. It would take him less than a minute to reach the emergency exit by the stairs. He slipped out of his room and walked rapidly towards the stairwell. The door to the nurses' room was slightly ajar and he could hear two women talking. At all costs he must not run. He reached the stairs. One of the lift bells sounded and the light went on above the lift door. It would open at any moment. Stachelmann leaped down the stairs two at a time, to the half-landing with the emergency exit. On the last stair but one he slipped and fell heavily on his tail bone, suppressing a cry of pain. Sitting there on the landing he looked upwards. Out of the lift stepped a man with white hair and a grey jacket, who started walking towards Stachelmann's room. Stachelmann ducked down, and as soon as the man was out of sight he got to his feet and hobbled to the emergency exit. The man would discover very quickly that Stachelmann was not in his room. Either he would wait there, which was risky, because someone other than Stachelmann might appear at any moment. Or he would leave the hospital, probably the same way he had come.

Stachelmann was ahead, enough to enable him to find a temporary refuge. Some hotel, under a false name. No one would find him tonight. Unless the man wasn't working alone but had accomplices who might follow him. Stachelmann didn't see anybody as he left the hospital via the emergency exit. Standing on an expanse of lawn, he heard a car being started up in the car park round the corner. He hid behind a bush, but the car did not come past him. Creeping along beside the wall of the building, away from the car park, he came to a corner and looked cautiously round it. There was the main entrance. He stood still and waited. Everything was fairly quiet. After about a quarter of an hour a man emerged from the hospital and walked out on to Luisenstrasse, his hair shining white under the entrance lights. Stachelmann set off in pursuit. I'm crazy, was the thought that kept echoing in his mind, but his legs kept going. His quarry walked along the street towards the Zinnowitzer Strasse underground station, without haste or any backward glances. He went down the steps to the underground. Stachelmann followed, but kept his distance. When the man reached the platform, Stachelmann waited behind a pillar. An elderly woman walking towards him eyed his clothes critically. Looking down at himself, he realized that they were covered in dirt from his fall on to the rails. A train came. The man did not get on until everybody had got out. Stachelmann took care to stay outside his field of vision, and got on the train one carriage ahead of him. He sat at the front of the carriage, from where he could keep an eye on the platform and see where the man got out. The route map on the inside of the carriage told him that he was on route U6. When the next stop proved to be Oranienburger Tor he knew that the train was heading for Alt-Mariendorf. At the Friedrichstrasse underground station he saw the man on the platform. He was hurrying towards the exit for Pariser Platz. Stachelmann quickly got off the train and followed him. He continued to tail him as he walked briskly towards the Brandenburg Gate, past the entrance to the Russian Embassy where two policemen were patrolling, and into the Hotel Adlon. Approaching the hotel doors and looking through the glass, Stachelmann saw him at reception being given a room key. Then he moved out of sight, probably going to the lifts. Cautiously Stachelmann entered the foyer. Something's certainly got into you, he thought. He looked round and then stepped up to the reception desk. An expensively suited hotel receptionist examined him, his face impassive.

'Hello. Could you tell me the name of the gentleman who just collected his key?'

The receptionist looked at him; Stachelmann had forgotten what a state his clothes were in. 'I am not able to give you that information. But if you would care to leave a message, I will have it delivered to the gentleman at once.'

Stachelmann took a fifty mark note from his wallet and laid it on the counter.

The receptionist gave him a reproving look. 'Sir, this is the Hotel Adlon.'

Stachelmann put the banknote away and left the foyer. Once outside he checked to make sure the man in the grey jacket wasn't following him, and decided to head for the Mitte district. He dared not go back to Haus Morgenland: he would only be safe somewhere where he could register under a false name. As he passed the Humboldt University, the base of his spine and his knees were hurting. On Karl Liebknecht Strasse he turned left towards Spandauer Brücke. He found a cash machine and withdrew a thousand marks. Now and then he looked round, but saw nothing. He turned off into a side street and waited a few seconds. Then he swung round, but no one was in sight. There was a sound of breaking glass. He gave a start and looked in the direction from which the noise had come. A man was staggering past on a woman's arm. She was shouting at him, while he mumbled incoherently.

Stachelmann walked on, without knowing where he was going. He was tired and hungry, and had lost his bearings. His knees would not hold out much longer; at one point he almost went over on his ankle. At the end of a narrow street he saw a red neon sign flashing on and off, and headed towards it. It read 'Hotel Elvira'; the tubes in the second L and the R had gone and were not flashing with the rest. The door was open. Stachelmann climbed the three front steps. A man was sitting at the counter, fast asleep. Behind him hung two rows of keys, one above the other, with brass-coloured tags attached. Stachelmann banged on the counter. The fellow was snoring and stank of schnapps. Stachelmann banged harder, and he opened his eyes and blinked. Then he yawned, producing an even stronger reek of spirits. He ran his fingers through his hair, reached round behind him, took a key and laid it on the counter. From under the counter he fished out two threadbare-looking towels. 'Room 16, first floor. Three hundred marks in advance,' he said. 'For that you can sleep on until tomorrow morning.' He looked past Stachelmann, towards the door. 'Where's the lovely lady?' he asked.

Stachelmann counted out three hundred marks onto the counter and climbed the stairs. When he found the room, he went in and lay down on the bed. The intermittent blinking of the neon sign flashed in through the window. He lay on his back, exhausted and aching, unable either to think clearly or to fall asleep. The continuous hum of the city permeated the room.

He had, after all, fallen asleep at last. When he woke up, a pair of black eyes were staring at him. 'You get up, end of night,' said the woman, who was wearing a light blue headscarf. She glanced at the towels lying beside him and shook her head. Getting up, he viewed himself in the mirror above the washbasin, which must once have been white. He looked at his clothes, and could understand the Turkish woman's reaction. She was running her feather duster over the chair and bedside table. A person who had spent a night alone in a brothel, lying on the bed in filthy clothes, must be wrong in the head. There had been pity in the woman's eyes.

'Would you like to earn two hundred marks?' Stachelmann asked her.

She laughed. 'I cleaner, should I call other lady?'

Stachelmann shook his head. He pointed to her, took two hundred-mark notes from his purse and held them out to her.

She gave him a stern look. 'I not whore.'

Stachelmann got scared. If he made her angry, he'd be in the soup. 'No, no.' He pointed to the bed and made a gesture of negation. 'Something else, just helping me.'

The woman looked at him.

Stachelmann pointed to his clothes. 'I need a clean shirt, and trousers, underwear and socks.'

'I should buy?'

'No, they are at my hotel.'

She did not understand. It was indeed unfathomable that Stachelmann should wake up in one hotel and have his clothes in another.

He wondered whether to give her money for a taxi. He decided not to, she might attract attention getting out of a taxi. And it might occur to her to demand more from him if he gave the impression of being too free with his money. He gave her his room key from Haus Morgenland. She would finish her work at the Hotel Elvira and then go straight to Lichterfelde and bring back a change of clothes from his room there.

'You write me paper,' she said.

At first he did not grasp what she meant, but then he nodded. She left the room and returned with a notepad and a pen. He asked her name, and then wrote that Aisha Yüksel had his authority to fetch some clothes on his behalf, and that he had given her his room key for that purpose. He signed the statement and handed her the piece of paper. He warned her only to show the paper in the hotel, and even then only if she was asked to do so. Often, he knew, there was nobody on the reception desk and Aisha might manage to slip in and collect his things without being noticed. Then he could be sure that she was not being followed and leading the murderer to him.

'Maintenance?' Aisha asked.

Stachelmann shook his head. 'I had a girlfriend,' he said. 'Unfortunately I didn't know that she was married.'

Aisha made a sympathetic face, 'She not told you?'

Again he shook his head.

'That sad.'

He nodded.

'And now husband of girlfriend after you?'

Stachelmann drew his hand horizontally across his throat.

'He do better kill girlfriend. Girlfriend lie.'

He shrugged.

They agreed to meet that afternoon at two. Aisha left to finish her work. Stachelmann went down to reception. This time there was a younger man sitting there, with brown hair that was thinning at the temples. He was studying a magazine full of pictures of naked women.

'I need to keep the room until about three o'clock,' Stachelmann said.

The man nodded and said, 'Three hundred marks in advance, including towels.'

Stachelmann laid three one-hundred mark notes on the countertop. This trip to Berlin was proving to be expensive.

His mobile rang. He pressed to accept the call, and heard: 'Anne here, where are you?'

Stachelmann started up the stairs. 'In the hotel.'

'I thought you were working in the Archive. I suppose you've decided to go for the nightlife instead.'

'Absolutely,' he replied. 'That's my real reason for being in Berlin. But you didn't want to come.' Fear of the killer had blown away his shyness. He surprised himself. Everything seemed crystal clear.

'Aha,' said Anne. 'And what's the name of the establishment where you spent the night?'

'I believe it's called the Hotel Elvira. It's pretty sleazy. Three hundred marks a bed, towels included.'

Anne was silent.

Then she said, 'You're having me on.'

'Not at all. How's the Legend?'

'Tell me, that stuff about the Hotel Elvira is just a joke, isn't it?'

'No, I prowled about half the night and ended up sleeping here. And now I'm waiting for a Turkish cleaning woman to fetch me some clean clothes from my hotel in Lichterfelde.' He was pleased that she seemed jealous. He could hear her breathing. 'The night before that I spent in hospital. This isn't a research trip, I'm having an adventure holiday in Berlin.'

'Start again from the beginning. I don't understand any of this.' She sounded worried.

He gave her a brief outline of events.

'Why don't you go to the police?'

'Actually, they came to *me*. They don't believe a word I say.'

'What about Ossi?'

'He doesn't, either.'

Anne said nothing for a few moments. 'Shall I come?'

'I thought Bohming was using you to build up his legend even more.'

'And how. But it could always happen that my grandmother becomes terminally ill.'

'Grandmothers do sometimes have their uses.' He was touched by Anne's offer, but she couldn't help him in this. 'No, it's nice of you, but I'd rather be murdered on my own.' He made an effort to laugh, as though he had made a joke. The fear kicked in again.

'As you like, but the offer still stands.' She sounded disappointed.

'No, it'll be enough if you come to the funeral.'

She hung up.

Stachelmann stared at his mobile and cursed himself. There were times when he was just trying to be funny but ended up hurting someone's feelings. For a few moments he thought of phoning Anne back, but then he decided not to. It would be better if she stayed in Hamburg. Back in his room now, he lay down on the bed and stared at the ceiling. In one corner hung two spiders, small bodies, long legs, not moving, their web shimmering in the light. He christened them Amalie and Alberta. He closed his eyes and pondered. Weird things had happened to him in Berlin. His would-be killer was staying at the Adlon. He could have led the police to him, at any rate as far as the hotel foyer, and they could have waited there until he appeared. Of course the man would have denied everything, and Stachelmann had no evidence against him. The fact that he had turned up at the hospital? He'd have been sure to have a good explanation. Or he would just have denied it. Or said nothing, and the magistrate would have had to let him go. There was nothing, nothing at all, against him, except for Stachelmann's conviction that the man was out to kill him. He cursed his fear. Hornblower would have been just as afraid, but would not have let his fear get such a grip on him.

He went down to reception and got the porter to fetch him a classified telephone directory. Under the heading 'Personal Security' he found a number of entries, and opted for 'Meyer, Personal Protection and Information-gathering'. He dialed the firm's number. It was answered by a woman with a screechy voice and a thick Berlin accent. Stachelmann heard her shout, 'Gustav, c'mere, a job.' Stachelmann hung up.

He would have to clear up the affair by himself. He could afford a bodyguard for a few days, perhaps a couple of weeks, but then he would be broke. He lay down again on the bed. Amalie had crawled a few inches towards the wall, while Alberta was still just hanging idly on the ceiling. Spiders, too, had different personalities. He opened the window, hoping that some flies and mosquitoes would get caught in the web. Then he fell asleep. In his dream, he vainly tried to run away from a monster that was snapping at him with drooling jaws. His shoulder was being shaken; it wasn't the monster but Aisha, who had returned with a shopping bag. She put it down by his feet and said, 'Nobody see me. Hotel empty.' She pointed to the bag. 'Put in toothbrush also and comb. Bag you can keep.'

Stachelmann got to his feet, shook her by the hand and gave her the two hundred marks. When she had gone, he showered and put on fresh clothes, brushed his teeth and felt much better. He put the dirty clothes into Aisha's bag and went downstairs. When he laid the key on the counter, the receptionist did not even look up from his magazine. By the time he was out on the street, his depression had evaporated. He went to the nearest underground station, Turmstrasse, and after two changes arrived at Lichterfelde-Süd. The trains were crowded. Stachelmann was free of pain, and was savouring these few hours before it would inevitably return.

Reaching the Archive, he went into the cloakroom and locked his shopping bag away. Then he approached the entrance to the reading room. Through the glass door he could see the two men from the Hamburg Finance Department. They had their backs to him, and were busy reading documents. He entered the reading room, caught sight of Bender and beckoned him out to the corridor. Bender gave him a questioning look, but then came over.

'Herr Bender, how much longer are those two going to be here in the Archive?'

'Until this evening, Herr Carsten told me.'

'After that, can I see all the files they've been reading?'

'Well, no, at least not the ones they want copied. They're in a hurry and their needs are being given top priority.' Bender seemed angry. The two men were probably getting on his nerves. Special requests. Officials hate special requests.

'What if you let me take a quick look? After all, the stuff can't all be copied at once, if there's so much of it.'

'That's true, but the documents are going to be copied by a firm that will be collecting them all this evening.' He looked sternly at Stachelmann. 'What do you actually want them for?'

'To be honest, I don't exactly know. My fear is that those two are looking for the same thing as me. But they probably have a better idea of what it is. In any case, I very much doubt that they're really from the Finance Department.'

Bender's jaw dropped. Then he demanded, 'Whatever makes you think that? I was even phoned by someone from the Hamburg Finance Senator's office. Really, Dr Stachelmann, if we hadn't known each other for so long…' He returned to the reading room without completing his sentence.

Stachelmann left the Archive building and went to the library in the former chapel of the cadet school. He sat down, at a little distance from two other men who were reading, and considered what to do. It seemed impossible to get hold of the documents that the pair from Hamburg were studying. He toyed with the idea of luring them out of the reading room with a telephone call, but they would return the files to the issue desk before leaving the room to accept a call. In a few weeks' time he might be able to discover, with the aid of the borrowing slip attached to each file, what it was that they were interested in. For that he would need to know both their names, of course, but Bender would give him that information as soon as they had left for Hamburg. But Stachelmann was too impatient to wait that long—besides, it was not certain that the same borrowing slips would still be on the files when he saw them again. And he couldn't *afford* to wait that long. If those two had something to do with the killer, he would have to reckon with another attack. He still could not understand why they should attack him, but he might discover a motive in the documents that were going to be taken away for copying this evening. He had memorized some of the reference numbers. He needed to find the files. And then, in a flash, he knew where.

* * *

They sat facing each other. Ossi lit a cigarette, and Carmen pulled a face. 'All this smoking is really foul,' she said.

'I haven't improved in that respect. Ulrike hated it, too. But she was tolerant enough to put up with it.'

'And let herself be poisoned by you? Passive smoking is almost more unhealthy than doing it yourself.'

'We'll argue about that later.' Ossi took a sheet from the file lying in front of him and read aloud: 'Helmut Fleischer, sold his business to Holler in 'seventy-five. Norbert Enheim, sold in 'seventy-six, murdered by person unknown. Karl Markwart, sold in 'seventy-six, died three years ago of lung cancer.'

Carmen shot him a reproachful look. 'Probably shared a room with a smoker.'

Ossi brushed that aside. 'Otto Grothe, sold up in 'seventy-eight, is now a dithery old man. And a non-smoker, so he's got every chance of dying a brave death from some other cause. I've spoken to Grothe, and I don't see how he can get us any further. Otto Prugate is hiding something. He also sold up in 'seventy-eight. Johann-Peter Meier, sold up in 'seventy-nine and is still alive. Where?' Ossi leafed through the file. 'That's right, in Dockenhuden. We need to pay him a visit—unannounced. Ferdinand Meiser sold up in 'eighty and is buried at Ohlsdorf.'

Carmen looked at him enquiringly.

'That's the main cemetery. Gottlob Ammann, sold up in 'eighty-one, still alive. I think that's the lot. I'll suggest to Taut that somebody should go through the companies register to see whether Holler bought up any other firms.'

'The companies register covers the last four decades. That's slave labour. I bet I'll be the one saddled with it.'

Ossi grinned. 'If you're nice to me, that could be avoided.'

'I thought only other countries had corrupt cops.'

'No, No. You get them everywhere, it's a sort of international club.'

'And you're the big boss.'

'You flatter me. The big boss is always the most corrupt. I'm working on it, but I've got some way to go before I can beat the competition in Russia or South America.'

'Keep at it, you'll get there,' said Carmen.

'Right then, Ammann and Meier,' Ossi resumed. 'We'll get hold of them this afternoon. And while we're busy stirring things up on the property dealing scene, I'll give Taut a call and get him to let somebody loose on the companies register.'

'And then you'll have me in the palm of your hand.'

'Absolutely,' said Ossi.

Meier lived in a spacious villa in Dockenhuden, not far from the Elb-chaussee. In front of his house stood a black Mercedes, the current s Class model. Recessed into the white housefront was a black door with a brass knocker that Carmen banged vigorously a number of times. Before long the door was slowly opened by a tall, thin, black-suited manservant. 'Yes?' he said.

'We would like to speak to Herr Meier.'

'Herr Meier zu Riebenschlag.'

Ossi looked at Carmen. She was trying not to laugh. 'That's right—Herr Meier,' he repeated, holding up his police warrant before the butler's eyes.

The butler's face twitched almost imperceptibly. 'If you would care to follow me.' He led the way into a room that was supposed to be a library. The walls were lined with old books, many of them leather-bound. Ossi glanced at a few of their spines. 'All antiquated stuff,' he said. 'Ranke, Freytag. I ought to pinch them and give them to Stachelmann.'

'Stachelmann?' Carmen asked. 'Is that your historian pal?'

'You've cottoned on to that, too, have you? There's no keeping anything from you, is there, little Miss Nosy. Yes, that's my histo-rian pal. He gets weird ideas sometimes. The latest thing is that he fell in front of a train in Berlin, and now he thinks somebody's out to kill him.'

'Sounds like a fun character, I must meet him some time.'

'You've got very odd taste.'

'I'm sure he isn't as boring as you are.'

Before Ossi could answer, the door opened. A tall man came into view, straight-backed, with wiry, short hair and hard, sharply defined features. He wore white trousers, a short-sleeved white shirt and a red sweater, all expensive-looking. He stopped a few steps away from Ossi and Carmen and said, 'You are from the police?'

'Murder Squad,' Ossi replied, and introduced Carmen and himself.

The man made no comment.

'You are Johann-Peter Meier?' asked Carmen.

'I am Johann-Peter Meier zu Riebenschlag.'

'Until nineteen seventy-nine you owned a property dealing company, which you directed under the name of Meier.'

Meier nodded.

'Since when have you been calling yourself Meier zu Riebenschlag?'

'I do not *call* myself that, that is my name. I was adopted in nineteen eighty-three by Herr zu Riebenschlag.'

'Why?' Carmen could not disguise her astonishment.

'Has it anything to do with your enquiry about my company?'

'What did you pay Herr *zu* Riebenschlag to be able to bear his name?'

Meier looked at her disdainfully.

'Why did you sell up in 'seventy-nine?'

'I would not have sold if Holler had not been keen to buy. He pressed me and then threatened me. He clung to me like a burr. I couldn't shake him off. By the time I came into the office each morning, he would have already driven my secretary to distraction or filled up all the tape on my answering machine.'

'You sold up because Holler was getting on your nerves?'

'Yes.'

'I can't understand that,' said Ossi.

'Very possibly not,' replied Meier. His tone was bored, condescending.

'And after the sale Holler forced you to pay back part of the sale price to him.'

Meier gave Ossi a look of surprise. 'One could see it that way,' he said.

'You mean you returned part of the sale price voluntarily? I don't understand.'

'Possibly not.'

'Herr Meier, we're investigating a murder. So our inclination to let ourselves be trifled with is rather limited. Perhaps you'll answer our questions now, and that can be the end of it. We could of course meet again at police headquarters if that suits you better.' Carmen's tone was at least as superior and condescending as Meier's had been.

'A murder?'

'Several murders, in fact,' said Ossi. He marveled at Carmen's quick-change skills.

'If you notify me of your wish to interview me, you must use my proper name. Otherwise I shall not come.'

'Herr Meier zu Riebenschlag, we don't want to play games. Above all, we have no time for them. If you continue to avoid giving us proper answers, we will have to assume that you are in some way implicated in our case. That being so, perhaps we should apply for a warrant to search this house straight away. You are not short of staff to clear up afterwards.'

Ossi had let Carmen proceed in her own way, but she was on thin ice here. There was not a shred of suspicion against Meier, and even a charge of concealing a felony would be ridiculed by the state prosecutor. However, her ploy might possibly have the desired effect on Meier.

Meier turned to Ossi. 'He found things to object to.'

'Holler did?'

Meier nodded vigorously, his hair bobbing up and down against his forehead. The roots were brown.

'What sort of things?'

'He claimed that the portfolio of clients was not as good as promised, and a few other things. He said I had made promises to people that he had to accept liability for after the sale.'

'What, for instance?'

'He showed me a contract I had agreed to with a house owner, an exclusive contract, by which I had committed myself to selling the house within a certain period of time.'

'And if you had failed, you would have had to pay him compensation?'

'Yes, but the house is on Harvestehuder Weg, by the Alster. The chance to handle the sale of such a property is like winning the lottery.'

'And that's why a dealer would sign a contract like that?'

Meier shrugged. 'What else can you do? I would have managed it alright. But Holler said I had failed to mention the contract to him and that under the penalty clause he had had to pay a hundred and fifty thousand marks. I don't know if he actually paid it. He did sell the house, though, just a few weeks after coming down so hard on me.'

'You feel he took you for a ride?'

'The swine cheated me, that's the truth. Only I can't prove it.'

'You're the third person to allude to that particular animal. The last one put it even more strongly.'

Meier was taken aback, but then grinned. 'I'm not surprised. I hate to think just how many people he's conned.' His eyes rested on Carmen, then Ossi, then again on each of them in turn. 'Ah, I see. You expect to find the murderer of Holler's daughter among the people Holler has defrauded.'

Ossi looked searchingly at him. 'Would you look anywhere else?'

'No, that's exactly where I'd look myself. It wasn't me, though. I will admit that my sympathy is not unbounded, but it shouldn't have been the daughter who was killed.'

'If you didn't do it, who did?' demanded Carmen. 'You've just described to us what your motive would be. Plenty of murders are committed for half the motive that you have.'

'Well, yes, I might have done it, and the swine would have deserved it, too, but I'm wealthy enough not to worry about money I've lost. Now and then I read in the papers about Holler's generosity, everything from Bread for the World to Amnesty, and then there are these extraordinary murders in his family. Why should I join in the killing? There's enough without me adding to it.'

The door opened and a young blonde woman entered the library. She wore a tight blouse and equally close-fitting trousers. 'Excuse me, chéri,' she said. 'Will you be needing the Porsche today?'

'It's in for servicing, my love. Didn't I tell you?' Meier asked in a sickly-sweet tone.

'No, you didn't,' she said huffily, and stalked out.

'That guy's a complete phony,' Carmen pronounced. 'Did you see that he's dyed his hair white? That's weird. And the floozy was straight out of Hollywood. Meier zu Riebenschlag!' She emphasized each word and chuckled. 'What a great job we have! We meet types that would never cross an ordinary person's path. But admit it, you fancied the floozy.'

'Oh, absolutely, chérie,' said Ossi. 'She's got everything in the right places.'

'Chauvinist pig,' said Carmen.

'I'll show you how nice I am.' He got out his phone, dialed and waited. 'Hi, Werner. I want you to send somebody to look at the register of companies. All of Holler's acquisitions and sales of companies since nineteen seventy.' Ossi listened for a few moments, then said, 'No, I need her here. We're doing the rounds of Holler's victims.' He listened again. 'No, really, she can't right now. What's that? The taxi drivers? You've found one? That makes two pieces of good news. One, we've got a witness, and two, Kamm and Kurz are free to tackle the companies register.' Ossi grinned and hung up.

'Say thank you,' he said.

'Thank you,' said Carmen. 'And what were you grinning at?'

'I'm a very cheerful person.'

'You've kept it well hidden up to now.'

'A police officer has to be equal to all sorts of challenges. You'll learn that in time. Oh yes, they've found a taxi driver who's had our man in the grey jacket in his cab. We'll call in at headquarters and then go and have a cosy chat with Herr Ammann.'

* * *

The newspaper lay open on the kitchen table. On the local page there was a picture of Enheim. Kohn sat on his chair, staring at the photograph. The face was unfamiliar, but he knew the name, from a time far back in the past. 'Those people are worse than vultures,' he could hear his father saying, his voice trembling with fury and despair. 'And one of the worst is Enheim.' One of the worst of them was Enheim: why had his father said that? His father bore no hatred against anyone, he was a timid and polite man. Kohn did not know, or did not remember, what his father had meant. He could just have let the matter rest—Enheim had probably deserved to die, had deserved a cruel death and the fear preceding it—but he grew restless. He put on his jacket, folded the newspaper and tucked it into his inside pocket. He set out for the Jewish Centre in Schäferkampsallee. There were still old people around who might know the name. Enheim.

On the way to the Centre he remembered Goldblum, whom he had not seen in a long while. They had never called each other by their first names, always by their surnames, yet they were on terms of close familiarity. Goldblum had helped Kohn on his return from England. He had shown him how to lodge a claim for compensation with the finance authorities, even though nothing might come of it. He had found Kohn a lawyer who knew his way around the jungle of the compensation and restitution legislation. If anyone had information on Enheim, it would be Goldblum. And if *he* didn't have any, he would know someone who did.

Goldblum had let Kohn into his secret. In his cellar he had a crate of plastic explosive and a packet of potassium cyanide. The explosive was from England, he had bought it on the black market, just as he had the poison, straight after the war. You could get anything you wanted on the black market then. There were plenty of soldiers who couldn't resist the temptation: they stole army property and got phenomenal prices for it. It had been a British soldier who had offered the plastic explosive for sale. Goldblum had paid with a diamond necklace that had belonged to his mother, who had been gassed. 'I can blow up a few of them with this. It gives you a good feeling. If I catch up with one of those out-and-out Nazis who were "just doing their duty", I'll shove a hundred grams of explosive under his backside. Just imagine, Kohn, on New Year's Eve. That'd be a sight worth seeing.'

But Goldblum had never actually put on his New Year's Eve firework display. Many Jews could not sleep without tranquillizers because they felt guilty for having survived. Goldblum's tranquillizer was the plastic explosive. The knowledge that he could use it at any time gave him strength.

As for the poison, a leading Nazi had sold it to him when he saw that he need not fear execution. Goldblum had heard that some Jews had tried to poison German war criminals in a prison camp in Nuremberg. They had sneaked into the bakery that supplied bread for the camp, but the doses of arsenic they'd used had been inadequate, and the former masters of life or death had spewed their guts up, but that was all. That leading Nazi was now a big noise in the management of the port of Hamburg; the cyanide lay unused in Goldblum's cellar.

Goldblum had told Kohn about the poison and the explosive. So one day Kohn had surreptitiously got hold of the cellar key and had a copy made, and had gone down into the cellar and helped himself to what he needed. Goldblum had not noticed, or possibly had chosen not to notice. Sometimes Kohn even thought that Goldblum had been inviting him to make use of the stuff in the cellar, not directly, but by means of hints.

Later he had lost touch with Goldblum, who had grown more and more taciturn and was often in a world of his own, staring at nothing in particular. The last Kohn had heard was that Goldblum had moved.

In the secretarial office at the Jewish Centre sat a grey-haired woman wearing silver-rimmed spectacles. She gave Kohn a friendly look.

'Good morning. I'm trying to find Herr Goldblum, I'm afraid I don't know his first name. He's an old man, my age.'

'Well, there aren't many Goldblums here nowadays, so we can find out some details if he's registered with us.' She went over to a filing cabinet and leafed through the file cards. 'Yes, here he is,' she said. 'We have only one gentleman of that name, at any rate.'

'So he's still alive.'

'Certainly,' she said. 'You understand, though, that I can't give you Herr Goldblum's address just like that. You'd have to have a very good reason.'

'He helped me, many years ago, when I came back here from England.'

She scrutinized him. 'I believe I know you. You're Herr Kohn, aren't you?'

Kohn nodded. He vaguely remembered a woman who had assigned returners to lodgings and families.

'You and I also met at that time. I was involved in helping people who had been sent away under the Kindertransport scheme. It's very nice to see you again. What a pity you didn't keep in touch with us.'

'I'm sorry,' Kohn said.

'No, no, don't worry about it. I don't think Herr Goldblum will mind if I give you his address.' She looked at the file card. 'He's a resident at the "Indian Summer" home for the elderly in Niendorf. I'm afraid his state of health isn't very good.' She wrote down the address of the home. 'Perhaps I should phone them in advance.'

Kohn nodded.

She picked up the receiver and dialed a number. When someone answered, she asked, 'Could I speak to Herr Goldblum, please? Oh, I see, that's not possible. Well, would you tell him that Herr Kohn is coming to visit him? Fine.' She put the phone down. 'Herr Goldblum isn't well, but you can visit him.'

Kohn took the piece of paper with the address, thanked her and left. The residential home was on Pommernweg. It was only a few stops on the underground to Niendorf Nord. As he walked to the underground station he grumbled quietly to himself. The rain was soaking through his jacket and he could feel the dampness on his skin.

The home had once been an imposing turn-of-the-century villa. The door was locked, so he rang the bell. After a few moments the door opened and he found a tall, fat man staring at him with protuberant eyes.

'Good morning, I should like to see Herr Goldblum,' said Kohn.

'Room eleven,' the man replied, pointing to the stairs.

Kohn stepped inside, and the door was closed behind him. The stair carpet was worn. Room 11 was on the second floor. On the corridor wall hung an aerial photograph of a shoreline. The brown paint on the doors was cracking in places. Plaintive cries emanated from one of the rooms. Kohn knocked on the door of room 11. There was no response. He cautiously pressed down the handle, opened the door slightly and peered into the room. A bed, a washbasin, a table and two chairs were visible in the dim light that entered through brownish windowpanes. Even with the sun shining it wouldn't look much better, Kohn thought. Only when he opened the door to its full width did he see Goldblum, who was sitting in an armchair behind the door, a stick grasped in his hand as though he were about to strike a blow with it. Two strands of white hair hung down over his forehead; apart from that he was bald. A hooked nose seemed to thrust itself towards Kohn.

'What do you want?'

'It's Kohn, I've come to see you. I need to talk to you.'

Goldblum shut his eyes, opened them again immediately and said 'Don't get the idea that I'm not on my guard.' Then he stared at the wall. 'Kohn,' he mused. 'I've known a few Kohns in my time. Some went to the gas chambers. One came back from England. You're the one from England. I helped you. You think I'm an old fool. I'm old and slow, but I'm no fool. The people from the Jewish Centre lured me into coming here, with promises that they didn't keep afterwards. Liars, all of them. But I'll get out of here. I didn't give up my own home even though they put a lot of pressure on me. They told me exactly how much money I'd save if I didn't have to pay the rent anymore. But they haven't got me to that point yet. I'm old, but I'm not an old fool who can be ordered about. The last people to throw me out of my home were Adolf's lot. And they *were* the last.' He laughed like a goat. 'Come here, Kohn, sit down, pull up a chair. You won't have come just to keep me amused. That would be taking gratitude too far.'

Kohn took a chair and sat down facing Goldblum.

'Come closer, Kohn,' he said.

Moving the chair nearer, Kohn could smell the old man's foul breath.

'Do you know somebody called Enheim?'

Goldblum burst out laughing. 'I read about it in the paper. He's dead, murdered. I'd have danced for joy if I were still capable of dancing. I hope he suffered before he died.'

'Who was Enheim?'

'His father was one of the party's "Golden Pheasants"—he had the Golden Party Badge. The Enheims were some of the greediest vultures of the lot. The moment they smelled carrion they homed in on it at once. All quite legal, all done strictly according to the letter of the law. First they got to work on people who needed to sell because they wanted to leave for America or Palestine. They squeezed the little Yid dry.' Goldblum tried to demonstrate the action, but his crooked fingers would not close into a fist. 'They agreed contracts in front of a notary. And when the synagogues went up in flames, they piled on the pressure even more. They stripped our people of anything that looked valuable. They paid for the things and always drew up contracts. I believe they backdated some of the contracts so that nobody should get the idea that they weren't legal. There were actually some Nazis who didn't believe that the Thousand Year Reich would last a thousand years, so they backdated the agreements, if possible to before nineteen thirty-five, before the Nuremberg Laws. The Enheims weren't the only ones who got up to those filthy tricks, but they did their share. And, as I've just seen in the paper, they managed to hang on to at least a part of the fortune they made—they weren't victims of restitution. It's staggering. But why are you asking me about them, Kohn?'

'My father mentioned the name, back then.'

'Was he one of Enheim's victims?'

'I don't know. When the people came to take our house and furniture away from us, I didn't hear Enheim's name.'

'Oh, there were so many of them. I don't know if you know, but they auctioned some of the furniture to "members of the German nation" right in front of the houses it had come from, and other things at the harbour. And sometimes suitcases, heaps of them, brought from the east. The contents went to Aryans who had been bombed out.'

'Goldblum, who do you think killed Enheim?'

'A righteous man,' said Goldblum. 'It can only have been a righteous man, Kohn. Who else?'

Chapter thirteen

Stachelmann parked his Golf near the Archive entrance. Then he went and sat down in the Italian restaurant opposite the main gate and ordered an espresso. He felt a new man in his fresh clothes. After he had waited half an hour they appeared. The two men from the Hamburg Finance Department emerged from the entrance gate and set off westwards down the Finckensteinallee. When they were out of sight, Stachelmann paid for his coffee and went back into the grounds of the Archive. He sat down on a bench and waited, keeping an eye on the entrance to the reading room. He switched on his mobile. It bleeped, and he listened to his voicemail: a message from Ossi. He called him back, and Ossi asked him about a man with white hair; Stachelmann gave him a brief account of what he knew, then hung up. He laughed. Ossi had asked him what he was doing now. He was planning a break-in, he had replied. And once again Ossi had not believed him.

He remained sitting on the bench for over an hour. He was afraid, and looked around from time to time. At last a red delivery van approached, with 'Reiter Copying Service' written on the side. It stopped, and the driver jumped down and disappeared into the

Archive. Stachelmann went closer to the van and jotted down the address written beneath the company name. Then he left the Archive grounds and sat waiting in his own car. When the van turned out on to the road, he started up his Golf and followed it. He had no trouble keeping it in sight as they drove at a moderate pace in the direction of Zehlendorf, where the van turned into a side street and stopped outside a gate marked 'Reiter Copying Service'. Stachelmann parked a few yards further on. The street was Edithstrasse. He had time to spare and decided to take a stroll around Zehlendorf.

A shower of rain forced him to shelter in a shopping arcade, where he came across a shop selling electrical goods. He bought a small but powerful torch. Next door he found a bookshop. He looked around, studying the new titles, and bought a detective novel by an American woman writer whose name was new to him. More often than not books like this were disappointing, but occasionally you were pleasantly surprised. He should have brought a Hornblower with him; he decided to put one in his car at the next opportunity, in case he found himself again with a few hours to kill. It was a little before seven. He wouldn't be able to put his plan into operation before one in the morning, and even then it would be pretty risky. For a second he wondered whether it might not have been a better idea to keep a watch on the grey-jacketed man. But then he decided that he was doing the right thing. He had to find out which files were involved.

He had had sashimi in a Japanese restaurant in Zehlendorf for supper and gone for a final stroll. Now he was sitting in his car, reading. The detective story was a letdown: some publishers would translate any old rubbish that came from America. His legs hurt, and he could feel pressure in his right eye. He cursed—he had forgotten to bring his drops. By tomorrow the eye would be inflamed. The pain in his back was from the chair at the Japanese place. He gulped down two pills. It was a quarter to one. He was growing more edgy. He got out of the car. The moon gave very little light, but, annoyingly, a street lamp lit up the copying firm's gate. The windows of the houses round-about were in darkness. Even so, some insomniac might just happen to be looking out at the street. The copying firm's compound was separated from the street by a wire mesh fence. Stachelmann walked along it, pulling at the mesh here and there until he found a spot where there was some give. He looked all round—there was no one in sight. With all his strength he pulled the top of the fence downwards, and kicked up with his left leg while pushing off from the ground with his right. He more or less rolled over the top of the fence and landed on the asphalt in the yard. There was a clatter; his torch had fallen out of his trouser pocket. He put it back in and stayed lying flat on the ground. Trying to ignore his pain, he waited to see if there was any movement anywhere. What he feared most was that there might be a guard dog—but a dog would have starting barking before this, when he was pulling at the fence from the outside. He stood up and walked towards a door. It was padlocked and impossible to open without tools. He cursed under his breath: he had had ample time to buy some. Moving round the outside of the building, he came to a garage. This had a door that he could open, and inside he saw the same van that had collected the files for copying. In the faint glimmer of light he made out a cupboard; it was not locked, and it contained a wooden box full of tools. He switched on his torch for a moment, and its beam fell upon rags, pliers, a big screwdriver and a hammer. He picked out the hammer and screwdriver and an oily rag and took them back to the padlocked door. Pushing the screwdriver between the metal plate and the wood of the door, he covered the handle of the screwdriver with the rag and struck it with the hammer. With a grating noise, the screws pulled free. The wood was rotten, and after only a few blows he was able to remove the plate. The door squeaked as he pulled it open. He went inside, drawing the door back into the frame behind him, and put the tools down on the floor. He switched on the torch for a moment, and found himself standing in a passage with three doors opening off it. The first led to a toilet, the second led into a storeroom, and the third into a high-ceilinged room with shelves going all the way up the walls. Between the sets of shelves there were photocopiers and a long table and chairs. Stachelmann sat down next to one of the copiers and considered what to do next. The blinds were closed, but even so the light of his torch might be visible from outside. A light that moved around was bound to arouse suspicion, so he put the torch in his pocket and switched on the main light in the room. Neon tubes up on the ceiling flickered, and then it was bright as day.

He looked along the shelves until he came to a stack of four files labelled NS 3. On top lay a form which read: 'Ordered by: Peter Carsten, Finance Department, Hamburg, Gorch-Fock-Wall 11.' The second man's name was not given. Stachelmann moved the stack of files to the table, sat down again and opened the first one. He could see immediately that these were documents from Pohl's personal office, mostly correspondence. Opening the other files, he laid them side by side on the desk and moved from one to another, leafing through the documents they contained. He was afraid of being caught, and was intent on getting an overview as quickly as possible. Most of the letters he found in the second file came from Hamburg. He skimmed their contents. The writers were SA and SS officers. All the letters told the same story. A Nazi party official would be forcing a Jew to sell him his property, or to give it to him, which in view of the pitiful purchase prices came to much the same thing. The state, usually in the shape of the Finance Department, would enter a protest on the grounds that the confiscation of enemy property was the sole prerogative of the Finance Administration of the Greater German Reich. The Nazi official would then write to his bosses asking them—in light of his services to the Nazi cause—to intervene on his behalf and obtain an exemption for him.

Stachelmann carried on leafing through the documents. His eye was caught by a letter from a district economics adviser with a flamboyant signature that seemed an expression of self-confidence bordering on egomania. SA Standartenführer Robert Enheim was protesting, in this letter dated 19 April 1941, against an attempt by the Hamburg Finance Department to take from him a house and plot of land that he had purchased legally from a Jew who had 'travelled east'. Since the contract of sale dated from before November 1938, the sale had been concluded before the law had required that enemy property be confiscated by the state. Enheim reminded SS Gruppenführer Pohl of the days when they had fought side by side for the Party. He had also written, he said, to SA Obergruppenführer Lutze and was even considering informing the Führer himself about the injustice being perpetrated by a 'soulless bureaucracy' which 'we had believed the National Revolution had utterly rooted out'.

Enheim—Stachelmann had seen that name before. Where, hmm, that would come back to him. He made a note of the file number, NS 3–1/2015, and took a closer look at one of the photocopiers. They were more complicated than the machines at the university or in copy shops. He found a red switch and pressed it. There was a humming, and then the sound of a mechanism coming to life. Lights of various colours blinked on and off. Stachelmann fed Robert Enheim's letter into an opening marked 'Insert', found a 'Copy' button and pressed it. The sheet of paper disappeared into the machine, there was a swishing noise and the letter reappeared in a tray on the opposite side of the machine. He found the copy in the space underneath. He copied the second page of the letter, put the original back into the file, and folded the copies and put them into his inside jacket pocket. He looked through the papers in the other files. Many of them related to what historians have since called 'unofficial Aryanization'. Exploiting the desperate situation of Jews facing emigration or deportation, Nazi functionaries and other plunderers were buying up their businesses, houses and plots of land at ludicrous prices but following the proper legal procedure. This was giving rise to disputes, with the finance authorities insisting on their right to seize enemy assets, as the Nazis called Jewish-owned property, to enrich the coffers of the state. This by no means suited the private profiteers, who called for 'justice' and appealed to anyone who might help them achieve it. The 'old fighters' from the years before 1933 brandished their golden party badges. They hadn't fought for the 'brown revolution' only to have their booty snatched away by some finance office. And certainly not by the very same tax officials who had served the Weimar Republic.

From time to time Stachelmann had come up against the question of what became of the property of people who were taken into captivity and murdered. It was an issue on the periphery of his *Habilitation* thesis. Research in this area was not making much progress, not least because in 1988 the West German government had extended the period of secrecy for finance office documents.

Otherwise the brown muck would have come pouring out of the cellars of the finance authorities on to the streets. Many people could not face the fact that Jewish assets were not stolen by Germany, an abstract entity, but quite concretely by the German finance offices, acting under the law. It was the inconspicuous little civil servant 'only doing his duty', before 1945 and since.

Battling against his fear of being discovered, Stachelmann leafed through more of the documents. Another letter captured his attention, four pages long this time. As he skimmed through it, his heart began to pound. He read the names Holler and Enheim. The letter was from the Central Office ss Courts and was dated 26 June 1941. It was evidently a reply to a letter from Pohl to Obergruppen-führer Friedrich Alpers, the head of the Central Office ss Courts. Stachelmann took the letter out of the file and photocopied it.

Something rattled. He jumped, and sweat broke out on his forehead. He leapt to the light switch by the door and turned it off. He forced himself to stand still and listen. There was no sound but the hum of the copier. He crept over to the machine and switched it off. A loud voice, a shout. A drunk. Cautiously Stachelmann opened the entrance door and peered out. The drunk was leaning on the fence and throwing up. Between bouts of vomiting he was babbling something unintelligible. Having fallen to his knees, he used the fence to haul himself upright again. In a house opposite, on the second floor, a light came on and a voice rang out, 'Quiet over there! Or I'll call the police.'

'Asshole,' came the bellowed retort. 'Come down and I'll smash your face in.'

Stachelmann hurried back to the copying room and put the files back in their place. As far as was possible in the dark, he checked that he was leaving the room exactly as he had found it. Then he was back at the door. He felt around on the floor for the metal plate and the tools, and then on the door for the screw holes. He held the plate up to the door and gently tapped the screws partway into the holes. Then he drove them home with the screwdriver. It wasn't likely to hold, but it might be good enough to conceal the break-in. There were other reasons why a lock might work loose. And why should anybody think of a break-in when there was nothing missing and no sign of disturbance?

Then he saw the blue light. He crouched against the wall next to the doorway. The police car was driving slowly past the fence. After a few yards it halted, its flashing light colouring the copying firm's compound intermittently. He heard the drunk mumbling, and then started at the sharp shout of a policeman. Doors slammed, and then the police car drove on. He waited in case it turned round and came back, but the sound of the engine faded away into the distance.

He crept across the compound to the fence, recoiling as he smelled where the drunk had been sick. He had no choice, this was where the fence was low enough. He pulled it downwards and left the yard with a flying roll. Landing on something slippery, he lost his footing, and fell flat on his face in the pool of vomit.

* * *

Ossi and Carmen drove back to police headquarters. Sitting with Taut in his office were Kurz and Kamm and an older man in a battered black leather jacket. He faced Taut across the desk. Ossi positioned himself in a corner, while Carmen took the one remaining chair. The man at Taut's desk was making an inordinate fuss, as if someone had accused him of a crime.

'I can't call the police every time I have a passenger.' He threw his arms in the air.

Overemphatic and affected, he reminded Ossi of a theatrical impresario.

Taut was calmness itself. 'No, Herr Görner, we don't expect that of you. We're not accusing you of anything. We're grateful for your willingness to help us. With your assistance we shall most certainly catch our man.' He sounded like someone telling a child that Mummy and Daddy will be back soon.

'I will, that's my public duty.' Görner nodded vigorously.

'We'll take you to our artist, who will produce a facial likeness based on what you tell him. We'll use that picture to try and catch your passenger.' Taut nodded to Kurz.

Kurz stood up. 'Please come with me.'

Görner, too, stood up and they left the room together.

Taut groaned. 'What a windbag! I wonder what'll come out of his session with the artist.' He turned to Ossi. 'How did you get on?'

Ossi laughed. 'Great. It was like an American soap, a cross between "Dynasty" and "I Dream of Jeannie".'

Taut looked at him and shook his head.

'Meier's a crank. He's got a thing about titles and status,' Carmen interjected. 'And he's got a girlfriend who's much too young for him and...' Her hands described two big curves.

'Now who's being sexist?' Ossi challenged.

'I was only expressing what you think,' Carmen retorted.

'I see our new colleague contributes something to our working atmosphere. What a bonus,' Taut commented. Then he grinned. 'It was about time somebody exposed your dirty mind,' he told Ossi.

Ossi raised both hands.

Taut picked up the telephone and pressed a speed dial button. 'Why isn't Stroh here? I put in a request two hours ago for him to be brought over here,' he said. His tone was serious. 'Maybe our man in the grey jacket drove the Mercedes, too.'

Ossi threw him an enquiring look. 'What makes you think that?'

'Hasn't it struck you that two people involved in our investigation into the Holler case have been murdered? Couldn't it all be part of a plan?'

Ossi suddenly felt hot and sat down abruptly. His thoughts were in turmoil. Taut's suggestion had made him recall his last phone conversation with Stachelmann. Stachelmann had also been involved with the investigation, and nobody outside the police knew that his involvement had ended. Maybe his story of an attempt on his life hadn't been so mad after all.

'I'll be right back,' said Ossi. 'I need to make a phone call.' It sounded more like 'Leave me alone.' Carmen looked at him in puzzlement, but Ossi waved aside any question she might have and left the room. He practically ran to his own office, looked up Stachelmann's mobile number in his notebook and dialed.

'You have reached the mailbox for Josef Maria Stachelmann. Please leave your message after the tone.'

Ossi cursed, waited for the tone and said, 'Jossi, ring me straight away.'

He returned to Taut's office. From the corridor he heard Carmen laughing. As he entered the room, Carmen was telling the story of their visit to Meier. 'He hates Holler as much as Grothe does. Maybe Enheim did, too. But that's something we'll never know.'

Taut looked at Ossi. 'What's up?'

'I tried to get hold of Stachelmann. He phoned me a day or two ago and told me somebody had tried to kill him. I didn't believe him. That was a mistake. I did let our people in Berlin know about it, but I don't think I gave them the impression that it was something they should take seriously. Damn!' Ossi kicked the chair over.

'Are you crazy?' Carmen demanded.

Instead of answering, Ossi righted the chair and sat down.

'Did you get hold of your tame historian?' asked Taut.

'No, I left a message on his mobile.'

'So he'll be in touch. Why are you getting so steamed up about it?'

'Because if it was an attempt to kill him, it won't be the last.'

'Are you a clairvoyant?' asked Carmen.

'No, but I can't help feeling that we're dealing with something big. It's a web, and the question is this: is Holler the spider or the fly?'

'If he's the spider, he belongs to a hitherto unknown species,' said Taut.

'Oh, I see, Professor, I didn't realize you were an entomologist.'

'A senior officer in the German detective force knows about everything.'

The door opened, and two uniformed officers brought Oliver Stroh into the office. He was unshaven and his eyes were glazed. Spittle drooled from his mouth.

'What have you done to him?' asked Taut.

'Nothing, he was like this when we found him in his apartment,' said one of the officers.

'And of course Herr Stroh has come here of his own accord because he's so keen to help the police,' said Taut. 'Isn't that right, Herr Stroh?'

Stroh dangled in the two policemen's arms without replying.

'I tell you what,' Taut said to them. 'Take Herr Stroh and sit him down in a cell. But don't lock the door, he's a guest. Give him a slap-up meal and lots of coffee. And if he wants a shower, that's fine by me.'

The officers looked at him in amazement, then retreated with Stroh.

Ossi's mobile rang. 'Winter.'

'Stachelmann, what's up?'

'Where are you?'

'I'm just planning a break-in for tonight. Shall I tell you where, so that you can alert your police friends here?'

'Don't talk rubbish.'

'It's not rubbish.'

'Did you tell the Berlin police everything about the attempt to kill you?'

'What a silly question. According to you there *was* no attempt to kill me.'

'No need to get huffy.'

'You either think I'm getting huffy or you reckon I'm a fantasist. Think of another alternative. That might simplify things.'

'Listen, this is important. We're looking for an elderly man with a grey jacket.'

'And white hair. I've noticed him too,' said Stachelmann. 'He's been my inseparable companion on some of my travels. Right now he's staying at the Hotel Adlon, if that's any help. That's where I saw him last, anyway. In his spare time he shoves people under trains.'

'Just a minute.' Ossi put his hand over the speaker of his mobile. 'Our man may still be staying at the Hotel Adlon in Berlin. Get the Berlin police onto it straight away, tell them to pull him in.'

Taut picked up the phone.

'Do you know his name?' Ossi continued.

'No,' Stachelmann answered. 'All I know is that he has a grey jacket and white hair. A rather unsoldierly haircut, or un-policeman-like, if you prefer. Anyway, longish hair, curly at the ends. The guy's a sun-worshipper, too. I believe he's not the only old gentleman like that in Germany. Anything else?'

'Jossi, don't be like that! I'm sorry, I was wrong.'

'If you hadn't thought I was a nut, you wouldn't have to apologize now.' Stachelmann hung up.

Ossi turned his mobile over in his hands for a moment, toying with the idea of phoning back. But he decided against it; he did not feel like trying to appease someone who was in a bad mood. He knew these episodes of old. It would only be a few days, at worst, before Stachelmann was his normal self again. People don't change, he thought; that's good, and not so good. It would be quite sufficient if they shed their lousy traits and kept the better ones.

'You two go and talk to the other property dealer. What was his name again?' Taut asked.

'Ammann,' said Carmen.

'You'd better tell him that our killer takes a special interest in anybody who is part of our investigation. And Herr Ammann will be, if you go and see him. I'll have somebody keep an eye on Grothe's door, and Meier's too. And the same goes for Ammann. Perhaps it's unnecessary and the fellow at the Adlon will be our man. But we could be barking up the wrong tree.' Taut got to his feet, which only ever happened if he needed to go to the toilet, or was going off for something to eat. He detested the canteen and the fodder that police stuffed down themselves when on duty. He had a sophisticated taste in food, too expensive a taste for a policeman, really. Once in a while a snack bar would do, though. 'And you lot watch yourselves. One dead officer in the department is more than enough.'

'We'll do our best,' said Carmen.

Ossi shook his head as they left.

Gottlob Ammann lived in Hagedornstrasse in Eppendorf. The whole area looked freshly polished. The lawns were closely mown, the paths swept, the housefronts white, blue or green. There was nothing resembling a common style—each house had a different appearance from all the rest, each came from the catalogue of a different builder, who had promised his clients domestic heaven on earth. Carmen laughed when she saw the houses. 'They were playing with Lego here,' she commented.

Ammann lived at number 3a. Ossi rang the bell, and the door was opened by a short, portly man with strands of thin hair on his head. A fleshy nose almost formed an arch over his mouth.

'What do you want?' His tone was suspicious and ill-humoured. His voice sounded strangled and too high-pitched.

Ossi showed his warrant card. 'Good afternoon, police, criminal investigation department. Kommissar Winter, and this is Kommissar Hebel. You are Herr Ammann?'

The man hesitated, then opened the door wide. 'I am Ammann, come in. You've taken your time.' He stepped to one side. 'I phoned you a week ago, but nobody came.'

Ossi and Carmen took a step into the hallway. The walls were covered with reproductions of oil paintings. A runner muffled their footsteps. Ammann showed them into the living room and gestured towards the sofa. Ossi and Carmen sat down side by side.

'You have come about my dog?' Ammann asked.

'We are investigating a murder. It concerns the Holler family. You'll have heard about it?'

Ammann nodded assent.

'In nineteen eighty-one, I believe, you sold Holler your property company?'

Ammann nodded again. Then he raised his eyebrows. 'And why have you come to see me?'

'We are calling on all the property dealers whose firms Holler took over. Those that are still alive,' Carmen said.

'Quite,' said Ammann. 'We're not getting any younger.'

Ossi stood up and walked over to the window, which faced towards the back. Looking out, he gave a start. On the patio lay a dog, somewhere between a collie and a terrier. It had evidently been dead for some days, since the first signs of decomposition were plain to see. 'There's a dead dog out there,' he said.

Carmen looked at Ossi as though he had gone mad.

Ammann's face did not flicker. 'That's Bello. He was run over last week, in this street. It's a twenty mile-an-hour zone, but nobody keeps to it. Some car came roaring down the street, wide tires, deafening noise, and killed my Bello. I phoned the police, but do you suppose they're interested in that sort of thing?' He sounded quite composed.

'So why is the dog still lying out there?'

'I can't bear to be parted from him. Do you understand?'

'No,' said Carmen. 'It's dangerous to leave dead bodies lying around.'

Ammann showed no more reaction than if she'd read him an extract from the rail timetable.

'We need to know why you sold your company to Herr Holler,' said Ossi.

'There's nothing complicated about that. Business was only so-so, and Holler offered a reasonable price. That's the way it goes, in times of crisis the owners of small businesses have to be glad if they get bought up. Plenty go bust and end up in debt. I didn't have to face that.'

'But some time after the sale Holler came along and demanded a repayment.'

'Yes, but it wasn't much. He was right. I hadn't been keeping my client list up to date during the last few months. I hadn't been able to hang on to my secretary. And then there was a plot of land and two houses in the package that were in a pretty bad state.'

'But surely Holler looked at everything before the sale. Or did he buy the houses and the client portfolio blind?'

'No, no. But it's not unusual for problems to show up months or even years after a sale, problems that even the seller didn't know about himself but for which he is liable.'

'As a property dealer, how did you come to own houses? And why did you sell the real estate as well as your firm?'

'That's not unusual either. The real estate belonged to the company, it just got left over, as it were, after a transaction.' He shook his head gently. 'Left over,' he repeated. He seemed pleased with the phrase.

'Can you imagine anyone having such a hatred of Herr Holler that he would kill because of it?' Carmen asked, as matter-of-factly as if she had been asking about the weather.

'I really don't know him, beyond the business contacts I had with him. How should I know who wishes him ill? I read about him from time to time, he gives to charity without making a song and dance about it. That's rare nowadays, when every Tom, Dick and Harry want to become a celebrity. Maybe he's got a bad conscience and something to hide. Maybe he doesn't want media attention, maybe he gives so generously because he's been up to something and is saving up brownie points for whatever final reckoning is coming. Maybe, maybe, maybe. How should I know? Isn't that your job? Don't we citizens pay our taxes so that you can catch murderers, including the madman who killed my Bello?'

Ossi sat on the sofa listening while Carmen led the questioning. His new colleague was self-assertive, pushy, she ignored his seniority. She took charge of the questioning, and made a good job of it. He had to put up with her behaviour. She asked questions that he wouldn't have thought of. Some of them seemed rather peculiar—but the case they were poking around in was even more peculiar. If they were ever to find a solution, this was probably the only way to go about it. Rule nothing out, ask any question at all, however stupid it might seem. He was starting to feel sick, he either had to get out of this room or throw the patio door open. It was far enough away from the dog's corpse. He stood up and addressed Ammann: 'May I open the door?'

Ammann shuddered. 'You have no idea of what can come in from outside. What you think of as air is a toxic cocktail of carbon, benzene, formaldehyde, arsenic, and heaven knows what else. Better to put up with a bit of stale air than let yourself be poisoned. I only spend time outside if I really have to.'

'Didn't you walk your dog?' Carmen demanded.

Ammann shuddered again. 'Good grief, I wouldn't have dreamt of it!' He looked searchingly at Carmen, his face darkening. 'I suppose you think it was my fault that my dog got run over? So that's the way it is, first you don't send an officer round, and then you blame the victim. Fine police methods those are!'

'It's your dog that's the victim,' said Carmen. 'But that's not our concern.' Standing by the patio door, Ossi took a handkerchief from his trouser pocket and mopped his forehead. There was nothing he wanted more than to get away from this madman and his house.

But Carmen still sat on the sofa as though she were glued to it. The stench and the heat did not seem to trouble her.

'Let me just give you an idea of our investigation,' she said. 'We are questioning some of the property dealers who sold their firms to Herr Holler between twenty and twenty-five years ago. They all say the same thing, it's as though they'd coordinated their statements. You are saying essentially the same as Grothe and Meier. And no doubt Enheim would have told us the same, too. Only he, unfortunately, is dead. Perhaps the reason he's dead is so that he *shouldn't* tell us his story.' Ossi was startled: she was right, that wasn't a bad idea. What had made her think of it? And was it wise to let Ammann in on it? Carmen continued: 'The story about the slump in the property market, Holler's offer, and the so-called "deficiencies" and "problems" that were used as grounds for a repayment of part of the sale price. Some of the dealers see Holler as God Almighty, others hate him without telling us why. And yet they all tell the same tale. There are two possible explanations.'

Ammann shook his head. He seemed paler, though perhaps that was just Ossi's imagination. Ammann's left hand, resting on his knee, was trembling.

'Explanation number one: it's all true. In which case I believe in the Easter bunny. Explanation number two: it's all lies. All the dealers who sold to Holler have agreed the story among themselves, or alternatively Holler put a knife to their throats: "One wrong word and you're for it." And Enheim was going to say a wrong word. Is that how it was?'

Ammann shook his head. The hand on his knee trembled.

'Do you know what it makes you, if you cover up for a murderer? Do you know what the judge will give you?'

Ammann shook his head.

'I don't know precisely, either, but you'd certainly go down for it. And how much poison do you think prison air has in it?'

'Stop,' cried Ammann in a voice that was even more of a squawk than before. 'You're trying to intimidate me. You're not allowed to do that.'

'I *am* allowed to. Can't you see I'm doing you a favour? I'm trying to make sure you don't have to breathe in quantities of poison for the rest of your life—benzene, carbon, arsenic.'

Now Ossi understood. It was time to give her his support and increase the pressure on Ammann. 'When did you last speak to Herr Holler on the telephone?'

Ammann opened his mouth to answer.

'Before you tell us a lie, we have a list of all the telephone calls that Herr Holler has made in recent months,' Carmen warned.

Ammann shook his head again. He reminded Ossi of a puppet with someone continually pulling the strings attached to its head. He sat there, shaking his head.

'When did you last speak to Herr Holler on the phone?'

'A week or two ago.'

'Can you be more precise?'

'It was the day after his daughter was killed.'

'Did he call you?'

Ammann nodded.

'He called you on the day after his daughter died?' Carmen had him on the hook and was reeling him in.

'Yes.'

'And what did he say?'

'I can't remember exactly.'

'You're lying,' said Carmen. 'If you go on lying to us, we'll take you down to headquarters.'

The only one demonstrably lying is Carmen Hebel, thought Ossi. But her tale of a list of phone calls was a stroke of genius. And of course they couldn't arrest Ammann. Up to now he'd been lying, at worst; there was no evidence of complicity in a crime. Ossi was amazed at the way Carmen had broken through the barriers. Beginners had their advantages, they hadn't yet got into a rut. He was beginning to get an inkling of what had happened, of what this was really all about.

'He told me I shouldn't take the repayment business amiss. He was in a terrible state.'

'So he calls you up after twenty years and tells you not to hold the repayment against him.' From Carmen's tone it was evident that she did not believe a word of it. 'That's nonsense.' She was losing her temper, which was a mistake. Ossi could feel the line slackening. She almost had her fish hooked, but her anger was giving him a chance to escape.

'If you think I'm talking nonsense, you can leave. And if you consider it worthwhile, you can call me to a formal interview.' He had raised his voice.

'I'll tell you what we think,' Ossi said amiably. 'We think that you wouldn't have admitted speaking to Holler on the phone if we didn't have the list of his calls. You must admit that we could have laid a trap for you, by asking about phone calls first and then springing the list on you. You see what I mean?'

Ammann gave a slight nod. He sat there like a block of stone.

'But we don't want to trick you. We've got a series of murders to solve, and we need information quickly, or else there'll be more people killed. We've questioned various property dealers who sold their businesses to Holler. They all tell us the same story. A sale, followed by a repayment—every time. That might reasonably happen once, but not every single time. And another thing that's striking is that all the dealers we speak to turn defensive when we get on to our friend Herr Holler. I don't understand that either. I'd like you to explain it to me.' Ossi spoke as if to a child.

'Did you ask Enheim, too?' Ammann's voice was faint.

'No, he was dead before we could put any questions to him.'

'Are you sure?'

'Frau Hebel and I went to question him and found his body.'

Ammann nodded, he believed it. 'I can't tell you more than I already have. Truly I can't.' He was almost pleading.

'You can't, or you daren't?'

Ammann shook his head. 'Please go. I have to see to my poor dog.' His eyes were glistening.

'For goodness' sake tell us something, this is murder we're dealing with here!' Carmen was cross and spoke sharply.

Ammann sat in his armchair, shaking his head.

'Come on,' Ossi said to Carmen.

Carmen turned to Ammann. 'We're putting an officer on your door. To protect you.'

Ammann stared at them uncomprehendingly.

'Two people who were involved with our case have been killed.' She swung round and followed Ossi to the door.

'Sadist,' Ossi said to her.

They drove back to headquarters. Oliver Stroh was sitting in Taut's office. Freshly shaved, and above all sober, he was barely recognizable. His eyes were still slightly red. He slouched on the chair in front of Taut's desk. Taut was in his own seat.

Taut gestured towards another pair of chairs as Ossi and Carmen entered. Their role was to remain silent.

'You say you saw the black Mercedes come shooting out of Wesselyring, lurching from side to side and with tires screeching. And then it drove straight at the woman, as if the driver was actually targeting her.'

'Yes, I'm sure he meant to kill her. He was waiting round a corner and started moving the moment she went to cross the road. Honestly. I saw him waiting there before I popped in to the pub for a quick one. He gave me a nasty look, I can tell you, so I didn't hang about.'

'I believe you, don't get me wrong, only it's not easy to imagine a person deliberately running someone over.'

'That's how it was, though.'

'And where were you standing when she was knocked down?'

'I was coming out of the Hop-Flower. I'd had a beer or two. I was just going to cross the road. Then I saw her, standing with a man over on the opposite side of the road. They were talking. Then she turned round and went towards the road. She called out something to him. She'd just got one foot on the road when I heard the screech. I didn't know where it came from at first, but then I saw the car. The same Mercedes that had been waiting before, hurtling towards her. She didn't immediately realize what was happening, then bang!' He smashed his fist into his palm.

'And the driver, did you recognize him?'

Stroh leaned back in the chair. 'I'm not sure.'

'But you got a look at him while he was waiting. That's what you just said.'

'Yes, well, it was a man.'

'Young, old?'

'Old.'

'How did you know?'

'He had white hair, receding, a bit on the long side.'

'And a tanned face?'

'That's right, actually, now you come to mention it.' He turned towards Carmen, as if expecting confirmation.

'Couldn't he have been young but wearing a wig to make him look like an old man?' Carmen suggested.

Stroh turned his chair in her direction. He ran his eyes over her; nothing in her expression revealed how revolting she found him. 'That would make him a very clever operator. Bright, like me.'

'It's possible, isn't it?' said Carmen.

'Possible in theory, but not him. He was an old geezer, you can tell the difference.'

'How?' she asked.

'He had an old face. Lines. And an old nose.'

'How do you define an old nose?'

'It's sharper, it was a beak.'

'So you think, considering everything you saw, he must have been an old man.'

'Exactly.'

'How old?'

'How should I know?'

'Over sixty?'

'Definitely.'

'Over seventy?'

Stroh nodded. 'A real old crumbly, ancient.'

'Would you know him again?'

'Don't know.'

'You've helped us a lot, Herr Stroh,' said Carmen. 'Many thanks.'

Taut cleared his throat. 'Do you know this gentleman sitting next to Frau Hebel?'

Stroh glanced at Carmen and then at Ossi. His eyes rested on Ossi for a while. He frowned, then said, 'Possibly. I'd rather get an eyeful of her, though.'

The patience was palpable in Taut's voice as he asked, 'I can understand that, but this isn't a beauty contest, is it?'

Stroh laughed; it was repellent. 'Then I'll take another look at him.' Ossi sat motionless as Stroh directed his gaze towards him.

Stroh took another look at Carmen before turning back to face Taut. 'No, don't know him. He's a cop, though. Not that I've had anything to do with cops, I'm an honest man.'

'Apart from a GBH and a few other little matters.'

'Crap. That was a miscarriage of justice. There was a joker in the pub wanted to pulp me. I got my defence in first, that's all. That's what I told the lady judge, but she was a man-hater. She sent me down because I'm a man. Anyway, that was years ago.'

'Eighteen months,' said Taut.

'That's what I'm saying.'

Ossi stood up and left the room. He went to the coffee machine and took a mug of coffee back to Taut's office. As he opened the door, Stroh looked him in the face.

Carmen protested, 'You could have brought one for me.'

Stroh said, 'He looks like the guy who was talking to the woman before she got run over. It's just struck me. Similar, anyway.'

'You've got good eyesight,' Taut said in a friendly tone.

'I'm proud of it,' said Stroh. 'I wouldn't swear to it. But it could have been him.'

'It was,' Taut confirmed.

Ossi went out again and fetched another coffee. On his return he handed it to Carmen with a bow.

Taut said, 'You didn't bring one for me?'

And Stroh asked, 'Or me?'

Taut's phone rang. He picked it up. 'Right, I'll be there,' he said, hanging up. 'And you two are coming, too,' he added to Ossi and Carmen. 'Herr Stroh, could you possibly wait a few moments until we get back?'

Taut went out to the corridor with them. 'You pulled that off brilliantly,' he told Carmen. 'Usually I can't stand being interrupted when I'm questioning somebody, but it's results that count.'

'I messed up with Ammann, though,' she replied. 'We'd almost landed our fish, and then I let the line go slack.'

'Do you fish?'

'My grandfather did.'

'Ah,' said Taut.

'I don't think the business with Ammann was that bad,' said Ossi. 'I'm not sure how close we were to having him. And anyway, even without more information from him we have a pretty good idea that Holler acted strangely, at the very least, with his orgy of acquisitions, and that he set up the repayment version of events with Grothe and the rest.'

'Is there any proof?' demanded Taut.

'No, but we know we're right.'

Carmen nodded. 'No question about it, there's something fishy there. And we'll see what friend Holler has to say on the subject.'

'First you two can come with me and take a look at what the taxi driver and the artist have been up to. And then we'll compare what the taxi driver and'—he turned to Carmen—'your boyfriend Stroh have told us.'

Carmen gave a snort.

'Come on,' Ossi teased her, 'that was almost a love scene just now with your beloved Oliver.'

'So that's your idea of a love scene, is it?' Carmen retorted. 'Perhaps I ought to feel pity for you!'

'Before *you* turn into Mother Teresa and *you* talk any more nonsense, let's all go and look at the art exhibition,' said Taut, without a hint of a smile.

The taxi driver had a self-satisfied look. When Taut and his colleagues opened the door, he said, 'That's him, definitely.'

It was an old man with white hair that covered the upper part of his ears, and an angular, rather large nose. Further details were noted alongside the image. The eyes were black, he was about five feet five inches tall, and slim, almost skinny. His face was suntanned. His age was put at over seventy, possibly even eighty or more.

'How did he move?' Taut asked, after studying the picture.

The taxi driver shook his head.

'He got in and out of your cab. Did you see him approaching you or moving away? At the airport, for instance.'

'That's right, at Fuhlsbüttel, I saw him walking towards my cab. But only for a few seconds. I was sitting in my car waiting for the next fare when he came out of the terminal. He caught my eye because his brown skin was such a contrast to his white hair. Old people do sometimes look odd.' He laughed. 'My mother does, for one.'

No one joined in with his laughter.

'I saw him at the exit from the terminal and then again as he put his bag into my trunk, he didn't want any help. He had an old-looking face and a slim build, and seemed quite strong and wiry.' He looked at Taut, waiting for some sign of appreciation. 'The way he moved was younger than he looked. He had a springy sort of walk, like somebody who does sport.'

'And you don't know where he was from?' Carmen asked.

Taut shook his head.

'I told the Kommissar that already.' The taxi driver pointed to Taut.

Taut said, 'Let's stick to your description for a minute. You say he moved like a young man. With a springy kind of walk.'

'Exactly, and his voice was young, too. Something sharp about it. Short and to the point. He didn't say hello or good-bye, and he didn't tip, either. And he was wearing gloves. Thin, dark leather gloves. Odd sort of guy. I tried to make conversation, about the weather, the usual sort of thing. I might as well have been talking to the Merc.'

'You picked him up at the airport and took him to Jupiter-weg.'

'That's what I said.'

'And he got out there without a word?'

'Yes.'

'Do you remember anything else about him?'

'No.'

'If you do later, please get in touch at once. You've been very helpful indeed.'

They sat together in Taut's office to discuss where they were with the investigation.

'At any rate,' said Kurz, 'Ulrike and Enheim were killed by the same man.'

Taut sat slumped at his desk, apparently lost in his own thoughts.

'We've started a search for the guy with the just-back-from-holiday face,' said Ossi. 'We think he's been around in Berlin, too. According to what my historian pal says, he tried to kill him as well.'

'Have the Berlin police found out anything?' asked Kurz.

'The description fits a guest who stayed just one night at the Adlon hotel. The details he put on the registration form are false. Nobody knows where he is now. But at least it seems that the identikit picture is quite a good likeness. Perhaps the hotel porter could help us make it even better,' suggested Carmen.

'Good idea,' said Ossi reluctantly. That had occurred to him too, but Carmen had got it out first. She didn't always think faster, but she had a quicker tongue.

'No, it's a really bad one,' said Taut. 'Supposing they're two different people after all, we'd be messing up the only real lead we've got, the descriptions that the taxi driver and Stroh have given us. We can rely on them—they match up perfectly. Who it was getting up to monkey tricks in Berlin, we don't know yet. It was probably our man, but we can't prove it. We all know how unreliable reactions to an identikit image can be. You shove a rough sketch under the nose of some hotel worker who sees a thousand faces every day, or put pressure on somebody who's in a hurry, and he'll recognize anything for you. Ossi, ask the Berlin police to knock up a picture of their own with the hotel porter. And then we'll have two images to use, instead of combining different people's impressions into a hybrid that would really just be the sum total of our errors. Okay?'

Ossi nodded. He thought Taut was splitting hairs, but at least this way they would avoid one possible mistake. Even if it was an unlikely one.

'Do we know how he left Enheim's apartment and the Adlon?' Taut enquired.

Nobody answered.

'Do we know whether Identikit Man has anything to do with the Holler murders, and if so, what?'

Silence.

'So we've got nothing but the identikit image and the descriptions provided by a taxi driver and a drunk. We suspect that the man that the image is supposed to represent is implicated in the murders of Ulrike and Enheim. He may have something to do with the attack on Stachelmann. And perhaps with the Holler case.' Taut looked at Ossi.

Ossi said nothing.

'If there even *was* an attack on Stachelmann. Plausibility is the enemy of curiosity. I made that up myself, but it wouldn't disgrace a Chinese sage. Unfortunately Confucius and Co. didn't have much experience of crime-solving, so they haven't left us any clever sayings on the subject. If they had, we might be surplus to requirements, which wouldn't be so great either. Nobody wants to be superfluous.'

Ossi hated these pseudo-philosophical monologues. As a rule Taut said very little; it was only when they were getting nowhere with a case that he started making speeches. Perhaps their purpose was to distract and provoke his listeners, which might lead to their gaining a new perspective on the crimes, although Ossi doubted it. It was just that some people went quiet when they were stumped, and others talked a lot.

'If the old fellow in the grey jacket who was picked up from the airport *is* our killer, then it's possible that he took a plane out again after committing his murders. So he could be anywhere between

Beijing and Honolulu. That's really encouraging. We'll knock up an international arrest warrant on the basis of our identikit image and the description from the taxi driver. Kurz and Kamm can do the rounds of the airport, all the check-in desks and the people on passport control. Got it?'

Kamm nodded. Kurz was looking out of the window.

Taut turned to Ossi. 'This Holler is a queer bird. Buys companies and then a few months later wants part of the purchase price paid back to him. The forensic accountants tell us he did that in every case. Has Holler got something to do with Enheim's murder?'

Ossi shook his head. 'I doubt it. His alibi is sure to be perfect. At the most, all we've got against him is that for some time he's apparently been phoning the property dealers he once bought up. He phoned Ammann, anyway. But my bet would be on the usual sort of dodgy business deals. Holler as a killer just wouldn't make sense.'

'Tell me what *does* make sense about these cases.'

'Fair enough, but why should Holler murder, or get someone else to murder, somebody who paid money back to him? Assuming the sale of Enheim's business ran along the same lines as the others, there's no motive. And there's nothing in the accounts to suggest that it was any different from the others. All we actually know is that Holler has lost his wife and two children. If it was the same killer each time, then the newspapers are right and murders two and three are our responsibility because we were too stupid to catch the murderer after the first one.'

'Has anyone else had any brainwaves?' Taut looked at his fellow officers. 'Well then, Ossi, take your loud-mouthed colleague and go and pay another visit to Holler. Put pressure on him, never mind if he goes snivelling to the Chief about it afterwards.'

*   *   *

Leopold Kohn lay on his bed, remonstrating with himself. You've let yourself be distracted. What has Enheim's death to do with you? You need to finish your task and you're running out of time. But the visit to Goldblum had unsettled him. Was there someone else making sure that justice, justice in its truest sense, prevailed? Not legal arrangements that protected the guilty—statutes of limitation, lack of evidence—but punishment that inflicted as much pain as the crime. An eye for an eye. Only when Holler was as utterly alone as Leopold Kohn, only then would justice have been done.

He thought of the remote control. He had ordered, at considerable cost, a remote control unit, transmitter and receiver, from a specialist mail-order firm, to be sent to him by express delivery. It had a range of over five hundred yards, and the quality of the signal would barely be affected by any obstacles between the transmitter and the receiver.

Who had killed Enheim? He could not get the question out of his head. Had it been Holler? In the paper Kohn had read that Enheim had sold his business to Holler, many years ago. Enheim was a bastard who deserved to die. And Holler deserved it every bit as much.

A sudden terror seized Kohn. He began to shake all over, gripped by fear. What if the unknown killer took his revenge on Holler as he had on Enheim? Then he would kill Holler and rob Kohn of the fulfillment of *his* vengeance. If he couldn't complete his vengeance, his life would have had no purpose. His thirst for revenge had given him the strength to kill strangers who had become guilty because they lived with a guilty man. Guilt is handed down if the guilty one is not driven out of his family; ignorance is no shield against retribution. That was justice. The thoughts raced through Kohn's mind. He had to protect Holler, had to make sure he did not die too soon. Holler must live, must have a long life, must feel how long the pangs of grief can torment a man, biting deeper and deeper.

What could he do? He moved towards the telephone and picked up the handset, but then put it down again. Reaching for his jacket, he went out. He walked as far as Dammtor station and caught an s 11 train for Blankenese. At Altona he got out and went to the nearest phone box, where he dialed the number for the police. 'Give me the murder squad.'

A woman put him through to the officer in charge of response unit 3.

'Taut,' announced a calm voice.

'Is that the murder squad?'

'Yes.'

'Are you dealing with the Holler and Enheim cases?'

'Yes.'

'Take steps to protect Holler. Otherwise he will be killed. Just like Enheim.'

'Who are you?'

'Someone who knows that Holler is in danger. Protect him!'

Chapter fourteen

Stachelmann's eyes were burning from tiredness. He got into his Golf and drove back to Haus Morgenland, hoping that his pursuer had given up the chase. 'Don't be a wimp,' he muttered under his breath, trying to conquer his fear. 'Just go into the hotel through the back entrance, don't turn any lights on, slip into your room and have a shower.' Once inside his room he locked the door, but fear still lurked in every corner. He undressed and had a shower, and then took some clean clothes from his suitcase. After that he fetched the copied documents from his jacket pocket, sat down at the desk and started to read.

The first document was a letter, dated 19th April 1941, from SA Standartenführer Enheim, economic adviser to the NSDAP district administration in Hamburg, to Pohl, who was then head of the SS Central Office. It was clear from the tone of the letter that Enheim had known Pohl for some time. He wrote that the Jew Robert Israel Zucker had travelled east in November 1939, but he did not know exactly where he had gone.

> *I am writing to ask you, esteemed party comrade Pohl, to discover the whereabouts of the Jew Zucker and to obtain confirmation*

from him that I purchased his former property, 53a Grindelallee in Hamburg, in a legally incontestable manner and prior to 8th November 1938. I attach the documents relating to the purchase.

Stachelmann had not found any documents attached.

When you, esteemed party comrade Pohl, have obtained this confirmation from the Jew Zucker, would you please send it to the Finance Department in Hamburg, for the attention of Oberscharführer Schirmer, who has offered me his support if I am able to prove that my purchase of the property in question, 53a Grindelallee, is legally incontestable. If I cannot prove this, the property reverts to the Finance Department, or to the German Reich, and I risk losing the money I paid.

The other document was a letter dated June 1941 from the Central Office ss Courts to Pohl. Skimming through it, Stachelmann came across the names Holler, Grothe, Ammann, and Meier. After briefly closing his tired, burning eyes to rest them for a moment, he read it right through. It was a reply from the Central Office ss Courts to a letter that Pohl had written. The Central Office ss Courts informed party comrade Pohl that

after consultation with the Reichsführer ss, the decision has been taken to halt the proceedings against Sturmbannführer Holler, Hauptscharführer Ammann, Meier and Grothe, and the other party comrades. There are no grounds in law to object to the purchases made by these deserving comrades, who had given meritorious service. In the present heroic epoch, in which the ss faces immense challenges in the struggle against our enemies both within and without, it would amount almost to undermining the morale of our armed forces if these unnecessary and defamatory proceedings were to be pursued any further. The Reichsführer ss has promised to lay the matter before the Reich Minister of Finance. Instructions have also been sent to Gestapo headquarters in Hamburg to ensure the compliance of the Hamburg Finance

Department in this regard. You may therefore rest assured that the case will very shortly be closed.

Stachelmann lay down on the bed, still trying to keep his tiredness at bay. It all seemed perfectly plain. Enheim and some friends of his in the ss had obliged Jews to part with their property. Astute as they were, they made it appear as though they had bought just any house or plot from just any Hamburg citizen. If one did not know that from 1933 onwards Jews were squeezed out of public life, that the gradual exclusion of the Jews from the economy meant that Jews were robbed of all their property and driven abroad, until, with the outbreak of war, murder took the place of emigration—if one did not know this and much more besides, one might really believe that these were legitimate deals for the mutual benefit of both buyer and seller. But they were forced sales, often to Nazis who were anxious to seize an opportunity for self-enrichment before Jewish property was confiscated by the state, but who went through the proper forms, with the appropriate entries in the land register. Stachelmann recalled discussions about this in his seminars. What some students did not grasp at first was that the main threat to the Jews, before the extermination began, did not come from the hordes of sa men eager to see Jewish blood on their knives, nor from the Gestapo with its nighttime arrests and its torture cellars, nor from the courts handing out punishment for 'racial pollution'. The main threat came from the finance authorities, the officials who could wipe out a person's livelihood with the stroke of a pen. Before murder came wholesale robbery.

The two documents Stachelmann had copied were evidence of a tussle over Jewish property between the Hamburg Finance Department and these members of the ss. The Finance Department had gone to the Central Office ss Courts and denounced the ss men: the usual accusation in such cases was corruption and seeking pecuniary advantage. The ss men had acquired property to which the state laid claim. Jewish property counted as enemy assets, the confiscation of which was the prerogative of the state. The Central Office ss Courts, the ss's internal investigating body, had examined the case, and after interventions from Pohl and the Reichsführer of the ss, Heinrich

Himmler, the proceedings were discontinued, and these fighters on the Jewish front won a heroic victory.

Stachelmann knew of such cases. Particularly crafty Nazis had approached Jews, browbeaten them, threatened them, physically attacked them, blackmailed them, made them fear for their lives and those of their families, and finally presented them with a contract of sale. Even craftier ones had adopted a different method. They promised Jews that they would take care of their property for them until better times came. When better times did come and the war was over, these benefactors of the Jews fell prey to amnesia, a disease which ran rampant in Germany after the defeat in 1945, worse than any Asian flu. Suddenly the new owners did not recognize the old ones, and Germans found themselves unable to remember whose things they had bought in the streets or at auctions. And the financial authorities continued to stick rigidly to the letter of the law.

Stachelmann knew the names Enheim and Holler, but not the others. Enheim and Holler were property dealers; Enheim had been murdered—so Stachelmann had read—and Holler had lost his wife and two children. Who were Grothe, Meier and Ammann? Hamburg ss men, evidently, who had robbed Jews and had got into trouble with the authorities as a result. He would find out more when he got back to Hamburg. Or perhaps even sooner.

Before he knew it he had fallen asleep. Now the sun was shining in his face. He blinked and closed his eyes again. He remembered the documents he had copied. What should he do now? Return to Hamburg, or go on to Weimar? He opted for Weimar. Getting up, he plugged his laptop into the telephone socket, waited for the Internet to be connected, and then called up the online directory enquiries site. When he typed in 'Ammann', the screen showed three listings in that name. There were a larger number of Grothes. There was no point in looking up such a common surname as Meier.

Holler and Enheim were property dealers. Holler junior had inherited his firm from Holler senior, the ss man. The sa officer Robert Enheim had stolen Jewish property, and if Norbert Enheim was his son, then the cases were similar. So after the war the ss plunderers became property dealers, having very possibly acquired their start-up capital through a theft that Himmler and the ss court had covered up for them. Though Stachelmann's copied letters did not absolutely prove this, it seemed perverse to interpret them in any other way.

Stachelmann dialed Ossi's number on his mobile.

'Winter.'

'Stachelmann here. Was the murdered dealer called Norbert Enheim, and was his father's first name Robert?'

'Why do you want to know? The Chief will go mad if he even suspects that you're poking your nose into our case, and I'll go mad, too.'

'Keep your hair on. Anyway, I gave you a hot tip earlier. Don't be difficult, just answer my questions, there's a good chap. We're not talking state secrets here.'

Ossi snorted. 'Okay. Norbert is right; I don't know about Robert. I'll find out and let you know. And if you find out anything that could help us, you let *us* know. Otherwise there'll be trouble.'

'You're stuck, right?'

'It's a tough case.'

'I thought so, otherwise you wouldn't be so cooperative.' Stachelmann hung up.

He packed his things, paid his hotel bill and set off. It was a long way to Weimar. At times he was driving on uneven surfaces, sections of freeway from GDR days that hadn't yet been turned into road works. He kept checking the rearview mirror to see if he was being followed. It didn't look like it. There were bottlenecks where the traffic stacked up and Stachelmann frequently came to a standstill, which gave him time to think. An idea took root in his mind: that of an old conspiracy that had lasted right up to the present. He lacked evidence, but was determined to find it.

His mobile rang. It was Ossi.

'Yes, you were right, it *was* Robert. How did you know that?'

'Pure chance. Robert Enheim was in the SA in Hamburg.' Stachelmann turned into a parking and picnic area, and stopped his Golf behind a caravan.

'I see,' said Ossi. 'And my old man was a lieutenant in the Wehrmacht and a big Hitler fan. So what?'

'So the key to your murders lies more than half a century in the past.'

'Nonsense,' answered Ossi. He laughed. 'I admit we're still stuck, but we're beginning to see a glimmer of light. A number of dealers sold their firms to Holler, and in every case there seems to have been some trouble about the sale. At least, *I'd* call it trouble when the seller is made to return a couple of hundred thousand marks of the sale price. So I reckon that didn't go down too well with one of the dealers and he flipped.'

'But that doesn't explain Enheim's murder.'

'No, we're not clear about that yet. Maybe two or three of them wanted to take revenge on Holler, and Enheim refused to go along with it. Or perhaps Enheim threatened Holler, and Holler knew somebody who could do the job for him.'

'What are the names of the other dealers?'

'Helmut Fleischer, Karl Markwart, Otto Grothe, Otto Prugate, Johann-Peter Meier, Ferdinand Meiser, Gottlob Ammann.'

'And you're quite sure I can't help you?'

'Well, the Chief's sure, anyway. He'll never forgive you for the exit you made. But even leaving that aside, murders nearly always have very simple motives, and they're usually linked to something that's happened very recently. Unless it's some family matter—then hatred and desperation *can* build up over many years. In our case it's not a row between relatives, but a madman who's decided to wipe out a property dealer's family. And we've also got a former property dealer, an old man, sitting at his desk with his head shot to pieces. Perhaps Enheim and Holler cheated someone together, or at any rate somebody sees himself as their victim, or whatever. Take it from me, serious crimes are caused by jealousy, envy, blackmail and money. Not history.'

'If you say so,' said Stachelmann and hung up. He was fed up with being lectured.

The parking area was almost full. The whole country seemed to be off on its holidays. Children were charging about among the cars, and people were walking their dogs along the bank that separated the car park from the woodland. From the freeway came the roar of traffic.

Stachelmann felt that he was closer to the truth than the police were, but they didn't want his help. He laughed to himself. The police chief was a career-obsessed idiot and his subordinates were a bunch of dimwits. Well, they'd soon see which of them managed to solve these murders. A group of ss men in Hamburg had enriched themselves by taking Jewish property. Stachelmann was not surprised that the names Ossi had read out were the same as those in the copied documents. There had been a dispute between the ss mafia and the Finance Department. The ss men had turned to Pohl for help, and he had obtained Himmler's backing. These were, after all, men of the Reichs-führer's own elite, and a Finance Department could not be allowed to harass them and denounce them to the Central Office ss Courts. This much seemed clear to Stachelmann, and it should be possible to deduce more. Why had it been necessary for Norbert Enheim to be killed? He was the son of a 'golden pheasant' who was not an ss man, but a senior official, an economic adviser to the Party.

Stachelmann realized how little he knew. Each thing that he discovered or guessed only threw up more questions. The further he delved into the matter, the deeper he sank into chaos. His elation gave way to despondency.

His mobile rang.

'How are you?' It was Anne.

What should he tell her? He did not know how he was. A moment ago his mood had been buoyant, and now he was cast down. 'So-so,' he said.

'Where are you?'

Fleeing from my murderer. Searching for truth. 'I'm in a free-way parking area, having a break. Then I'll carry on to Weimar.'

'Is the traffic bad?'

'Yes, but I'll get there alright.'

'Did your researches in Berlin throw up anything useful?'

Actually, I know all I need to know for my *Habilitation*. I'm failing to get it done not for lack of material but because I'm not cut out to be a historian. Strange things have been going on since I arrived in Berlin. What would have happened if Anne had come with me? 'Yes and no,' he said. 'I didn't really find anything new on my topic. But I discovered something quite different. Something that may link up with those murders in Hamburg.'

'You can't get them out of your head, can you? Don't you think that catching murderers is what the police are there for? We historians don't catch murderers, except ones who've been dead for years.'

Stachelmann had to make an effort not to laugh, as if she had made a good joke. Instead he asked her, 'How are you getting on with preparing for the conference? It starts at the weekend, doesn't it?'

'Yes, and Bohming wants me to go with him. But basically all the work's done. He'll give a splendid lecture, asking all the questions and providing none of the answers. He'll show deep concern but not commit himself to any point of view. He'll present himself as the superior being who embodies the metaphysical nature of all scholarly debate, the Hegel of the twenty-first century. One who doesn't resolve contradictions because he thinks contradiction is necessary.'

'And you had to write out all this rubbish for him?'

'Oh, he did contribute, in particular by giving fabulous directives. A great role model for a trainee historian.' She laughed. 'But stop changing the subject! What are you actually doing in the archives if you're not looking for material for your *Habil*?'

'I've come across some names that are connected with the Holler murders. For instance an SA fellow called Robert Enheim.'

'The murdered property dealer?'

'No, his father. At least, Norbert Enheim's father was called Robert.'

'So what does that suggest to you?'

'I think that in Hamburg there was a group of Nazis who took Aryanization as a personal invitation to help themselves to Jewish property. The Finance Department wanted to take it away from them, but with the help of Himmler and Pohl they were able to hold on to it. We ought to find out whose property it was they took. And we ought to find out why they were still able to keep it after nineteen forty-five, even though under the compensation and restitution legislation that was brought in they were required to notify registerable transactions.'

'Notify what?'

'Registerable transactions. That's what the legislation called any purchases of property or possessions people made from Jews during the Nazi period.'

'Oh yes, I know that, I just didn't quite catch what you said. The reception isn't brilliant. So you think that if you track down their victims, one of them might be the person who killed Enheim and the members of Holler's family.'

It hit Stachelmann like a blow between the eyes. It was so obvious, why hadn't he thought of it?

'Are you still there?'

'Yes.'

She was right. The recent crimes might have their origin in other, earlier crimes. Crimes that had not been paid for, at least in the view of the surviving victims. This was a new lead. But did it rule out other possibilities? Like a quarrel among former Nazis over the booty? The whole thing might be quite different from what he supposed.

'Hello? Josef, you seem to have vanished.'

'I was just thinking.'

'You don't usually take that long.'

'I'm getting old,' he said. But where did those two characters from the Hamburg Finance Department fit into this scenario? 'You've given me an idea which I'll follow up as soon as I get back to Hamburg.'

'Let me be your muse, O Master. However you propose to liberate the world from crime, I'll be fighting at your side. The vacation's messed up anyway.'

'I don't need you to make fun of me, I can do that for myself. But I'll take you at your word. When I'm back we'll give the Hamburg Nazis a good shaking up. They won't know what's hit them!'

'Let's do that,' she said. 'But only if you're not offended anymore.'

'Offended? I don't know the meaning of the word. Bye!'

He looked in the rearview mirror. The car that had been parked behind him had gone. The mirror was now filled with a Polish version of a Fiat. It belonged to a couple with three children. Luggage on the roof. The children were playing close to the car, while the parents sat on a bench, holding hands.

Stachelmann's back began to hurt. The pain travelled from his tailbone to the top of his spine and then round to his chest. Stachelmann swallowed a tablet and waited. Once the tablet seemed to be working, he drove out of the parking area; the traffic was flowing normally now. He found a classical music channel on the radio. Looking in the rearview mirror he saw a silver-grey Opel close behind him. Something caught his eye: the driver of the Opel had white hair. Stachelmann eased off the gas. The Opel maintained the same distance behind him. Stachelmann increased his speed, and so did the Opel. He waited for the next parking area and left the freeway again. The Opel followed. Stachelmann drove to the end of the car park and came to a halt; the Opel stopped at the beginning of it. The driver stayed at the wheel. Stachelmann got out and walked towards the Opel, until he was just a few car lengths away from it. He saw an elderly man, who was fiddling with something in the car and not looking in his direction. Nevertheless, Stachelmann felt that he was being watched. Not daring to approach the Opel more closely, he went back to his Golf and got in. He started the engine and waited. In his rearview mirror he could still see the Opel, with the driver sitting at the wheel. Then a truck towing a trailer moved in between them. Stachelmann stepped on the gas, raced on to the slip road and filtered into the flow of traffic. He moved into the fast lane and flashed his lights at the car in front, forcing it into the nearside lane. He couldn't help grinning: now you're driving like one of those idiots. An exit was signposted: Beelitz. When it was still five hundred yards ahead, he moved into a tiny gap in front of a lorry. Horns sounded angrily behind him. He took the exit lane and at the end of it turned left, took the bridge over the freeway and joined it again in the opposite direction. At the next exit he left the freeway again. He looked in his mirror: no sign of the Opel. It was unlikely that the driver would have seen him leave the freeway.

He drove fast in an easterly direction, turning off at several junctions. At Hennickendorf he parked his car in the shade of a lime tree and got out. The village consisted of a handful of houses, plus a few animal sheds and barns. Some of the houses and outbuildings were very dilapidated. He looked up a driveway which led to a vast collection of sheds that had once belonged to a collective farm, the 'Friedrich Engels Livestock Production Unit'. The sheds must have been empty for years now. The yard contained only wrecks of cars and a rusty stroller, and there was broken glass on the ground. It was very quiet. On the road through the village a few chickens were pecking about on the asphalt. As a student, Stachelmann had once been to the GDR on a group visit organized by Heidelberg communist activists. The superiority of socialism was impressed on them. They visited a collective farm, and Stachelmann would never forget the words with which the collective's chairman greeted his visitors: 'Comrades, even in livestock farming man is at the centre.' That had been a long time ago. This time he was fleeing from a madman who was intent on killing him.

Why? Even while he was still in hospital Stachelmann had puzzled over this. There were three possibilities. Either the fellow was simply a lunatic and had chosen Stachelmann as his victim because he didn't like the colour of his hair. Or it had something to do with his investigations. Or Stachelmann himself was the lunatic, and only imagined that he'd been pushed off the platform because he was suffering from persecution mania. He didn't rule out that possibility. The Opel had been following him—or was that just his imagination? The sequence of events, the apparent chase, could easily be viewed as a series of coincidences. He had heard of people who tried to relieve the boredom of freeway driving by attaching themselves to the tail of another vehicle. They felt better in company.

These ruminations did not get him any further. If the man did want to kill him, he might make another attempt in Weimar. But how did he know that Stachelmann was in Berlin anyway? And why, in heaven's name, had such an obvious question only just occurred to him?

At the side of the road was a small graveyard with a wall around it. He sat down on the wall, in the shade of the lime tree.

Who knew about his research in Berlin and Weimar? Bohming, Anne, Renate Breuer, perhaps one or two other colleagues. Perhaps the students had got to hear of it, but that was hardly likely. Had he mentioned it in his seminar? No. He had meant to talk about it in order to foster an interest in archive work among the students. But in the end he had said nothing because he was afraid Alicia might follow him.

Then he remembered his visit to Holler. He had told Holler, in passing, as if to justify his position as a historian. He often felt impelled to justify himself when there was no occasion for it.

A dirty old green tractor came roaring and rattling along the cobbled road. It was pulling a trailer, and the two children riding on it stared at the stranger.

If Holler feared what Stachelmann's research might bring to light, then he had a reason to kill him. Perhaps it threatened Holler's livelihood: Stachelmann might discover something that would ruin him. No, he contradicted himself. How old might Holler be? Let's say late forties, early fifties. He couldn't possibly feature in the documents that Stachelmann was reading. And Holler knew that. But his *father* did feature in them. Herrmann Holler had been an ss officer and had got rich by acquiring Jewish property. He had enlisted the help of Himmler and Pohl in order to hang on to what he had stolen. And now two of his grandchildren and his daughter-in-law had been murdered. And Robert Enheim's son was dead, too. The policewoman had been run over. Someone had pushed Stachelmann onto the railway tracks; he remembered the old, suntanned face, or had that been just a bad dream? And perhaps Ulrike Kreimeier had been on the trail of the murderer or murderers and had been killed as a result. He wanted to think that all these things were connected. But he had no proof.

If the various cases *were* connected, then he himself was the next victim and a murderer was after him—the kind of murderer who had no inhibitions about killing children. The man was a monster.

He tried to arrange his thoughts logically, the procedure he always adopted when faced with a problem to which the answer was not obvious. As he did so, his hands began to tremble, he felt a cramp in his guts, he found himself going hot and cold and he broke out in a cold sweat. It was a few moments before he realized what his body was signaling. It was sheer terror: never in his life had he been more afraid than now. If his working hypothesis was correct, and if the murderer did not even think twice about killing police officers and children, then Stachelmann would remain in mortal danger until the case was solved. Whether the Opel had been tailing him or not, death would be waiting for him in Weimar. The murderer would not fail a second time. He would take even greater risks than before, because he was bound to assume that Stachelmann had discovered something.

Stachelmann looked around. It was early afternoon, and the lime tree's shadow was starting to spread across the graveyard. Shielding his eyes with his hand, Stachelmann looked along the road. In the distance he could see a silver car, indistinct in the shimmering air. Almost paralyzed, he stared at the approaching car, which trailed a cloud of dust in its wake. An impulse told him to flee, but his body would not move. He no longer felt the heat; he simply gazed at the car. At the wheel sat a man with white hair. It was an Audi, in metallic silver. At last Stachelmann was able to make out the registration: the driver was a local man. The car drove past, covering Stachelmann in dust.

It was a moment before he realized that he was crying. He had slipped off the wall and was leaning with his back against it, sitting on the grass verge. He touched his eyes and felt the tears on his hands. He took a handkerchief from his trouser pocket and wiped his face. He was shaking. He forced himself to take deep, regular breaths. A shadow fell across him. In front of him stood a dog, looking at him with its head cocked on one side. Stachelmann felt weak as he got up, though he was not trembling so much now. He placed one foot in front of the other, paying attention to his breathing. As he opened the car door he felt a rush of hot air. Getting into the driver's seat, he reached across to the other side to open the passenger door, and sat in the draft. The dog had followed him and was sniffing at the driver's door.

Stachelmann got out; the dog was peeing on the front tire. He took his briefcase from the trunk, and had to rummage in it to find his address book. Turning to 'D', he dialled Anne's mobile number. She answered at once.

'Can I come and stay with you for a few days?'

She did not answer immediately. 'What's up? Has something happened to you?'

'You could say that.' He tried hard to make his voice sound normal.

'You sound as if you're ill.'

'I'm fine. I'm even still alive.' He laughed.

'Have you had an accident?'

'No. All I've had is an idea, but it's landed me in deep trouble.'

'Where are you?'

'In some wretched little place in Brandenburg or Sachsen-Anhalt.'

'I thought you were going to Weimar.'

'So did I until I had this thought.'

'Forgive me for saying so, but you seem to be talking nonsense.'

'That shows you the state of mind I'm in. Can I come?'

'Yes.'

'What about the conference?'

'I'll sort that out somehow.'

For the first few miles of the drive to Hamburg he was sure he would end up in the ditch. But he gradually found himself shaking less and was able to concentrate on the road. Now and again he looked into the rearview mirror. He only stopped once, for petrol. Then he drove on at top speed. Later, whenever he heard the expression 'tunnel vision', he always thought of that drive round the Berlin Ring and on towards Hamburg. It was still light when he parked the car in a side street close to Anne's apartment. Not too close, he thought, in case someone's following me. He climbed the stairs to her place and rang the bell.

Anne appeared in the doorway. 'Good Lord, you look terrible! Have you been drinking?'

He shook his head and went in. He pulled the door closed and turned the key.

She stared at him as if he were a being from another planet.

He went into the living room and collapsed on to the sofa. She came over and stood facing him. 'Are you hungry? Thirsty?'

'Something to drink, please.'

She came back with a bottle of mineral water and two glasses. She filled the glasses and passed one to him. Then she sat down in an armchair diagonally opposite him. She watched him drink; water ran down his chin and he wiped it away with the back of his hand. She gently shook her head. 'What have you done?'

'Nothing, at least nothing I know of. I told you, someone's after me and wants to kill me. And on the road to Weimar he was tailing me. Or I think he was, anyway.'

She looked him in the eye. 'Who?'

'I don't know. I have a suspicion, but it's hazy to say the least.' He briefly recounted all that had happened.

She looked confused, clearly not knowing what to make of his story. Standing up, she went over to the window. 'But there must be some explanation.' She looked down into the street. 'Did anyone follow you here?'

On the way back to Hamburg Stachelmann had kept checking the mirror. 'No, I would have noticed.'

'I don't read many detective stories, but even I know that it's possible to follow somebody unobtrusively.'

'I shouldn't have come here,' said Stachelmann.

She shook her head. 'You couldn't go home. Perhaps they're already there waiting for you.'

'They?'

'Whoever. Now I can repay your hospitality. I've got a good sofa.'

'And what about the conference?'

'I've disappeared. Family crisis.' She giggled.

He was tired and was feeling the effect of his exertions. His legs felt heavy.

She looked out of the window again, and then said, 'I'm sure you must be hungry.' She went off without waiting for an answer.

He could hear her at work in the kitchen.

He woke up when a ray of sunshine shone on to his face. There was an aroma of coffee. He heard footsteps in the hall, and Anne came into the living room, grinning. 'I ought to punish you by giving you our supper for breakfast. You fell asleep last night almost before I'd set foot in the kitchen. But as I'm too compassionate and hospitable for my own good, I'll give you a proper breakfast.'

Stachelmann looked down at himself. He was lying on the sofa in the clothes he had been wearing the day before. He had had a good sleep, and could not remember dreaming at all. He wasn't in too bad a shape. Gradually memory returned. He did not feel as helpless as last night: the fear had lost some of its grip on him.

'And if you like, I'll buy you some decent clothes. I can lend you a few marks.'

'We can discuss that movement on the international financial markets after breakfast, if you can put up with me being smelly until then.'

'There are worse things,' she laughed. 'For instance there's the notorious slayer of document-hunters.'

'Any woman with an ounce of proper feeling wouldn't make jokes about my coming to a sticky end.'

They ate their breakfast.

'And what next?' asked Anne. 'I think you should go to the police.'

'No, they think I'm mad.'

'It's no good taking offense.'

'Listen, I went to the police. I reported the attack on me. I told Ossi, and a young greenhorn from the Berlin police came and sat by my hospital bed and dutifully wrote down my tale of woe. But they didn't believe a word of it.'

'What if you really insist they take it seriously?'

'Waste of energy. I've no wish to make an ass of myself. I know more about the Holler affair now than the police do, and I'll carry on and find out the rest.' He told her about breaking into the copying firm. He went into the hall and got the copied documents from the inside pocket of his jacket.

She read them through. 'I don't quite understand...'

'Neither do I. But it's quite clear that there was a group of Nazi officials who made eliminating Jews from the economic sphere their own personal business. They robbed Jews who were emigrating or were being sent to the gas chambers, but gave their deals an appearance of legality. And I think that they were able to keep at least part of the loot after the war. They spent the rest of their lives as highly-respected citizens of Hamburg. That's what I know, or think I know, so far. And it's quite a lot. Even if I can't prove any of it.'

She nodded. 'And what do you propose to do now?'

'I'll find out whether any of these honourable gentlemen are still in the land of the living. And if one of them is still alive, I can ask him about what went on then.'

'I'll help you.'

'You'd better not, it's enough if *one* of us gets pushed under a train.'

'But I can keep an eye on you, since you have this tendency to stumble.'

'So you don't believe me either.'

'Not a word.'

'The ideal basis for our future collaboration. Have you got a phone book?'

She went to fetch it.

Stachelmann leafed through it. Under 'A' he found 'Ammann'. 'There aren't many Ammanns, let's start with them.' He dialed the number, which rang several times before someone answered.

'Is that Herr Ammann?'

'And who are you?' It was an old man's voice.

'I'm sorry, I forgot to give my name. It's Dr Stachelmann.'

Anne raised her eyebrows and grinned. She pressed a button on the telephone; her hair brushed his face as she did so.

'And what can I do for you?' Now Ammann's voice could be heard in the room.

'A colleague and I are conducting some research for the university into the history of the city of Hamburg. Right now we're dealing with the Second World War. Someone told us that we should speak to you, you'd have things to tell us about it. You were in the city administration at the time, weren't you?'

The reply was slow in coming. 'You could say so. But I don't know what I could tell you. I wasn't in a position of authority.'

'That's not what I was told.'

'Who by?' Amman's voice sounded at once anxious and aggressive.

'I have to protect my source,' Stachelmann said. 'We promised to keep his identity confidential. We'd do the same in your case, if you'd prefer that.'

'I'm not interested. I don't know anything that would help you.' He hung up.

Stachelmann pressed 'redial'.

'Yes?'

'Dr Stachelmann again. I'm sorry, we got cut off. So much for modern technology! I forgot to mention the most important thing. I have a document here which refers to a Hauptscharführer Ammann. That's you, isn't it? And I don't suppose you'd be happy to read in the papers that former ss Hauptscharführer Ammann is in the same mortal danger as a certain Herr Enheim, whose father was an sa Standartenführer.'

Silence. Stachelmann could hear Ammann breathing heavily. 'We'd like to call on you. How about this afternoon?'

'Come at two o'clock. My address is in the phone book.' Ammann sounded as if he had aged in the course of the conversation. He hung up.

'I'll just go and buy you some proper clothes and a toothbrush,' said Anne. 'There are some shops just round the corner from here. You stay here and watch from the window to make sure no one follows me.'

Stachelmann opened his wallet and gave her four hundred marks, which she put into her purse. He went to the window and kept an eye on her as she went off. There was no one following her. Seen from a distance she looked even more slightly built. Eventually she disappeared round a corner.

The door to her study was open, and after a brief hesitation he went in. It was quite small. On the longer wall was a bookcase reaching to the ceiling, with the books arranged alphabetically by author. Under 'S' he found his own two books: his doctoral thesis about Buchenwald concentration camp, and a paperback entitled *Forgetting and Repressing*, a polemic against the attitude of most West Germans after the war. He took the doctoral thesis from the shelf and opened it. Leafing through it, he saw that various passages had been marked, in some cases with an exclamation mark in the margin. It was the same with the paperback. He put the books back on the shelf and, returning to the living room, sat down on the sofa. The two copied documents were on the table. He must find a safe place for them.

Anne was carrying various plastic bags when she returned. 'These should fit you,' she said. 'A bit on the big side, if anything.' She put a bag on the coffee table and went into the kitchen. Stachelmann emptied it out on to the sofa. Two shirts, a pair of trousers, socks, some underwear: very nice. There were no price tags on the clothes. Stachelmann leaned against the kitchen doorpost. 'I still owe you some money, don't I?'

'No, it was about time you had some new clothes. I don't like suits either, but even jeans have an expiry date.' She clapped her hand to her forehead. 'Oh, I almost forgot.' She handed him a toothbrush. 'And now off with you to the bathroom, you stink, Dr Stachelmann.'

She left the apartment to fetch her little Toyota. He waited at the back entrance and got in quickly as soon as she brought it round. At the university, she found a parking space close to the Philosophers' Tower. They went into his office; Stachelmann had the copies of the documents in his hand and was wondering where to hide them. Struck by a sudden thought, he left the room and went to the photocopier. The machine warmed up quickly and he copied the documents and put the new copies into his jacket pocket. Back in his room, he looked at the mountain of shame, took a folder at random from the middle of the pile, and buried the Berlin copies among the papers already in it. Then he put the folder back into the pile.

'And you'll be able to find those again?' Anne mocked him.

He did not reply.

He quickly looked through the mail on his desk. A letter from the Federal Archive aroused his curiosity. He opened it: it was a circular addressed to all users of the Archive.

> *I regret to inform you that a considerable number of documents will be unavailable for use for the foreseeable future. Through what is either a most unfortunate accident or a criminal act, the copying firm to which the Federal Archive entrusted the copying of documents for users has burned down and many documents have been destroyed. Most regrettably, an unusually large number of documents were in the firm's possession at the time of the fire. The Federal Archive is making every effort to replace the destroyed files wherever possible. However, we have to assume that in the case of most of the burnt documents no copies exist. Unfortunately many of these documents were scheduled to be transferred to microfiche only in the coming months...*

He passed the letter to Anne, who read it and whistled. 'Now that *is* interesting. Someone must have been playing with matches just after you were there.'

'It would be quite a coincidence if the documents had just caught fire spontaneously.'

She was a good driver. He sat in the passenger seat and thought about how best to tackle Ammann. He was nervous about this meeting. Perhaps Ammann was mixed up in these murders. Perhaps he had killed Enheim. It was even conceivable that Ammann was the one pulling the strings in all this madness that both the Hamburg police and now he himself were caught up in.

With a street map open on his lap, Stachelmann directed Anne to Hagedornstrasse in Eppendorf. Managing not to lose their way, they arrived on time. Parked on the other side of the road was a police car with two officers sitting inside.

'So this is the kind of place a serial murderer lives in,' said Anne when they were standing in front of Ammann's house.

Ammann opened the door at the first ring. He *is* mad, Stachelmann thought as he saw him peering out through the crack.

'Are you Dr Stachelmann?'

'Yes, and this is Frau Derling.'

Ammann motioned to them to come in. The smell in the house was overpowering. Stachelmann could see that Ammann was afraid. He showed his visitors into the living room and gestured towards the sofa, while he himself sat down on the edge of an armchair and looked at them. 'Well?'

Stachelmann put his copies of the documents down on the coffee table. 'These are some of the documents that we are keeping at a secret location. We obtained them by chance, by a very fortunate chance.'

Ammann stared at him without moving a muscle.

'We've only brought these copies with us to give you an idea of the kind of material we have. We'll gladly show you more another time.'

Ammann still did not move. A bead of sweat glistened on his forehead.

'Now won't you tell us a bit about the war?'

'What should I tell you?' He spoke in a low voice.

'Well, how you combated your enemies, the Jews.'

'The Jews weren't my enemies, at least not the majority of those who lived in Germany.'

'But the ones in other countries.'

'They boycotted us. From the beginning they stirred up hostility towards the new Germany. In America and England, all over the world, they were shouting, Don't buy from Germans! So some people in Germany blew a fuse. It's no wonder, when a nation has been trampled underfoot for years. Just think of the Treaty of Versailles!'

'It was because of Versailles that you took the Jews' property from them?'

'It was enemy assets. That wasn't *my* decision, that was Goering with his Four-Year Plan. The Führer wanted the Jews out of Germany. He had his reasons. And all those who wanted to go, we let them.'

'Quite a number of them, yes,' said Stachelmann. 'But most of them you killed.'

'There's no proof of that! And it's nothing to do with me. In any case, they were our enemies. I surely don't need to tell you how world Jewry reacted to the Führer's accession to power.'

'And so, as you said, some people blew a fuse. In November nineteen thirty-eight, for instance.'

'That was Goebbels. He persuaded Hitler—the Führer never refused him anything. Later Hitler regretted it. And Goering was furious, and so were Himmler and Heydrich. Goebbels was a zealot, always in overdrive. We in the ss obeyed the Führer's orders, and Himmler saw to it that everybody toed the line.'

'Himmler doesn't seem to have kept such a close eye as all that. How else can you explain the fact that you weren't hauled up before the ss court?'

Ammann was taken aback for a moment. Then he said, 'For the simple reason that I bought the house and the plot legally, even under the strict rules of the ss. Say what you like about us, we did things by the book. Not like today.'

'At least nowadays people don't find themselves going up in smoke,' remarked Anne.

Ammann laughed. 'Take a look at Ohlsdorf crematorium sometime.'

Stachelmann felt like hitting him. He knew these people who came up with their own slant on their past so that they could live with it. You don't sleep well with mass murder on your conscience. They were slowly dying off; Ammann was obviously one of the tough ones. There was no point in trying to change his attitudes. People like him had a conscience-salving lie ready in response to any question, because they had already put these questions to themselves. There was nothing to be got out of Ammann by having a debate with him. His sort only responded to pressure.

'Okay, so now we know your version of the story. There's just one problem. After the restitution legislation was passed you ought to have informed the authorities that you had *bought* a house and a plot of land from Jews.'

'Nobody asked me. Nobody approached me about anything.'

'You were supposed to come forward and report it yourself.'

'I don't know anything about that.'

'Just imagine people reading in tomorrow's paper that the former ss man Gottlob Ammann robbed Jews and after nineteen forty-five avoided making restitution.'

'I didn't rob anybody.'

'How much did you pay?'

'I don't remember. But it was the market price.'

'But as it happened, the market price for Jewish property had pretty much gone through the floor.'

'That wasn't my fault. I'd like you to go now.' Ammann stood up. His forehead was damp.

'Surely not. Do you really want to read in tomorrow's *Abendblatt* about those highly moral dealings you engaged in?'

'I sold that property long ago.' Ammann sat down again.

Stachelmann could not see the point of that remark. 'I know, but that doesn't alter the fact that an injustice took place.'

'An injustice—who can say that after so many years? Were you there? Can anybody judge without having been there?'

'What do you think of Stalin?' asked Anne.

Stachelmann was annoyed: this was a distraction when he was just beginning to get somewhere with Ammann.

Ammann looked at Anne in confusion. 'Why do you ask me that? We've no need to talk about that criminal just now.'

'How do you know Stalin was a criminal? You weren't there.' Anne shot this question at him before Stachelmann could intervene. His anger faded. She had cracked Ammann's resistance, even if he would never admit it.

Ammann's eyes held the look of a man cornered. 'That's different,' he protested weakly.

'You sold the Jewish property to Holler.'

'How do you know?'

'Our documents go beyond nineteen forty-five,' said Stachelmann. He hoped that Ammann would swallow this lie, too. Ammann was a coward, the sort who only turned into a murderer in murderous times. After 1945 he had broken the law, but not killed anybody. 'The man who killed Enheim might kill you too. Did you know Enheim?'

Ammann took the question calmly. 'I knew old Enheim very well, but I hardly knew the son.'

'When was the first time you saw Norbert Enheim?'

'At a celebration—well, at his christening, in fact. Holler was his godfather.'

'Herrmann Holler?'

Ammann nodded. 'That's not a crime, is it?'

'Did the godfather take an interest in his godson?'

'I've no idea, it was shortly before the end of the war and I had other things on my mind besides watching what other people's godparents did.'

'Is it correct to say that you and Holler were members of the same group?'

'We didn't have much to do with each other at work.'

'That's not what I meant. Did you have contact with each other outside work?'

'Not really. We sometimes met at the police sports club. Holler and I liked playing volleyball and handball.' Ammann stood up, and ran a hand through his hair. Evidently some thought had occurred to him.

'And who else was in the group?'

'Group, group, it's an exaggeration to call it that.'

'Grothe, Enheim, Holler, Prugate and a few others.' Stachelmann said it with as little emotion as if he were reading out a tax assessment. 'Perhaps you prefer the term circle of friends?'

Ammann took two steps towards the window, turned on his heels and took two steps back. There's something on his mind, thought Stachelmann. Should I go on putting pressure on him, or should I wait and see what he comes up with? He watched Ammann, whose thoughts seemed to be elsewhere. He saw Anne watching the movements of the former ss man as he marched to and fro. Their eyes met. Anne raised her eyebrows. Stachelmann raised his hands slightly for a moment. He didn't know what was going on inside Ammann's head. Was he being overwhelmed by memories?

Ammann came to a sudden stop. Pointing a finger at Stachelmann, he said, 'I'm not sure I caught your name. Stachelmann, was it?'

Surprised, Stachelmann nodded.

'Do you know a Paul Stachelmann?'

Stachelmann wanted to thrust the question aside, but it closed in on him remorselessly. As if his head were being moved by someone else, he nodded.

'Then no doubt you forgot to include that name when you were listing the members of our—what was that nice expression you used?—our circle of friends.'

Stachelmann shook his head.

Ammann laughed. 'The name means something to you, I'm sure. Was he your uncle? Your father? Well, let's hear it!'

Ammann's voice had grown sharper, with a mocking undertone. It had probably sounded like that when he had worn his ss uniform. 'No answer is an answer, too.' He laughed. 'Sometimes the truth catches up with you just when you'd rather it didn't, isn't that so, Dr Stachelmann?'

Stachelmann made an effort to control his anger. He was angry with himself. He had let his father fob him off with only half the truth, and although he had had his suspicions, he had let it pass. Now Ammann was punishing him for that lack of courage.

'Yes, there was a circle of friends, of patriotic German men, in Hamburg, and those that you named all belonged to it. There were some others you left out, besides Paul Stachelmann. It was wartime, man, you can't imagine that, can you? Wartime—your life on the line every day, every night, every hour. War is a particular way of experiencing life. It left its mark on whole generations. And then someone like you comes along, a product of the Economic Miracle, and tries to tell us what's what. Any minute you'll be bringing up all that stuff about the Jews. I'll say it again, even if you can't understand it, war is a particular way of living. The Jews were our enemies. It was them or us, that's how it was. They declared war on us, and we defended ourselves. That's all there was to it. Oh yes, we lost the war against the unholy alliance of world Jewry and Bolshevism, though of course I see Bolshevism as no more than a part of world Jewry. I need only name Trotsky, Litvinov, Radek, and whatever the rest of them were called.'

'We're leaving,' said Stachelmann. He couldn't take any more of this. Anne raised no objection. They heard Ammann laughing as they left. 'You cowards!' he said. 'Give Paul my regards, it's ages since I've seen him.'

The police car was still outside. Anne got in behind the wheel of the Toyota and drove round the corner. She parked at the roadside and switched off the engine. Looking sideways at Stachelmann, she said, 'A direct hit.'

A direct hit indeed. Stachelmann felt humiliated. It was his own fault, he shouldn't have let his father get away with giving only partial explanations. Hadn't his father also said, 'It was wartime'? No, it wasn't wartime when that Nazi 'circle of friends' was robbing Jews. The war started later.

'It's your father,' said Anne.

Stachelmann nodded.

'You can't help it.'

'Yes and no.' He told her about the conversation he had had with his father.

'Most people don't dare to ask about it at all,' she said. 'I was much readier than you to let myself be fobbed off with half-baked explanations. I'm sure my grandfather has also got a shady past. You were prepared to risk creating a breach between you.'

'It depends what you think the person has done. Was your grandfather an ss man, possibly a murderer, or at the very least somebody who robbed Jews? A mere 'follower' who went on being cowardly after nineteen forty-five isn't in the same category. What matters is *what* someone is keeping quiet about—just cowardice, or involvement in actual crimes. We're talking about robbery, extortion and murder. That's really bad. And it was also really bad the way that man was able to make me look stupid. Thanks to my father's lies.'

'That was awful. All the same, he did confirm your suspicions. We're a good bit further forward.'

Stachelmann's agitation subsided. She was right; the visit to

Ammann had been both a defeat and a success. 'But we know nothing about the murderer or murderers, and nothing about the person who pushed me off the platform in Berlin.'

'But now we can consider what might follow from the things we *have* found out. I think we're dealing with a quarrel among a gang of crooks and their descendants. Let's say Holler junior swindled his old man's cronies. He knew something, and what he knew was enough to make the rest of the gang hand over part of their loot. And what was the loot? It was what they had extorted in the course of their own private Aryanization programme, with the protection of Pohl and Himmler and ultimately, after some initial resistance, with the blessing of the financial authorities. It would be interesting to know why the Finance Department caved in. Even during the Third Reich they weren't known for doing that. I once did some research on Goering's Four-Year Plan; they grabbed everything they could get their hands on, and Goering didn't kowtow to the ss. But that's just by the way. Back to my theory, which I'm still not quite happy with, because there are some aspects that don't fit. Why were Holler's wife and children killed? It may have nothing at all to do with this, but I don't believe that. And the murder of Enheim fits perfectly with my hypothesis, and possibly the murder of the policewoman does too. Are you sure that it *was* a murder?'

Stachelmann looked at her. Her eyes were shining, and she had obviously given all this considerable thought. He listened to her assessing and arranging his ideas. He could have hugged her.

She went on: 'And Ammann was frightened, my God, he was frightened. Otherwise I'm sure he wouldn't have been so aggressive. He's probably afraid of suffering the same fate as Enheim. But I don't see where the attempt to kill you fits into all this. And why were the documents in Berlin burned? Because we might find the murderer in them? Let me just speculate a bit. The policewoman was on the murderer's trail, he realized it and killed her. But how did he know? No idea. And how did he find out that *you* were on his track?'

'I wasn't, he was on mine.'

'How things really are is irrelevant. What matters is what the murderer *thinks*. Obviously he thinks you have some idea of who he is or what's going on. That's not actually the case, but somehow he's got wind of something that he doesn't like one bit. Who knows about your research in the archive?'

'Ossi, and a few people in the department. Perhaps Bohming has been gossiping, but let's ignore that possibility for now. My parents know, but we needn't start suspecting that my father set a killer on to me.'

'Perhaps he mentioned it to someone.'

'He could have, but I doubt it.'

'And those are all the people who know?' asked Anne.

'No, you didn't let me finish, those aren't all. Holler knows. I told him.'

'Oh, my God!'

* * *

Holler was as polite as ever.

'I'll be blunt, Herr Holler', said Ossi. 'You know something about the murders that you're not telling us.'

Holler shook his head. He looked at Ossi suspiciously. His expression said: what *is* this nonsense? 'I hope you don't mean what I think you mean.'

'Yes, I do.'

'I've told you from the outset that you should not be directing your enquiries against me but catching the murderer. The more I think about what you are insinuating, the more offensive I find it. In case you have forgotten, my wife and two of my children are dead. I am the one who is suffering. I am not a murderer, or are you suggesting that I killed them all? It would hardly surprise me at this point if you started to believe that.'

'We're not suggesting that,' said Carmen. 'We just feel certain that you know more about the murders than you're telling us. That's all.'

'What gives you that idea?' Holler was calm again.

'We believe that the murders are the outcome of a quarrel between property dealers. You've made enemies through your business practices. Someone you've done business with thinks he's been cheated. Something snaps, he wants to take revenge, and to do it in the most effective way. And so he kills not you but the people you care about. Any other explanation would be too far-fetched.'

Holler gave her a questioning look.

'Only you know whom you have harmed most. Before a person kills three people he sends out some signals. He wants you to realize how much you have injured him, and he wants to be able to see you suffer. Perhaps at the time when he sent the signals you paid no attention or didn't see him as a threat. But I refuse to believe that you haven't thought about this every night for the past two years, and that in thinking about it you haven't formed at least some idea of who it could be, or must be. If so, you share the responsibility for each of the crimes that have happened since you first recognized the significance of those signals.'

Ossi was afraid that Holler would be angry. But he remained calm. He sat in his chair looking up at the ceiling. 'I see. You regard me as an accomplice.'

'Not in the legal sense,' Ossi said. 'But you're more involved in this than you're prepared to admit. The longer you keep silent and obstruct our investigations, the greater is your share of the guilt. Surely that's quite plain. Did you suspect Enheim?'

Holler laughed. 'I can see where this is heading. You want to pin Enheim's murder on me. If you go on like this I shall hold a press conference and let the public see how the victim of the worst crime in Hamburg is being treated. And what the police are doing to find the murderer. Have you any more questions? In case you should say afterwards that I've been hiding something again.'

'You didn't answer my question,' said Ossi.

'Well, what do *you* think? Of course I lie awake at night asking myself who could be doing this to me. But in all those nights I have not managed to work out the identity of the murderer. And up to now I always thought that was the job of the police. You took my books, you can see from them how much I pay in taxes to prevent the things that have happened to me from happening. Perhaps I'll succeed in identifying the murderer when he appears in front of me and kills me too. After all, that would seem to be his plan.'

'So you *have* decided on one particular scenario,' said Carmen dryly.

'What do you mean?'

'That you believe that the murderer wants to kill your whole family, including you. But there are other possibilities.'

'Oh yes?'

'For instance, I think it's just as likely that the murderer plans to kill all your family *except* you.'

Holler took a deep breath. A flush spread over his face. The artery in his neck throbbed. 'And I am the chief suspect.' His tone was sarcastic.

'Not at all. That's one possibility, but the other is that this way you're being hit harder than if you yourself were killed. And in addition you spend the rest of your life fearing that you *will* be killed.' She spoke calmly, almost casually. 'We can't give you total protection for the rest of your life. In your own interests you need to make up your mind to help us. Tell us what thoughts you've had. After all, you know more than we do. And you're not telling us what you know, because if you told us the truth you wouldn't appear in such a good light.'

Holler stood up and took a few aimless steps. 'It must be one of those dealers.'

'One of those whom you favoured with demands for repayment?' asked Ossi.

Holler gave an almost imperceptible nod. 'But I don't know which one.'

'Don't try to tell us that there isn't one particular name in your mind.'

'I suspected Enheim.'

'But he's dead now. Nothing further has happened since then.'

'Why did you suspect him?' asked Carmen.

'Because I had a major dispute with him. I had to threaten him with legal action.'

'Over the repayment.'

'Yes, he sold me a piece of property that was no good. In retrospect I realized that I should have examined it more closely. I trusted him, but then we discovered the dry rot. Complete renovation, have you any idea what that costs? It's cheaper to build from scratch. And Enheim refused to lower the price. He abused and threatened me. He was a hot-tempered man and he frightened me. It's a wonder he agreed to make the repayment.'

'I'm still surprised that there were repayments made in connection with every single one of those sales.'

Holler shrugged.

'So who did kill Enheim, and who killed Ulrike Kreimeier?' asked Ossi. 'Have you any thoughts about those cases?'

'Perhaps Enheim learned by chance that your colleague had found out something about him. And after that he got into an argument with someone.'

'Was Ulrike investigating Enheim?' asked Carmen, when they were back in the car.

'Don't think so.'

'You liked her, didn't you—or perhaps it was more than that.'

'Yes, more than just liking.'

* * *

Kohn had no difficulty in fitting the toy car with the more powerful remote control. Now he could steer the jeep with its huge wheels from several hundred yards away. And he could detonate the explosive at the touch of a button. He did not know just how violent the explosion would be; he had filled the car's every cavity with plastic explosive. It must be enough—too much, if anything. Kohn would be sorry if the nanny was injured; he could only try to ensure that the car was some yards away from her when he triggered the explosion. He had linked the detonator to a wire, which would start to heat up on receiving a command from the radio control unit. He had tried it out: it worked like a small immersion heater.

The forecast had promised sunshine for the next day. It would be warm and dry, and the little boy would be playing in the garden as Kohn had seen him do during the past few weeks. Tonight he would push the car through the fence and the hedge. Then tomorrow morning he would return there and wait for the right moment to set the car moving towards the boy and activate the detonator.

What would he do when he had completed his task? It frightened him to think of it. Death was waiting for him. He hoped he would die content, having closed the account that his enemies had opened. Not many people achieved completion in their lives before they died.

That night he went to Elbchaussee, where he tried to look like someone just going for a late evening walk. What could be more innocuous than an old man with a walking stick and a rucksack? A police car was parked in front of Holler's gate. Inside it sat two policemen, one of whom was yawning, showing all his teeth. The other turned his head towards Kohn, but soon looked away again. Kohn turned the corner, looking about him the whole time; there was no one to be seen. A few days earlier he had discovered a gap between the fence and the ground, and now he pushed the car through it. He leaned against the fence and looked around once more. Still nobody. Using his stick, he pushed the car into the hedge. He had expected it to be quite easy, but the hedge was denser than he had thought. He had to pull the car back out again using the handle of his stick, and try again at a different spot. This time it worked: there was no more resistance and he knew that the jeep was safely on the other side. For a moment he feared that it might have tipped over, but no, it was standing upright on its wheels—he could see it in the moonlight. He looked all around him again. Then he headed back towards the S-Bahn station.

Chapter fifteen

Where are the documents?' asked Stachelmann.

'What documents?' asked Anne.

'The ones I brought back from Berlin.'

'You put them in your pocket.'

'Well, I may have done. But I've looked everywhere—they're not there.'

'I don't know. Could they have fallen out of your pocket in the car?'

'I can't imagine that I'd put documents in my trouser pocket. I've already looked in my jacket.' He clapped his hand to his forehead. 'Damn! I left them behind at Ammann's place.'

'It doesn't matter. After breakfast you can get the ones from your office and copy them again.'

Stachelmann stretched.

'You've had a bad night,' she said.

He nodded.

'Your face is quite grey.'

It had been a terrible night. Lying on a strange bed was often painful for Stachelmann. Anne's sofa had turned into an instrument of torture.

'Tonight you'll sleep in my bed and I'll sleep on the sofa.' Her tone admitted of no contradiction.

'Aye, aye, cap'n!'

His back ached so much that he could hardly sit. Almost every joint in his body was hurting, and every movement produced a stabbing pain. He ate a slice of bread and raspberry jam and then walked over to where his jacket was hanging on the coatrack in the hall. He searched through all his pockets for his tablets but could not find them. He emptied his briefcase out on to the floor; among the papers there were some empty strips that had once held tablets. His vertebrae were pressing inwards, and with every breath he drew his chest seemed about to burst. When he breathed in, it felt as if his rib joints were being pushed against a bed of nails. He felt constricted, as though someone behind him was viciously drawing the corset of pain ever tighter around his chest. He lay down on the floor. He was perspiring.

Anne was alarmed. 'What's wrong with you?' She knelt down beside him.

'It'll pass,' he said.

She looked at him in astonishment. 'Wouldn't you rather lie down on my bed?'

'I certainly would!' He made an effort to grin. Carefully he got to his feet and went into her bedroom.

She sat down on the edge of the bed. 'Shall I call a doctor?'

'No, but could you bring me my mobile, please?'

She came back with her cordless phone.

'No, my mobile, please, it's got my doctor's number stored in it. It's in the inside pocket of my jacket.'

Lifting her eyebrows, she went to get it.

Stachelmann selected his rheumatologist's number. He was lucky and got the doctor straight away. He requested a prescription for Indometacin, and asked for it to be sent round by courier to Anne's address.

When he had ended the call, Anne said, 'I could have gone to fetch it.'

'Well, I don't want other people running errands for me. I won't have it.' It came out more brusquely than he intended.

She flinched. 'But perhaps you'll be able to live with yourself if I take the prescription to be filled?'

'I'm sorry,' he said, taking her hand.

She pulled it away and put it on her knee. 'And what's this illness called? What kind of medication is it? If you don't find these questions too intrusive.'

'Rheumatoid arthritis,' he said. 'With me it starts in my back and if it's feeling spiteful it spreads to all the other joints and various parts of my insides as well.'

'So it's rheumatism. My grandma had that.'

'I'd be prepared to bet that your grandma had *osteo*arthritis, which firstly is terribly painful, secondly results from wear and tear on the joints, and thirdly is often called rheumatism. But it's quite different from rheumatoid arthritis. Rheumatoid arthritis isn't caused by wear and tear on the joints but is an autoimmune disease. The joints aren't worn, but inflamed. The immune system decides that your joints aren't yours but are foreign bodies that it has to attack. That's what's happening at the moment.'

'But it's not only the pain that's making you irritable.'

'No, it's because I don't like talking about it, but sometimes I have to, and even then people don't understand.'

She took hold of his hand. 'I did understand some of it.'

'Good,' he said. The pain was spreading from his hip joints to his knees and ankles.

'How long have you had this?'

'About fifteen years.'

'And it can't be cured?'

'No, but sometimes it gets better, or to be more exact the episodes can stop for a few years at a time, or even stop for good. Or else it doesn't get better, and just stays as it is.'

'Normally no one would guess that you've got it—after all, everyone gets a bit of backache now and then.'

'That's the way I want it.'

'But there are advantages in telling people. You men have such a horror of attracting sympathy!'

'Idiot.'

She laughed.

The doorbell rang. Anne came back into the bedroom with an envelope in her hand. 'The prescription's come,' she said. 'I'll just run over to have it filled.' She did not wait for an answer.

In ten minutes she was back. In one hand she had the packet of tablets and in the other a glass of water. 'How many?'

'Three.'

She pressed out three tablets from a strip and gave them to him. He swallowed them and drank some water.

'Now you'll feel better,' she said.

'The pain will die down soon but the weakness will remain. With any luck I'll be more or less all right tomorrow. I'll try and have a sleep now.'

He did feel weak when he woke up the next morning, but he was a little better. Cautiously he got up and went into the kitchen. A spasm of pain shot through his left leg. He stopped for a moment, then continued as the pain abated. He could smell tea. Anne was in the kitchen, pouring tea through a strainer into a teapot, and had her back to him.

'Aha!' she said when she became aware of his presence. 'Back in the land of the living?'

'Good morning,' he said. 'Yes. The dead don't feel any pain.'

After breakfast they went to the History Department. They walked slowly, as his legs still hurt. In his office he pointed to the mountain of shame. The documents were heaped up, side by side and on top of each other. 'If only I knew where I put those copies!'

She stared at him open-mouthed. 'Please don't tell me you've forgotten.'

He thought about it. 'In a blue folder, I think.'

'There are at least five blue folders,' she said. 'And I hate to think how many more that we can't see.'

'I put them into one that was in the middle of the pile.'

'Then we only need to leaf through a few thousand pages.' She laughed. 'You really are chaos personified.'

He nodded. 'Sometimes I think so too.'

'Let's get on with it, then,' said Anne. She pulled out a folder with a blue cover and sat down at his desk. She opened the folder, but then looked across at Stachelmann, who was leaning against the table with the mountain of folders on it. 'Are you happy for me to look at these things, or do you feel it's industrial espionage?'

'Feel free to sniff around among my valuable sources. May you be granted the wisdom to understand them.'

'I suppose you think you're something very special, Dr Stachelmann.'

'I'll let history be the judge of that.'

She gave an admiring whistle. 'The greatest historian since Leopold Ranke! I feel honoured. What am I looking for? What was the heading?'

'The economic enterprises—the WVHA.'

'In other words the SS, Herr Pohl and the concentration camps.'

'Well remembered, Frau Derling.' He, too, took a blue file and sat down on the visitor's chair, opposite Anne. They leafed through the documents in silence.

Anne stood up. 'Shall I bring you a coffee?'

He nodded.

She came back with two mugs, laughing. 'Do you know who I just saw in the courtyard? Hand in hand, two hearts beating as one?'

He shook his head.

'Your girlfriend,' she said.

'Who?'

'That angelic creature from your seminar, the one who wanted to die for her love of you.'

'Alicia!' he said. 'And who was the man?'

'Kugler from Politics!'

'The heartthrob?'

'Exactly.'

'That's a match made in heaven.' Stachelmann laughed. 'I'd forgotten all about her, and yet she was the first woman who ever wanted to die on my account. And not every man can say that.'

'Before you get carried away by conceit, let's get on with the job.' Anne took a folder from the stack. 'Dust everywhere. You can't have looked at these for ages.'

'You could say that.'

'There's something here about the creation of Buchenwald concentration camp.'

'You can copy it when we've found the Pohl documents. I could kick myself for not having copied more documents in Berlin. I was in too much of a panic.'

'I wouldn't have dared to break in in the first place.'

'And now all the documents have gone up in smoke, and God only knows whether there are any copies somewhere else.' It would have been so easy to run the whole pile of Pohl's correspondence through the photocopier. And now here they were, desperately hunting for just two letters.

'This is interesting,' said Anne. 'Here the SA and the SS are arguing over who should guard concentration camp inmates.'

'Put that folder to one side when you've finished going through it, and then pick out anything that's of use to you.'

They went on searching but did not find the Pohl documents.

'I can't understand it. Surely no one can have come in here and pinched those papers.'

'They'd have made off with the whole pile. They'd hardly spend hours here rummaging through it.'

Stachelmann took half of a pile from the table and put it on the floor. For so long I've put off working my way through the mountain of shame, he thought. And now here I am dismantling it because I can't find two letters that I hid in it.

'Stapo Headquarters, Hamburg,' it said on the folder that was now uppermost on the table. It was green. He took it over to the desk with him. Anne looked up. 'Are you colour-blind as well?'

He shook his head. 'Look,' he said. He showed her the cover of the folder.

'Stapo Headquarters, Hamburg,' she read. She looked at him curiously. 'Documents from the Gestapo in Hamburg. What about it?'

'Well, it's just possible we may find our friends in one of these papers.'

'And you didn't even remember you had them.'

He shook his head. 'Well, I did, in a general sort of way.'

'And how long is it since you last looked at them?'

'A long time, far too long.'

She looked at him as if she were about to ask him something, but kept quiet. She was taking folders of documents from the piles and making new piles on the floor.

'What are you doing?' he asked.

'I'm sorting this stuff, just roughly, according to the headings. After all, the Herr Doktor did pen some immortal words on the file covers, which are probably meant to indicate what's in them.' She held up a folder. 'This is the third one with papers from the Hamburg Gestapo. If what it says on the cover is correct.'

'Let me see,' he said.

She gave him the file. 'I thought we were looking for Pohl's billets-doux.'

'They could be in any of the folders.' His back was aching; sitting didn't do it any good. But the weakness had vanished as if it had never been.

'So you *are* colour-blind!'

'Not at all, I just thought I'd put them into a blue folder.'

'Senile, then. I read somewhere that those old-timers in the SED Politburo took geriatric tablets to keep them healthy. And they did live to a grand old age. Perhaps you ought to try some. Another tablet or two a day wouldn't make much difference.'

He groaned aloud. 'How on earth did I saddle myself with you?'

'Bad luck.'

He stood up, paced up and down a bit, then sat down again and opened the file Anne had passed to him. It was about internal

Gestapo matters—promotions, reprimands, complaints, work rotas, plans for filling posts. He flipped through the pages. Something caught his eye, and he went back to it. A diagram representing an organizational structure. With a fine black pencil someone had drawn a set of boxes, each with a name written inside it. Staffing of Stapo HQ Hamburg, as at 16 April 1941. He read the names: Grothe, Prugate, Fleischer, Meier, Meiser, and at the top of the diagram Sbf. Holler. There were further names that meant nothing to him.

He read the names aloud.

She looked at him, wide-eyed. 'It's what you suspected.'

'Yes. But it's not every day that a suspicion turns out to be spot on.'

'Where's Enheim's name?'

'He wasn't in the Gestapo or the ss, he was in the Gauleitung. But he had connections with the ss mafia, no doubt about that. And they had an accomplice in the Finance Department, too.' Stachelmann had a clear picture of the conspiracy. He lacked proof, but as far as he could see there was only one way that the pieces of the jigsaw could be made to fit together. Of course he could not see the whole picture, only a part of it. 'But all this still doesn't solve the main question: who murdered whom, and why? I'm no lawyer, but I'm pretty sure that what we think we know would never stand up in court. All we know is that some people who worked in the same department conspired to get rich on the property of Jews. At least that's what I deduce from those copies from Berlin which are in here somewhere, and that diagram. Or let's put it like this, I *believe* that that's how it was. It's not proven, and it happened far too long ago for anyone to be prosecuted now. You don't have to be a lawyer to know that. And what has Maximilian Holler to do with it? Who killed Enheim, and Holler's wife and children?'

'Let's keep on hunting through your unread documents.' She tried to make a joke of it: 'It's a tale of revenge,' she said.

'Uh-huh,' Stachelmann agreed. 'I think so too. But who's trying to take revenge on whom? Was one of the ss mafia cheated? Or is there a victim who survived and who's now turned into a serial killer? There's another thing, too: they're all old codgers. I can't really imagine them, crutch in one hand and shooter in the other.'

'People live a long time nowadays. You should go to Majorca—they're all there, boasting about their heroic deeds on the eastern front. Or South America—there's a colony of old Nazis there to this day. I've just read a very illuminating book by one of Goebbels' former press officers. It was published recently in Kiel. He always puts the word "Jews" in inverted commas, Germany was forced into war, and anyone who doesn't believe that is a victim of the re-education imposed by the victor nations and their collaborators. Hard to believe it, but those attitudes are still around.'

Stachelmann was surprised at how much she knew.

'I once did some work on all that,' Anne went on. 'The escape of the Nazi heroes—sometimes with the Vatican's assistance—to exotic South America. Argentina was the country of choice. They have a really good life there, they do business with kindred spirits back home, and on April 20th, the Führer's birthday, they have a booze-up. That's what those old people do. So why shouldn't one of them carry on murdering?'

'Murdering children?'

'Why not? They did it before. It's nothing out of the ordinary for them.'

'I still can't quite imagine it. And who killed Enheim?'

'I don't know, but I'd say the same person who murdered the children. He and Enheim had a quarrel, God knows what about. And if someone thinks nothing of killing people…'

'Maybe,' said Stachelmann. 'But that doesn't answer the crucial question. Who is it? He must have a specific motive. Let's suppose the others swindled him, or he thinks they did. Old Holler is dead, so he takes his revenge on the son. That's the first bit I don't believe. It's completely mad. And instead of killing the son he makes him watch his family being wiped out. You've been reading too many detective stories.'

'I've read too much about the Nazis,' she answered. 'And I don't like detective stories. You're more of a fan of Lord Hornblower, aren't you?'

'The things you know.'

'If one's invited into your bed, I suppose it's permissible to look at what's on your bedside table. But, to change the subject, I'm hungry. You could take me out to the Italian restaurant.'

He shook his head. 'No, later. I haven't finished here.'

They spent the next couple of hours silently reading Stachelmann's documents.

Anne threw down a folder on to the table and rubbed her eyes. 'Well, I've had enough of files. We've been sitting here in the dust all day without eating. That's a form of torture. Tomorrow is another day. I'm off now. You can come round to my place when you've swallowed enough dust. I'll even give you a dessert. Bye.'

He could not understand how a person could run out of curiosity so soon. The mountain of shame was half dismantled, and now it would not let him go. He needed at least to have held each folder in his hands. The copies dated from a time when he used to order them on spec as he combed through archives. Most of them were still unread. What he had here was a chaotic collection of documents that got him as worked up as he had feared they would. They contained truths. Not always in a pure form, but what was the point of being a historian if he could not sift out the truths from all that paper? He carried on, picking up one folder after another, looking at its contents, closing it, putting it aside, then returning to a previous one because he had belatedly had a thought about it.

On the table, at the bottom of a pile, he saw a faded brown paper folder. He drew it out. On the cover he read, in his own writing, 'Gestapo file'. He cursed himself, not for the first time. He should have indicated more precisely what was in the folders. 'Gestapo file' might mean anything or nothing. He opened it and began to leaf through the contents. Copies of handwritten notes, interspersed with some typed sheets. *Rosenzweig, Fuhlentwiete 24, 2370 RM, Goldblum, Laufgraben 3.* From the heading of an internal memo Stachelmann deduced that these papers also came from the Hamburg Gestapo. The handwritten notes contained names, addresses, telephone numbers. *Bronstein, Grindelberg 36, 2thd—Mahler, Hoheluftchaussee 16a, 3500—Meyer, Mittelweg 93,800 RM.* There was a scribbled memo,

Phone Of. Schirmer!!! Kohn!!! Stachelmann turned over more sheets. *Enheim 8 P.M. at Anchor.* His eyes were smarting. He had been sitting hunched up and the pain was coming back. He screwed up his eyes, paced to and fro, stuck his head out of the window. He could hear the traffic noise from Mittelweg and Rothenbaumchaussee. It was getting dark.

He sat down at the desk again. A mosquito buzzed around his head, and he tried to swat it, but missed. He went on leafing through the papers. One bit of paper read, *Rosenzweig—5000 RM*. On another there was a name and address, and beneath it *7000*. Then a letter, just a few lines long. Stachelmann gave a low whistle as he read the letter heading. The letter came from the WVHA, and was signed by Pohl.

> *Dear Party Comrade Holler,*
> *With the help of the Reichsführer I have settled the matter according to your wishes. But I shall expect a favour in return! After the final victory, if not before!*
> *Heil Hitler!*
> *Pohl*
> *SS Obergruppenführer and Waffen- SS General*

Stachelmann leaned back in his chair. He had found another small piece of evidence. First the documents in Berlin, and now Pohl's letter to Herrmann Holler. Perhaps they were all linked. What matter could Pohl have settled for Holler with Himmler's help? That the Hamburg SS mafia would be able to carry on with its robberies? He turned over more sheets. Every so often he came upon further names, addresses, sums of money. And short memos: *Rosenzweig! Schirmer!* Schirmer—Stachelmann had seen that name earlier. He went back. Yes, Schirmer held the rank of Oberscharführer. Stachelmann looked for the diagram. He cursed: it must be under a whole pile of things. He found it on the floor. Schirmer's name—like Enheim's—was not there. So the SS men had accomplices in other departments. Or else the diagram was incomplete. Stachelmann found another letter addressed to Herrmann Holler. He had run up debts in a canteen, 12 Reichsmarks and 32 Pfennig. This file of documents must be

Holler's—no one else would have received this letter, or if they had they would not have kept it. What was the meaning of the names, the numbers, the addresses? RM stood for Reichsmark. Did the sums of money represent purchase prices? Some of the names sounded Jewish: Rosenzweig, Goldblum, Kohn.

Before the mass murders, many Hamburg Jews had lived in the area surrounding Grindelhof street, and up to the night of the pogrom there had been two synagogues close by. What could the references in Holler's papers signify? He needed to discuss this with Anne. He tucked the folder under his arm. In the doorway he turned back and stared at the chaotic mess of documents which only a few hours earlier had been the mountain of shame. For the past few years it had been growing, and the higher it got the more Stachelmann had feared it. Now it had been destroyed. A few folders which had formed its base still remained on the table; the rest were either on the floor or on his desk.

One isolated sheet had fallen to the floor. Stachelmann bent to pick it up, and read the jottings on it. *Stachelmann*, there was the name. He banged his fist down on the table. Then he leaned back and closed his eyes. He took the copy and put it into his pocket.

He rang at Anne's door. It was a while before she opened it. Her hair was flattened on one side and she looked sleepy. 'Where have you been all this time?' she asked, yawning.

'Come with me.' He took her by the arm and led her towards the living room. Puzzled, she peered at him sideways. As they passed the kitchen door she pulled away.

'I'll just get a bottle of mineral water.'

He sat down on the living room sofa. She came in with the mineral water and two glasses, and sat down next to him. He opened the file. 'This seems to be Herrmann Holler's file.' He turned over the pages, and she read in silence. He told her what he thought some of the notes meant, and she nodded. Pushing his hand away, she turned back to an earlier sheet. Thoughtfully, she turned over page after page. She read, closed her eyes, read on. She pointed to the letter from the canteen manager. 'That clinches it,' she said. When she had a page lying in front of her that listed names, addresses and sums of money, she snorted. 'The only way this makes sense is if Holler and his accomplices bought those properties from those people at those prices. Of course I don't know what the purchasing power of the Reichsmark was then, but it seems to me that the sums were only paid to give the transactions an appearance of legality. Are those people still alive?' She answered her own question. 'Probably not.'

'But if even one of them is alive, he'd be able to tell us more,' said Stachelmann. 'Only he'd be extremely old.'

'How would we set about tracking one of them down?' she asked.

'Let's go to the Jewish Centre, they should know of any survivors.'

'But not tonight. We're going to sleep now. In my bed. I promise not to jump on you.'

When Stachelmann came out of the bathroom and into the bedroom Anne was lying on her stomach, the quilt leaving her shoulders uncovered. She was breathing deeply and evenly. By her side, a quilt and a pillow were waiting for him. Moving gently so as not to disturb her, Stachelmann lay down on his side. He closed his eyes. What if the murderer was one of those named in Holler's document, he thought. He would have reason enough.

'Breakfast is served,' she said. She was standing in the doorway in her dressing gown, smiling radiantly at him. 'You're a real dormouse, it's almost midday.'

It was some moments before Stachelmann really came to. Anne had opened the curtains, and sunshine was falling on the foot of the bed. A ray of sunlight caught Anne's hair, which was still tousled. The thoughts which had drifted away in the night now came back to him. He was nearly there, he could sense it. It was always like this when he was close to solving one of the minor enigmas of history, even if it was an enigma only to him. That was the fascination of documents that he was the first archive user to see. He could feel the tension in his stomach. He had slept well; the pain had retreated to his back.

He got up and followed Anne into the kitchen. On the table was a note with the address of the Jewish Community Centre: 27 Schäferkampsallee. Anne had found it in the telephone book and had already enquired about their opening times. After breakfast they got dressed and left the apartment.

'Have you made a note of the names?' Anne asked.

'I don't need to, I remember them.'

They took the underground and got out at Schlump. A lady with grey hair and silver-framed glasses greeted them pleasantly. Stachelmann introduced himself and Anne as historians researching what had become of Hamburg Jews in the Third Reich, and she did not ask for any further details.

Stachelmann said: 'I have some names which I hope may mean something to you. Let's start with these: Goldblum, Mahler, Rosenzweig, Kohn.'

She opened a drawer containing a card index and searched through it. 'Josef Goldblum is still alive, I know that because someone asked about him quite recently. Herr Goldblum lives in an old people's home. It has a silly name—Indian Summer. It was Herr Kohn who asked about him. So at least one member of each of those families survived.' She spoke calmly, but sadly. 'The others were deported to the East, to Theresienstadt, then Treblinka or Auschwitz. Josef Goldblum had stayed here in hiding until the British took Hamburg. He was barely more than a child; I've no idea how he managed to stay alive. He never talked about it to anybody. Leopold Kohn had been in England—he went over on a Kindertransport in nineteen thirty-nine. He came back in the early nineteen fifties, but has hardly had anything to do with us. There are some who aren't interested in our community.' She sounded slightly annoyed. 'Some have even lost their faith.' She looked first at Stachelmann and then at Anne. 'Why am I telling you all this?' She left the question unanswered and turned back to the card index. 'Rosenzweig, no, there's no one of that name here. There could be various reasons for that, but probably there's no one left of that family.' She continued searching. 'Yes, and Mahler, there were several Mahlers. I know one couple, but they moved here some years ago. They came back from Israel: some people just can't cope with living in a strange country.' The woman paused. 'I shouldn't really be telling you this, at least not all of it. But you need it for your research. You know, in general no one shows any interest in us. From time to time they wheel out Herr Spiegel—he's the President of the Central Council of Jews in this country—and that's it. Another sop to their bad conscience and a boost for our car sales in America.'

Stachelmann listened, trying to keep his excitement in check, but it was not easy. They had found the names of two survivors, just like that. Two men, Goldblum and Kohn, whose names had been on Herrmann Holler's list. Perhaps they had already hit the jackpot.

'Could you possibly give me Herr Kohn's address?' Stachelmann asked politely.

'I'm not allowed to do that,' the lady said. 'I've already told you more than I should.'

'Funny woman,' said Anne, when they were outside again.

* * *

'This isn't getting us anywhere,' said Ossi.

She did not answer, just sat in the passenger seat looking out.

'Supposing we get a warrant for Holler's arrest?' she said at last.

'How do you propose to get one?'

'You're right, it was a stupid idea.'

'Let's try leaning on Grothe. And if that fails we'll have another go at that silly ass Meier zu Riebenschlag.'

'Do you know what I think? We're going round in circles. Of course feuds between dealers are a possibility. But it could be something else altogether. You told me about the attack on your friend, the one with the funny name. What if that's significant, and the whole thing has a totally different explanation?'

'Oh sure, maybe some little green men from Mars are behind it all. They've landed here and they particularly like to bump off the wives and children of property dealers, or if they can't get any of those they push potty historians off railway platforms.'

She said nothing, and turned her head away from him.

'Sorry, there's no need to get into a huff. But just imagine we pull Holler in for questioning and get nowhere. The Chief will go ballistic and the press will make mincemeat of us.'

She looked at him. 'Don't talk nonsense. If we're on the wrong track we need to stop at once and look around for a different lead, even if the Chief does go berserk. He's only thinking about the elections anyway. And if we get savaged by the press, that's just too bad. I think we should go and see Grothe now, and if that doesn't get us any further we go to Taut and say we've come up against a brick wall. And then we have another chat with your historian pal, assuming he hasn't fallen under a train by then.'

'Okay,' said Ossi. She was right. Much to his annoyance, she was making him feel he was being obtuse and pig-headed.

* * *

They were at the old people's home. 'Herr Goldblum's in the lounge, it's coffee time,' said a plump, dark-haired young woman. She pointed to a door at the beginning of a dark corridor. Leading the way, Stachelmann knocked at the door and opened it. They found themselves in a wood-paneled room with white curtains. On the walls were pictures with a nautical theme. Some old people were sitting at round tables, with white crockery in front of them and gleaming metal thermos jugs in the middle of each table. At the first table they came to, Stachelmann bent to ask an old woman, 'Excuse me, I'm looking for Herr Goldblum.'

She looked at him crossly. 'Whatever d'you want *him* for?' Speaking made her spray sticky cake crumbs from her mouth.

'It's a family matter, in a way.'

The old woman studied Stachelmann from top to toe. Then she turned and pointed towards a French window. 'He's probably outside, sitting in the sun and staring into space.'

Stachelmann and Anne went to the French window. On a terrace of concrete paving a man was sitting in a chair positioned sideways on to the building. His legs were propped up on another chair. A blanket of a dirty-brown colour covered his stomach and legs down to his knees. Stachelmann noticed he had a big nose. When he opened the door the man did not react.

'Good afternoon,' said Stachelmann.

The man did not stir. His eyes were open and he was gazing straight ahead. Stachelmann could not tell what he was looking at.

'Are you Herr Goldblum?' Anne asked, moving into his field of vision.

He looked at her, and then his eyes strayed to Stachelmann but immediately returned to Anne. 'Have you come to propose to me?' His voice was hoarse and thin. It was not easy to understand what he said.

'Later, perhaps,' Anne said.

'So I have a chance?'

'Anyone has a chance.'

'Nonsense. Don't take me for a fool.'

'Are you Herr Goldblum?' asked Stachelmann.

'Who wants to know, and why?'

'We're from the university, we're historians looking for survivors of the Holocaust.' Stachelmann hated that expression.

The old man smiled. One incisor was missing. 'I've never told anyone how I survived, and I'm not going to now. After all, it might stand me in good stead another time.' His laugh sounded more like a death rattle.

'We want, if possible, to find all the Hamburg Jews who have survived,' said Stachelmann.

'You won't have to look for long, then.'

'Do you know of any others besides yourself?' asked Anne.

'Why don't you go to the Jewish Centre?'

'They sent us to you,' said Stachelmann, hoping that Goldblum would swallow the lie.

'I don't believe you,' said Goldblum. He looked mockingly at Stachelmann. 'They won't even send anybody to my funeral.'

'Do you know Leopold Kohn?' asked Anne.

'I might,' answered Goldblum.

'He survived too,' said Stachelmann.

'It's possible,' said Goldblum.

'Do you know where he lives?' asked Anne.

'It's in the phone book.'

'If you're so grumpy I won't marry you,' Anne said.

'You wouldn't marry me even if I were the life and soul of the party.' He went back to staring into space.

Anne shrugged her shoulders. 'Pity,' she said, and walked away. Stachelmann followed her.

'Do you think he goes around killing children? Or pushing you off train platforms?' asked Anne.

Stachelmann shook his head.

'Let's have a look at Herr Kohn, then,' said Anne.

'And what if he's just another old man who talks a lot of drivel?' Stachelmann had been so hopeful, which made his disappointment all the greater. A stupid idea, to go looking for a murderer in an old people's home. He pictured Goldblum going around with poison capsules to murder people. Ridiculous. And Kohn, too, must be an old man. He had been sent to England as a child in 1939. Supposing he had been six years old then, he would now be about seventy. A mass-murdering pensioner. Yes, it *was* ridiculous. But what were they to do? They had to try and find him. There was a telephone booth on the corner, and Stachelmann went in and looked in the phone book. A lot of the pages were torn, but under K he found Kohn L., Hansastrasse 47c. That must be him. For a moment he considered ringing him. No, it was better to pay him a surprise call.

'Let's go straight there,' said Anne. 'It's practically round the corner from my place.'

The front door of the apartment building was not locked. They climbed the stairs. Age had stained the oak wood a dark brown, and the banister bore a sprinkling of black patches. The door on the second floor was marked 'Kohn'. As Stachelmann rang the bell, Anne took his arm. He heard footsteps: slow, firm. Through the opaque glass he could see a tall figure. The door opened and a strongly-built man with white hair was looking at them enquiringly. He reminded

Christian von Ditfurth

Stachelmann a little of the old man in Berlin who had pushed him on to the rails. But this was not the same person.

'The people at the Jewish Centre directed us to you. We're from the university and we're working on a research project. We're trying to find out how many Jewish survivors there are in Hamburg who lived here in the Nazi period. You are Herr Kohn, I believe?'

Kohn nodded.

'Could we possibly ask you a few questions?'

Kohn looked at them for a while with intelligent eyes, and then nodded again, though he did not seem very keen. He stepped aside and motioned to them to come in. 'And what sort of questions would those be?' His voice was firm and strong.

'We want to know how you survived. And what things were like for you after nineteen forty-five. Whether you encountered hostility, and whether anybody helped you.'

The man had led them into the kitchen. It was simply furnished; a row of white units along one wall, a window in another, and in the middle a table with four chairs. They sat down at the table.

Stachelmann asked, 'Herr Kohn, what was that time like for you?'

'Aren't you going to take notes?'

'No, not for the moment. The two of us'—he pointed to Anne—'will assess our interview with you back at the department, and then I hope you'll allow us to come again. There's a proper form for our research project. We would fill it in together with you, if you're in agreement.' Stachelmann hoped that Kohn would not see he was lying. He felt rather proud of the way he had handled the awkward question.

'I see,' said Kohn. 'Isn't it a bit late for your project? Most of the survivors are dead.'

'You're right, but unfortunately it didn't occur to anyone to look into this before.'

Kohn looked at him curiously.

'Where were you at the time of the Nazi dictatorship?' asked Anne.

'Kindertransport,' said Kohn. 'Perhaps you've heard of it.'

305

'Yes,' said Stachelmann. 'Just before the war a few thousand children were taken over to England. But the British didn't want the parents.'

'Well, children are so sweet, aren't they,' said Kohn.

'And when did you come back?'

'Quite late, not till nineteen fifty-one.'

'That *was* late,' said Anne.

'None of my family had survived. I nearly stayed in England for good. I did go to Hamburg in forty-seven or forty-eight, but I went back to England again.'

'Because you didn't find any of your family,' said Anne.

'It was almost unbearable in Hamburg. Everyone dead, the city destroyed and the Nazis practically in control again.' His voice got louder. 'The same policemen who took my family to the trains heading for the East were there in the police stations. The tax officials who robbed us were still raising taxes. The block wardens who spied on people were leading their lives as perfectly ordinary citizens. The public prosecutors and judges who sent some of us to prison for "racial pollution" when some patriotic Aryan denounced us, were now the guardians of the rule of law in the new Germany. The university professors who had demonstrated the superiority of the Nordic race were still giving lectures. And the vultures who exploited our desperate situation and took our property in exchange for mere pocket money or nothing at all were becoming the captains of the Economic Miracle.' By the end he was almost shouting. Kohn stopped and looked around, startled. 'I'm sorry,' he said. 'It's the first time I've talked about it for years. I didn't know...'

At first Stachelmann had recoiled, but then he had begun to feel a growing sympathy for the man.

'You see, we weren't rich, but I would have been able to go to university, we could have afforded that.'

Silence.

'But surely there were compensation tribunals?' said Anne.

'You had to lodge your claim with the tax office—the same people who had fleeced you before. And if they wouldn't help you, which often happened, you could take your case to court. But you had to prove your claim. I couldn't do that, at least not in the eyes of the law. I had no documentary evidence, it had all been burnt. The big bombing raid in nineteen forty-three, you know? The land registry, where my evidence was, burned down. And the tax office said the same thing had happened to the tax records and the records of the transfer of ownership. That may have been true or it may not. And *you* try and find Jewish witnesses. All gone up in smoke. The judge said he was sorry. "We have to act in accordance with the law," he said. I can still hear him saying it.'

'So the property that used to belong to your parents—who owns it now?' asked Anne.

Kohn looked down at the floor for some time. Then he lifted his eyes, just for a second, but long enough for Stachelmann to see the fury that consumed this man. He had never seen such a look: it registered despair combined with hatred. Whenever Stachelmann subsequently heard of someone's face being distorted with rage, he would think of this moment, of Leopold Kohn in his kitchen, wrestling with his rage. Getting the words out with difficulty, Kohn said, 'I don't know. And in any case it has nothing to do with your research project.' He sounded as if he were stifling a scream.

All of this had escaped Anne's attention. She had been expecting her question to produce information, and was confused at not getting it.

While they sat there in silence, Stachelmann looked around the kitchen. On the floor, next to the bin, was a box with a picture of a large-wheeled jeep, one of those outsize remote-controlled model cars. Next to the stove with its four steel hotplates were some tools and a remote control with its telescopic antenna only half extended.

'For your grandson?' asked Stachelmann, glad of a distraction.

Kohn looked at him, startled. 'Oh—yes,' he said.

'How old is he?' asked Anne.

Kohn said nothing, then said, 'Fourteen, no, thirteen.'

'Is he your daughter's boy, or your son's?'

'Please go now,' said Kohn.

Stachelmann hesitated but then stood up.

'When can we come back with the form?' asked Anne.

'Just go, and don't come back.'

Stachelmann looked at him, puzzled.

'Go!' Kohn's voice was trembling with the effort it cost him to control himself.

On the pavement Anne stopped and shook her head. 'That's really weird,' she said.

'Did you see his eyes?'

'No—yes—of course. What do you mean?'

Looking back at the house out of the corner of his eye, Stachelmann took hold of her upper arm and pulled her along. 'He's at the window watching us.' Once they had turned the corner he said, 'There was a moment when I thought he had the eyes of a madman, of a person running amok.'

'Oh, have you done comparative studies of people like that? What do a person's eyes look like when he's running amok? I must have overlooked the foam coming out of his mouth.'

Stachelmann felt a surge of anger. 'Believe me, he's insane. He's filled with such hatred—'

'He's just an embittered old codger, that's all. He hates the people who robbed and killed his family. He doesn't like to be reminded of it, and we reminded him. There's nothing more to it than that. To you the poor chap's a mass murderer just because he gets upset. People get incredibly upset about far less than that. But for Dr Stachelmann, with his great knowledge of the human psyche, it takes only one look to solve all the murders that have been committed in Hamburg in the last five years. Josef, don't get carried away. I suggest you take me out to supper, there's a Vietnamese place just around this corner.'

'No,' said Stachelmann. 'I'm going to wait here and see what Kohn does next. Perhaps he'll lead me to something interesting.'

'You're nuts,' she said. 'Well, I'm going to go home and make myself something to eat. I'll put a key under the mat for you in case you come along later. And because you're so terribly ill you can sleep in my little bed with me. But only if you're good.' She turned and left.

Stachelmann leaned against a tree. Here he could watch the entrance to Kohn's building without immediately being seen. Then he had an idea. On his mobile phone he dialed directory enquiries and asked to be put through to the Jewish Centre in Hamburg. He instantly recognized the voice of the lady they had spoken to. 'Excuse me, when did Frau Kohn die?'

'You mean the wife of Leopold Kohn?'

'Yes.'

'He never had one. Not to our knowledge.'

'And where do his children live?'

'I must say, you ask some very odd questions.'

'Herr Kohn hinted at something and I didn't want to be too intrusive, as you can imagine…'

'He has no children as far as we know. But you should ask him yourself.'

Stachelmann ended the call. This didn't prove anything, but it opened up a small gap in the fog. Who was the model car really meant for? Standing didn't do Stachelmann any good, the joints in his back, hip and legs hurt. He tried shifting his weight from one foot to the other, but that had no effect on the pain. A van came out of Hansastrasse, trailing a dark cloud of diesel fumes, and cut in front of a bicycle. The cyclist shouted abuse and shook his fist; the driver waved a hand dismissively. An old woman struggled along the pavement on two sticks, managing a bag as well. She stopped every few steps. Although she was on the opposite pavement, Stachelmann could see her panting with the effort. He wondered how often she walked along here. A shrieking horde of children passed him; he caught sight of yellow ribbons on plaits. His eyes followed the children. If only one could stay as young as that forever. No cares weighing you down. He remembered his days as a student. Several times he had been on the point of giving up. It had seemed like a never-ending torture, not the history part of it but the German studies he was forced to do as well: you were not allowed to study history on its own, at least not in those days and not in Heidelberg. Ossi had found it harder still. He wanted to be at the forefront of student politics, and never missed a demonstration or meeting. He always wanted Stachelmann to come along too, and Stachelmann seldom managed to resist. And once he was at the meeting nothing else mattered but the fight for the political line they stood for. And then he fought as hard as Ossi. A stabbing pain shot down his back and into his legs. He gasped for air and then went on walking, taking bigger steps but over a small area, to and fro, to and fro. He must not lose sight of Kohn's door. The street wasn't busy, but Kohn might vanish in an instant if Stachelmann didn't keep a close watch. And Kohn mustn't see him.

The longer he waited, the more he felt he was wasting his time. If Kohn went anywhere at all it would probably just be to the local shop. Where else would he go? If that happened Stachelmann would wait for him here again tomorrow. But then his conviction returned that Kohn would do something today. His eyes had given him away. Whatever Kohn was planning to do, he was involved in these murders. And Stachelmann would keep following him for as long as the vacation made it possible. He thought of his *Habilitation*. He ought to be sitting at his desk now, sorting through his documents. Still, he consoled himself, at least the mountain of shame had been destroyed. And he had read a number of the documents in the course of looking for the missing letters from Pohl's office. The mountain had ceased to be quite such an alien presence in his room. It was hardly even a mountain anymore.

He almost missed him. Kohn emerged from the house with a plastic bag in his hand, and walked towards Mittelweg. Stachelmann limped after him, taking care not to get too close. Kohn did not look round, and Stachelmann followed him to Dammtor station. Kohn quickly climbed the steps to the platform, where he stopped and waited for a train. Stachelmann stayed on the steps until a bunch of noisy people came up behind him, and then he let them push him up to the top. One of them was playing a trumpet, making an ear-splitting noise. He waited; Kohn had his back to him. An S-Bahn train arrived, destination Blankenese. Kohn got in and Stachelmann got into the carriage behind. Through the window of the door connecting the carriages he could see Kohn from the back. The old man was sitting on the right-hand side, next to a young girl with small earphones in her ears. Stachelmann stood at the window of the connecting door. Before each stop he looked to see if Kohn was making a move. A drunk was lying on the seat at the front of Stachelmann's carriage. He was snoring; then he opened his eyes and burped, and brown liquid dribbled out of his mouth. The man smelled of schnapps and dirt. His tousled hair was filthy. Stachelmann felt sick.

Just before they reached Klein-Flottbek station Kohn stood up, still clutching his plastic bag, moved towards the door and opened it when the train stopped. He went down the steps and set off in the direction of Elbchaussee. Stachelmann remembered coming here with Ossi when they had gone to visit Holler. Kohn turned into Holz-twiete and stopped about two hundred yards from Holler's house. Then he went towards the building site on the other side of the road, which was deserted by this time. He made straight for a gap in the fence and positioned himself behind a builders' truck. Stachelmann squeezed through the gap after him, using the truck as cover, and then crawled behind a bush that was to Kohn's rear; now he was only a few hundred yards away from him. Kohn had a pair of binoculars trained on Holler's garden, which could be clearly seen from here. In the soft early evening light the windowpanes gleamed golden. Birds were twittering, and a lawnmower buzzed in the distance. Kohn stood motionless with his eyes fixed on the garden.

There was a flash of light from the house as the French window opened. At the same moment a taxi drove past the building site. It was impossible to see, against the light, whether it was carrying a passenger. A woman came out on to the terrace, holding a child by the hand. Kohn reached into his plastic bag; a moment later he had a gadget in his hand with a long telescopic antenna. At first Stachelmann thought it was a radio, but then he recognized it as a remote control. Black. He felt himself go tense. His ankles hurt so much that he could barely stand. Paralyzed for a moment by shock, he suddenly saw it: a model jeep was heading towards the woman and the child, who had both stepped on to the lawn. The child was the first to notice it. He pointed and said something. The woman shook her head, and then she too saw the jeep approaching them. Now Stachelmann knew what was about to happen. He leapt on to Kohn's back, and they both fell to the ground, Kohn landing on his stomach with Stachelmann on top of him. His hand was still holding the remote control, his thumb had already flicked a switch. There was a loud, sharp, bang. Stachelmann pulled at Kohn's arm, Kohn let go of the remote control and turned on to his side. Stachelmann fell next to him. He was astonished at the old man's strength. Kohn sood up and kicked Stachelmann in the face. As he lay flat on the ground Stachelmann saw another man approaching. He had white hair and a sunburned face and wore a grey jacket. Something glinted in his hand. Kohn emitted a roar, which came from deep inside him and sent a shudder running down Stachelmann's back. It consisted of a single word: 'Holler!' Kohn threw himself at the other man. There was a bang, and Kohn stopped short as if he had collided with an obstacle. He swayed and he yelled, an inarticulate yell that was pure noise, an outpouring of pain, shock and rage. He fell to the ground. Stachelmann looked at the newcomer, and now he saw the gun in his hand. He stood up and ran, painful as it was. Then it struck him—he knew this man. He had seen him before: it had been in Berlin, first at Friedrichstrasse station and then again when he had followed him to the Adlon. Stachelmann's face hurt enough to make him forget the pain in his ankles. Still running, he glanced back over his shoulder. The man was not following him and was no longer in sight. Stachelmann forced himself to stop and cautiously went back, using the builders' vehicles as cover. Kohn was lying on the pavement, not moving. Stachelmann looked round; the other man had vanished. He stood beside Kohn, looking down at him. Kohn was groaning softly. There was a crater in Holler's lawn where the jeep had exploded. Stachelmann could not see anyone, but could hear a child crying.

He bent down to Kohn, who was lying on his side. He felt his neck and thought he detected a faint pulse. Kohn opened his eyes. He looked past Stachelmann. Blood was trickling from his mouth, and a thin red stream coloured the pavement, where it mingled with the dust and flowed slowly and thickly across the kerb and on to the road.

'Why?' asked Stachelmann. Silly question, he thought. He knew the answer, at least in general terms.

'He trampled on my toy car,' Kohn whispered, getting out only a word or two at a time.

'He robbed your family back then.'

'He trampled on my toy car.'

'And so you kill a woman and children who had nothing to do with it?'

'Who else should I kill? I didn't know Holler was still alive. I'd never seen him again until today. And now he's killed me too.'

Stachelmann found himself able to think again. He called the emergency number on his mobile and asked for an ambulance and the police. 'Send Kommissar Oskar Winter here, quickly.' Where were the policemen who were supposed to be guarding Holler's villa? They had probably rushed into the garden when the jeep exploded.

'Why did you murder the children?'

'Why did those people gas my parents?' Kohn was speaking more slowly. A tremor passed through his body. 'What was I supposed to do?' He closed his eyes and said nothing more. He looked peaceful, not like a man who had spent most of a lifetime tormenting himself with thoughts of revenge. Stachelmann looked up. Old Holler came out of the garden gate, looked around and recognized Stachelmann, froze, hesitated, then abruptly turned away and ran off in the other direction. Stachelmann left Kohn where he lay and followed Herrmann Holler. For a moment he thought he had lost him. He ran to where he had last seen him. Holler was just turning into a side street, and Stachelmann followed him. He was afraid of Holler's pistol, but still he ran, overcoming his pain. He could hear his breath rasping. His nose hurt: Kohn had kicked him hard. Perhaps Kohn was dead, or perhaps the emergency doctor would save him. Holler looked round, stopped and aimed the pistol at Stachelmann. Stachelmann heard the bang. He stopped too, and then jumped behind a tree and watched Holler from there. Holler pocketed the pistol and started running again, with Stachelmann pursuing him. At a corner Holler turned to the right, and Stachelmann reached the spot just in time to see a taxi driving off. Holler was in the back seat, looking through the rear window; the taxi was travelling at speed. It was only now that Stachelmann noticed the taxi rank. He ran to the cab at the head of the line, jumped into the passenger seat and shouted, 'Follow that taxi, and fast!'

The taxi driver turned his bulky body to face him, tapped his sweating brow and said, 'You've been watching too many films. I'm very attached to my driving licence, more than I am to my wife. Where do you want to go?'

Stachelmann had long since lost sight of Holler's taxi. He slumped down in the seat.

'What's the matter?' asked the taxi driver. 'I know, I'll take you to Fuhlsbüttel airport, if that's all right. That's a nice long drive.'

'No, I'm not going anywhere,' Stachelmann said.

'Well, I'd reconsider that if I were you. The thing is, I heard over the radio that my colleague is driving that gentleman to the airport. And you seem to have some business with him, am I right?'

'Yes, go on! Fast as you can!'

'Now take it easy, it's no good rushing, the roads are clogged up. I know a few rat runs, let's give it a try.' He shifted into drive—the car was an automatic—and moved off.

I must call the police, thought Stachelmann. He reached into his pocket for his mobile.

It wasn't there. He looked on the floor, next to the seat: it had vanished. It must have fallen out of his pocket. He saw the taxi driver's mobile resting in its cradle. 'Could I make a call?' he asked, pointing to it.

'If you pay for it,' said the driver. 'Time it by the clock there. Let's say two marks a minute.'

'Thank you,' said Stachelmann, trying to take the mobile out of the cradle.

'I'll do it,' said the driver. He pushed Stachelmann's hand aside and freed the phone from the cradle.

Stachelmann keyed in 110.

'Emergency services,' said a woman's voice.

'I'm chasing a murderer!'

The driver looked sideways at Stachelmann and raised his eyebrows.

'Please tell me your name and where you are.'

'Josef Maria Stachelmann. I'm in a taxi, we're on our way to the airport. We're following Holler.'

'Who is Holler?'

'The murderer.'

'And who has he murdered?'

'Leopold Kohn.'

'And you are Herr Josef Maria Stachelmann?'

'Yes.'

'And I'm Mother Teresa and if you get off the line immediately, Josef Maria, I won't have you prosecuted.' There was a click.

The driver looked at him again, ran his hand through his damp hair and sighed.

Stachelmann asked, 'Do you know the number of police headquarters?'

The driver shook his head, but then spoke into his radio microphone. 'Switchboard, I need the phone number for police headquarters.'

'42860. Is there a problem?'

'No, everything's fine.'

Stachelmann had already dialed the number. 'Kommissar Winter,' he said when someone answered. 'Give me Kommissar Winter of the murder squad. Quickly!'

'Putting you through.'

There were a few beeps. At last someone answered. 'Murder Squad.'

'Stachelmann. Give me Kommissar Winter, quickly.'

'Kommissar Winter isn't in the building just now.'

* * *

The interview with Grothe had been as unproductive as most of their previous meetings with the dealers. They were heading back to police headquarters when Ossi's mobile rang.

'Kamm here. Some lunatic rang up a while ago, I think he was called Stachelmann. He was trying to get hold of you. I fobbed him off. He said he'd solved the Holler case and was pursuing the murderer.'

'You idiot!' yelled Ossi. 'Why didn't you give him my number?'

'If I gave your number to every madman who calls, we'd be in a fine mess. Anyway, I've told you now.'

'When was this call?'

'About a quarter of an hour ago.'

'Where was he calling from?'

'It sounded like a mobile. He said something about the airport.'

Ossi hung up. He wrenched the wheel of the Passat round. 'Find the blue light!'

Carmen released her seat belt and groped around on the back seat. She found the magnetized blue light and reached out through the window to put it on the roof. With the blue light and the siren going Ossi cut his way through the congestion in Hoheluftchaussee. He cursed and swore. First at Kamm, then at drivers who blocked his way. He gave Carmen his mobile. 'Try to get hold of Stachelmann. I wish I'd stored his number in my phone. He's called Josef Maria Stachelmann.'

Carmen started contacting the information services of the mobile phone companies, and at the second attempt managed to get the number. Stachelmann's mobile rang, but there was no answer.

With a squeal of tires, Ossi stopped outside the terminal entrance for scheduled flight departures. They rushed inside.

* * *

The driver charged ten marks more than was on the meter. Stachelmann paid and hurried into the departure area. Where should he start looking? At check-in. He ran past all the airline desks; no sign of Holler. If Holler wanted to take a flight, he would have to go through the entrance to the gates. An illuminated sign above the entrance gave the gate numbers. Stachelmann stood behind a revolving postcard stand in front of a newsagent's and waited. What if Holler was already on his flight? That was hardly possible, Stachelmann reassured himself. It would be an extraordinary coincidence if a plane happened to be standing there ready to go just when Holler needed it. At the very least he'd have had to buy a ticket, or change his ticket if he already had one. I've got a ninety percent chance of catching him, Stachelmann thought. Or better.

A woman in a fur jacket passed him. She must be mad, he thought—it was about eighty-five in the shade. His eyes followed her. The black jacket had a rich sheen, it looked expensive. The woman disappeared into the crowd. At the entrance to the gates there was a short queue of people waiting to go through the personal and baggage security checks. Then just the other side of the queue Stachelmann caught sight of a forehead with white hair above it. Standing on tiptoe, he was able to recognize the face. He ran towards the queue. By the time Herrmann Holler recognized Stachelmann it was too late. In one mighty bound Stachelmann pounced on the old man. Holler gave a yell and then hit out.

Stachelmann felt himself being grabbed by the shoulders and pulled to his feet. A young man was shouting something incomprehensible at him. He saw a tattoo on the man's muscular upper arm: it had the name 'Vera' set inside a rose. 'Leave him alone! Police!' shouted the tattooed man. Holler broke free and ran towards the exit. The man with the tattoo watched him go, and Stachelmann pulled away from him and ran after Holler. As he emerged from the terminal he could see Holler running across the car park, perhaps three hundred yards ahead of him. Pretty fast for an old man, Stachelmann thought as he chased after him. Holler reached a patch of grass that was separated from the car park by a hedge. He knelt down, reaching into the hedge. Stachelmann was close behind him now. Suddenly Holler had a pistol in his hand. In the distance a police siren could be heard. Stachelmann looked round. The tattooed man and two others were running across the car park, but they were too far away to do anything. Holler aimed the pistol at Stachelmann. Then he looked past him, and Stachelmann saw the shock in his face; the police sirens were very loud now. Herrmann Holler put the barrel of the gun into his mouth, and there was a sharp report. Blood spurted from the back of his head.

Someone put an arm round Stachelmann: it was Ossi. Then Stachelmann fainted.

Chapter sixteen

Stachelmann woke up in a room in the Eppendorf hospital. He did not know how long he had slept. No one had been allowed to visit him, a nursing sister told him with some amusement: Kommissar Winter had ordered absolute rest. Stachelmann left the hospital the following day, and went to ground in his apartment. He rang Anne to tell her what had happened. Anne said little. She only contradicted him when he said he was responsible for somebody's death. After that he stopped answering the phone when it rang, which it did frequently.

He telephoned the Finance Department, pretending to be looking for a relative. He gathered pieces of information and fitted them together until he had completed the jigsaw.

Ossi turned up at his door. They only exchanged a few words. With some difficulty Ossi got him to promise that he would go to police headquarters. 'They're really impatient to hear all about it.'

Stachelmann kept his word. When he arrived, Ossi, Carmen, Kurz and Kamm were assembled in Taut's room. Taut was picking his teeth when Stachelmann came in.

'Come in, take a seat here next to me. We were just talking about you.'

Stachelmann sat down at one end of the desk.

'You solved our case, at least as far as it could be solved. Leopold Kohn was a serial killer: he killed three members of Maximilian Holler's family. But you saved the lives of the little boy and his nanny.'

'And what about Enheim?'

'It was murder, that's quite clear. And it's equally clear that the murderer was old Holler. But we'll never be able to prove it. All the same, our witness, a man called Mortimer, did identify Herrmann Holler at the mortuary.'

'Leopold Kohn wasn't a murderer in the usual sense. It was despair that led him to kill. Exactly what Herrmann Holler did in the Nazi period, how much he may have contributed to the extermination of the Kohn family and others, we shall probably never know. But I do know that Herrmann Holler first destroyed Leopold Kohn and finally murdered him.' Stachelmann had given this a great deal of thought in the past few days. 'Kohn is a victim first and foremost. Herrmann Holler is a killer.' He turned to Ossi. 'Why did old Holler shoot Enheim?'

'We don't know. But I suspect Enheim felt that the exploitation had gone on long enough.'

'Well, this is how I see it,' Carmen broke in. 'Enheim was short of money, and had the bright idea of demanding the reimbursement back from Holler junior. I mean those strange repayments that were made in relation to all Holler's purchases. And Enheim probably thought, why shouldn't I make it all public? Holler junior would lose his halo and I'd lose my good name. I'd be losing less than friend Maximilian.'

'There's probably more to it than that,' said Stachelmann. 'From the late nineteen thirties onwards there was a group of ss men and other Nazi officials who were carrying out their own personal Aryanization programme.'

'Aryanization?' Kamm queried.

'Robbing Jews because they were Jews.' Stachelmann felt a momentary surge of anger. He took a piece of paper from his inside pocket and read aloud: 'Helmut Fleischer, Karl Markwart, Otto Grothe, Otto Prugate, Johann-Peter Meier, Ferdinand Meiser and Gottlob Ammann were members of the Hamburg Gestapo. Robert Enheim was a Standartenführer in the sa and a big cheese in the Nazi Party district administration. They all robbed and plundered together. They had a contact in the Finance Department, a man called Schirmer, who was also a member of the 'Black Order', the ss. He probably did his best to ensure that any papers that might provide evidence of those robberies disappeared. Schirmer still held a high position in the same department after the war.'

'How do you know that?'

'Easy, I just made a few phone calls. Schirmer retired in the late seventies. But he still kept in contact with his old colleagues. When I went to the Archive in Berlin, he sent two guys ahead of me who pretended to be Hamburg Finance Department officials, with all the right papers and so on. That was simple for him to organize. And my guess is that those two have something to lose. Perhaps they're living in houses that belonged to Jews. You'll have to find that out, I don't want anything more to do with it. I bet you that Schirmer will just play the innocent and you won't be able to pin anything on him. I bet, too, that Peter Carsten, which is the name the man I spoke to at the Archive gave, doesn't exist. But to return to our Nazis. They had accomplices in the police force—because it was the police who made sure that the Jews didn't give any trouble when they were being deported to the extermination camps, whether directly or by some roundabout route, for instance via Theresienstadt. This Nazi mafia decided what they wanted to get their hands on. And the loot had to be shared out among everybody involved; the division was probably worked out long before the victims had any idea of what was going to happen. When it had all been agreed, the Jews were sent their deportation orders. The police made sure that the orders were delivered to the victims and that they all duly set out on their journey east. Schirmer destroyed the documents in the Finance Department—insofar as the Brits and the Yanks didn't do it for him, with their bombing raids—think of Operation Gomorrah.'

'What?' said Ossi.

Stachelmann had to pause in his narrative. 'That was the name given to the air raids in the summer of nineteen forty-three, the terrible fires.'

'Oh, yes,' said Ossi.

'So after the war, thanks to Schirmer and his Anglo-American helpers, no documents could be found relating to any of the cases in which our mafia men had been involved, and that's why Kohn's compensation claim got nowhere. The same thing happened to other people, too. But in most cases the matter ended in the gas chambers. Where there's no plaintiff, there's no case to answer.'

'So in Hamburg some property still belongs to people it shouldn't belong to?'

'Yes, for instance a certain Maximilian Holler. You haven't been able to prove anything against him, and I don't see how anyone could. He inherited his father's loot.' He turned to Ossi. 'You said something once about that mysterious account with the eleven million marks in it. I'm convinced that Maximilian Holler knew all about it. And another thing: I think that those dubious reimbursements can only be explained if we take it that Holler junior blackmailed his father's fellow mafiosi. There was money to be had there, and he took it. It was a sort of membership fee for the Aryanizers' club. I assume that he channelled it to his father by some devious means. After all, *he* needed something to live on. Grothe and Co. owed their livelihoods after nineteen forty-five to Herrmann Holler. He had organized the robberies and used his contacts with Pohl and other prominent people to cover them up. And there had probably been an agreement among those private Aryanizers that when the loot eventually came to be sold a kind of commission would be payable to Herrmann Holler.'

'How can you possibly know that?' asked Ossi.

'I can't prove it, how could I? But can you think of any other explanation for those repayments? Ockham's Razor—'

'What's that?' asked Ossi.

'Well, it means that it's a matter of common sense—there's no other reasonable explanation. Let me go on with my speculations. Everyone thought that old Holler was dead, and so the fee would no longer be payable. It must have been quite a shock for those gentlemen when Holler junior persuaded them to sell and then held out his hand. If he had demanded the fee from the outset, some of them might have refused to sell. After all, Holler junior wouldn't have looked all that good himself if it had come to a showdown. He was heir to the ringleader. On the other hand, that's all he was—the heir. He could have explained his charitable giving as his secret penance for his father's misdeeds, or, better still, he could have pleaded ignorance and might well have got away with it. Unlike Herrmann Holler's accomplices—they would have appeared in a really bad light. They could hardly have claimed to know nothing. No, Holler junior was in effect demanding payment of the commission which the dealers had agreed with his father. And only Enheim resisted.'

'What a foul hypocrite Holler is!' said Carmen.

'Worse than that,' replied Stachelmann. 'Because in the case of Enheim he actually got his father to murder him. First the old man tried to intimidate Enheim—that was the purpose of his visits to him. When that didn't work, he killed him. Probably Enheim threatened to blow Holler senior's cover. It might seem surprising that only one of the blackmailed dealers put up any resistance, but for the fact that they had all been individually guilty of plundering Jews. What we have here is basically a falling-out among thieves.'

'And what about Ulrike?'

Stachelmann shrugged his shoulders. He turned to Ossi. 'You told me at the time that you had a witness. Show him Holler's body. I bet he'll recognize him.'

'And why was she killed?' asked Taut. Then he banged on the desk with his fist. 'My God, we've got that hair! Has no one thought of comparing it with one of Herrmann Holler's? Go on, see to it!' Kamm left the room.

'I think that Ulrike Kreimeier must have rung Holler junior and asked him some question that made him panic. Perhaps she suspected the historical roots of the tragedy,' said Stachelmann.

'There were a couple of indications of that in her papers,' said Taut. 'But perhaps Maximilian Holler only jumped to conclusions. What she said made him *think* she was on his trail.'

Stachelmann's mobile phone rang. It was Anne.

'I'm in a meeting just now, I'll call you back,' said Stachelmann.

'But I'm not free again until next week. Bohming is working on an article for one of the major journals.'

Stachelmann said nothing.

'But you *will* come next week?' asked Anne.

'Yes,' said Stachelmann in a strangled voice.

He could hear her breathing. 'You've still got a toothbrush here.'

'Yes,' he said. A small ray of light, of hope. He ended the conversation and looked round. The others seemed hardly to have noticed the phone call.

'So old Holler was watching over his own estate. I imagine the two Hollers agreed that the father needed to die. That was easily arranged. Presumably they were scared that it would all come out. Herrmann was living in Majorca under a false name, and when things started to get too hot he flew over here and dealt with the matter in true Gestapo style,' said Taut. 'We've got his false passport and his air ticket. That all seems clear enough.'

'Talking of things getting hot, old Holler probably also arranged for those two phony finance officials to pick out the most incriminating documents in the Berlin archive and order copies, and then he himself paid the copying firm a visit to torch them,' said Stachelmann. 'Not a bad scheme. They were afraid I'd be on to them as soon as I started rooting around in the archive. Have you checked whether Holler junior telephoned his father in Majorca?'

'Yes,' said Taut. 'We did that yesterday. We got nothing, of course. We can't pin anything on Junior. Unless one of his blackmail victims is prepared to talk. About those dubious repayments, for instance.'

'I don't see that happening,' said Ossi. 'They're more likely to get Holler to pay some of it back to them. There aren't many like Enheim.'

'And old Holler tried to kill me in Berlin because I'd mentioned to his son that I was going on a research trip to the Federal Archive. The old man must have blown a fuse.'

'I'm sorry I didn't believe you,' said Ossi.

'This is all very instructive, but we've no evidence,' said Taut. 'We can't prove anything against Holler. If we tried, it wouldn't work, and everyone would be after our blood—the press, the Chief, and Kriminalrat Schmidt. Maximilian Holler has lost his wife and two children and we'd be trying to pin something on him which we'd even have some difficulty in proving against his father. Besides, everything apart from the murder happened too long ago and comes under the statute of limitations. Sometimes this job really makes you sick. Is it the same with yours, Herr Stachelmann?'

Stachelmann nodded. But not for the same reasons, he thought. He said nothing.

'But why didn't Kohn kill old Holler years ago, when he was officially still alive?' asked Carmen.

'I don't know,' said Stachelmann. 'Revenge is a strange thing. Perhaps it all only came to a head when it seemed that old Holler had drowned in Majorca. Maybe Kohn had always put it off, out of fear, or because he had doubts. Or perhaps he only learned of all this more recently.'

'And then he discovered that the son was living in high style on the proceeds of robbery, and putting on an act as the Holy Man of Hamburg. We found some newspaper cuttings in Kohn's apartment. He saved everything he could find about Maximilian Holler. I think it was the son's hypocrisy that finally turned Kohn into a murderer.' Taut stood up. 'You can understand how he might react that way, the whole thing is a monstrous injustice.' He held out his hand to Stachelmann. 'I'm most grateful, Dr Stachelmann.'

Stachelmann was embarrassed. He hesitated, but then shook Taut's hand.

'It's a scandal, a bloody scandal,' said Carmen.

* * *

That evening found him sitting in his parents' living room.

'So you've come, I'm glad about that,' said his father. 'I suppose you understand now what I said to you last time.'

'Oh yes,' Stachelmann said. 'I understand perfectly.' He laid his briefcase on his lap and took out the folder. 'This seems to be a kind of personal file kept by Sturmbannführer Herrmann Holler. A lot of people are mentioned in it. Gestapo officers, tax officials and policemen.'

'Ah,' said his father.

'You're in there, too. The bit about you was written in nineteen forty-one or nineteen forty-two, or at any rate it's among other pages that date from that period. It says, "Stachelmann, fit for active service, to be conscripted." There's a tick against it. But you *weren't* sent to the front: you did something for Holler to buy yourself off. Would that be the correct interpretation?'

His father looked at him for a long time without speaking.

'Shall I bring some wine?' his mother asked from the doorway. She had probably been listening; neither of them answered.

'I was about to be called up,' his father said. 'To go to Russia. It was after the battle for Moscow. Everything was going badly. The men were dying like flies. They needed reinforcements. Then suddenly this Gestapo man came and said, we'll put you in the police, then you won't have to go to the front. And in return you'll just do us a favour now and then. At the time I thought, the Gestapo, they look after law and order, you have to help them. After all, I've never denied that I was in the Party. I only realized later that Holler had manipulated me. He'd got me just where he wanted me: if I didn't do as I was told I was off to Russia. By the time I saw how deeply involved I was, it was too late. So there I was in the police, and from time to time I helped Holler.'

'By making sure that certain specific Jews were on the transports to the east.'

'How do you know that?'

'Actually, it was just a guess. I can picture it in my mind. I don't like what I see, but there it is.'

'If I hadn't kept an eye on those Jews someone else would have done it. They'd have been deported just the same.'

Stachelmann stood up.

'If I hadn't done it, you would probably never have been born,' said his father. His voice sounded plaintive.

Stachelmann walked straight past his mother to the front door. He opened it, got into his car and drove home.

Afterword

I would like to thank Gisela Gandras for her critical reading of the manuscript and for making suggestions which have improved the book. She also contributed the psychological profile of the killer; the author alone is responsible for the fact that it did not help solve the case. I am grateful to Dr Herbert Brehmer for specialist advice. My thanks also go to Nikolaus Wolters, who improved the manuscript by his meticulous editing, and I thank him for it. Any remaining errors are my own responsibility.

The characters and events in this book are, of course, fictitious, except for those that are historically documented. I might not have needed to invent them if all the tax offices in Germany had made their documents from the period of the Third Reich available for inspection.

About the Author

Christian von Ditfurth, born in 1953, is a historian. He lives and works in Lübeck as a freelance writer and editor. He has published numerous non-fiction titles on politics and history, and in recent years, several highly acclaimed novels. *A Paragon of Virtue* is the first in a series of books featuring Dr Stachelmann. It is the first of Ditfurth's books to be published in English.

The fonts used in this book are from the Garamond family

The Toby Press publishes fine writing,
available at leading bookstores everywhere. For more
information, please visit www.tobypress.com